"What do you think you're doing?"

Charlie's voice sounded way too fucking sexy.

Vince anchored his fingers into her hair and brushed his nose along the curve of her neck. That smell—sweet flowers and temptation. It drove him crazy.

"Appearances need to be maintained, right? Besides, you make me want to live dangerously."

Her brown eyes narrowed on him, scanning his face as if weighing her options. "Oh, what the bloody hell."

Charlie wrapped her hand around the back of his neck and pulled him against her mouth. Her tongue dove in before she eased back and nipped Vince's bottom lip. And that did it. Any control he possessed, shattered. He firmed his grip in her hair and immediately took over the kiss.

D0017157

Acclaim for April Hunt's Novels

HOLDING FIRE

"Passionate chemistry and nonstop drama drive Hunt's second book in the adrenaline-charged Alpha Security series."
—Publishers Weekly

"4 stars! The suspense is ever-present...and the heat between the hero and heroine is intense."
—RT Book Reviews

"April Hunt has me hooked!"
—HerdingCats-BurningSoup.com

"April Hunt has quickly become one of my one-click authors. Her daring heroes are so damn charming. And with sassy, take-charge women by their sides, it makes for one hell of a ride."
— NallaReads.com

HEATED PURSUIT

"Smartly balances slow-burning passion and explosive high-stakes danger. This book kicks off an adventure-packed romance series, and readers will eagerly anticipate the next installment."
—Publishers Weekly

"4 stars! Fast paced and intriguing."
—RT Book Reviews

HARD
JUSTICE

ALSO BY APRIL HUNT

Heated Pursuit
Holding Fire

HARD
JUSTICE

APRIL HUNT

FOREVER

NEW YORK BOSTON

Copyright © 2017 by April Schwartz
Excerpt from *Heated Pursuit* copyright © 2016 by April Schwartz
Cover photography by Claudio Marinesco
Cover design by Elizabeth Turner
Cover copyright © 2017 by Hachette Book Group, Inc.

Forever
Hachette Book Group
1290 Avenue of the Americas, New York, NY 10104
forever-romance.com
twitter.com/foreverromance

First Mass Market Edition: August 2017

Forever is an imprint of Grand Central Publishing. The Forever name and logo are trademarks of Hachette Book Group, Inc.

The publisher is not responsible for websites (or their content) that are not owned by the publisher.

The Hachette Speakers Bureau provides a wide range of authors for speaking events. To find out more, go to www.hachettespeakersbureau.com or call (866) 376-6591.

ISBNs: 978-1-4555-3952-9 (mass market), 978-1-4555-3951-2 (ebook), 978-1-4789-1626-0 (audiobook, downloadable)

Printed in the United States of America

OPM

10 9 8 7 6 5 4 3 2 1

*To my very own Alpha Man—the heroes
in my books pale in comparison to you*

ACKNOWLEDGMENTS

Writing this series has been a blast from the very first written word, and I couldn't have done a second word (much less three books) without the support of my family. To my Mini Me, who proudly announces to her teachers and every adult at school that her mom writes "smoochie books"; and my Mini Alpha Man, who shows me, every day, glimpses of the loving hero he's going to make for some lucky (and VERY-far-into-the-future) girl. To my own Alpha Man, who's stood behind me from the time I said, "I want to write a book!" To my mother, my sisters, my "second" parents, I've never once felt like I was climbing for this dream by myself because you were always there waving your pom-poms in the air.

Sarah E. Younger, my Agent of Awesome. Your photo should be in the picture dictionary under AMAZING. You're equal parts dragon-slayer, therapist, and sister... and I'm inclined to add ninja warrior princess to the list as well.

THANK YOU! Because of you, I can always say that I'm a published author.

Madeleine Colavita, my editor extraordinaire. You plucked me from the din and gave my Alpha men—and women—a home at Forever. With your support and guidance, I've been blessed to leave a stamp on this world in the form of Rafe, and Trey, and Vince. THANK YOU SO MUCH! And to everyone on the Forever team, from the intern to the exec, the business-oriented to the artist, THANK YOU for all of your hard work delivering each book baby into the world.

To my amazing best friend and CP, Tif. You kept me sane through another plotting session, through drafting and edits, and you didn't once think, "I'm changing my phone number" (at least not that I know of). THANK YOU!

To all my amazing writing friends, to #TeamSarah, to my #GirlsWriteNite crew: Tif Marcelo, Rachel Lacey, Annie Rains, and Sidney Halston. You ladies rock, and I'm so glad we have each other on this crazy ride.

And to all the readers and reviewers and bloggers who take time out of your day and pick up a book, THANK YOU! You're the reason I write well into the night, drink way too much Snapple, and sometimes have inappropriate conversations in my head with my characters.

Keep reading! Keep reviewing! And keep Alpha-ing up!

HARD
JUSTICE

CHAPTER ONE

Clutching her semiautomatic to her chest, Charlotte "Charlie" Sparks crouched behind a decapitated tree. Rivulets of sweat dripped into her eyes, and any pink-tinted locks of hair not glued to her head whipped across her face. She blinked through the sharp sting, slowly wrangling both her vision and her concentration back into focus.

It wasn't the time or place to dwell on what had happened the last time she'd stepped onto this field—the time when she'd moved too suddenly; the time when she'd been spotted; the time she *still* hadn't managed to live down.

"Everyone in position?" Alpha leader Sean Stone's voice rumbled from the tactical communication piece tucked behind Charlie's right ear.

"Good here." Chase Kincaid, Alpha's medic, started off the round-robin of affirmatives that included lead negotiator Trey Hanson. But they wouldn't need Trey's expertise this time around because tonight was an all-out war. No negotiat-

ing. No prisoners. Survival of the fittest. Let the best man—
or woman—remain standing.

"Ready," Charlie muttered when her check-in turn came
last.

At barely five-foot-three and a hundred and twenty
pounds, stealth not only came easier to her than it did to her
oversized counterparts, but it fooled more than one Neanderthal into labeling her a damsel.

She loved proving those bloody bastards wrong.

"It's a go," Stone announced. "I repeat, it's a go. Fast and
light. Eyes on the prize."

Keeping low to the ground, Charlie breached the heavy
thicket of trees and headed immediately toward the immense
boulder on her left. She skirted around the rock's perimeter
until she saw her target—right there in all its beautiful Day-
Glo glory.

Less than fifteen yards away, the opposing team's orange
flag swayed in the May evening breeze. It was an easy sprint.
A quick dash. Hell, she could spit and reach it with inches to
spare.

"I have my eyes on the prize," Charlie notified her team,
keeping her voice low. "But it's suspiciously quiet—and out
in the open."

She scanned the area and came up empty—no oddly
shaped shadows, no suspect movements. To the untrained eye,
the area was devoid of human presence . . . but Charlie knew for
a fact there were at least six other people out there with the
same two goals—either get the flag or keep *her* from getting it.

"Hawkeye, you have a bead on me?" Charlie addressed
their lone sniper.

"Got your position locked," Logan's voice chimed back.
"Everything's clear from your eleven o'clock to four. You're
the hottest thing out there, darlin'."

Charlie rolled her eyes at the ridiculousness of the double entendre, something at which the Texan excelled.

"You get what I did there?" he asked after her prolonged silence. "I'm reading heat signatures and you just so happen to be British Barbie."

"I think I have one too many tattoos to be considered a doll," Charlie said.

"So you're Badass British Barbie."

"Call me a Barbie one more time and you'll get a first-hand glimpse of how those steer on your family ranch feel on castration day."

"Harsh, darlin'. Really harsh." Logan chuckled. "Stop flirting with me and go get us that win—and take no freaking prisoners."

A small smile danced across her lips. "Not planning on it."

Charlie stepped—and cringed as a twig crunched beneath her heel. Irritated that she'd let herself get distracted, she listened for any signs that she'd been compromised. After a solid thirty seconds of hearing nothing but rustling leaves, she kept going.

Ten feet from victory, a mountain-sized commando stepped into her path—too damn close for her not to have heard a damn thing. Charlie screeched to a halt.

Vincent Franklin.

Where the bloody hell had he come from?

Charlie had dealt with cocky, too-gorgeous alpha-hero types every day and managed to keep her sexual fantasies down to nil—until Vince had joined the team. The former SEAL commander always seemed...*more*. More intense. More combustible. And more than capable of awakening the sexual libido that had been in remission a lot longer than she cared to admit.

From his piercing hazel eyes and commanding presence to every tattooed inch of his body, the man was the epitome of Doom and Brood and would look dangerous donning flannel pj's and a pair of bunny slippers. Put him in head-to-toe black camo and a throw a cap over his shaved head?

He looked *lethal*.

Neither of them moved as his gaze traveled up and down the length of her body, each pass tightening the mouth she'd fantasized about more than a few times through the course of the year. His hands, wrapped around his gun, flexed, diverting her attention to the full sleeve of colorful tattoos decorating both ridiculously corded arms.

Those bloody arms.

Some women coveted a broad chest with pecs that could make a quarter bounce—which Vince had. Some women fantasized about a firm, hard ass with a slight curvature perfect for palming—which Vince also had. And some women drooled over calloused hands, a symbol of hard work and talent in something other than pushing papers—which Vince *also* had.

But as delightful as all those attributes were to any red-blooded woman, Charlie was an arm girl. More specifically—*forearms*. When every hand-flex and wrist-rotation resulted in the gliding movement of ripped, corded muscle, something happened in her brain that shorted her circuits and sent a warmth straight to her lady goods.

Unfortunately for Charlie, Vince's arms not only managed to short out her brain cells, but set them—and her body—ablaze. Like they were now. By the time she realized that drool had started collecting at the corner of her mouth, Vince's lips gave a little twitch, which for him was practically an award-winning smile.

Charlie recovered from the shock of seeing it by drilling

him with her best glare. With his gun already at half-mast, he could fire a round into her safety vest before she even took aim. "What are you waiting for? An invitation? Go ahead and get it over with."

"You managed to get this far." Vince gestured toward the flag flapping behind his shoulder. "Finish what you started. I'm not going to get in your way."

"I'm closing in," Chase's voice murmured in Charlie's ear mic. "Keep him distracted."

Charlie plastered an unassuming smile on her face and watched the former SEAL go on high alert as she took a small step closer. Good. She liked that she could make him nervous. Well, maybe not nervous...*edgy*.

She refused to pull her gaze away from his. "Do I look like I was born yesterday, Navy?" Another step. "The second I turn my eyes away from you, you're going to fire off a round, and then I'm out."

"You need to work on those trust issues, English."

A truer statement had never been uttered.

Another step and her vest brushed against his when she took a deep breath. "I have a name, you know. And it's not English."

"Maybe I'll learn it when you realize mine isn't Navy."

"What if I shelve Navy and come up with something even more annoying?"

"You do and I'll switch English to *Crumpet*."

Vince shifted. In the overstretched, gaping folds of his vest, Charlie saw her opportunity—and took it. She drilled the butt of her paintball gun into his left torso and gave it a twist for good measure.

"Low blow," he grunted. "But so's this."

His arm hooked around her waist, dragging her flat against his body a split second before he spun them right.

Charlie's back met the bark of the nearest tree, both her hands and her gun effectively sandwiched between their chests.

Damn smart blimey bastard.

"You should've left when I gave you the chance. Now where the hell are you going to go... *Crumpet*?" Vince murmured against her ear.

Hell if she knew. He trumped her in size a few times over. Charlie squirmed and twitched. Vince only held on tighter... but in order to anchor her against the tree, he widened his stance, leaving his family jewels vulnerable.

"Sorry, *Flipper*, but you asked for this." Charlie leaned back a fraction of an inch and lifted her knee straight up between his legs. Even mountain men couldn't shake off a direct shot to the juniors.

Vince released her, doubling over on contact with a low, hissing growl. Charlie leapt forward, quickly yanking the flag off its perch, and whistled. "Game over!" she shouted, gleeful.

Defeated groans and victorious shouts echoed around them as the teams started stepping into the small clearing. Charlie turned toward Vince, prepped to gloat and maybe see if he required medical attention. But instead of seething in pain, the man had his gaze resting squarely on her arse.

Each step Charlie took toward him amped up her degree of mad. "You better not have let me win, or my knee's going to feel like a tickle compared to what I'm going to do next."

He kept his face impassive and shrugged. "You got really fucking close. You deserved to win."

"No." She shook her head angrily. "I would've deserved to win if I'd gotten the flag without being seen. I can win on my own. I don't need some He-Man type giving me a free pass. Next time you can take the shot, take it, and stop staring at my bloody arse."

Charlie turned and stalked away before she did more than knock her knee into his man bits. But on her tenth step, she heard Vince's low mutter, "Maybe I like staring at your bloody arse."

Her patience dragging on the ground, Charlie spun and squeezed the trigger. A handful of bright pink paint splattered on Vince's chest pad—dead center.

"What the hell was that for? The game's fucking over, English," Vince growled.

She fired another shot dangerously close to the bottom edge of his protective gear. A few inches lower, or with slightly off aim, and he would've been walking funny for weeks. "The first was for the arse comment—because my behind is not yours to ogle. And the second was for calling me English. *Again*."

Charlie stormed off the field, where her foul mood was intercepted by two of her best friends.

Having joined in on the game, Penny, the first to drag one of the Alpha men into the pits of love and happiness, was decked out in black camouflage much like Charlie herself. But Elle, waddling slowly over tree limbs, toted around a protruding pregnancy belly instead of a paintball gun.

Grinning, Penny bumped into her shoulder. "You're getting soft on us. I thought for sure you were going to shoot a blast of paint straight into his crotch."

Elle snorted on a chuckle and carefully stepped over a mossy tree branch. "We placed a bet on it. Although I don't know who wins, because we both bet crotch. Maybe we can all share an ice cream sundae and call it a draw."

If it had been one of the other guys who'd taken it easy on her, or if she'd known he was wearing manly protection,

Charlie would've done as Penny had suspected. But she didn't want to permanently dismember the guy. Not to mention, aiming toward Vince's crotch meant looking at his crotch, and her imagination needed no additional encouragement in picturing the infuriating man sans camo and padding.

Reaching the end of the paintball field, Charlie chanced one final look over her shoulder and immediately collided with a familiar piercing gaze. Depending on his mood, the shade either darkened or lightened. Most women would have drowned in their depths and died happy, but Charlie reached for her metaphorical life vest and held on for dear life.

A man was the last thing she needed now that she'd finally proven herself worthy of being on Alpha's frontline—especially a man like Vince Franklin.

CHAPTER TWO

Everyone had lost their damn minds—including Vince. That was the only excuse for what had happened at the paint-ball range earlier in the day. But in the light of a full moon, the crazy started spreading like the fire he'd put out in the bar's bathroom only two hours into his shift—and the fuck-ery hadn't stopped there.

So far, he'd broken up three fights—one of which resulted in a phone call to the local sheriff's department—fished a drunk coed out of their Dumpster—*don't ask*—and dodged no less than a dozen ass-grab attempts by Bea Nicholas and her quilting circle.

Vince filled one order after another, slowly making his way to the end of the bar where the head Grabby Hands her-self waited, more mischief sparking in her eyes the closer he got. He reached beneath the counter for a crate of clean mugs and received a sharp sting on his left ass-cheek.

This night couldn't end any fucking sooner.

Forcing a deep breath, Vince slowly stood and locked the older woman in his sights.

"Behave, Bea." He pointed a warning finger at the eighty-some-year-old.

"Oh, honey. I've spent most of my life misbehaving. I can't change now," she teased, not a speck of remorse anywhere to be seen. Her crew of ladies howled in laughter behind her. "Besides, it was an accident. My hand slipped."

Her friends continued their hyena-type laughter. *Jesus.* Octogenarian misfits, the entire damn lot of them.

"When your hands start developing a mind of their own, it's time to water down the drinks," Vince said dryly.

"Now, there's no need to get hasty." Bea looked appalled at the idea of being cut off. "I'll tell you what, hon... agree to be the male model for our senior art class, and I bet you'll find my hands will keep to themselves."

He didn't want to fucking ask, but the words left his lips anyway. "Don't people pose naked for those kinds of classes?"

"Your point?" Bea wiggled her eyebrows suggestively.

"What's wrong, Navy? Afraid to shed your skivvies for a roomful of art enthusiasts?" came Charlie's sultry, English-accented voice. *Goddamn, it was the voice of a phone sex operator*—not that he knew what one of those sounded like.

Charlie, taking a break from her girls' night across the room, whipped up two simultaneous batches of frozen margaritas and slid one pitcher Bea's way along with a saucy wink. "You're way too adventurous for Navy, Bea. You'd run circles around him."

Vince shot the pink-haired thorn in his side a glare. "Because I don't want to pose naked in front of a group of women with a fondness for pinching my ass? Like you'd do it?"

"I did. Last week."

The mug in his hands slipped, splashing beer all over his jeans and shoes. *Charlie. Naked. No clothes.* His dick twitched at the mental image, one he should be familiar with by now considering he'd pictured it at least twice a fucking week. Hell, more.

"Dropped something there." Charlie grinned. After lifting his jaw back into position, she hopped over the counter again, taking a full tray of drinks back to the other side of the room.

Vince forced his eyes off the sway of her ass and turned to a smirking Bea. "She didn't seriously pose for you all, did she?"

The older woman sipped her margarita. "She sure did. She even promised to come back for couples' week. I'd ask if you wanted to volunteer, but when I told him we'd already secured our lovely Charlie, that ridiculously handsome Beau brother, from the construction company in town, immediately offered his services. Maybe you could be his understudy...if he calls in sick."

Vince caught himself grinding his back molars at the thought of Charlie posing with the oversexed douche. The guy had so many notches on his post that the damn thing couldn't stay upright—and he boasted about each and every one of them.

"Behave." He gestured to Bea's group's replenished margaritas. "Or I really will confiscate your drinks."

Vince returned to his orders, walking away from the chorus of chuckles.

The town of Frederick didn't have much in the way of a tourist flow, which made spotting the stranger at the end of the bar easy. Somewhere in his mid-thirties and dressed in a suit and tie, the man should've been in a boardroom instead of a country dive.

"What can I get you?" Vince asked.

The stranger's attention remained fixed on the other side of the bar. Vince followed the man's gaze, annoyance stirring his gut when he realized he was watching Charlie and the girls.

Vince cleared his throat and didn't bother with pleasantries. "You need to either order a drink or get off the stool. Patrons only."

Preppy Boy finally turned around. "I'll take an ice water."

Vince waited for the punch line, but when it didn't come, he reached for a glass. He'd no sooner turned toward the tap machine when Preppy's eyes slid back toward Charlie. He plunked the water down, making it splash on the countertop. "What else?"

"Nothing." Preppy Boy reached for his drink. "Actually, you could hit me up with a little bartender gossip. The blonde? With the pink hair? Is she here most nights?"

Vince crossed his arms over his chest and heard his jaw crack.

At his silence, Preppy spared him a quick glance. "Oh, come on. You know, the hot little number who was over here a few minutes ago? The one with the perfect rack and killer ass?"

"I know who you're talking about. I just have no intention of answering you, and if you knew what was good for you, you'd keep your distance."

Preppy cocked up a suspiciously well-groomed eyebrow. "Are the two of you an item or something? Or are you playing the part of the big bad protector?"

"She's not an item with anyone, and I don't need to protect that woman from anything when she can do it all on her own. Just saving you the embarrassment of getting shot down—or knocked down. With her, it could go either way."

Preppy took a sip of his drink. "Thanks for the advice, friend, but I can handle it—and her."

Vince leaned closer to the bar and to the stranger, throwing a little extra menace into his tone. "Let me make myself a little clearer, *friend*. She's not the type of woman who's going to be handled—by you or anyone else. As a matter fact, none of the women in this joint are, so if you're looking to cause trouble, you best walk away while you still have the use of both your legs."

Vince almost wanted the ass-hat to argue because, not having been in the field for more than a week, he could use a little action. Unfortunately, Preppy stayed silent and gave a slight nod. Vince turned back to the waiting customers, barely missing an *innocent* Bea-grab, when his gaze caught a familiar pair of brown eyes watching him from the other side of the room.

Fuck. He really should start thinking about taking his own advice.

* * *

Charlie ripped her eyes away from the bar before the three women she'd claimed as best friends called her out on her distraction. Again. Despite the fact that they'd all met less than a year ago, they sometimes knew her thoughts better than she did, a side effect of having girlfriends to which she wasn't yet accustomed. Any childhood friends she'd collected growing up had been kids whose parents had decided to stretch their legs at the same rest spot.

Learning through life experiences. That's how her mom had once described their vagabond existence, hopping from country to country, never staying in one place for longer than a week or two. No classrooms. No school dances. No best friends—until now, which was why she tried bloody hard not to chase them away with her snark.

"Stop staring a hole through me. *Please*." Charlie narrowed her eyes, focusing on the bull's-eye in front of her. The dart flew from her fingers and missed its mark by three damn rings.

"I'll stop staring when you tell us the truth," Penny bartered from her perch on the stool. Fingering her red hair, she studied Charlie before throwing her attention toward Rachel and Elle. "You guys see it, too, right? I mean, I'm not completely off my game?"

"Definitely hiding something," Elle agreed with a nod.

Rachel, at least, gave Charlie an apologetic look. "You have been a little off tonight."

Charlie didn't want to lie—something *had* been different since she'd stepped into the bar. Normally, meeting up with the girls meant a male-free night of fruity drinks, dirty jokes, and relaxation. Tonight, she simply felt plugged in...like her body was on a constant alert, prepped for something to happen.

She almost blamed Vince for the source of the itchy, hyperaware tingle on the back of her neck, but his attention warmed her body from the lady bits out; it didn't make her feel like an entire colony of ants were doing the Irish jig on her spine.

"Fine." Penny sighed. "You don't want to tell us what's on your mind. At least explain what you did to poor Vince when you went over to get our pitcher. He went from looking annoyed to shell-shocked, and then...I don't know what that was when you walked away."

"I may have mentioned my posing for Bea and the ladies at the rec center," Charlie admitted.

Elle's nose wrinkled up, the blonde deep in thought. "But

why would that make him look like he'd walked in on his parents having sex?"

Rachel burst into laughter, nearly falling off her seat. "You didn't tell him what kind of posing you were doing, did you?"

Charlie chuckled. "If his mind chose to go the dirty and naked route, who am I to steer him in the right direction?"

"Wait," Penny interjected. "You posed nude?"

"My hands did. They were studying the bending of joints or something and needed someone who didn't have arthritis yet. But my point's that I—"

"Love seeing Vince squirm."

Charlie shrugged, barely hiding her own grin. "A girl's got to have a hobby, doesn't she? Besides, I don't know if you noticed, but it's pretty damn hard to get a reaction out of the man. I have to take advantage of every opportunity that comes my way."

Rachel's attention shifted across the room. A ghost of a smile hovered over her lips. "I don't know. He looks pretty reactive to me."

Charlie couldn't help but follow her friend's gaze, and instantly regretted it. Rachel was right. Locked in their direction, Vince's hazel eyes not only pierced through the room, but through her.

"I need the loo." Charlie handed over the remaining darts to Elle. "Don't shoot someone in the arse—at least until I get back and can drive the getaway car."

"Hey," the pregnant blonde complained, "my aim's not that bad."

"Love, you couldn't hit a barn big enough to park a semi…but we love you anyway."

Charlie forced herself into a slow, easy stride, but halfway across the room, that damn watched feeling came back.

She performed a quick eye-sweep of the room. Sports and hunting seemed to be the focus of more than one discussion. Nothing unusual. Nothing out of the norm—until she saw the stranger.

In a sea of flannels and hunter jackets, his pressed pants and pin-striped shirt stuck out. He leaned casually against the end of the bar, smiling at her from over his drink. Something about him made her hair stand up on end, but she passed quickly and headed down the long hall toward the ladies' room.

She took her time using the facilities, washed her hands, and then splashed her face with cold water for good measure. When she came out, Pressed Pants was leaning against the far wall.

"The gents' loo is down the way." Charlie gestured toward the other end of the hallway—*after* she'd made sure he didn't have any friends with him.

"Not here for the bathroom. How about I buy you a drink?"

Charlie cocked up a single eyebrow. "Do you always follow women to the bathroom so you can ask them that? And before you answer, know that was a rhetorical question. I'm not interested."

She turned to walk away, but his hand landed on her elbow. Instinct ripped her arm from his hold, and she spun, using the fifty or more pounds he had on her to pin his arm behind his back and plant his face into the wall.

"Did I give you permission to touch me?" Charlie growled.

"Jesus Christ. Intense much?" the stranger's voice sounded muffled. "I thought you looked stressed. Figured it would unwind you some."

"I don't need unwinding," Charlie lied. She released her

hold and stepped back, forcing her breathing to slow as she turned toward the main room. "You're barking up the wrong tree, love. I'm sure there's someone else who would love to take you up on your offer, but I'm not that woman."

"And I think you are...Charlotte."

Charlie froze at the mouth of the hall before she turned around. Pressed Pants was no longer smiling—and he no longer had the condescending man-on-the-prowl look. Something else glittered from his eyes, and it zapped a fierce—and brief—bolt of panic down her spine.

"I tried doing this the easy way, Miss Hughes." He smiled, obviously enjoying the fact he'd caught her off guard. "Oh, I'm sorry. You go by Charlie Sparks now, am I right?"

"Who are you?"

"I work for someone who's been searching for you for a long time. And I have to admit, we almost gave up. Your talent behind the computer hadn't been fabricated in the least."

"Trust me, there's nothing I can do for you."

His lips pulled back into another grin. "But there is, which is why we should be sitting for a talk—in private."

Twelve years suddenly seemed like yesterday. Charlie's world started going dark, the walls getting tighter around her. The only thing preventing her from going under was a familiar pair of hazel eyes watching her from the other end of the bar.

Vince's attention flicked from her to the stranger and back, not missing a beat despite being half a room away.

Charlie grabbed the stranger's arm and tugged him down the hall to the bar's small corner office. She needed to deal with this—preferably without witnesses. Once she found out exactly what she was dealing with, then she'd decide how high the shite was going to rise.

CHAPTER THREE

Thump-thump. Wack. Thump-thump. Wack. Someone wailed on a sparring bag, the sound reverberating through Alpha Security's corridor as if it was on the overhead communication system. The closer to the gym Vince got, the louder the low grunts became. Logan and Trey, two of his Alpha teammates, hovered outside the door, which left a handful of possibilities as to the owner of the serious aggression.

"Why are you two girls hiding out here in the hall?" Vince smacked Logan on the back and peeked into the training room.

The snug fabric hugging the ample curves of her breasts like a fucking glove, Charlie bounced on the balls of her feet in a hypnotic to-and-fro movement. A little blue jewel winked at him from her belly button as she pivoted her hips and turned her torso into a punch.

Frowning, Vince watched the way she attacked the sparring bag, as if it had insulted her mother, and she showed no signs of slowing despite the dewy glow sliding over her skin. "How long has she been at this?"

"An hour." Trey, obviously displeased, nodded toward the left. "And before that it was about thirty minutes of Scooter time—give or take."

Vince glanced over to the life-sized dummy they kept on hand for weapons training, and winced at the half dozen throwing knives sticking out of his neck. And his chest. And his groin, exactly where his dick would be fucking shish-kebabed if he'd been human.

Logan's gaze tracked the way Charlie drilled fist after fist into the sparring bag and added, "And she was in Stone's office before that."

"Door open or closed?" asked Vince.

"Closed. For half-a-fucking-hour."

Fuck. Nothing good ever came out of being summoned to the boss's office. And Vince couldn't help but tally the time clock and realize that the chain of events had started soon after she'd hustled toward the back room with Preppy Boy.

"Did either of you ask her what happened?" asked Vince.

The guys looked at him as if he'd sprouted a dick in the middle of his forehead.

"Does it look like we have a fucking death wish?" Trey questioned. "Jesus. I have a kid on the way, one I'd like to watch grow up, and raise alongside my future wife. No way am I sticking my head anywhere near the lion's mouth."

"She's five-foot-nothing."

Logan shook his head, chuckling low. "Dude. You've been on the team for a while now, and it's like you haven't learned a damn thing. Charlie makes some four-star generals seem like domesticated pussycats."

He was inclined to agree. Though petite Charlie was no

wilting flower. He'd been on the receiving end of her sharp wit more times than he cared to count, not to mention her roundhouse. But that wasn't where her edge stopped.

The most exquisite ink work he'd seen in a damn long time wrapped around the right side of her torso and slid beneath the band of her yoga pants. The understated beauty of rich brown tree limbs and pink cherry blossoms was as gorgeous as it was fitting. Hard and soft. Stark and gorgeous. All of it fit Charlie to a tee.

"You're overextending your arm on the punch." Vince stepped into the gym, aware that his friends hightailed it in the opposite direction the second he'd opened his mouth.

Chicken shits.

"I don't recall asking for your bloody advice." Not bothering to look in his direction, she drilled another series of punches into the bag, no doubt envisioning his face floating in front of her.

"The friendly thing to do would be to say 'Thank you, Vincent. You saved me from having my arm in a sling for four weeks.'"

"If you want friendly, go upstairs." Charlie nodded above them to where the bar was in full midnight swing. "I'm sure there's a blonde or brunette or redhead looking to be the next member in the Navy Boy fan club."

Thwack. Kick.

Hell, she was right. He could go up to the bar and, within five minutes, have a willing companion for the night. Once upon a time, he wouldn't have thought twice about it, and the fleeting sexual release would've easily smoothed away the constant edge that always hovered beneath the surface. Now it left him cold.

"You almost sounded a little jealous there, English. Careful, or I may get the impression you care." Vince took position behind the sparring bag and held it in place, knowing he was living dangerously but not giving a shit.

As expected, she kicked precariously close to his right hand. "There's nothing to be jealous about. I could get a bad dye-job and fake boobs if I wanted, but flying around like a deflated balloon if something sharp pokes me in the chest isn't my idea of fun."

At the mention of her chest, his eyes dropped to her cleavage. Hell, he couldn't help it. He was a man, and the two secured globes looked pretty damn close to perfection. Unfortunately, she noticed his shifted attention too.

Charlie twisted, winding up for another roundhouse, but this time didn't pull back. Before he registered her aim, the top of her shoe connected with his ear, making it ring like a church bell.

Vince released the bag with a growl. "Jesus Christ, woman. You're a fucking nuisance."

Hands on her curvy hips, she stepped into his space, the top of her head barely hitting his chin. Mighty Mouse with a bad attitude. "Oh, please. You're a big bad SEAL and you can't take a little tap?"

"You want to turn this into a hand-to-hand sparring match, *English Muffin*? Fine with me."

She ducked his frontal assault and spun, her foot impacting two inches above his knee. The damn thing buckled and gave her the upper hand for about five seconds. Vince took his time, blocking each of her moves while he waited for the one that would regift him the advantage. When her eyes shifted left, he spun right. Now behind her, he pinned his forearm across her collarbone and anchored her back against his chest.

"Are you done yet?" His lips brushed over the shell of her ear. Every one of his internal alarms went ape-shit, including the one between his legs, which was semi-hard and nestled perfectly against the small of her back.

Fuck, he couldn't help it. All night watching her, then picturing her posing nude. He could only keep his body in check for so goddamned long without having at least one minor slip.

Charlie stilled for about two seconds, her backside moving into a slight sway. And hell if she didn't do it again, the second time pulling a low groan from his throat. His grip lightened to step away, but it was too late. Two small hands yanked down his arm, and a set of teeth bit into the flesh of his hand.

"Fucking-A," Vince howled, releasing her quickly.

Charlie ignored his colorful curses and swayed her ass over to her water bottle. "Yep. I'm about done now."

Vince opened his mouth to comment, but movement at the doorway caught his attention.

Stone stood off the mat, arms folded across his chest. And fuck, he didn't look happy. "I need you in the meeting room. Now. And Charlie, I want your ass in there in another ten."

Vince nodded, not having any clue how much of the show he'd seen.

He tossed Charlie a glare before leaving the room, and followed Stone deeper into the underground labyrinth that was Alpha Security headquarters. They had not only a training room, but a shooting range, offices, and a meeting room that made the Pentagon look half-assed. And all of it built into a section of the Blue Ridge Mountains. To the outside world, Vince and his team were business owners and bouncers who'd taken over the running of a much-loved neighborhood bar. To a select few topside, they were the men who got shit done when the government's hands were metaphorically—or logistically—tied.

The meeting room was empty when they got there. "You want a bag of ice for that hand?"

Vince glared at his boss's smirk. "Maybe a tetanus shot. Look, about what happened in the training room, I—"

"This isn't about the training room, although it does involve Charlie."

Stone wasn't an easy guy to read—at all. But his silence spoke a thousand fucking words. "What about her?"

"I've offered her a primary position in a case."

Vince narrowed his gaze on his boss. Having been champing at the bit for a real field assignment, the mouthy Brit should've been walking around HQ busting their balls and gloating. "If you've assigned her a case, then why the hell has she spent the last hour neutering Scooter? What the hell kind of case is this?"

Lips pressed in a tight line, Stone looked grim. "DHS. More specifically, human-trafficking, with a possible link to agency corruption."

Vince's eyes widened. That sure as hell wasn't what he'd expected to come out of Stone's mouth. "In the Department of Homeland? Shit. And you think English can track the perps electronically or something?"

"That would be fucking nice, but no. It's a bit more complicated. I'm not sure what you know about Charlie pre-Alpha, but—"

"Nothing, and it's bloody well going to stay that way." The woman herself stood in the doorway of what she and Penny had once dubbed the Room of Testosterone. Her brown eyes shifted to him before traveling back to Stone. "Sorry, I didn't think I should wait and chance missing all the fun. And I'm glad I didn't. What's Navy doing here?"

"I told you that if you decide to go through with this, you'd have a partner." Stone nodded toward Vince. "Franklin's yours."

Charlie's calculating gaze slid to him before returning to their boss. "No way in hell."

"If your backup isn't one of ours, it doesn't happen. I'm not letting you go back on the inside without someone we can trust standing next to you. I'm sorry you're having a problem with that, but that's how it's going to be."

"What about Logan?"

"With you away, I need him running operations here."

"Chase?"

"Out on a surveillance gig. Rafe's on another assignment too. And I'm not sending Trey, knowing his mind would be back here on Elle and the baby. Franklin's your second. You can either accept it and sit down to hear the rest, or I can call our contact at DHS right now and tell them it's a no-go. Your choice."

Charlie trying to pass Vince over in favor of one of the other guys chafed him raw. Being one of the newest to the team didn't mean he was a fucking rookie. In his years of service, he'd seen and done things that would give a person's *nightmares* nightmares. Fuck, he still woke up most nights in a goddamned cold sweat.

Charlie sat two chairs away, refusing to look him in the eye. He didn't even know exactly what the assignment entailed, but he was suddenly hell-bent on making sure he was there for its duration, whether she liked it or not.

"Charlie was approached tonight by a DHS agent looking for assistance with one of their dying cases. They're about two steps away from writing it off and calling it a loss," Stone addressed Vince.

It took him a moment to register what his boss was saying and to connect the dots—to Preppy Boy. Vince shifted his attention to Charlie. "The dipshit with the chinos was a DHS agent?"

Charlie nodded, still not looking his way.

Vince turned to his boss. "Okay, so why the hell are they approaching English? That kid was barely out of diapers there's no way in fucking hell he's high enough on the DHS food chain to know about Alpha."

"They didn't approach Alpha Security. They approached Charlie because they believe she's the inside they've been lacking. *I'm* making it an Alpha Security issue. I contacted our department liaison and told him that *if* she decides to go through with it, it'll be us taking point. Actually, taking the fuck over. Color me surprised when he sounded relieved. They've lost three agents trying to get on the inside of the Franconi crime organization, and the fourth, their deep-cover agent, is suspected to have switched jerseys."

"Franconi?" Vince's eyes narrowed. "Why do I know that name?"

"Most people do unless they've been living under a rock."

Suddenly, it clicked. "Why the fuck would Charlie have insight into a human-trafficking ring led by one of the East Coast's most notorious crime lords?"

Vince stared down Stone. Stone looked expectantly to Charlie. And Charlie finally flashed her dark brown eyes Vince's way and admitted, "Because Arturo Franconi's my uncle."

* * *

"Uncle." The truth of that word sliced up Charlie's throat like razor blades. Her aunt's marriage to Arturo Franconi meant he'd been gifted guardianship of eight-year-old Char-

lie when bad weather and a twisty road took both her mother
and her aunt away with one veer of the steering wheel.

Growing up in the middle of a crime cartel hadn't been
the type of life experiences her mother had had in mind
when they first set off across the globe, but Charlie had been
subjected to it nonetheless . . . for eight years, until she'd gotten the final push to make a quick, clean break.

"You may want to close your mouth before a fly beds
down in your tonsils," Charlie addressed an obviously
shocked Vince. "Yes, Arturo's my uncle, but only because
some judge in Florida signed a marriage license."

Vince's gaze snapped back to Stone. "You've got to be
shitting me right now."

"Wish I was," Stone answered. "If you and Charlie decide
to do this, you rely only on each other and no one else.
There's no way in hell we're going to take a chance that the
deep-cover agent is still loyal to the feds."

And *that* was something that Charlie couldn't yet wrap
her head around. "I know DHS said Brock Torres has become like Arturo's appendage, but I can't see it. I know
Brock, or at least, I thought I did. He couldn't stand the fact
that his father worked for Arturo *before* he left for the Army,
and he hated it even more when he got out. Him working for
the organization—cover or not—is really hard to picture."

Stone slid a large manila envelope down the table.
Surveillance photos. Each image ignited a flash from Charlie's past, erasing nearly a decade in an instant. Except for
the obvious aging of her uncle's colleagues, the first few
pictures didn't make her blink more than once. The one of
Brock, however, made her pause. And stare.

Every second of the last twelve years was etched on the
hard lines of his face. In one particular photo, her one-time
friend stood next to Arturo, looking oh-so-comfortable as

they spoke, heads bowed low in conversation. Or maybe she should say her one-time *supposed* friend, because he'd evidently been on the job when he befriended her all those years ago.

Stone stood, locking Charlie in his sights. "The only reason I didn't put a stop to this right off the bat is because of you. I feel for the women being taken, too. I do. But I was dead serious. You and Vince either do this together, or you don't do it at all. Figure out if that's something the two of you can do without killing each other and let me know. I'll be in my office."

Stone walked out of the meeting room, making Charlie painfully aware she was alone with Vince. There wasn't a doubt in her mind that he'd try demanding answers to the questions firing around in his head. Whether or not they'd be ones she'd answer was less certain.

Vince leaned back in his chair, arms folded across his chest, and stared at her. He didn't say a word. Not a mumble. Not even an audible sigh. He merely waited, as if he hadn't just found out she'd been raised by a man who made hardened criminals piss in their britches.

Needing to move, Charlie stood and began pacing the length of the room before she caught herself and picked a spot a safe three feet away. "I suppose you're expecting me to plead my case on why I want to go."

"No, but if you think pleading may be necessary, then I'm curious why you think going's a good idea."

"It's *not* a good idea," she said honestly. "Actually, I think it's a horrid idea, and I can't express to you how much I don't want to do it."

He blinked, trying to understand. "Then why are we even talking about it? Stone's leaving the decision in our hands. If you don't want to do it, you say no. It's that simple."

"It's not simple. At all. Because if I'm in a position to find those nine missing women and prevent others from being abducted, then that's what I bloody well need to do. Otherwise, we're part of the problem."

"What problem?" Vince needed to know.

"Apathy. The whole '*Well, it doesn't involve me directly, so I'm keeping my nose out of it*' mentality that's been known to plague humanity."

"And what about putting yourself at risk?" When she didn't answer, Vince stood, his towering height forcing her gaze north. Before he realized it, he was inches away from crowding her personal space. "I can't imagine a man like Franconi was happy about letting you walk away."

Charlie snorted. "It's not like he had a choice."

Vince raised a brow, his curiosity piqued.

Charlie sighed, knowing she needed to tell him *something*. "I've had a fondness for computers for as long as I can remember—a fondness my uncle liked to utilize from time to time to help him slip out of tight spaces. Thinking how naive and trusting I was, it makes me cringe. But when I was fifteen, I wised up, stopped helping, and started working *against* him. The man's seriously techno-illiterate. It let me construct a ticket to freedom...which I used when I was sixteen."

"So in other words, you blackmailed him."

Charlie shrugged. "What I did, *worked*. I left, and he knew if anything ever happened to me, all the information I'd collected through the years would get to the authorities. To this day, he doesn't know exactly what I have on him...which, between you and me, wouldn't have been enough to buy him five to ten years. I was a little too good at keeping his nose looking clean."

Vince stared at her as if trying to read her memories. Too

intuitive for his own bloody good, he no doubt knew she was leaving something out. And she was. Oh, she'd used her computer savvy to magic her way out of his life, but she'd been forced to leave Miami and cut all ties before she'd drummed up enough damaging evidence against him.

After her own abduction, Charlie focused on nothing but living.

CHAPTER FOUR

Nothing good ever came out of flying by the seat of your pants. Vince had learned his lesson the hard way eight years ago when one of his calls led to a good man's death. Ever since, he prided himself on collecting all the data, constructing a plan, and sticking to it. They'd been in Miami for a total of six hours, and Charlie had already slid his plans through the fucking shredder.

He flipped through their wrist-thick file on Arturo Franconi and his horde of merry convicts, and tossed it on the bed.

"We need to talk about tonight," Vince called through their hotel suite's bathroom door. "I'm not convinced this is the way to go."

"And I told you, it's the *only* way," Charlie's muffled voice came through the door.

"And it's a logistical fucking nightmare. Too big a space. Too many bodies. There's no way in hell I'm going to be able to track the comings and goings *and* watch over you. I'm one man."

"Then I guess it's a good thing I'm a woman because we can multitask—and I don't need to be *watched over*."

The bathroom door flew open. Vince nearly swallowed his damn tongue. Her yoga pants and exercise tank gone, Charlie's navel-plunging dress not only didn't have a fucking neckline, but it dipped into a severe V, showing off her twinkling belly button ring—and skin. A lot of fucking skin.

"That's what took you so long?" The words escaped his mouth before he could stop them. "For the degree of clothes you're not wearing, it should've taken you five seconds to get ready."

"Wearing less requires more maintenance."

Charlie strutted past him, making him choke on what was left of his own goddamned spit. Not only was her outfit backless, revealing the feminine top curve of her ass, but each sway of her hips gifted him a glimpse of her cherry blossom tattoo.

"Where are you planning on strapping Gregor?" Vince watched her pick up her Glock and pack it back in its case.

"Nowhere. As much as it pains me to leave him behind, we can't go in armed in the traditional sense, so I'm resorting to the backup." She pulled out a pair of throwing knives and a thigh holster and caught him mid-ogle. Her voice dropped to a low purr. "Want to help me secure them into place?"

Yes.

"No." Sweat dampened his forehead despite the fact their suite was air-conditioned to the nines.

Charlie chuckled as she propped her booted foot onto the edge of the bed and began adjusting her blade holster. "So what were you blathering about logistics?"

Vince cleared his throat and got his mind off Charlie's legs and back on their night's plans. "The point of being here is to make sure you get on Franconi's radar."

"Wrong. We're here to find information on the abductions and whoever's responsible."

"How's going clubbing going to make that happen?"

Charlie pulled out the list of suspected hunting grounds from their file and not-so-gently smashed it against his chest. "DHS managed to link most of the reported disappearances to these three popular, Franconi-connected clubs. I thought you were going to brush up on the details while I got ready."

"I read the list." Vince ground his molars.

"So what would you rather us do? Sit in a car outside the club and stare at the exit?"

That was scarily close to what he had planned.

"You do realize this city practically has a limitless number of clubs, right? All with multiple egress points. We can't keep our eyes trained on them all—even using recording surveillance. We need to focus on the clubs with the most activity and try to figure out what we're up against—why *these* clubs are the ones that keep getting hit. And we can't do that while sitting in a car. As for getting on Arturo's radar, he's going to know I'm in town before we sip our first drinks—if he doesn't already."

Charlie finished tucking her throwing knives into place against her thigh and let her dress drop. "Any unsightly bulges?"

Not beneath her dress. Behind his zipper was a different story. He'd been fighting off a hard-on since she stepped out of the bathroom looking like La Femme Nikita. Usually there were any number of the guys around to keep his head on straight. Charlie Sparks was most definitely not *one of the guys*, something Vince Junior was evidently starting to realize.

She turned, mistaking his discomfort for disbelief. "What is it that has your panties in a twist, Navy? Does taking a back seat to a woman really bother you that much?"

"You're not a woman. You're English." Vince tried reminding himself that this was Charlie he was picturing half-naked and oh-so-fuckable.

Her brown eyes sparked with a flame of annoyance. Or hell, an explosion. "Sorry to disappoint you, love, but if I'd had a penis, I would've been let into the boys club a hell of a long time ago. But penis-challenged as I am, I'm the one with the inside scoop. I know how Miami works. And I know how Arturo and his brood of miscreants work too. You're going to have to trust me. *This* is what we need to do. Walking up to his front door and ringing the doorbell won't do anything except ensure we end up like those out-of-commission DHS agents."

"It's not about trust."

"You mean if you were partnered with Logan on this assignment, you'd be questioning his decisions right now too?" At his silence, she snorted, rolling her eyes. "Yeah. I didn't bloody think so."

"He can sometimes be annoying as hell, but Logan isn't in the habit of flying off in all directions. If we come up with a plan, I need to trust you'll follow it."

Charlie settled her hands on her hips and shot him a daring look. "And what if following the plan puts innocent people—or us—in danger? You expect me to go by the rulebook? Sometimes going in a different direction is what you need to do to get the job done."

He glared. "There's a time and place for going off-script. You don't do it because you're bored and looking for a little action."

"I'm glad you think so little of my judgment."

"I told you before, it's not about—"

"Me. Yeah, I got the memo but I'm not buying it." Charlie lifted her chin and ground her teeth. One step closer and she'd be near enough to drop his ass to the ground. "Maybe we should put a hold on this conversation before pretending to be infatuated with one another becomes a lost cause. As it stands right now, we're going to need a miracle if we're going to convince anyone we're headed down a wedding aisle and not death row."

Vince stepped closer, keeping his face blank. Charlie's, however, wasn't. A hint of something flickered in her eyes as she watched him stalk toward her. By the time he stopped, inches shy of her fuck-me heels, it had vanished.

He traced one calloused hand provocatively over her silk-covered hip, and cupped her lower back, tugging her flush against him. Her palm braced for impact, colliding with his chest.

"What are you doing?" Charlie's voice sounded low and breathless, something he'd only heard after she'd attacked the sparring bag for an hour or more.

"Why? Am I making you nervous?"

"No." The twitch of her left eye said otherwise. "I'm *disturbed*. There's a difference."

"I'm about to propose to my fiancée." Vince reached into his pocket and pulled out the ring. It had been a last-minute, spur-of-the-moment grab before he'd left his apartment in Pennsylvania, one he still wasn't sure was a good idea.

Charlie stared at his hand, her body gone still. "What's *that*?"

"For such a smart woman, I'd think you'd recognize a ring when you saw one."

"But why do you have it?"

"Can't have anyone, especially your uncle, questioning

my loyalty to you, now can I?" He slowly slid the simple princess-cut ruby onto her finger. When it was in place, he kept hold of her hand. "It's not a traditional ring, but you're not a regular diamond kind of woman, so I thought it was fitting."

For once in the year he'd known her, Charlie was speechless. Her eyes locked on the platinum setting and the small baguettes nestled on each side of the rich red stone. "It's . . . gorgeous. Who did Stone let do the shopping? Penny or Elle?"

"No one. It belonged to my grandmother."

She startled out of her awe, shaking her head emphatically as she tried tugging the ring off her finger. "Nope. No way in bloody hell are we using family heirlooms when there's perfectly presentable cubic zirconia out there in the world."

Vince trapped her fingers beneath his. "Yes, we are. Don't you think your uncle would be able to tell the difference between the real thing and a knockoff? Or, more importantly, wouldn't he expect *you* to know the difference and deal with anyone who tried pulling the wool over your eyes?"

"We are not using family jewelry for an assignment," Charlie hissed.

"You can either accept the ring, or we'll swing by a tattoo shop and get my name tattooed on your ass. Your choice."

"Like hell will I ever let a man brand me." Charlie scowled.

"Then the ring it is . . ." Vince's large thumb stroked over her knuckles. "What's wrong, English? Not thrilled about being the future Mrs. Franklin?"

Goddamn, those words sounded foreign even to his own ears. As a Navy grunt, he'd been too young to think about tying himself down, but now? Now he was too damn jaded. He couldn't expect someone else to haul around his baggage, much less a no-nonsense woman like Charlie.

"Not thrilled with the idea of being Mrs. Anybody. I fought too hard to convince Stone to give me a chance in the field. I'm not about to let some random Neanderthal muck it up." She glanced back to the ring, and cringed. "Seriously, Navy. There's some pretty real-looking costume jewelry out there. It's not like I'm going to let Arturo put it under a microscope."

"Ring or ink, English. Besides, it's not like I slid it off someone's finger to use it, or that it's going to be put into use anytime in the near future. This is the most action it'll ever receive."

Vince knew he'd latched onto her common sense when she blew out a long sigh. He kept her hands trapped in his a beat longer before letting her pull away.

"Fine. Consider us engaged," Charlie announced. She threw their rental keys at him a little harder—and higher—than necessary, but he caught them easily. "But I swear to God, if I hear one crack about practicing for the goddamned honeymoon, this ring's going to be introduced to your colon—previously owned by a grandmother or not."

An hour later, Vince pulled his truck into the valet line at Miami Heat. People strutted up and down the sidewalk, already blitzed out of their minds. "Looks like we're late to the party."

Charlie peered out of the window and chuckled. "These guys haven't even started. Give them another hour or two to hit their peak."

That's what Vince was afraid of. Give him something to shoot, punch, or blow up and he was in his element. Expect him to socialize with a horde of twenty-somethings at a trendy Miami nightclub and "awkward" didn't begin to explain how he felt. "Old" came close—really fucking old. At thirty-six, he didn't fit into this kind of crowd. Charlie, on the other hand, meshed like she fucking belonged.

Vince slipped out of the truck just as she swung open her door. A group of college-aged boys turned the corner, one of whom immediately latched his lurid gaze onto Charlie's toned legs.

"Hot damn, baby." The kid whistled. His gaze flickered to Vince. "Why don't you ditch the geriatric and come party with us?"

"Unless you want this geriatric to rip those lips off your face, keep walking," Vince growled.

The kid and his friends laughed but kept going. At some point during the exchange, the pimply faced valet attendant extended his hand to Charlie.

"I got her. You get these." Vince's bark made the teen jump.

"Yes, sir." The valet caught the keys Vince tossed his way and hustled over to the driver's side.

Every inch of Charlie's body brushed along Vince's as he plucked her off her seat and set her back on her feet. The hair on his arms lifted as if he'd touched pure electricity, and in a way, he had. Charlie. A live wire. Jolting. Heat-inducing.

Her teeth trapped her bottom lip in a sexy nibble. Vince couldn't help but glance down to her mouth, seeing that he wasn't the only one overtaken by a sudden burst of awareness.

"If I'd been the one to offer my hand to you, you would've taken a hunk of flesh out of it with your teeth," Vince half-joked.

She smoothed the front of his shirt, a coy smile dancing on her lips. "Not a hunk. Maybe just a little nibble."

Sucking in a groan, Vince wrapped an arm around her

waist and guided her away from the truck as another large group of college-aged kids stumbled past.

Charlie let out a strangled noise.

"What?" Vince looked at her, confused.

She bit the corner of her mouth, obviously trying to withhold laughter. "You and the look of excruciating pain plastered all over your face. You can't tell me you've never prowled the bars looking for a good time."

Vince steered them toward the entrance of the club's outdoor patio. "Yeah, a million fucking years ago. And I didn't have to *prowl* for anything. Good times always came to me."

This time Charlie snorted with her chuckle, and the sound of it made his lips twitch. It was goddamned cute, though he would never admit it aloud and risk a punch to his kidneys.

"It's a wonder headquarters hasn't blown up from testosterone toxicity," Charlie murmured as they stepped to the end of the club's red-roped line.

The bouncer manning the entrance took a lazy-eyed stroll over Charlie's body. "You two together?"

Vince cocked a glance to his arm, still wrapped snugly around her waist. "What do you think?"

"I think it's too damn bad. But you both can go on in. And if your lady's interested, there's a bar-dancing competition sometime within the hour." He eyed Charlie's legs. "You're a shoe-in for first fucking prize, sweetheart."

Vince would've loved nothing more than to swipe the smirk off the bastard's face, but Charlie intervened, threading her fingers through his, and thanked the man for the invite. The people in line grumbled their protests as the bouncer opened the gate and let them onto the club's patio.

Miami Heat lured in a who's who of the rich, famous, and privileged. Whereas the indoor section of the club catered to the couples dancing to the loud, theatrical pound of the music, the outdoor patio was a pool party on 'roids.

White Christmas lights wrapped every palm tree and, and, as if Miami wasn't hot enough, bamboo torches lit up the patio's perimeter. Humidity didn't seem to be keeping people away, because the line wrapped around the circular bar was three people deep, and growing.

"Don't people have anything better to do than spend their money on overpriced booze?" Vince asked, inspecting the sea of drunk people.

Charlie lifted her brow. "In Miami? No. It's all about twenty-dollar drinks and lots and lots of skin. You're such a people person, Navy. It's a wonder you don't have an entire entourage surrounding you all hours of the day."

"And you're such the sparkling social gem, huh?" Vince said dryly. A pair of overly bronzed women skirted past, outrageously wearing less than Charlie. "I wasn't the one who nearly made the pizza delivery boy cry because he mistakenly left behind my order of fried mushrooms."

"No, but now I'm sure that Christopher will never forget them again. That's the difference between us. I don't see any point in hiding my displeasure, where you take the whole brooding in silence thing and turn it into an art form."

"Some things can't be changed by making a scene."

Charlie turned toward him, the side of her breast brushing against his chest. "No, but sometimes it can make you feel a lot bloody better. Unleash the beast, Navy. Or at the very least, loosen the reins. You may be surprised at what happens."

When he'd been with the SEAL teams, Vince wouldn't have hesitated to let off a little steam—and without prompting. But both time and experience had taught him the error of his ways. He'd learned it at the end of his Navy career, had it drilled into his head working for bail enforcement, and now with Alpha, it had become almost second nature—except when Charlie was in close proximity. Then all those lessons flew out of his fucking head.

"You want to make ourselves visible?" Vince slipped his hand over her hip and veered her toward the dance floor. "Hope you can dance in those stilts."

CHAPTER FIVE

As if diving into the club scene wasn't bad enough, Vince played Charlie's bluff like a concert cellist. She'd known before accepting the assignment that being back in town would test her in every way imaginable—and probably a few which he hadn't yet drummed up. But she'd underestimated her own level of paranoia—paranoia she couldn't afford to let Vince see, because the second she did, she'd be back on the Alpha jet and headed to headquarters.

No way in bloody hell was she abandoning those missing girls to the circus DHS had been running for the last few months.

Vince's large hands settled on the bare patch of skin above the curve of her arse—and he began to move. Charlie forgot all about the paranoia. Heat eased through her body as her breasts brushed against his chest with each magical sway.

A body his size wasn't meant to move this smoothly.

Her heart skipped, pounding beneath her breastbone, nearly double-time compared to the slow beat of the music. Vince looked...unaffected. Beneath her sweaty palms, which rested on his chest, his heart thudded, nice and even...and slow.

"Where did you learn to dance?" she asked. At the sight of Vince's lips sliding into a naughty smirk, her knees went wonky.

"I'm a SEAL."

Charlie blinked, waiting for more. "Which means what? They teach you how to waltz during Hell Week? Or that you know how to do it all?"

"Not all, but most. And if Hell Week involved waltzing, more soldiers would've rung that damn bell and walked the hell home," Vince joked. "But once a SEAL cares enough about something to put it on our to-do list, we make sure we master it. Life. Job. Hobbies. We don't do any of this half-ass shit. Once upon a time, I had a wedding to go to, and I didn't feel like making an ass out of myself."

Charlie couldn't wrap her mind around Vince taking dance lessons, maybe surrounded by little girls wearing tights and pink tutus. A coming smart-arse comment died on her lips the moment someone bumped into her from behind.

She gasped, taken by surprise. A couple danced around them without so much as a glance in their direction. Charlie tried reining in her shock, but Vince saw the startle.

His body went on alert despite the fact that he never once broke their rhythmic movement. "What's up? You see something?"

Yeah, she saw her paranoia roaring back.

"Nope. All good here," Charlie lied.

Miami Heat might not have been the club she'd visited on her last night in Miami, but it possessed the same meat market feel: a sardine-packed dance floor and nearly palpable sexual haze that had people flocking to it in droves. One difference, other than not needing her expertly made fake I.D. to get through the doors, was that instead of a gang of "friends" watching her back, she had six and a half feet of obnoxious Alpha operative.

It isn't like last time, Charlie told herself.

And she wasn't as naively helpless as she'd been at sixteen. If someone came up behind her nowadays, she'd neutralize them first and ask questions later—or not at all, depending on how badly they ticked her off.

"All right, all right, all right, my little club hoppers," the overexcited DJ's voice bellowed over the club PA system. He stood on a small corner stage, waving his arms to get the crowd's attention. "It's time to turn the heat up in this joint with some sexy tabletop moves. Any and all lovely ladies who'd like to strut their stuff for a chance to win the Golden Fucking Ticket—a year of *free* admittance into some of Ocean Drive's hottest clubs—come down to the bar. I'm sure we have a few gentlemen in the crowd who wouldn't mind giving you a boost."

Stay or leave. Charlie didn't like either option, but Vince's questioning gaze didn't go away, making the decision for her.

"Looks like that's my cue," she murmured, stepping away.

Vince caught her arm, spinning her back. "What the hell are you doing?"

"You were right. There's too much happening here to get noticed by playing the part of the wallflower. I need to put myself in the limelight." With a somewhat gentle thumb twist, she effectively loosened his grip and smiled. Rising to her toes, she sandwiched his whiskered cheeks between her palms and tugged him into a hard kiss. "Enjoy the show, love."

Charlie regretted volunteering for the dance-off before she even made it over to the bar. Two men waited by the counter, easing every contestant onto the high surface. She waited her turn and thanked them for the lift.

Get noticed. She should've factored in her penchant for looking like a clumsy clown in anything higher than the heel of her combat boots. It was times she found herself in these kinds of situations that she regretted her big mouth, and judging by Vince's scowl, he was none too happy about it either.

Lips clamped tight, jaw flexing, he looked like he wanted to throttle someone. Probably her. Maybe the drunken frat boy flashing a wad of ones at her feet. Navy was not a happy camper.

"All right, ladies, it's time to show us what you're made of," the DJ's voice echoed through the club. "Just remember, we're a family establishment, so let's keep it clean." He chuckled. "Oh wait, we're not. Which means you can get as dirty as you want! I'm sure our judges won't have any problems with it, right?"

The DJ gestured to the right, where five men and one woman sat, all decked out with nearly similar matching smirks. People whistled and cheered, getting louder when a sultry, steady beat rumbled from the speakers.

"Move or get off." The young woman next to Charlie dug a pointy elbow into her side.

Barely of legal drinking age, the brunette swayed her hips, nearly knocking into Charlie a second time. The coed's grin stoked Charlie's temper. Since she couldn't shove the girl off the bar and get away with it, there was only one thing she could do.

Win.

Charlie planted her feet into position and moved. It took a minute, but she eventually got into the music, swaying her hips to the beat. That's when Brunette Barbie upped the ante with an arse-in-the-air bend Charlie had once seen done in a strip club.

The crowd ate it up. They cheered for more, which the brunette gave without a second thought. Determined not to get shown up by a sorority girl, Charlie slid her hands up her body, and while sifting her hair off her neck, arched her back. Male cheers erupted around her. Charlie gifted a small smirk to the woman next to her and got a scowl in return.

Charlie temporarily forgot she was dancing on top of a bar. Everything faded into the background, even Vince, as she and the brunette tried to outdo one another.

As the song started winding down, Brunette Barbie elbowed her aside and did a walkover backbend that thoroughly displayed her neon pink G-string for a good twenty-second count.

Healthy competition or not, no way was Charlie flashing her bits to every Tom, Dick, and Troll in the place—even if she didn't have knives strapped to her thighs.

"Come on, baby. Shake it! You can show her a thing or two. Work it. Show us those gorgeous titties!" Standing by her feet, the frat boy wrapped his sweaty fingers around her ankle.

"Back off." Charlie easily dislodged his hold with a flick of her leg. But the kid was relentless. No sooner had she centered her balance back on her heels than his hands returned. "Let go before I'm forced to hurt you."

"Oh, I want you to hurt me, baby. Hurt me so damn good."

She flicked him off again. This time, her heel caught on

the lip of the countertop. Instead of falling on her arse, she controlled the tumble by hopping down. Her ankles buckled on impact and a sharp sliver of pain shot up her legs from the jolt.

"Now, that's what I'm talking about," the jerk slurred. His hand slid beneath her dress and cupped her arse.

"Remove your hands before I remove them for you," Charlie ordered firmly.

"Ooh, baby. You've got a fucking hot accent. Threaten me again." His fingers bit painfully into her rear cheek. "Come on. Threaten me like you mean it."

"I *do* bloody mean it." Reaching behind her, Charlie grabbed his elbow and the back of the kid's shirt, and face-planted him against the bar top.

"What the hell are you doing?" he bellowed, sounding a little more sober. "You're breaking off my fucking arm!"

"And it would serve you right." Charlie sharpened the angle at which his arm was pinned behind his back. People around them watched as she leaned close. "Did I give you permission to put your hands on me?"

"Oh, please. You were strutting your—"

"Did. I. Give. It? No, I did not."

"Let me go," the frat boy lookalike whined, realizing she meant business.

"Depends. Are you going to touch any more women without their consent? Or are you going to act like a gentleman . . . or at the very least, a decent human being?"

"Fine. Yes. I'll behave—just let me the fuck go already!"

They'd built up quite the audience, some people wearing smirks of amusement while others mouths gaped in shock. It wasn't how she planned to get noticed, but she'd take it.

A split second after releasing the groper's arm, another hand hauled the drunken guy upright by the scruff of his shirt. Mouth twisted into a snarl, Vince drew his fist back, prepped to make contact with the kid's nose.

Charlie quickly stepped into the line of fire.

"You don't need to do that, love. I took care of it." She dropped her hand over his fist and slowly lowered his arm...and her voice. "Vince. Think, okay? As much as I'd like to see this arse with a broken nose, it's not worth the assault charge."

Or the flak they'd get from Stone.

"You didn't do a good enough job. The bastard's head is still attached to his fucking body." Basement-low and ominous, Vince's tone sounded as if he was about to remedy— and remove—it.

More than once, Charlie had wished for a first-row seat at the uncorking of the usual Man of Cool. Something told her that if she didn't intervene, she'd get that wish fulfilled tonight. More green than hazel now, Vince's eyes hardened, his nostrils flaring.

"Hey. Look at me." Charlie pinched his whiskered chin between her fingers and turned his murderous glare her way. Five seconds elapsed before he shook off whatever the hell spell he was under and released a deep breath. The Vince she knew slowly returned.

"Good," she said after gaining his full attention. "Now release the arse-hat and let's finish what we came here to do."

"We're done for tonight." His clipped tone dared her to argue. And she wanted to—boy, did she. But something told her it would be in vain. *Pick your battles, Charlotte*, a phrase her mother had once favored, fit the moment well. This was one battle she didn't feel strongly enough about to warrant arguing, so she let Vince have his way—for now.

Vince released his hold on the college kid, and the guy immediately scrambled away.

"Hey there!" The DJ, his thousand-watt smile blaring at Charlie from two feet away, approached, holding out a golden trophy in her direction. "Congratulations, sweetheart. You're the proud recipient of the Golden Legs Award, and free admission to Miami Heat and eleven of our Ocean Drive colleagues. Would you like to keep the party going and give our guests an encore performance?"

"No, she fucking would not." Vince ripped the trophy from the DJ's hand and spun them toward the exit.

As far as first assignments went, things could've been worse.

CHAPTER SIX

Vince wasn't waiting for the valet to bring the truck around. He grabbed the keys from the pimply-faced teen who'd parked it and hoofed it toward the lot.

Two more seconds without Charlie's intervention and he would've plowed his fist through that college kid's face, and it wasn't about playing the fucking hero. Not really. She handled punks like him on a daily basis. Hell, she could bring down a man double her size without breaking a sweat.

But Vince had watched her get on top of that bar and his mind had gone blank—a complete white sheet. And then she'd *moved*, and the sway of her hips had breathed new life into a goddamned techno-song...not to mention his dick. *That's* what pissed him off the most.

He had no damn business getting hard over his partner. Over *Charlie*. He wasn't in the position—or condition—to start anything with anyone. Not when he couldn't sleep through the fucking night without waking up in a damn swimming pool. And even if that shit stopped, it couldn't be English. She tested his control while awake nearly as much as his nightmares did when he slept.

"Dammit, Navy," Charlie cursed from behind. Her heels clacked on the pavement as she followed him at a fast clip. "What the hell was that?"

Him fucking up.

"Nothing." Vince saw the truck in the far back corner of the lot and lengthened his stride.

"It didn't look like nothing to me. I had it handled."

"Having some drunk bastard kid groping your ass is you handling it?"

"Your caveman vision must be seriously blurred because I had the smarmy bastard's face eating the wood counter. I was handling it just fine," Charlie shot back.

He snorted, knowing he was acting like a prick but not giving a damn. Pissing her off seemed to be his fail-safe tactic. If she was yelling at him, he spent less time thinking about the other things he wanted to do with her mouth.

When they reached the driver's side door of the pickup, Charlie's hand latched onto his arm. Even in the dark lot, her eyes swam with countless emotions—so many it was impossible to decipher them all. Except anger. That Vince saw right away.

"Is this how it's going to be the entire time we're here?" she demanded crossly.

"Hot and muggy?" he joked humorlessly. "Probably."

"*You* jumping into the thick of things like I'm not a grown-arse woman and then pouting when I call you out on it? Because that kind of backward thinking isn't going to work for me."

"I know you're a grown-ass woman. And I know you can handle yourself," Vince all but growled.

"Do you? Because your little show back at the club says otherwise. If you can't find it in your thick skull to trust that I know what I'm doing, then we may as well call Stone right the hell now and get Logan down here. I am not risking those women's lives because you can't get your misogyny gene under control."

"You're not fucking replacing me." Vince crowded her, pushing her back against the truck. An internal warning system blared to life in his head, and he ignored it, stepping close enough so her breasts became crushed against his chest.

"Then start thinking with your head, not your testosterone pouch!"

Vince knew she meant caveman thinking, not sporting erections, but the words could have a double meaning. And both versions meant trouble for him.

His gaze dropped to her mouth, and her pink tongue flickered out, wetting her bottom lip. He wanted to nibble that plump lip until it throbbed in the most delicious way imaginable despite the fact that he shouldn't, for a million fucking reasons. But hell if he could summon up any of them at the moment.

Vince slid his hand through the back of Charlie's hair, moving slowly so she could stop him at any time. When she didn't, he held his mouth inches above hers. "That's the fucking problem, English. Around you, sometimes I can't fucking concentrate at all."

"And that's *my* fault?" she demanded to know.

"Yes." Vince brought his lips to hers, and on contact, pierced his tongue into her mouth. His mind shut off everything except one thing:

Charlie.

She gripped the back of his head and returned the kiss

with her typical fierceness. Their tongues melded. Their hands roamed over muscles and under clothes. Despite her being three-quarters undressed already, Vince wanted to see—and touch—more.

A sharp nip to his lower lip pulled a groan from his throat. *Fuck.* This wasn't the time or place for this, and it looked like fate agreed because, off to the left, gravel crunched beneath the soles of someone's shoe.

Charlie pulled back, lips swollen and breathing heavily. Her gaze shifted subtly around their perimeter. She'd heard it too.

A steady gait usually meant innocent intentions. These steps were calculated and inconsistent...like someone trying to be discreet.

Charlie's eyes locked on his, and damned if her throat didn't convulse. But Charlie? Nervous? That shit didn't happen.

"You know I hate it when we fight, baby." Vince started the performance for their shadow-lurking audience. He slipped a pink lock of hair behind her ear and followed it with his mouth. Skating his lips over her cheek, he murmured, "You with me?"

"*Mm.* I'm with you, love." Charlie tilted her head, giving him more room to feast.

She shivered in his arms, and he couldn't help but wonder if it was real or manufactured. There wasn't time to wonder long. Her palm danced up his chest, fingers catching on his left nipple piercing.

Her voice purred. "Maybe you can make it up to me. Three grovels should do it—and maybe a Dwayne Johnson movie spree."

Three grovels. Vince nearly chuckled at her way of telling him they had three Dwayne Johnson visitors—or men they shouldn't take lightly. Under normal circumstances, it would be child's play. But normal meant he had his gun...which he didn't.

Vince reached for the truck's door. "Let's hole ourselves in our room for the rest of the night, and I'll start the groveling process."

"Afraid that's not going to happen," came the unfamiliar voice.

Charlie startled, playing along to the game that they'd been taken by surprise. Vince turned and got a good look at their voyeurs. In jeans and dark hoodies, they didn't exactly dress like pillars of the crime community. But they were spread out, strategically creating a semicircle that locked them against the side of the truck.

Trained thugs, or instructed by someone with at least half a brain.

Vince lasered his gaze on the leader—the one who'd spoken. "You care to tell my why?"

"Someone wants to talk to your girl."

Charlie sidestepped from between Vince and the truck. "*Woman*. I graduated from training bras a while ago. And I'm not a particularly chatty person, so I'm afraid your someone is going to be disappointed."

"Look," Vince added, "we don't want any trouble."

"There's only going to be trouble if you make it, my friend." The head thug took a step closer, the move making his buddies stand up straighter. At Vince's side, Charlie's weight shifted as she prepped for action.

"Do not bloody touch me." Charlie's voice snapped Vince's gaze left.

Thug Two had slunk closer, brave enough to make a grab for her elbow. Charlie easily skirted around the hold—and that's when trouble started.

A shadow rushed forward. Vince blocked an incoming fist, retaliating with an uppercut to the jaw that made his opponent stumble. Charlie's soft curse momentarily stole Vince's concentration. She was efficiently dealing with her own attacker when her brown eyes shot over his shoulder. "Your three o'clock!"

Vince whipped right just as a kick came flying toward his head. Fucking-A. He was done holding back. Punch, kick, and toss, he hurled the incoming assailant headfirst into the truck's door, cursing at the dent it left behind before turning back toward the leader.

In his peripheral vision, Vince witnessed Charlie's perfect roundhouse smack Hoody Three off his feet.

"Stop playing around with the bastard and get in the truck," Vince barked.

"Little busy, Navy." One high-heeled kick to her thug's knee, and the man howled, staying down.

"Charlie! Enough!" came an unfamiliar bellow.

Both Vince and Charlie stopped their attack—and so did the three sniveling men lying at their feet. A fourth figure stepped out of the shadows. Though tall, his lanky form didn't have anything on the muscled thugs they'd put on the ground.

Charlie's eyes narrowed in on the new arrival, studying him a few seconds before her mouth went slightly slack. "*Eric?*"

Shaggy blonde hair, mismatched baggy clothes. The new arrival couldn't have been older than mid-twenties. "It's good to see you, Char."

She glanced at the men now climbing to their feet. "Are these friends of yours?"

"They're more like pups in training."

"They have a really sucky trainer."

Eric, with his hands shoved deep into his jeans, fidgeted. "He wants a word with you."

"I'm sure he does," Charlie quipped dryly. "Give me a good reason why I should care."

"I know things didn't end well between the two of you—"

"You think?" She waited a beat, glancing Vince's way before turning back to the kid. "Fine. We'll go. But I don't need an escort."

Eric shifted his feet, his gaze bouncing between the two of them. "I—I don't think the invite was for the both of you."

"Then she's not fucking going anywhere," Vince growled.

Charlie placed her hand on his arm. The touch instantly soothed his still-rising adrenaline. "I'm not going anywhere without my fiancé. If he doesn't go, I don't."

"Jesus Christ, Char. Are you trying to get my ass beat? You know he hates fucking surprises."

"Too bloody bad. What's it going to be?"

At Eric's reluctant okay, Charlie pulled the truck keys from Vince's pocket. She was already sliding behind the wheel, making him hustle to the other side. His ass barely hit the seat when she peeled out of the parking spot.

"Do you want to tell me what the fuck that was all about?" Vince demanded. "Or who the fuck Eric is? Fuck, skip all of that and tell me who the hell we're going to surprise. Arturo?"

"Torres," Charlie stated simply. Her knuckles turned white as she gripped the steering wheel tighter.

"Torres, as in Brock Torres, the deep-cover agent? Arturo's new bosom buddy?"

"Eric used to follow Brock around when I lived in Miami. He was a bit of a computer nerd—too smart for his own good."

"Sounds like someone else I know," Vince muttered.

"Apparently he's still walking in Brock's shadow."

"Then he can't be too smart, can he?" Vince opened the glove box and pulled out his Sig.

Charlie eyed him from the driver's side. "You can't take that."

"The hell I can't. We're about to confront a suspected grade-A asshole. No way I'm not going in hot." He made sure it was loaded and stuffed it into the back of his jeans.

"And what's your reasoning for having a gun shoved in your pants? You're a bar owner and I'm your bartender fiancée—not exactly occupations that require an armory attached to our bodies."

"Tell me Brock Torres is tame as a fucking pussycat and I'll *maybe* consider leaving it behind?" He waited for the reply he knew wouldn't come. "No? Then if you can have a knife strapped to your inner thigh, I can have my goddamned gun."

She opened her mouth, no doubt to say something snarky, but closed it again and focused on the road. That Eric kid's words rang in his head… "*I know things didn't end well between the two of you…*"

Charlie hadn't shared the specifics of her past with the undercover agent. She wasn't one for sharing—period. Vince couldn't help wondering if maybe there was a bit more to their relationship than what was in those DHS intelligence files.

It didn't matter that she'd been sixteen when she'd left. Sick as it was, assholes in authority roles took advantage of kids all the damn time, and if Brock Torres really was the type of guy to go against his agency, he wasn't exactly busting at the seams with morality.

Vince would keep his gun in his pants—for now. But one wrong look and all bets were off.

* * *

Charlie steered the truck through the Miami streets, almost on autopilot. Day one of her first formal mission and she'd not only forced herself into a club, but made out with her partner, got jumped in the parking lot, and was now topping off the night by confronting her least favorite lying arse.

Life couldn't sink any lower in the hole. Strike that—sure it could—because she'd yet to lay eyes on Uncle Dearest.

Nestled between the docks and the industrial district, Brock's tattoo shop definitely wasn't located in a place where anyone with a strong attachment to their wallet would take a casual stroll. But even twelve years ago, most people in the area had left him alone. Being a scary-ass former Special Ops soldier and the son of Franconi's second-in-command gave him the title Man Not to Fuck With—to everyone except Charlie.

To Charlie, he'd been a friend. An older brother. Someone who cared about her, not because of what she could do or who she was related to, but because she was Charlotte Ann Hughes. That's what she'd believed right up until Stone had burst her well-maintained bubble back at headquarters.

Charlie pulled the rental in front of Inked Up and cut the engine. There wasn't any point to being stealthy. Despite her threatening to end him, she knew Eric would've alerted Brock she was on her way—and pissed. But she didn't expect to strut right through the front door.

Vince trailed her, hot on her heels. "You have a plan here?"

"Not shooting someone in their bloody arse," Charlie murmured.

She flung open the front door, a harsh jingle announcing their arrival. Behind the counter, a young tattooed girl paused in her flirting with the heavily pierced man in front of her and looked up. As Charlie headed toward the door leading to the back rooms, she jumped off her little stool. "Hey, you can't go in there!"

"Watch me."

Arms folded across his chest, the girl's friend puffed up like a peacock and stepped into her path. "You heard her. No one's allowed back there unless you're a customer or an artist."

Charlie barely resisted sticking her fingers through his bull-ring nose piercing and flinging him to the side. "Step aside. Seriously. I am not in the mood."

"Step aside or what? You think your scrappy self is going to do any damage to me? Honey, I take dumps bigger than you."

"You may want to listen to the woman," Vince's gruff warning came from behind.

Charlie kept her gaze locked on Metal Face and took a step closer. "I did you a favor by asking you to step out of my way. But now I'm telling you—if you want to keep that ridiculous thing attached to your face, you'll move. Now."

He must've seen the truth in her eyes. He lifted his hands in mock surrender and took a step to the left. "Bloodthirsty little wench, aren't you?"

"You've got no fucking idea," Vince muttered beneath his breath.

Charlie burst through the back doors and stalked into the depths of Inked Up. She already knew where Brock would be...the far back room, where he saw his *special* clients.

Behind the closed the door, the faint whir of a needle told her he was definitely in there, and he wasn't alone. Charlie didn't give a damn, flinging the door open and making the woman—who was naked from the waist down and sprawled on the chair—jump.

"What the hell?" Blondie's eyes narrowed, but she didn't make any dash to cover her bare goods. "Get the fuck out of here!"

"I'm not going anywhere, love." Charlie remained planted in her spot. "But you're going to have to put your panties back on and finish up another day."

"Like hell." She turned to the man hunched between her legs. "Brock!"

Charlie allowed herself to finally look up. Just as she'd feared, twelve years melted away. Instead of being a newbie Alpha operative, able to incapacitate men twice her size, she stood, frozen, and mentally forced her heart down her throat as Inked Up began melting away...

CHAPTER SEVEN

Miami
Twelve Years Earlier

*C*harlotte turned her back toward the group of girls waiting for her outside Illusions and glared at her living shadow.
Thanks to the loud pound of music spilling from the club
and onto the street, she didn't have to worry about the Glam
Squad overhearing Brock being Brock.

"It's a mistake, Char," he said yet again. "It's a big goddamned mistake."

"No, it's Illusions," Charlie corrected. "I don't know
what your bloody problem is. You've been here before, probably a million times. Why is it an acceptable place for you to
hang out and not me?"

"Because I'm not a sixteen-year-old girl," Brock
snapped. He threw out an angry arm and pointed to the club
in question. "Do you think just because your uncle owns this
place that you're going to be safe in there? Wrong. You're
even more of a target than your dim-witted friends. And why

the hell are you even hanging out with them? I thought they were all on your shit list."

"Excuse me for wanting some kind of normalcy in my life, and some of us can't exactly be choosy in the friend department. It's them or Tina, and you know how much I can't stand my cousin. I'd rather bathe in a tub of flesh-eating bacteria than hang out with her."

"If you go in there, you're on your own," Brock warned.

"So go! It's not like I'm alone anyway." Charlie gestured off in the distance to where there were no doubt at least a handful of her uncle's guards. Even when she snuck out, like tonight, they always managed to find her.

Brock stormed off, spewing curses. Charlie felt a twinge of guilt, but ignored it with a reminder to herself that she needed unwinding time in the worst way. These girls weren't exactly her first choice of nightclub companions...they were her only choice. Not too many clamored for the chance to get chummy with Arturo Franconi's niece, and those who did usually wanted something.

"Hey! Are we going in or what?" Sandy Madison, the leader of Miami Prep's social elite, called out.

Charlie pushed her shoulders back and strutted to the bouncer. He gave her a once-over before nodding and letting them inside.

Illusions catered to the elite—and to those who believed they were. Music pounded like a second heartbeat. Strobe lights blinked and swerved over the sea of dancing bodies. It was like any other night, except the confrontation with Brock had put Charlie in a bad mood. With each song, the girls she'd come with distanced themselves even more. And she couldn't blame them. Heck, she didn't want to hang out with her either.

"I'm going to the bathroom. Anyone want to come?"

Charlie shouted to the group, receiving four shakes of the head.

She left them to flirt with a group of guys and headed toward the back of the club. One look at the long line for the women's bathroom and she bypassed it to go around the corner to the zero-wait men's.

"If anyone's in here, you'd best cover up the junk," Charlie shouted in warning before stepping inside.

She made quick work of using the facilities. While washing her hands, she contemplated a believable excuse as to why she had to go home, and after finally thinking of something that didn't sound too God-awful lame, she exited the bathroom. Two steps out the door and she crashed into someone walking past.

"Shit. Sor—" Something covered her mouth...a hand.

Charlie dug the soles of her sneakers into the floor, trying to stay rooted to the spot as someone dragged her backward, away from the club and toward the emergency exit.

"Stop fucking struggling," a voice growled against her ear.

No way in hell. She watched the movies. She saw what happened when kidnapped girls got into cars. Charlie squirmed. She elbowed. She pushed her mouth deeper into the hand covering it, hoping to take a bite.

Nothing worked.

She was overpowered.

And a few seconds after a sharp sting pierced her neck, Charlie was also really, really tired. Her vision went fuzzy, her muscles weakening.

"Get the fuck over here and get her legs," someone barked, his voice sounding muffled and far away. "We have to get her out of here before someone fucking sees us."

"Shit," came a second voice. "You doped her?"

"Had to. Little bitch is too spunky for her own damn good."

Voice two chuckled, his words sounding a lot more muffled as darkness started closing in around Charlie, "Yeah, well, that's soon going to become a thing of the past."

She drifted in and out—that's all she remembered. Every time she roused, another bite of pain came, and darkness wrapped itself around her again. Six times? Twelve? It seemed like a lifetime had passed when Charlie pried her eyes open and no prick of a needle followed.

She took a deep breath and choked on the urine-tainted air. She couldn't see. She could barely breathe. And thanks to the rough ties binding her hands and feet, and securing her to some kind of post in the ground, she could no longer feel much of anything—except the hollow ache of her stomach. It cramped as if she hadn't eaten in weeks, and maybe she hadn't.

Pain sliced up her throat every time she cried out for help. Just when she'd given up, light ripped through the enclosed space. It seared into her retinas, temporarily blinding her.

"We're going to get you out of here, Char," Brock's rough voice promised. Something broke away her bindings a moment before arms lifted her from the ground. "We're going to get you to safety, and then you're leaving Miami and never coming the fuck back."

* * *

The sound of flesh hitting flesh snapped Charlie to attention. Blondie, wide-eyed and livid, stalked away from Brock and the red handprint she'd left on his right cheek. Charlie used the distraction to take a deep breath, but it didn't go unnoticed.

Vince's hazel eyes studied her carefully, making her more uneasy than she'd ever been—except for that night at Illusions.

It *had* been Brock who'd rescued her twelve years ago. In a post-drugged state of dehydration and sensory deprivation, she'd thought she'd imagined his voice and hallucinated the distant sight of him in a swarm of law enforcement officers. But he'd been there, on the dock, when the door had been opened. His storming into Miami University Hospital in a panicked frenzy had been an act. He hadn't been called as an emergency contact. He'd known about her abduction because *he'd been working the case*.

Charlie had always prided herself on her ability to read people but she hadn't been able to see through the lies of one of the people closest to her. It made her wonder what else she'd gotten wrong. But the abducted women couldn't afford for her to throw herself a pity party. The job. The assignment. That's what she needed to focus on instead of a past she couldn't change.

Brock, rising to his six-and-a-half feet of prime badass, shot her a glare. "What the fuck are you doing here, Charlie?"

At his volatile tone, Charlie hiked her big girl panties back around her waist. "My presence was *requested*, remember? You provided me with escorts and everything. Glad to see you're putting Eric's computer talents to good use."

"You know damn well that's not what I meant."

Charlie flashed him Vince's ring. "We're scoping out honeymoon destinations. Trust me, Miami wasn't one of my first choices, but Vince has never been here. We'll be out of your hair in less than a week."

"You, of all people, know what kind of shit can go down in a week." Brock flicked a glance toward Vince and casually started cleaning up his workstation. "If you want to make sure your girl makes it to your wedding day, be on the first plane out of town."

Vince answered the dark tone with one of his own. "That sounded suspiciously like a threat."

"No, it's a fucking premonition." Brock slammed the tray of ink and whirled around, finger pointed toward Charlie. "I don't expect your little boy toy here to have any kind of a fucking clue, but *you* should know better."

"The circumstances still apply now as they did twelve years ago. If anything happens to me—"

"He's got terminal cancer, Charlie. Death row or a life prison sentence to a dead-man-walking isn't exactly a huge deterrent. Or are you taunting him? Do you want him to finish what he started?"

He went there.

Next to her, Vince's ears perked up. Yeah, she'd told him how she'd bargained for her freedom, but she didn't want a *complete* purge. If Brock continued on this path, she couldn't spin his words around. She couldn't control it, and the bastard knew it. But hell if she wasn't going to try.

"I haven't laid eyes or ears on you in twelve years, and that's what you're going to lead with?" Charlie attempted to steer the conversation away from its current direction.

"If it gets you gone quicker, then yes."

"It was a long time ago, Brock. It's in the past."

"Then why are you so pale, babe?"

He was right. Light-headedness wasn't something she experienced routinely, or at all. But really, it started now. The only way she could convince Vince it hadn't been a big deal was if she acted as though it wasn't.

Brock leaned against his desk, locking Vince in his

sights. "Did Char tell you how she spent her last night here in Miami?"

"Why do you even care?" Charlie inserted herself back into the conversation. "You keep warning me about leaving before Arturo finds out I'm back, but hasn't he already? I mean, you're using two of his men as your own private people-fetchers."

Brock's jaw clenched.

Crisis averted—for now.

"At first, I only recognized Eric. But now I remember. Two of those men from the parking lot used to be part of my uncle's thug squad. And like you said, he has an aversion to letting people go...which means you're either talking out of your arse about that whole shelflife thing, or you've gotten pretty close to Arturo while I've been away."

Brock stalked closer, stopping with a few inches to spare. "Get. The fuck. Out. Of. Miami. If you don't, I can't guarantee your safety."

"Good thing my safety isn't any of your concern. Don't *summon* me again, Brock. If you do, I'm not going to be so easygoing." Charlie spun around and left. She ignored the harsh glare from the girl out front, and didn't even enjoy the sight of Bull Ring guy warily moving to the other side of the room as she passed.

By the time she'd reached the sidewalk, Vince had caught up.

"Goddamn it, English." His hand latched on to her arm, bringing her to a stop. "What the fuck?"

Charlie counted to three before she met his gaze. Damn those eyes. They lasered through her with all the tact of a missile, roaming over her face, searching for...something. Being partners gave him the right to some kind of explanation. She couldn't give it...not right now.

Miami. Her family. Brock. Their mission. Thoughts and insecurities—old and new—shimmied their way into her mind.

Vince gifted her a slight nod, almost as if he knew where her head was at, and took the keys from her hands.

"Passenger seat." He opened the door, and waited for her to slide in.

That was it. No questions. No demands.

For now.

She didn't have high hopes of that lasting forever.

* * *

What Vince thought he'd known about the woman sitting in the truck next to him had been obliterated in a matter of minutes. One thing he was damn sure of: He didn't like Brock-fucking-Torres. He didn't like his attitude, or his seeming familiarity with Charlie. And she sure as hell didn't like how he'd transformed the mouthy Brit into a quiet church mouse.

A silent Charlie was an eerie Charlie because that shit just didn't happen. There'd obviously been something he'd missed during their little meet-and-greet, and judging by the silence from the other side of the truck, whatever it was, was a fucking whopper. Vince had two options: Let her get away with her obvious omission and keep his mouth shut, or open it and possibly get them both into a fuck-ton of trouble.

He flipped on his turn signal and aimed the truck toward downtown. "Are you planning on explaining what the hell happened back there?"

"I told you once already. Why I left has nothing to do with why we're here now. Let it go."

"I'm not letting anything the fuck go if it's not safe for you to be here," Vince growled. "Is Arturo going to make trouble for you? Do we need to make you disappear again?"

"No. That was Brock's attempt at a scare tactic. I told you, it's fine."

She didn't even look him in the goddamned eye, the first sign of a lie.

"Goddamn it, English." Vince scrubbed a hand over his face. "This assignment was a clusterfuck from the beginning, but now it's a clusterfuck soaked in goddamned gasoline. We need to change our plan of attack because there's no way in hell I'm letting your sweet ass out of my sight."

Charlie's gaze snapped to him. He wanted her to talk and he was about to get a fucking earful.

"Excuse me?" She kept her voice low, but sounded no less threatening. "I've been keeping an eye on my own arse since long before I came to Alpha, and I can continue to do it now, *and* long into the future."

"That go-it-alone mentality may have worked when you were a punk teen in Miami, but it's not going to fly here. At Alpha, we watch each other's backs."

"I don't need you to tell me what we do at Alpha. I've been with Stone since the start-up."

"Behind a computer," Vince snapped. He swerved around a slow delivery truck. "I know you don't like to talk about it, but the fact is you lack field experience."

"My apologies for not having been born with a penis," Charlie muttered under her breath. Her eyes locked on her side mirror and stayed there. "So you have all the field experience."

"I do."

"And because of that, you've really honed your observation skills, right?"

He nodded, glad she was finally starting to get it. "Exactly."

"So, Mr. Experienced, Observant Field Operative, does that mean you pegged the dark SUV that's been following us for the last four city blocks?"

"What the fuck?" He studied his rearview mirror, taking twenty seconds to take stock of their surroundings.

"Three car lengths back. Tinted windows."

"Yeah I see it." Now that she'd pointed it out.

Vince made a last-minute left, the wheels on the truck letting out a faint squeal. Charlie grabbed onto the oh-shit handle and threw him a glare. "You're so worried about my bloody safety, but you're the one who nearly gave me a concussion."

"Guess your boyfriend was serious about you getting out of town." Vince glowered. *Fuck.* That sounded like catty reality show shit even to his own ears.

Charlie didn't mention it, shaking her head. "Dark SUVs with tinted windows aren't Brock's thing. I put my money on Arturo. I told you we'd get noticed just by going to Miami Heat. And may I remind you that it's going to look a little odd if a bartender starts executing evasive driving techniques."

"Which is exactly why I'm not bothering to lose them."

Their tail followed them all the way back to the hotel, but they either were stupid or didn't care about the possibility of being spotted. Vince opted for the parking garage instead of the valet, noting that, after three car lengths, the dark SUV also turned into the underground lot.

"Stay in the truck until I come around to get you." Vince parked. He expected an argument, but Charlie stayed quiet as he came around to the passenger side door. He plucked her off the seat, much as he had earlier at the club, his fingertips brushing over the bare skin of her torso, and closed the door. But this time, he didn't let her go, leaning her body into the side of the truck before she could get into a reflexive defensive position.

"What do you think you're doing?" Charlie's voice sounded way too fucking sexy.

He anchored his fingers into her hair and brushed his nose along the curve of her neck. That smell—sweet flowers and temptation. It drove him fucking crazy.

"Appearances need to be maintained, right? Could you try and look more like a woman about to be ravished and less like you're about to aim for my junk?"

"After that 'sweet arse' comment? You come at me with those lips, and I will seriously bite them off your face *before* I go for your junk."

The corners of Vince's mouth twitched. "What can I say? You make me want to live dangerously."

Her brown eyes narrowed on him, scanning his face as if weighing her options. Obviously deciding on one, she mumbled, "Oh, what the bloody hell."

Charlie wrapped her hand around the back of his neck and pulled him against her mouth. Her tongue dove in before she eased back and nipped Vince's bottom lip. And that did it. Any control he possessed, shattered. He firmed his grip in her hair and immediately took over the kiss.

And he *did* take. But Charlie demanded from him as much as he took from her, entwining their tongues in a heated duel that vibrated him with need. He used the truck as his anchor and rubbed his body against hers, relishing the way her nipples hardened beneath the silk fabric of her dress. With a low groan, he coasted his free hand up her leg and guided it alongside his outer thigh.

A fucking down parka couldn't have kept him from feeling the heat between her legs, much less a few measly summertime layers. At some point his hands cupped her ass, and her slender legs wrapped around his waist.

Charlie's palms slipped beneath his shirt and up his torso.

Her clever fingers found the iron barbells piercing his nipples. She rubbed the right one before flicking it with her nail, and then doing the same to its twin. Vince released a lusty groan.

He could take her right now and die a happy man. And it didn't go without his notice that this was the second time in twelve fucking hours where he'd forgotten the time and the place—and whose mouth he couldn't seem to stop invading with his tongue.

Vince pulled back first, and when he did, almost dove in again for another taste of Charlie's red, swollen lips. Her brown eyes, hooded and hazy, peered up at him in a sexual fog. Evidently, he wasn't the only one who'd gotten caught up in the moment, and before they got snatched up in it again, he linked his fingers with hers and led the way to the garage elevator.

The sound of their breathing filled up the small space as they reached their floor. The second he buzzed them through the door, he released her hand. Hell, it didn't matter. His entire fucking body was still vibrating from their acting debut downstairs.

"I'm taking five." He left her standing in the main suite, glaring at his back, as he tried to calm his shit down and remind himself why getting wrapped up in Charlie Sparks wasn't in either of their best interests.

Once in the bathroom, he did something that would no doubt bite him on the fucking ass—if Charlie didn't kick it first. After turning on the shower, he pulled out his cell phone and dialed headquarters.

"What's up, doc?" Logan answered, by way of a greeting. "Want to switch places yet?"

"I need you to do me a favor."

Logan paused for a moment. "Where the fuck are you?

Niagara Falls?" A beat passed before he realized. "Shit, Franklin. You're going to ask me to do something that's going to get my ass reamed, aren't you?"

"And maybe bruised. And chewed. But she's not giving me a choice here. She's convinced everything is sunshine and fucking lollipops, and all I can smell is sewage. I need you to find out the events of Charlie's life up to and including when she left Miami. And I need you keep it on the down-low."

"*How* down-low?" Logan asked carefully.

"You and me. That's it. Not even Stone, for now."

Logan blew out a deep breath. "You can't ask her? Oh hell, never mind. This is Charlie we're talking about, but Christ, man. You like living dangerously, don't you?"

"I like knowing what can come at me at any given moment."

"If Charlie finds out we've been digging around in her past, you can pretty much guaran-damn-tee what's coming at you is her right hook."

"Maybe I can avoid it by playing the I'm-just-looking-out-for-you card."

"Nah, brother. Then you're going to be too damn busy dodging a right *and* a left hook."

CHAPTER EIGHT

South Beach. Land of young, tan skin. Oil. And heat. The reputation had nothing on the reality. Women strolled by wearing dental-floss bikinis, and way too many men wore those skin-tight swim briefs that left no one questioning their package size. Despite the vast crowd soaking in the sweltering morning sun, Vince's attention was snared by one particular nearly naked beachgoer.

Charlie.

The thorn in his side. The reason for his sleepless night—besides the norm.

She was lying on a lounge chair, her own bright pink barely-there bikini hugging her curves to perfection. Her breasts strained against the triangular fabric of her top, and her long, tan legs might as well have started beneath her chin. Until Charlie, he'd never known someone so petite could have legs that went on for fucking weeks.

They'd spent the better part of the morning by the hotel

pool, but when Arturo still didn't make contact after the fourth hour, they relocated. To the beach. It was almost worse than the fucking club, and only because he was keeping watch from a distance rather than up close and personal.

A group of guys strutted past Charlie's lounger, not bothering to hide their sexual ogling. Vince gripped the pier railing in front of him until the wood bit into his palms. Fuck. He couldn't blame them for appreciating the wonderland of Charlie's body. Last night, he'd done the same damn thing. Hell, he'd done more.

Even though he wasn't about to admit it aloud, their first tongue-lashing outside the club hadn't involved their covers or their assignment one damn bit. It had been need—plain and simple. He'd needed to feel her in his hands and on his mouth more than he'd needed his next breath. And despite happening under the guise of their cover, at some point during their second tonguing, it had been more about giving—and soaking in—pleasure, and less about their assignment.

Recipe. For. Fucking. Disaster.

Every woman who'd slid into his life, had left just as easily. Now their faces and names were all a blur—if he'd even gotten their names to begin with. They hadn't left behind any significant marks, and other than sating a temporary need, hadn't left behind any lasting impression. No emotions. No loss of control.

But Charlie? Even as colleagues, it took everything in him to keep his shit together—like what had happened in the parking garage. He'd lost his fucking head with a goddamn kiss.

Overstepping that professional line was a one-way road to hell for both of them. Something told him being with

Charlie would not only leave behind an impression, it would sear it into his DNA and bring a horde of emotions along for the ride. And he knew from firsthand experience that emotions led to wrong decisions. Emotions led to dead friends and living nightmares that always started the same—with laughter and jokes—and ended in smoke and blood.

When he focused, Vince could still smell the smoke from eight years ago. Insurgents, who'd managed to get the drop on base security, had sent a fucking bomb straight into the middle of camp while soldiers slept. No one knew what was happening around them until it was too late. Too many lives lost. Too few resources.

Vince's decision to go after those responsible had led to Rico "Watchdog" Padillo's name being added to the list of casualties. New husband. Soon-to-be father. He'd been a best friend and a brother. When Vince had watched his buddy's pregnant widow spread Rico's ashes along the shore, he'd vowed...

Never. Again.

No more losing sight of the big picture, complete with repercussions. And no way in fucking hell would he bring someone into the nightmare he lived every fucking day.

Logistics. Rulebooks. Game plans. Those were the methods by which he now lived his life. Anything that threatened that ordered structure couldn't happen. He wouldn't *let* it happen. Being with Charlie would not only threaten that vow, but obliterate it. He couldn't see beyond his own fucking wants when she was near.

"Vincent?" His name, whispered in a voice from his past, plunged Vince's body into ice.

He didn't move. He didn't breathe. Maybe thinking about Rico and his team had finally brought on the fucking hallucinations. But Vince forced himself to turn and came face to face with his past.

"Dawn." He stared at his friend's widow.

She looked the same, as if time hadn't flown by. Her dark hair was a little shorter, barely brushing her shoulders, but she'd kept her willowy figure—and her smile. She watched him warily, as if trying to predict his reaction to the blast from their past.

He knew how she felt.

Dawn's smile brought out the dimples Rico had been so damn fond of. "I was going to keep walking in case I was wrong. A few months back there was an embarrassing incident with a Chris Evans lookalike and—well, I can't go to my local coffee joint for a while."

He let out a soft snort in spite of himself. Same Dawn...yet not.

"What are you doing in Miami?" he asked.

"My mother retired down here so we're visiting for the summer. Although, I have to admit, I underestimated the amount of half-dressed people. I thought maybe all the television shows overestimated it, you know? Guess not."

We've.

A moment after he'd registered the word, a little girl skipped up to Dawn's side, her dark hair bouncing. Big brown eyes watched him as she adhered herself to the safety of her mother's legs.

It was like staring at a child version of Rico—in girl form.

Vince swallow the lump forming in this throat and, goddamn, it hurt.

"Mama." The little girl turned her heart-shaped face up to Dawn. "I want to go fly a kite. You said we could fly one of the long ones when we got here—and we're here."

Dawn tucked an unruly strand of curly hair behind her

daughter's ear. "I know, baby, and we'll do that in just a minute, but first I want to introduce you to Vincent. He was a friend of your daddy's."

That seemed to put the kite business on the back burner, because the little girl looked at him again, her curiosity piqued. "You were friends with my Daddy Rico?"

Vince's chest tightened, and it hurt to fucking breathe. Taliban torturers had nothing on this little seven-year-old's stare. He cleared his throat and awkwardly shifted his stance. "I was. He was one of the best ones I had."

"I'm Richelle. My mama named me after Daddy Rico because she said I looked just like him. Do you think I look like him?"

Vince's eyes bounced to Dawn, who smiled in return. When he looked back to his buddy's daughter, she was waiting patiently for an answer. "Yeah. You do. Except you're a hell of a lot cuter."

Shit. He probably shouldn't have sworn.

He grimaced and glanced at Dawn. "Sorry, I'm not used to—"

Dawn chuckled, waving away his fumbling apology. "Don't worry about it. I've been known to drop a bomb or two when I stub my toe."

A heavy dose of awkward shifted Vince's weight. He shot a glance back over the pier railing and watched an older man, significantly overdressed in a suit and tie, approaching Charlie.

Vince finally found his voice. "I've got to go."

Dawn's smile slowly melted. "Okay. Of course. Sure. You're probably busy."

"It was good seeing you again." His gaze flickered down to the little girl. "And it was nice to meet you...Richelle."

The little girl grinned, which made her look even more

like his buddy. Fucking-A, he needed air—ironic, since he was standing on a goddamn pier leading out to the Atlantic Ocean. He walked past, but Dawn stopped him, pushing a piece of paper into his hand.

She bit her lip, nervous. "Give us a call, okay? We're going to be in town for another few weeks. Maybe we can get together and catch up. I'd like to hear how the guys from the team are doing."

"I'm here working so I don't know how much free time I'm going to have."

"Okay. Well, keep the number anyway... in case you ever find yourself in our neck of the woods."

He nodded, not trusting his voice.

Vince couldn't have broken away fast enough, but he forced his feet into an easy glide, making his way toward the beach. It didn't take long to find the overdressed man hovering over Charlie, or the equally overdressed men that were spread out in a twenty-yard radius. Arturo's horde stuck out like sore thumbs.

Vince ignored his instinct to intervene. This was why they'd come... to create an opening for her uncle to make contact—which he was doing by sending his head of security, Anthony Torres. Vince stood back and watched, leaning against the pier's pylon as Brock's father made himself comfortable in the lounge chair next to Charlie.

Vince started the clock. Five minutes, and then he wasn't keeping his distance anymore. He'd already let down one important person in his life, and Rico had paid for that shortcoming with the ultimate price. No way in fucking hell would he let the same thing happen to Charlie.

* * *

In the last hour since Charlie had parked herself on the beach, she'd gained an uncomfortable knowledge about the open relationship of the young couple six feet away, and the current STD outbreak at the Oakdale Nursing Home. Oh, and a reminder that she hadn't missed the Miami humidity one bloody bit.

The scorching sun's only redeeming quality was that as soon as sweat dotted her brow, it evaporated. Behind her sunglasses, her gaze strayed toward the pier.

Vince had been keeping watch for as long as she'd been out here, which, in her opinion, was too damn long. But her boredom had nothing on his...or probably hadn't until the slender brunette had joined him.

For a moment, Charlie had thought the heat had her hallucinating the woman's presence. Vince Franklin didn't do small talk with strangers. He barely tolerated conversation with friends. But there he was, chatting up a gorgeous woman who could've easily stepped off the page of a swimsuit magazine—and then the brunette bombshell had executed a perfect note-pass.

It had been nearly effortless, something Charlie would've offered congratulations for if her stomach hadn't suddenly flipped on its side. Whether the woman was an old friend, a recent lover, or someone trying to pick him up, Charlie told herself it shouldn't matter.

It shouldn't.

Yet her teeth creaked from clamping them. Taking a page out of Vince's book, she deep-breathed herself away from shattered molars. Her focus needed to be on the shadow looming behind her right shoulder, not on lover boy.

Charlie Sparks the Alpha Operator wanted to confront the new arrival head-on. But Charlie Hughes, the once-wild-child orphan, needed a better tan.

Keeping her gaze focused on the ocean's gentle waves, Charlie reached for the nearby suntan oil. "Sorry, love, but you're interfering with my daily vitamin shot. Could you be a dear and move over a smidge?"

"Nah. I think I'll stay and prevent you the need for a skin cancer screening...Letty."

Only one person dared call her Letty. At the sound of his voice, weathered by countless years of puffing on her uncle's cigars, she turned in her seat. Her uncle's head of security— Brock's father—sat in the empty chair next to her.

Salt-white hair had taken over his head, and what she remembered to have once been fine lines etching his face had become more pronounced and brought friends. But still tall and broad, he looked like an older—harder—version of his son.

"Anthony." Charlie fought to keep her voice level, feeling his penetrating gaze through his mirrored sunglasses. Despite the fact that Anthony Torres presented a refined outward appearance, his cunning surpassed only that of her uncle. To show weakness or hesitancy was like opening an artery in shark-infested waters.

"You don't seem surprised to see me," Anthony pointed out needlessly.

"I knew it was a matter of time. I was just hoping it would be a *longer* amount of time."

"We may run by the old-school way of things, but this is still Franconi's city. Nothing much happens in it without him knowing." Anthony leaned his elbows on his knees. "Like you having a little run-in with Brock. Hope my son minded his manners."

Charlie snorted. "As hospitable as ever, although the company he keeps now leaves a little something to be desired. Glad it appears the two of you have called a truce, though. Father and son back together again, huh?"

"We have an understanding." Anthony's head cocked toward the pier, where Vince stood in the distance, watching. "I hear congratulations are in order. Why don't you wave him over here? I'd like to meet the man who finally tamed Wild Child Letty."

Charlie wouldn't let herself be taken in by the laid-back attitude, and when she waved Vince over, she saw in his stride that he was also prepping for a hundred different scenarios. Standing when he got close, she reached out for his hand and latched herself to his side. Vince didn't miss a beat, wrapping his arm around her waist.

"Anthony Torres," Anthony introduced himself. "I'm a good friend of Letty's uncle."

"Vincent Franklin. Fiancé."

Anthony's smile held little warmth. "I know. You don't think her uncle found out about his only niece's engagement and didn't look into the man she's going to marry, do you?" He turned back to include them both. "Arturo's inviting the both of you to brunch tomorrow morning. Ten o'clock at the house."

Charlie warned, "I'm not here for a family reunion."

"And yet you came back to Miami knowing that's exactly what you were going to get. Ten o'clock," Anthony repeated. "Arturo's looking forward to having both his girls there at the same time. And it may have been a few years, Letty, but your uncle's not so changed that he condones lateness in any form. See you tomorrow."

Charlie and Vince watched as he turned back toward the boardwalk. With their dark suits and goon-walks, both Anthony and his men stuck out on the scantily dressed beachgoers. Vince took the vacated seat and pulled Charlie onto his lap. She knew it was in case they were being watched, but it didn't stop the tingle zapping through her body and to all her barely covered lady bits when his hand landed on her upper thigh.

"Start talking," Vince demanded gruffly. "Now."

"About what? The fact that I was right? One night out on the town and we already have a meet with my uncle," Charlie smarted back in an attempt to gloss over the unexpected onslaught of nerves attacking her stomach.

She thought she'd mentally prepared herself to step back into her uncle's life, but the slight shake of her hand said otherwise. She draped her arm over Vince's shoulder and tightened her fingers, hoping he didn't notice.

"What are you worried about?" Vince asked, too damn observant. "The brunch invite?"

"*Invite*? You thought that was *asking*?" Charlie snort-laughed. "You mean you didn't hear the silent *We both know you don't have a choice so let's not keep pretending*? Granted, Anthony's always been a bit more tactful than the rest of Arturo's men. The others wouldn't have attempted to make it sound like there was an option other than saying yes."

"Yeah, I'm sure he's a real swell guy," Vince muttered sarcastically. "Father like son."

"Maybe that's one of the things bothering me." Charlie absently massaged her fingers into the back of his neck as she fought to make sense of her thoughts.

Vince flashed her a curious look. "What?"

"Brock has been undercover with DHS since he got out of the military, right? Which means he was an agent even when I knew him."

"Your point?"

"My point's that as long as I've known him, Brock's never gotten along with his father. Not before he left for the military, not after, and not even when he was apparently with the DHS. So what happened? What happened to suddenly make him get involved in Arturo's business *now*?"

"Assuming he hasn't changed sides? He did have a job to do. It's hard to do it if you're on the outs—easier to infiltrate from the inside. Which is exactly why we're here too."

Charlie knew he was right. In theory. Still, something was missing. Even the acting greats couldn't have put on a better performance than Brock. He'd legitimately hated everything his father and Arturo stood for and never hid the fact from anyone—especially them. So why would Anthony and her uncle think he'd experienced a sudden change of heart?

Or more importantly, what had he done to convince them?

CHAPTER NINE

At sixteen, Charlie bartered for her own freedom. Striking out on her own in a world that loved nothing more than to chew young women up and spit them out, she'd been resourceful. She'd *had* to be. But at barely eighteen, she'd used her resourcefulness and fondness for computers to skim money off a few well-endowed bank accounts—strictly for food, shelter, and other necessities. But she'd picked the wrong account—or more accurately, the right one.

Sean Michael Stone.

He was never supposed to question the minuscule amounts she skimmed every other month, much less be able to track her, but he did—and gave her an ultimatum: Use her smarts for good, go to school, and then work for him; or get comfy in a county lockup.

She'd chosen the first option and hadn't looked back since—at least until now.

Standing in front of the house that had been her jail from

the ages of eight to sixteen conjured feelings and memories Charlie hadn't thought about in a damn long time. According to Vince's employee file, he'd been to war zones in both the desert and the jungle, places all over the globe where he'd fought for his life and the lives of others. Charlie might not have toted around an AK-47 and covered her face in black camo paint, but this house had been her war zone all the same.

Arturo didn't do anything half-assed. "Ornate." "Ostentatious." "Outrageous." Those three words described his taste pretty accurately. His house, a mixture of Miami color and Greek grandiosity, welcomed visitors with a marble staircase that led up to a rotund, pillared porch and double-wide glass doors.

At the top of the stairs, Charlie glanced back at their rental truck, a good twenty feet away. They hadn't rung the bell. It wasn't too late to change her mind. She could still turn around, build another identity, join a nunnery… and let her uncle deconstruct yet another dream, the first being a lifetime of experiences with her mum.

Vince's hand settled on the small of her back, its warmth turning into a supportive wall. Charlie closed her eyes and took a deep breath. "You got this, English."

"Yeah, I know I do," she lied. "I'm just worried about you. This isn't any regular *Meet the Parents*."

"I can handle it."

A sudden silence hung in the air between them. Charlie couldn't meet his gaze. She gripped the purse in her hands a little tighter. Vince's fingers locked onto her chin and directed her gaze to him.

Disdain. Annoyance. Hell, even that horny look that occasionally clouded his eyes was easier to deal with than the concern staring back at her.

"You got this. *We* got his. We go in, make nice, then leave and continue on with our day. That's it." He made it sound so damn simple.

"I need in his office," Charlie reminded him.

It had been their first argument of the morning. Charlie wanted to use the opportunity of being in Arturo's territory to their advantage while Vince wanted simply to use it as a foundation for future encounters. Immediate versus eventually. Fast versus slow. *Charlie versus Vince.*

"We talked about this," Vince murmured. "It's too risky. He's not going to have any kind of useful intel lying around for anyone to come across. It's better to hold off and wait until we're in a better position."

"The women being taken from the clubs don't have *time* to wait," Charlie hissed. "Each day we sit around drinking mimosas gives these arseholes another chance to ruin someone's life. If I have an opportunity to get away from the table, I'm taking it. Either back me up, or I'm walking in there with an announcement that I've called off our winter wedding."

A low rumble slid out from his throat.

Patting his cheek, she stepped back and rang the bell. "Keep growling at me, and I'm going to fit you in a muzzle."

Nothing inside the house had changed in twelve years. Expensive artwork hung on the walls, and sculptures lined both sides of the corridor. Branson, her uncle's butler, led the way through the foyer and toward the back patio, where Anthony waited outside the sliding glass doors.

"Glad you showed." Anthony gave them a small nod, holding open the door.

"I'm not one for wearing cement shoes, so..."

Vince tensed, only relaxing when Anthony burst out into laughter. "Haven't lost the sense of humor, I see."

"Not a bloody bit. As a matter of fact, I'm trying to teach it to Vince."

Anthony chuckled harder, but he was alone in the joke. Firming his arm around her waist, Vince bent closer to her ear. "I think you're the one who needs the muzzle."

Charlie ran her hand up his chest and grinned. "Try it and see what happens, love."

Anthony was still chuckling as he walked them onto the patio.

Arturo Franconi, the once robust, most-feared crime boss south of the Mason-Dixon Line, looked like a different man than the one she'd left. He looked like *half* a man. He'd easily lost seventy-five pounds off his hulking frame, the lines bracketing his mouth deeper and more numerous, . . . and his pallor yellowed.

DHS's sources had confirmed end-stage liver disease, but they didn't say how far advanced it had become. Shock at her uncle's physical changes almost made Charlie overlook the man standing at his side.

Brock glared unapologetically at her and Vince until her uncle stood, keeping one hand secured on the tabletop.

"We'll talk about this later," Arturo said, dismissing Charlie's former friend. "It looks as though my long-lost niece has finally come home."

"I really think we need to nail this down now . . . sir," Brock stated firmly.

Arturo's eyes snapped back to the younger man. Dark and menacing—that was the uncle whom Charlie not-so-fondly remembered. "As long as there is life left in my body, I'm still the one who makes the decisions—and I believe I've given you an order. I told you what needs to be done. Now I expect you to get it done. Is there going to be a problem?"

"No . . . sir." Brock gritted his teeth.

"Then do it. And I don't want to hear any fucking excuses." With a flick of his hand, Arturo dismissed him again.

Brock stalked past her. "You still don't fucking listen," he muttered beneath his breath. Vince shifted his weight closer to her, obviously hearing the less-than-welcoming words.

"Come." Arturo gestured to the empty chairs. As Charlie and Vince sat, she sensed her uncle's gaze on her. "You've turned into a very beautiful woman, my dear. Of course, I shouldn't be surprised. Both your mother, Mia, and my dear departed Leslie looked the part of earth-bound angels."

Hearing him mention her mum and aunt turned Charlie's vision red. Her body tensed, and Vince, sensing the change, reached over and gave her leg a firm squeeze.

"And you"—Arturo turned toward Vince—"you're the man who believes he's good enough for my niece, a Franconi."

"I'm a *Hughes*," Charlie corrected, her jaw aching.

Arturo turned his cold, dark eyes on her. "You were a Franconi from the moment you stepped through my front door, all pig-tailed and wide-eyed."

"You mean red-eyed and shell-shocked. After all, my mum had just been murdered."

Arturo frowned at the reminder, but Charlie didn't care.

"I suppose I should apologize, Vincent. I'm sure Charlotte has explained to you that we haven't exactly been keeping up with the times. As a matter of fact, I think it's been...what? Ten years since she shed her family as though we were the common cold? I mean, changing her name...to Charlie *Sparks*?" He shook his head, *tsk*-ing.

"It's been twelve—as you very well know," Charlie muttered. "And my name is more Charlie Sparks than it ever was Charlotte Franconi."

"It's a wonder why you've even graced me with your presence if you find everything Franconi-linked so distasteful, my dear niece."

"If Anthony had made it a choice, I wouldn't be... *Uncle*."

Arturo leaned back in his chair. "Did she ever tell you how she became a part of my life, Vincent? It was both a shining moment and a dark cloud—she lost her mother, and I lost my wife—all in the course of minutes."

Charlie stared at her uncle. He *wouldn't*.

He took a sip of his champagne. "Eight years old is such a horrid time to lose someone so close to you. But as one does in times of great sorrow, you latch onto the family who remain. At least, that's what I did. I gave my daughter and my niece my whole heart, and do you know what put the next crack in it? The girl I thought of as a second daughter, one I'd raised as my own, thinking I could be so heinous as to be behind the death of my own wife."

"If I thought that, I wouldn't be here," Charlie forced her voice to work.

Finally, Arturo turned his attention toward her. "You no longer think I'm responsible for their deaths?"

"I no longer think you *ordered* them," she clarified. "I didn't say anything about not being responsible. They're gone because of who you are, what you do, and the friends you keep."

Arturo looked thoughtful for a moment before letting out a drawn-out sigh. His posture relaxed, shoulders releasing some of their stiffness. "That's one of the many reasons why I'm turning over a new leaf."

Charlie snorted. "Right."

"You don't believe me?"

"I'd sooner believe in the Easter Bunny. You're not the kind of man to go through life without having power over others. No way would you give that up," she pointed out.

"You're right. But it seems like fate has other plans for me." He gestured to his rail-thin body. "As you could guess, I'm not in the best of health. And since I can't take power with me to the grave, and both you and your cousin have no desire to take part in the family business as it works now, there's no reason not to use my final days putting things on the straight-and-narrow. Contrary to what you may believe, Charlotte, I do love my family, and the last thing I want is to pass something to you and Tina which may bring danger into your lives."

Too bad he hadn't thought that way twenty years ago, *before* someone tampered with the car her mother and aunt had been driving.

Before she left Miami, Charlie had gotten close to finding true answers as to who had called for the hit. It hadn't been Arturo, but *someone* had—someone with something to gain, either by flexing their power or creating a reason for retaliation. Charlie hadn't wanted any part of the life that had taken her mother from her way too soon—and still didn't.

The *click-clack* of heels on stone reached Charlie's ears as Tina, her cousin, turned the corner, looking no less gorgeous than the last time Charlie had laid eyes on her. Her skin-tight red dress, no doubt tailor made, hugged her curvy body, and her black wavy hair and flawless olive complexion leaned heavily on her Italian genes.

"So you really are here." Tina's dark eyes gave Charlie a critical once-over. "I thought Daddy lost his mind when he said you came back to town. I assumed you ended up buried in a garbage dump somewhere."

"Now, now, Tina," Arturo admonished. "That's no way to greet your cousin."

Tina dropped a kiss onto her father's cheek and did a double take as she turned her gaze on Vince. She propped her sunglasses on top of her head, letting her eyes feast on him from the waist up. "Well, hello there, gorgeous."

Charlie contemplated amputating her cousin's hand as she walked behind them, sliding her palm over Vince's shoulder as she passed. He got points for pulling away pretty quickly and received even more for draping an arm on the back of Charlie's chair.

Chuckling, Tina took the seat across from her father. "I can't possibly stay long or eat much. There are a few fires I need to put out."

"Anything you need help with?" Arturo asked.

"I've got it handled, Daddy. Just a little housecleaning that needs to be done." Tina leaned toward Vince, giving him a nice view of her cleavage—something that hadn't been there years back. "I own and run my own successful business. I hear you run one as well."

"Along with a few of my service buddies," Vince replied.

"I love ambitious men." Tina turned a false smile in Charlie's direction. "And what are you doing, Charlotte? Working as a drop-in volunteer at one of those salon schools? Not at a very good one, judging by the hair. Hopefully they give you some kind of hazard pay."

Charlie clenched her teeth and prayed for patience. "I'm a bartender...in Vince's bar."

"Oh, I'm so sorry to hear that." Placing a hand on the center of her chest, Tina feigned empathy. "I suppose it was a very rude awakening to find out you weren't half as smart as you thought you were, huh? What was it that you said when you left? That you wanted to make a positive difference in the world? I didn't know you could change the world with martinis. Maybe you'll show me how you do it while you're in town."

Charlie would love to show her all right... show her her fist and a dark closet.

As if reading her mind, Vince pried her fist open, finger by finger, and interlocked their hands to keep her from doing it again.

"Down girl," he murmured under his breath before gracing Tina with a hard glare. "Your cousin's an extremely talented woman. At anything she sets her mind to do. And the best thing about it—which is sometimes the most frustrating—is she demands to get it on her own terms. Handouts aren't her thing. It's one of the many reason why I care for her as much as I do."

Something in Vince's words sounded almost believable. Like he'd meant them. Or maybe it was the mimosas starting to course through her body. Thirty minutes and three orange juice concoctions later, Charlie needed to do something more useful than verbally sparring with everyone within a six-foot distance—except Vince. And didn't that shock the hell out of her because he was normally the first one she tried goading into an argument.

"I need to use the loo." Leaning over to brush a kiss on Vince's cheek, Charlie whispered, "Keep them busy."

"Charlie," he warned softly.

"Be back in a jiffy."

He looked like he wanted to throttle her, but she couldn't worry about his displeasure. The entire point of this meeting was to get information, not go on a trip down memory lane or be verbally accosted by the cousin from hell.

It took all of five seconds to note that nothing had changed about Arturo's security, including the dummy cameras. All ancient by prehistoric standards, they were visible to the naked eye, not hooked up to a live power source. Every night she'd had on the town as a teenager had been because of those things.

Charlie turned into the left corridor leading to Arturo's office and kept to the perimeter. Just outside the door, the same squeaky floorboard that had been present years ago squeaked under her shoe, indicating that not only had he avoided updating his security, but shunned house repairs too. She carefully stepped over it and slid into the office, unde-tected.

Natural wood bookcases lined the white, weathered walls of Arturo's office, making the space functional, but with the old-world Italian flair her uncle coveted. Sitting at the desk, she turned on the laptop. While she waited for the decrepit machine to boot up, her gaze snagged on an old photo.

She'd seen it before—one of her aunt, her mom, Tina, and an eight-year-old Charlie. All smiling. All happy. Two days after that picture had been taken, Charlie's two-week family reunion had ended up becoming a permanent stay.

Big world. One little girl.

Not exactly the stuff of which dreams were made.

"Throw yourself a pity party later, Char," Charlie ad-monished herself, jiggling the mouse as if it would speed up the hunk-of-junk computer. Without her around to keep things updated, Arturo's tech was in serious need of upgrades...and a new password.

The second the screen flashed to life, she grabbed a flash drive from between her cleavage and inserted it into the USB port. *Time to go fishing.*

Anyone who didn't know how Arturo's mind worked could have searched the hordes of files for days and not have a thing to show for it. But having cracked his system when she was thirteen, she easily found what they needed on his businesses—both the public ones and those he only financially backed—and started copying.

Charlie got into a routine of clicking and dragging, not wasting the time to read the open docs. There'd be time to sort through it all later. Outside the office door, the loose floorboard groaned under someone's weight.

She shut down the system moments before Vince slid into the room.

"What the hell are you doing?" He silently closed the door behind him before drilling her with the intensity of his disapproval.

"I told you that the best way to get into his files was to go directly into his files." Charlie pocketed the drive back between her breasts, noticing Vince's gaze tracking the movement. "He's not going to know I was here."

"Not the point. We agreed this was about making the first contact."

She came out from behind the desk and drilled a finger into the center of his hard chest. "No, *you* said we were going to take our sweet ol' time. *I* told you waiting wasn't an option. If opportunities don't pop up on their own, then we need to make them."

"And if someone caught you in the process?"

"Arturo's allergic to technology. Sneaking out of this house was always easy as pie, and I'm a significant degree smarter than my sixteen-year-old self. No one was going to catch me."

The same floorboard that had alerted her to Vince's presence alerted them to another. Charlie didn't blink. One tug on Vince's shirt and her mouth was on his, tasting the hint of coffee and mint on his tongue. He didn't miss a beat, walk-

ing them backward until her bum hit the edge of the desk.
Arturo's desk rattled.

Vince's mouth feasted on hers. The man could perform
a search-and-rescue of her tonsils any damn day he'd like.
Palming his rock-hard arse, Charlie tugged him even tighter.
He took the invite to get closer and slid his fingers beneath
the hem of her dress and up her thigh. A not-so-little—and
very real—moan slipped from her throat as the door clicked
open.

Tina's disgusted grunt barely inched them apart. "Ugh.
Really? Now I'm going to have to get the cleaners in here to
sanitize every square inch of this room."

Breathless from the intense kiss, Charlie reluctantly
pulled her mouth from Vince's. Her gaze dropped to his
swollen lips and before she dove back in for another round,
she was reminded they weren't alone by Tina's not-so-subtle
throat clearing.

Charlie flashed her cousin a naughty smirk, but didn't
move from Vince's embrace. "Sorry. You know how it goes.
When you find the man of your dreams it's practically impossible to keep your hands off each other. Or maybe you
don't know. I never did ask, Ti, is there someone special in
your life?"

"Yes. My father," Tina snapped. "If you both could please
put yourselves back together, Daddy's making plans."

Charlie wiped a speck of lipstick off Vince's mouth, and
he gently bit the pad of her thumb. Her eyes shot up to his,
immediately registering their still-sweltering fire. Maybe
they *had* gotten a bit carried away.

"What do you mean 'plans'?" Charlie turned, facing off
with her cousin.

Tina's smile didn't reach her eyes. "Daddy wants to sponsor a girls' day at the spa while he gets to know your boy

toy here. Personally, I say we don't and say we did. Or better yet, I'll go and say that it turned out you're allergic to grooming. I'm sure I'll have no problem selling that as an excuse."

Charlie clenched her teeth. "Fine. You tell me when and where, and I'll be there."

Tina's eyes narrowed. "You realize I said 'spa,' right? Not a tattoo shop? I won't let you embarrass me by asking Gustov to put more of that...whatever the hell it is...in your hair."

"Time and place, Tina. I'll even drive."

With a disgusted growl, Tina turned away and *click-clacked* out of the office.

Vince shook his head. "I don't know who's going to have it worse—me for getting grilled by your uncle, or you for having to put up with that."

"Me. Definitely me." Charlie sighed, turning around, and fixed his shirt, which she'd somehow managed to partially unbutton. She paused in re-dressing him and rubbed the back of her fingers over his stubble-laden jaw. "Do you want to switch? You could probably use a thorough exfoliating scrub...maybe a little man-scaping?"

"Fuck no." He snorted, glancing at the door where Tina had disappeared. "And be nice—maybe see if she knows anything about anything."

"Fine, but I'm taking the truck."

Vince's mouth opened to argue, and it made her laugh. "Seriously, Navy. I have to go to a spa—for *hours*—with the devil's spawn. I will be bloody damned if I'm left without an escape route."

CHAPTER TEN

Vince wrapped a towel around his waist and stepped out of the shower to the chorus of British curses coming from the suite's living room. A few more days of working with Charlie, and his vocab was going to expand by at least 50 percent—and considering he used to be in the Navy, that was saying a damn lot.

Ever since they'd returned from Arturo's, Charlie had been in a roaring mood, even threatening physical harm to the goddamned laptop itself. Escaping to the bedroom and hoping a little more time alone would chill her out would be the smart thing to do.

Too bad he wasn't smart.

He barely reached her before she hurled the laptop across the room.

"Give that back to me right the bloody hell now, Navy!" Charlie grabbed for it, and he lifted it further out of her reach. Sometimes being as tall as a mountain paid off.

"Calm the hell down, and I'll give it to you. We both know if you toss it, you're going to be pissed about it five seconds later. And then who are you going to take it out on? *Me*."

Charlie sank a fist into his gut. He lowered his arms with a grunt, and she ripped the damn thing out of his hands. "I don't need you to tell me what I'm going to be pissed about."

She plunked her small body onto the couch, cross-legged, and rested the computer on her lap.

"I take it things aren't going as well as you'd expected," Vince teased dryly.

She threw him a glare. "Really? *Now* you're going to try and grow a sense of humor?"

"Better late than never, right?"

Her attention dropped to his towel, and damn if his body didn't respond. Thank God she diverted it back to the computer screen or she'd have seen the terry cloth twitch. *Hyperaware*—that's how his body reacted whenever she laid those brown eyes on him.

He made his way around the back of the couch, putting an additional barrier between them, and leaned over her shoulder. "You can't find anything?"

She let out a sign and tucked a stray pink hair behind her ear. "Nothing useful. Everything I've come across so far makes it seem like Arturo really isn't talking out of his arse—that he's trying to make his businesses legitimate. Those that aren't hacking the change are slowly being shut down."

"So either there's something we're missing, or there's nothing there. You said before, Arturo's no angel, but selling humans doesn't seem like his thing."

"Yeah, but someone *is*. That's awfully ballsy to do in Arturo's turf—and all of Miami is his turf, not just the clubs on Ocean Drive."

A beep sounded right before a video chat request popped up from headquarters. Charlie clicked on it, and Logan's face appeared on the screen. "Hello, my love—" His words cut off. "Well, I was going to say '*my lovely*,' but you look like you've been on a week-long bender. Jesus."

"It amazes me how you're not taken, Callahan," Charlie joked.

"Amazes me and my gran too. I'm quite the catch."

"What do you need, Logan?" Vince asked, trying to get them back on track.

Logan's smile slowly faded. Fuckin-A. That was never a good sign.

"There was another abduction last night—this one outside a club called Hot Lips."

Vince arched a brow. "You know where?"

"Sure do. According to the DHS who questioned the witness, the abductee's friend saw her being hoisted into the back of a van, but the alley behind the club was too dark and she was too blitzed to give much detail—or any. She swears one of them looked like one of the Avengers."

"Well, that's credible," Vince joked dryly.

"I'm sending you what DHS gave us, but I'm warning you ahead of time. There isn't much."

"Any link to the two girls who disappeared last week? Or the ones before?"

"Nothing concrete. They look nothing alike and they're all from different backgrounds."

"You said nothing concrete." Vince caught onto the former Marine's words. "Does that mean there's something?"

"The two last week were friends, military brats celebrating the end of semester finals. One has a general grandfather and the other, a JAG lawyer father who's been retired five years now. Last night's, Tif Jansen, has a colonel uncle."

Charlie bit her lower lip, contemplating the new information. "So the last three have a military connection. It could be a huge-ass coincidence. I mean, the girls taken before this point didn't have military ties."

Vince leaned on the back of the couch, his arm sliding behind Charlie's neck. Her slight shiver gifted him a little thrill before he focused back on the assignment. "Okay, so we have at least a dozen abducted young women, the latest three of which have military connections."

"But you can't forget, Miami's a vacation destination. People flock here in droves, especially the young, I-have-nothing-better-to-do-with-my-money coeds," Charlie pointed out, half-turning in her seat to look at Vince. "I know what you're thinking, but Logan's right. We can't say it's a new trend in the pattern. It's horrible to think about, but human trafficking is big business here. But it *is* a business. The more grabs they make, the more money they can stuff in their wallets. Traffickers sure as hell aren't doing background checks on their targets."

"This whole damn thing is fucked-up," Vince muttered.

Charlie murmured in agreement, turning back toward Logan. "Send everything DHS gave you and maybe between the two of us, we'll find something else linking all the girls."

"You mean something other than being last seen at one of Franconi's clubs?" Logan asked. At Charlie's scowl, he backtracked. "You got it, darlin'. I'll send away. So, how's engaged life treating the two of you? Looks like a nice room. Double bed? Queen? King?"

"Logan," Vince warned.

"Hey, I'm curious how sleeping arrangements are working out for you all."

"Good-bye, Callahan." Vince reached over Charlie's shoulder and closed the video-link. Suddenly, he felt like he hadn't slept in ten damn years. He stretched his arm over his head, working out the coiled muscles in his back. "Bed sounds like a good idea."

Charlie looked at him like he'd sprouted a horn in the middle of his head. "Did you not just hear him? There was another kidnapping. We don't have time for things like sleep. We need to get to that club and see what we can find out."

"It's three in the morning. The club's closed. Hell, if there's been another abduction, it probably closed even earlier. You're not going to find out anything—and you're not going to be able to function tomorrow and make sound decisions without rest." He came around the couch and removed the computer from her hands. "Bed now. Worry later."

"I'll take the couch tonight, since I had the bed last night."

Vince snorted and pulled her off the couch in one tug. "I wasn't born yesterday, English. If I leave you here with your computer, you'll be back on it before the bedroom door even closes. It stays out here—with me. Now go and get at least four hours."

Charlie glanced to where his hands remained cupped over her elbow, not just holding her steady. His thumb, having a mind of its own, caressed the soft skin on the inside of her arm.

He dropped his hand, fisting it at his side, as if that would get rid of electric buzz that had started when he'd first touched her. No such fucking luck.

"You're getting awfully bossy, Navy... and hands-y," warned Charlie.

"I'm your fiancé, right? Looking out for your welfare it part of the job description. And before you start going on about sexism and equal opportunity, I'd be telling any of the guys to hit the sack too."

"Would you also be holding their hand?"

Vince shrugged. "If the assignment called for it? Maybe. Or maybe I like touching you. Ever think of that?"

Charlie's cheeks pinked. She stormed away in a mad huff, his name and a slew of curse words flying off her lips seconds before the bedroom door slammed.

"Was it something I said, sweetheart?" Vince called out. Something hit the door from the other side, making him chuckle.

That was one way to get her to run the other way.

Too bad his words held way more truth than made him comfortable. He liked holding her. Touching her. Kissing her practically sent him into fucking orbit. Hell, being close to her was starting to feel so damn natural he reached for her without thinking.

Maybe he should be turning around and running the other way too.

* * *

Sixteen clicks away from the forward operating base, they got their first whiff of smoke. At three, Vince and his team stood on the bluff overlooking the destruction and tried to decipher the charred remains. People below shouted and called out, alerting them to the fact that not everyone was gone, but there was a big-ass crater where the sleeping quarters used to be.

The bastards had attacked while everyone had been fucking sleeping.

"Franklin, over here." Rico gestured to the right where a small divot in the earth cut a rough road through the mountain.

Vince aimed his binocs toward the fast-moving group

of nine men—not theirs—all hustling like their lives depended on it. The mobile wagon with the military-grade rocket launchers on it pegged these fuckwads as the ones who'd tried taking out their friends.

Vince knew what Rico wanted to hear, but as team commander, it was his responsibility to give the order.

"We can't let them fucking go, V," Rico protested. The native New Yorker knew Vince better than anyone and immediately read the thoughts going through his head—and didn't have any qualms about questioning him, despite being outranked. "They smoked half the goddamn base."

"We should see who's alive and help where we can." Vince said the words he was trained to say, although he didn't agree.

"I'm no fucking nursemaid. My talents stray much more heavily toward kicking some insurgent ass." Rico nodded to where the group of nine men quickly hustled their way out of the valley. "If we wait too much longer, they're gone."

Every one of Vince's five-man team nodded their agreement. Return to base or hunt for a little retribution. An argument could be made for either decision, but goddamn it, some of those men and women had been prepped to go home next week.

Orders or emotions. Vince had to choose.

"Pack up and haul ass," he barked, his decision made. "Once they get out of the ravine, they're going to be practically impossible to find."

Two hours and one shoot-out later, they'd finally cut the bastards off, with meters to spare before they could've tucked tail and spread out into the mountain.

"They're retreating!" Rico shouted over the hail of gunfire, and despite the fact that he was crouched next to Vince

behind the boulder, he could barely hear his teammate. "Those assholes are getting the fuck away!"

"Like hell they are," Vince growled. "Eagle Eye," Vince snapped into his radio, "what are we looking at from the bird's view?"

"We got six at your twelve, hauling it east—and fast," Eagle Eye Sanders came online. "And we got two veering off, one north, one northwest. They want to split us up, evidently not as stupid as we thought."

Six and two. Split or not, it was still a piece of fucking cake. Vince divvied his team like he would on any other mission, and they immediately jumped to execute his orders. Next to him, Rico was anxious to get moving, too, and he couldn't blame his friend. People they'd come to call family were in the camp, and they had no idea if they were alive or dead. The only thing they did know? Their camp had exploded from the inside out, and these bastards were responsible.

"Let me cut off the ass from the northwest," Rico tried convincing him.

Vince shook his head. "Pairs. You know the rules. We head off the guy from the north and then cut west to get the straggler."

"And then we run the risk of him getting the fuck away. Come on, man. You know this is the only way to make sure we get every single damn one of those fuckers before they climb into a hole and disappear." Rico got right in his face. "We got this. No fucking problem, man. Ball up."

The smoke stench from their charred base still clung to Vince's nostrils. All those soldiers—mothers, brothers, fathers, sisters. All heroes. All taken out in the most chicken-shit way imaginable.

"Fine. Let's do this." Vince fist-bumped Rico and returned his grin. "Watch your fucking ass, man."

"Let's do it."

And they did. Seven fucking hostiles in ten minutes, a cakewalk for SEAL Team Five's well-oiled machine.

"Watchdog." Vince reached out to Rico via their comm system. *"Do you have a status?"*

"Maybe he can't give away his position," Callen, one of the other men, murmured as they stalked closer to where Rico had last announced his position.

"Watchdog, we're coming in on your flank. Don't fucking shoot us in the face."

They cleared the turn, and Vince raised his arm to signal his men to stop and take cover. Up on a rocky embankment, a distinguishable swatch of desert camo draped over a boulder.

"Stay here," Vince told his team and kept going, knowing his guys had his six.

The closer Vince got to the boulder, the more his stomach twisted in a fucking knot. It wasn't a lone swatch of camo...

Rico lay motionless, a growing puddle of red coating the rock beneath him. There was no need to check a pulse. With his face white and chest still, it was clear the gaping slash across his throat had drained him of all blood.

"Oh, fuck no." Vince's stomach rolled.

To his left, dirt and stone shifted. Vince spun seconds before Rico's killer jumped out from his hiding place, the knife coated with his best friend's blood lifted high, ready to plunge into his chest...

* * *

Vince couldn't fucking breathe. His chest tightened each time he tried sucking in a dose of oxygen, sharpening the pain to fucking panic levels before the desert heat slowly started melting away. Each passing second brought him more into the present.

Instead of the vast openness of the outdoors, white walls surrounded him—and a floor. His knees dug into the soft carpet beneath him. His thudding heartbeat, the soft tick of a clock, and something else filled the room—a garble.

Vince blinked, trying to fully identify both the noise and his surroundings, when something smacked against his shoulder. Frozen in horror, he stared at the sight of his hand wrapped around Charlie's neck.

"Fuck." He jumped up instantly, bile already coating his throat as she gasped and rolled, struggling to regain her breath.

Vince paced, unable to look at her. Goddamn. He'd not only knocked her to the ground and straddled her slender body, but he'd fucking pinned her to the fucking floor!

A series of raspy coughs had him reluctantly looking her way. Back on her feet, she still worked a little hard to pull in fresh oxygen—and she stared straight at him. Not wanting to scare her to death—again—he stopped a good three feet away.

"Are you okay?" he asked, voice gruff. If she wasn't, he didn't know what the fuck he'd do. When she didn't answer, he took a step in her direction. "Goddamn it, English...*are you fucking okay*?"

She flinched back. It was a small move, but noticeable—at least to him. Vince closed his eyes and counted to ten. When he dared look at her again, she'd been the one to approach *him*. "What was that?"

"I fucking hurt you," Vince croaked. He wanted to throw up, automatically touching the red welts forming on her neck.

"I'm fine." This time, she didn't flinch, or move. Her gaze

stayed locked on him, and she let him trace his fingers over her skin. Her voice sounded huskier than normal when she asked again, "Navy, what the hell was that?"

Vince growled softly, dropping his hand. "You're not fine. Look in a mirror and tell me you're fucking fine."

"I don't need a mirror. I'm breathing. I'll live. I'm fine. Now are you going to answer my question or are you purposefully going to act obtuse?"

This was why he never got involved with anyone seriously enough to warrant a goddamned sleepover. He walked away, needing space. "Never wake me up. Do you hear me? Leave me the hell alone."

She followed him into the small kitchenette. "It sounded like you were being chased by Freddy Krueger. Pardon me for trying to help your big bloody arse."

He spun around, nodding toward the now-noticeable finger marks on her neck. "My big bloody arse is just fine. Can you say the same? If you want to be fucking helpful, then the next time you hear Freddy Krueger chasing me, leave my ass alone and walk the fuck away."

Charlie stared at him as if telepathically trying to pluck his nightmare from his head. It was gone now. Mostly. All except the part when he'd woken up with his hand wrapped around her throat. *That* image would be burned into his memory vault forever.

"You need to let it go," he added through gritted teeth.

"If only that's how I was wired," Charlie muttered before adding, "But if that's how you want to play it, fine. Pretend away. Deep breathe or count to ten or do that meditation thing you like doing, but I don't have to stand here and listen to you talk stupid."

She grabbed the key card to their room and stormed off.

"Where are you going?" he called after her.

"Wherever the hell I feel like it. I either need to punch you a few dozen times or run a million miles," she snapped back. "Don't wait up for me."

Charlie left, her lack of presence making the room feel like one big fucking cavernous tunnel—and he didn't know where the other side led.

CHAPTER ELEVEN

Charlie punished the treadmill for a good hour and, when that didn't come close to working off her mad, she increased the pace and went for a second. Toward the end, the tight band around her chest finally started loosening.

She hadn't been angry when Vince knocked her to the ground. She hadn't been scared—at least not beyond the first few seconds of no oxygen. What she'd been most was worried. Despite how much he wanted it to be true, the man was definitely not fine.

She knew nightmares. For close to two years after her abduction, she'd slept with her room lit up like it was a spotlight for the Hubble. What made her furious was the whole I-shit-testosterone business—alpha freaking men.

Charlie smacked the off button on the treadmill and reached for a towel. In mid face-wipe, she glimpsed the tall figure standing just inside the hotel gym entrance.

"Voluntary physical exertion, Sunshine? And here I am

without a camera." Hands shoved into his pockets, Brock leaned heavily against the wall, watching. "How far did you just run?"

She shrugged. "Only twenty. I was going easy. It's been a long day."

"Ah. Brunch."

"Yeah, brunch. It went about as well as you'd expect." Charlie grabbed a bottle of water and downed half of it until she came up for air. "What are you doing here, Brock? More importantly, how did you know I was here, specifically? Or maybe I shouldn't bother asking, considering your new-found friendship with Arturo."

Brock didn't look amused. "Actually, you trained Eric well in the art of computer-sniffing. He found out where you were staying, and it just so happens I used to date the cute security guard on duty. She was all too eager to help me out for old times' sake."

Charlie rolled her eyes. "Some things never change."

"And some things do."

Brock stepped into the room and, for a moment, he looked like her old friend, the twenty-two-year-old veteran with a new outlook on life—and evidently, a new secret job. But had he ever been her friend? Or had she been a means to advance his career? His link to bringing down Arturo's organization? Had he played her so thoroughly? Was he playing the *DHS* now?

Either way she approached it, he was a traitor to some-one, which wasn't a characteristic she held in high regard.

"What the fucking hell is that?" The deep bellow snapped Charlie's head up. Brock stalked across the room, his eyes locked on her throat. "I'll rip off his balls and put them in a fucking grinder."

"Relax."

"The hell I will. Is that fucking fiancé of yours upstairs? Never mind. I'll find out myself." In full rage mode, he turned back toward the door.

Charlie grabbed his arm. "It's not what you think, so just back off."

"It's pretty damn hard to misconstrue fucking finger marks. Christ, Charlie. After all these years, you still haven't figured out the difference between a good and bad decision? Where'd the fuck you find this asshole? A prison yard?"

"You're not in a position to question my decision-making. After all, I did see you playing the part of my uncle's lapdog." At Brock's tightening jaw, she continued. "What? You didn't think I'd call you on it? The Brock I knew couldn't wait for the day when the entire Franconi organization went under."

"Yeah, well. The Charlie I knew would've never let a man do that to her"—he gestured to her neck—"and live to tell the tale."

Charlie scoffed. "We both know the Charlie you knew was a whole lot of talk and not a lot of action." *Which was one of the reason why she'd been determined to become full-fledged Alpha.* Never again would she let herself feel that helpless—*be* that helpless. "I don't have to stand here and explain things to you. Leave Vince alone, or you'll find out how much I've changed."

"Fine. He's a swell fucking guy. Wouldn't lay a hand on you. That doesn't mean he's not a bastard for bringing you back here after everything you went through."

Charlie turned away, both so he couldn't read her face and to get her room key so she could get the hell out of there, but it was too late. He'd seen.

"Goddamn it, Char. He doesn't know, does he?"

His incredulous tone stoked Charlie's already brewing emotions. "No! Because it's nobody's business but mine."

"What the hell are you trying to prove? Do you not remember that night? Because I sure as fuck do. I'll never get the image out of my head of you shoved into that filthy fucking crate, bloodied and bruised and prepped to be shipped God knows where."

"I remember it all in explicit detail. I don't need you repainting the picture for me," Charlie snarled, wincing at how dry her throat had become. *Five days.* That's how long the authorities said she'd been gone. "You mean in the hospital." Charlie forced her voice calm.

"What?" Brock looked momentarily confused.

"You said you'd seen me in the crate, but you didn't come until I told the authorities to call you—after they'd already taken me to the emergency room."

"That's what I meant," Brock lied oh-so-effortlessly. "The cops told me what those bastards had done to you. It still makes me sick to my fucking stomach."

That wasn't what he'd meant, Charlie knew, and it confirmed the fact that he'd been there when she'd been found.

She finished her water and tossed the empty bottle into the recycling receptacle in the corner of the room. "Is there anything else you want to discuss, because I have to say, sliding down memory lane wasn't exactly in my plans for the evening."

"If you're not going to leave Miami, then you need to be careful." Brock stepped closer, gripping her chin between his fingers.

Charlie didn't need a map to read Brock's mind. "I may not have much love for my uncle, but even I can't link him to what happened twelve years ago. It could've happened to any young woman in Miami."

"But you're not just any young woman, Char. You're Arturo Franconi's niece." He dropped a chaste kiss onto her forehead, something he'd once done a million times over...but it had been so long, and he'd done it so effortlessly, it took her by surprise. "Just be careful, Sunshine. I may not be around when you need saving."

"Good thing I've gotten used to saving myself."

* * *

Vince pushed his arms out in front of him and breathed through his nose. His muscles automatically glided through the repetitive motions as he shifted his torso to the side and did the same off to the right. Inhale and flex. Exhale and push.

Meditative tai chi was about as close as he got to drugs. His muscles now craved the beautiful, stress-relieving movements. That's what he sure as hell needed after watching Charlie storm out of the room two hours ago.

The door had closed, and there'd been an unfortunate incident where a vase met the floor. He'd regretted it the moment the glass left his fingers, but by then, it was too late. So he'd cleaned the mess, gotten rid of the evidence, and prayed a little meditation would sort out his head before Charlie returned.

If she did.

Their balcony suite, which conveniently overlooked the beach and the front of the hotel, allowed for prime viewing of everyone who came in and out of the resort. Even a few floors up, there'd been no mistaking Brock Torres and his merry band of hoodlums.

Fuck, for all he knew, Charlie could be downstairs at the hotel bar, reminiscing about old times with the ass-hat himself.

Behind Vince, the suite door opened.

Vince sensed Charlie's eyes moving over him as he slipped into another pose. Five minutes passed before she cleared her throat. "We need to talk."

"Talking defeats the purpose of clearing the mind," he said, being purposefully asshole-ish.

"Then unclear your mind and stop for a bloody minute," Charlie snapped.

He almost ignored her—*almost*. Turning around, he fought not to wince at the welts on her neck. They were still pink, in the obvious shape of a handprint, but there was a chance—though slim—they wouldn't bruise.

"How long have you had them?" Charlie questioned pointedly. "And don't insult my intelligence by pretending you don't know what I mean. The night terrors."

He knew what she meant. He folded his arms over his sweat-laden chest and waited for her to realize that her efforts to get him to talk weren't going to work.

She realized it quickly, giving an exaggerated sigh. "You want to play the macho card and don't want to talk about it with me? Fine. But there are people out there who specialize in treating PTSD."

Which Vince knew. Anyone who'd ever put on a uniform was warned of the downside of fighting for your country. He clenched his jaw until it creaked—but remained silent. Hell, he didn't know what to say, and even if he did, he sure as hell wasn't about to purge his nightmares onto her. The fact that they'd touched her as much as they had ripped a hole in his gut.

Charlie waited one breath, then two. Tossing her hands up in the hair, she stormed toward the bedroom. "Forget I said anything, okay? Forget I even care, and continue letting your bloody nightmares control your life!"

"Thanks, I will," Vince quipped, without an ounce of humor.

Charlie whirled around, anger sparking in her dark eyes as she stomped back. "And you say *I'm* a stubborn arse?"

"Among other things...but it's not personal, English. It's not something someone like you would get."

"No?" Her anger changed to something else, something Vince couldn't register until the words stumbled out. "For days, weeks...hell, months or more, you avoided going to sleep at every turn, right? Even now, you function on as little sleep as possible because as long as you keep moving, keep your mind busy, it's easy to delude yourself into believing everything's fine and dandy."

She paused, studying him, and continued to glare. Her throat seized, working harder at getting out her words. "But it's not sunshine and bloody roses, is it? It's hell and brimstone. Every time you close your eyes, you invite the shadows back into your life, and once they have you, they drag you under like fucking quicksand."

Vince listened. He watched. And then he realized—she wasn't speaking about him. If this was the only glimpse she was going to give him inside her own troubles, he'd take it.

Charlie subtly avoided eye contact. "It was bad. I get it. Maybe someone got hurt. I get that too. But you're not doing yourself—or anyone else—any favors by not talking about it."

"Spoken like someone who has some quicksand of their own, sweetheart," Vince pointed out. At risk to his digits, he cupped her chin and slid her gaze back to him, and surprisingly, she didn't tug away. "Why don't you tell me the real reason you left Miami? After years of being under Arturo's controlling thumb, what happened to finally make you head for the hills?"

Charlie's guard snapped back up in an instant. Pulling her chin from his grip, she drilled him with a look that could've frozen lava. "I wasn't talking about me."

"I think we both know that's the not the case. We're both fucked up. You just don't want anyone pointing it out to you. I'll tell you what, English. I'll show you mine if you show me yours."

"There's nothing for me to show."

"That's how we're playing it?" Her lack of trust conjured a rush of anger. "Then I guess you're going to have to deal with my broody silence—and remember to leave me the fuck alone when I'm sleeping."

"How did you manage working with a SEAL *team*? That's like five living and breathing humans who you have to trust on a daily basis."

At the mention of his former SEAL team, Vince neared his boiling point and stepped close, matching her glare for glare. "You know jack shit about my team."

"You're right. I don't." Charlie moved forward until her shoes bumped his. "But I'd bet Gregor they have something to do with your quicksand. Be careful, Navy. While you're trying to measure how deep mine is, you're already knee-deep and sinking fast in your own."

Boiling point fucking achieved. They moved at the same time, their bodies clashing together in a tangle of mouths and hands. Vince gripped Charlie's hips, holding her against his as he walked them against the nearest wall.

"You drive me fucking crazy," Vince muttered against her mouth.

"Feeling's mutual." Charlie took his lower lip between her teeth in a playful nip.

Vince growled. His fingers bumped the silver hoop in her bellybutton and glided up her bare torso. Her skin, like silk over his palms, was all beautiful, sleek curves. Her breasts, covered by her cotton sports bra, fit perfectly in his hand.

"What the fuck are we doing?" Vince stroked his thumb over her hardening nipple.

"Don't know. Don't care."

Fuck, neither did he—and that was goddamned dangerous. Shit happened when he didn't keep a lid on his emotions.

Vince gripped her hair, holding her still as his tongue slipped into her mouth, but with the release of a breathy moan, she stole his control. He palmed her ass, and her legs, already opening, wrapped around his waist. Hiding his raging hard-on became an impossibility because it pushed through his shorts and rubbed against her abdomen.

Charlie sucked in a quick breath. "Oh hell. This is a bad idea. A really, really bloody bad idea."

"The fucking worst." Vince dragged his mouth over her jaw. "Goddamn . . . you smell like fucking flowers and you've been down in that gym for hours."

Charlie arched, exposing the line of her neck to him even more. He nibbled and licked, enjoying the faint sting of her fingers digging into his shoulders. She anchored her body against his and swiveled her hips. The provocative move brushed her mound against the tip of his erection.

Vince ran the backs of his knuckles against her stomach and lower, making her tremble, right before he paused at the band of her stretchy pants. "One quick release. We'll burn this off and let it fizzle out. No discussion or play-by-play. Then we go about our business."

Panting, she pulled back just enough to unzip his pants and cup his aching cock. "Both of us."

Charlie's small fist wrapped around him and coaxed out a reflexive thrust.

Under normal circumstances, he'd fear for his fucking nuts having her this close to his genitals, but what was happening right then was anything but normal, and the only thing on his mind was Charlie's pleasure.

He breached her pants and received yet another shock to his system. "What the fuck are you wearing? Silk?"

A coy smirk pulled up the corner of her mouth. "Just because I don't like pastels doesn't mean I don't like nice things."

Vince dipped one finger through the damp folds of her pussy. *Drenched.* She was soaked through and getting wetter with each stroke of his fingers. When he brushed his fingertip against her clit, she pumped his cock. When he paused, she paused. They brought each other to the brink of their restraint and back, teasing. Tormenting. It was the best goddamned way to lose track of time—and reality.

Vince pushed his finger deep into her tight sheath, enjoying the way her body immediately clamped down, and pumped once...twice. After her body adjusted, he inserted a second, then a third. For every few thrusts, he gently rubbed her clit, and Charlie, beginning to squirm in his arms, gave the same degree of attention to his throbbing cock.

Her hand slid up his shaft from root to tip, slickening his rod with pre-come on the downward plunge. So slick. So good...not as good as being buried inside her would be, but they were rocking the goddamned boat of professionalism as it was.

Vince took her mouth in a kiss. Who needed to fucking breathe? They kept at it, their heavy breathing and damp bodies the only sounds in the room.

Her body tightened around his fingers, her hips moving faster.

"I'm not going to last much longer," Vince growled out against her mouth.

"Good, because I'm not lasting at all." On his hand, Charlie erupted. Head falling back against the wall, she rode out her orgasm and took him along with her in two more firm pumps.

Goddamn, he didn't think he could come this much, or this long. As he continued to empty himself, Charlie's body trembled in his hands. He rubbed her clit in soothing circles as they both road their highs back down to earth.

"Holy hell." Vince dropped his forehead to the wall just above her shoulders. Her heavy pants pushed her chest against his, and when he regretfully removed his hand from her panties, her moan made him go half-hard all over again.

It took everything in him not to carry her into the bedroom, where they could keep exploring this very bad idea.

"Well"—Charlie smirked, still breathless—"I'm not an expert or anything, but I think that was more stress-relieving than tai chi and running any day of the week."

It was. And that was going to be a huge fucking problem.

CHAPTER TWELVE

Charlie had found it impossible to sleep the night before. She'd tossed and turned, her mind too busy worrying that Vince would have another nightmare to truly fall into a deep sleep. And in the scant few seconds she managed to stop distressing about *that*, her thoughts leaned in the direction of their argument—and the wall interlude.

She still wasn't sure how *that* had happened, or how she'd managed to stay conscious after what was easily the best orgasm she'd ever had. *The* best, and it was handmade—pun intended. Now that the memory was hers to tuck away for cold, lonely nights, she and Vince could get back to business—and coffee.

Luckily for her, this morning linked them both together.

Sarah Yingst, the young twenty-two-year-old Miami barista who'd witnessed her friend's kidnapping the night before, was, curiously, already back at work.

Catering to both tourists and the social elite, Brewed

Awakenings boasted not only the best domesticated coffee in the city, but international roasts too. The line escaped the shop's front door, making those at the end stand out in the ridiculous Miami heat.

"You've got to be kidding me." Vince adjusted his sunglasses, and glared at the long line. "There's a million coffee shops around here. What makes this place so freaking special that half the goddamned city's here?"

"They serve *kopi luwak* coffee."

Vince aimed his sunglasses her way. "Did you just fucking swear at me?"

"Do you know what *kopi luwak* is, Navy?" She couldn't help but tease.

"Coffee, I'm guessing."

"*Expensive* coffee. Coffee made from a bean that's partially digested by an Asian civet." At his continued blank stare, she added, "It's a catlike weasel."

"So basically, the coffee here is literally shit coffee and everyone's insane."

Charlie laughed at his horrified expression, linking her arm through his. It was an automatic reflex and, as soon as she started to pull away, he locked it in place by pulling her closer. At her questioning look, he shrugged one broad shoulder. "We're on constant display. Eyes everywhere."

Right. Their cover. They needed to touch, sometimes to an extensive degree. But one thing that didn't necessarily need to happen was the ease with which it came. Leaning against him and joking around felt...comfortable.

But she couldn't afford to dive into hidden meanings.

"When we get up there, let me talk to Sarah," Charlie requested. The line moved another couple of feet.

"Okay...but why?"

"Because I'm me and you're..." She ran her gaze up and down his massive body, pausing at the tattoo-covered arms she secretly lusted over. "Well, to put it bluntly, you'll scare the girl mute."

Vince bristled. "I'll have you know that I'm a very approachable person."

Charlie's laugh ended with a snort. "Approachable like a skunk. Wait, no. You smell too good to be a skunk. A cobra maybe. Or a rattlesnake."

"You think I smell good?" Vince's lips twitched.

Yes. "No," she lied before shutting her mouth and pretending not to hear the jerk chuckle.

With twelve baristas manning the counter, the line moved fast. Thirty minutes after their arrival, Charlie placed their orders for two coffees—sans Asian civet droppings. Sarah Yingst stood at the register, her long, dark hair and blue eyes identifiable from the photo Logan had emailed the night before.

"That's twelve-fifty." Sarah extended her hand for the money, not even looking up.

Charlie handed over the cash and waited a beat. "You're Sarah, right?"

Sarah's attention finally lifted. Dark rings circled her blue eyes as she gave Charlie, then Vince, a wary appraisal. "Yeah. Do I know you?"

"Nope. We were hoping to talk to you—about last night."

Sarah glanced around the room, her anxiety skyrocketing. "I can't talk about last night. Who are you? Cops? I already told you everything I know."

"We're not cops. But if you can take a break or something, I really think you can help us."

Sarah bit her lower lip, looking nervous. When Charlie thought she'd tell them to take a hike, she gave a faint nod and headed toward an older woman stocking supplies. They talked for a minute before Sarah headed out from behind the counter, her purse in hand.

"Not here." Sarah gestured toward outside.

"Show us the way," Charlie agreed.

Sarah led them across the street to a small urban park. People ran by on the trail and, off to the left, a group of kids tried to erect a kite into the breeze. The young woman settled on a park bench, her purse tightly clenched in her hand. Charlie sat next to her, but Vince, ever watchful, remained standing, no doubt keeping an eye on everything around them.

"You're not cops?" Sarah asked again.

"We're not. But we are interested in what happened to your friend Tiffany. Your statement said you saw a pair of men throwing her into the back of a van, but that you couldn't remember what they looked like, or anything about the van."

Sarah's blue eyes narrowed as she fidgeted in her seat. "How do you know what I said in my statement if you're not cops?"

Vince dropped to his haunches and pushed his sunglasses onto his head. "Sarah," he said in a surprisingly soothing voice, "we're not, but we *are* trying to help. Your friend isn't the first girl to go missing from the Ocean Drive clubs, and if we don't find the people responsible, she's not going to be the last."

Sarah went back to biting her lower lip.

"Sarah." Charlie dropped a gentle hand on the young woman's arm. "We're just trying to help."

She seemed to contemplate her choices before nodding. "We weren't at Hot Lips like I told the detectives."

"Why did you tell them that you were?"

"I mean, we were there earlier, but then we went..." Sarah nervously played with her hands. "Part of the membership agreement is we don't talk about it to anyone outside of the club—unless we're sponsoring that person to become members themselves. That includes law enforcement. Any issues that pop up are supposed to be handled exclusively by the club ownership."

"What club is this, Sarah?" Charlie asked, supportively squeezing the girl's arm. "You can tell us. I promise we'll make sure no one knows you went back on the agreement."

"It's called Sinful Delights. It's a..." She cleared her throat, giving Vince an embarrassed glance before turning back to Charlie. "It's a fantasy-fulfillment club. It's all aboveboard. I mean, they're not doing anything illegal. Everyone there is there willingly. Heck, they pay outrageous membership fees to make use of the place. It's extremely exclusive."

"I've never heard of it and I used to live in Miami."

"It's fairly new, and it's not like they advertise. They get business by word of mouth. You have to know a member to get invited."

"And you're a member?" Charlie asked carefully.

"Me?" Sarah's eyes widened. "No. There's no way I could afford it. I'm a bartender there three nights a week."

"Did Tiffany work there too?" Vince asked. "I thought she was here on vacation."

Sarah nodded. "Visiting me. Even though I'm not a member, I'm given four free passes a year. They're only good for one night. I haven't used them. Truthfully, it's not my scene, which is why I stick to working behind the bar, but the pay's great. I was working last night, so I gave Tif one of my passes."

"So you weren't with her when she was taken," Charlie guessed.

Sarah's eyes welled with tears. "No. We were supposed to go together but then my manager called to ask if I'd work because one of the other bartenders called out sick. And the pay's *so good*. If they let me pick up extra, I can't say no."

"So she was by herself," Vince added.

"Yeah. It's normally a safe place, but I still asked a few of my work friends to look out for her. And before you ask, no, Tif isn't the type of person to go home with someone she doesn't know—and I found her cell phone in the back alley, smashed."

"And you reported her missing to your boss?"

Sarah nodded. "But I kept worrying about Tif's family— which is why I called the MPD. I'll get fired if my boss finds out I did that, but it's Tiffany. She's like my sister. I couldn't sit back and do nothing."

Charlie gave her arm a supportive pat. "No, if you can do something, you should do it. Which is what we're going to do. You said you had free passes? How would you feel about giving them to Vince and me? So we can check things from the inside?"

Sarah glanced at their surroundings before digging through her purse and pulling out a pair of black business cards. "These will get you the one free night's admission, but you won't get in after that without being ridiculously vetted—and able to flash the money."

Charlie picked up the card so that Vince saw silver embossed lettering. SINFUL DELIGHTS. That was the only thing on the card, except for an elaborately designed watermark.

Vince took the pair and put them in his pocket. "How much does a membership at an exclusive sex club go for these days?"

"Ten grand."

Vince's eyes grew to the size of saucers. "Ten grand a year? To get *laid*?"

"Ten grand a month—to have your fantasies brought to life," Sarah corrected.

Charlie grinned at Vince's look of mystified horror. "So where is this place? There's no address on the card."

"No address, no paper trail. But it's on Pier 28, the old Stone Work warehouse on Wharf Street."

Charlie froze, her smile slipping away just as her heart skipped a beat. It stumbled over a second before slowly easing into a somewhat normal rhythm. "It used to be something else. A long while back."

Sarah shrugged. "I heard it was another club back in the day, but I have no idea. That was way before my time."

Vince watched Charlie carefully, and when she didn't say anything, turned back to the young woman. "Thanks for helping, Sarah. We're going to do everything we can to find your friend. In the meantime, be careful, okay? Clubs aren't a safe space right now."

"It's not much safer out of them." Sarah stood, and after thanking them again, hustled back across the street to work.

Charlie and Vince waited by the bench.

"Are you asking yourself the same question I am?" Vince asked cryptically once the young woman was out of earshot.

Charlie dragged herself out of her funk. "What?"

"Sarah lied about where her friend was abducted because of her employer's rules."

"Yeah? So?"

"So aren't you curious if there are any others out there who may have lied about their activities that night to cover up what they were really doing?"

"You mean, maybe the other girls didn't actually disappear from the mainstream clubs after all? You're right…that does make me curious," Charlie agreed.

Also on her mind: whether there were truly such things as coincidences.

Because Sinful Delights—in its previously owned form, Illusions—was the very club she'd been abducted from twelve years ago.

* * *

Vince read people better than they could read themselves. Usually. But when he'd met Charlie a year ago, she'd fritzed out his magic power with a single bat of her brown eyes, and it hadn't been working the same since. Okay, so not a bat— *a glare*. A sharp, calculating, and pain-promising glare.

But sitting on that bench, she'd dropped the armor she'd toted around since they'd met, and he'd read something in her eyes that was pretty damn close to uncertainty—and it had happened around the time Sarah told them Sinful Delight's location. A blink later, the old Charlie had returned, dragging him to the car and to a store that had more leather than a motorcycle shop.

Vince cringed at his reflection in the dressing room mirror, thankful he was alone. No. Fucking. Way. Not in this time zone, hemisphere, or fucking universe.

"It's not happening, English," Vince rumbled, knowing Charlie stood on the other side of the door, waiting for his leather-clad ass to come out. "I'm wearing something I brought. End of fucking story."

"Come out and let me see."

"I'm not letting *anyone* fucking see me in this goddamned getup. They're uncomfortable. They're fucking tight. And we're in fucking Miami. I'm going to sweat my fucking ass off and then I'll need to be cut the fuck out of them."

"That's a lot of fucking happening—which I suppose is pretty apropos, considering where we're going tonight." The humor in her voice was impossible to miss.

"Glad you find this funny," Vince grumbled. "But you don't see these goddamned pants."

"No, because you're refusing to come out like some kind of prima donna. I'm giving you fair warning, Navy. If you don't come out. I'm coming in."

"I have the door locked."

"And you think that's going to stop me?" She let out an evil chuckle. "Oh, love, and here I thought we were getting to know each other so well. I'll make you a deal... You let me see how the leather pants look, and I'll show you my outfit."

"I saw what you're wearing."

"You saw what I was wearing *before* you stepped into that little cubicle. But while you've been throwing a tantrum, I've since changed. It's a little snugger, a lot shorter, and ridiculously more... freeing... than the other outfit. This one's a keeper."

Fucking-A. It was like she sensed his weakness. His hand barely touched the latch when she log-rolled beneath the door and stood, shrinking both the space in the room *and* in his leather pants. At least his mind shifted off the high likelihood of chafing his nuts.

Charlie's knee-high boots covered more skin than the rest of her outfit combined. Her top, more glorified bikini top than leather halter, revealed her twinkling navel piercing, and her short shorts barely covered the bottom curve of her ass.

Vince's mouth dried like the fucking Afghan desert. "That's what you're wearing?"

She gave her outfit a once-over, turning to look at her posterior in the mirror. "What? It's surprisingly comfortable—a lot more than that cat-suit thing I tried on before."

"Well, yeah. Because there's not much fabric to confine you. You can't wear that if I'm not allowed to bring my piece into the club," Vince stated adamantly.

She grinned wickedly. "They had a whip out there for sale. I bet you could bring it in and no one would question it. Or maybe I'll use it to complete my look . . . you know, accessorize."

At his pain-filled groan, Charlie chuckled and instructed him to spin with a twirl of her finger. "Let's see the goods. Strut."

"The goods are dying from asphyxiation," he grumbled, but did it.

Her gaze locked on him in an open ogle, and the attention made him that much harder. By the time he faced her again, he could've plowed a railroad spike into the ground with his dick. "I say we skip all this shit and wear jeans and tees."

Charlie lowered her voice. "Anyplace that has a ten-thousand-dollar cover charge expects more than the everyday casual."

He hated that she was right.

"We should change back until we're ready to hit the club. Do you need my help getting out of those pants? I left my butter in my other corset, but I could probably come up with something else," Charlie teased.

Invisible tension rose, something that was happening more and more frequently. And unlike before, when he could distract himself with a hard workout, ignoring his body's reaction to her nearness was becoming damn near impossible. What was worse—he didn't even try hard anymore.

At his silence, Charlie laughed and turned to leave, but the snug confines brushed her ass against his hard-on. Vince hissed, clamping his hands on her hips. Hell, he didn't know if it was to prevent her escape or to pull her closer.

A few layers less and they would've been in prime position for him to take her from behind, something Charlie must've realized too because she froze.

Her suddenly erratic breathing matched his own and, for the longest time, neither of them moved. Hell, if he moved, he'd probably come inside these damn pants, and wouldn't that be a bitch to clean the fuck up?

"We already had our stress relief, Navy," she reminded him. "One and done, remember?"

Meaning they shouldn't be about to rip each other's clothes off. His head got it—at least the one on his shoulders. His other one? Not so damn much.

Vince dropped his mouth to her shoulder, needing to taste her skin as much as he needed his next breath. By the time he reached her ear, she was trembling in his hands. "Funny thing about stress...it comes and goes, doesn't do the considerate thing and stay the hell away."

"I have no intention of becoming that person. I *refuse* to be that person," she stated, softly but firmly.

"What person would that be?"

"The one who, because she's a woman and sleeps with a man, people think slept her way into her job...or that she shouldn't be taken seriously."

Vince manually turned her to face him. "What the hell are you talking about?"

"I'm talking about how hard I've worked to get here, and not wanting to ruin it in the name of tension release. There's no way in hell I'm going down as the office tramp."

"You did not just fucking say that." He gripped her arms,

knowing she could've broken free at any time, and demanded her attention—and then forgot what he was about to say.

The woman staring at him through Charlie's eyes wasn't the woman who loved busting his balls every day at headquarters. This one looked uncertain. Out of her element.

It took Vince a moment to get his head and his mouth online and working together. "First," he said, barely keeping his voice to a faint whisper, "no one's ever questioned your right to be here. You worked damn hard for the spot, and it's yours. Secondly ... *tramp*? For having a fucking life?"

"People objectify women a lot differently than they do men. It's not like I condone it. It's just how it is."

"Well, fuck that, because you know everyone back home wouldn't think that of you ... at least, no one who mattered, and anyone who would can fuck the hell off."

She smiled, but the humor didn't reach her eyes. "Be careful, or you may give me the impression you actually like me."

"I do like you ... too goddamned much. It was never a matter of liking you."

It was how much she *affected* him—and being unsure if he was willing to pay the price for it.

Charlie cocked up an eyebrow and took a small, hesitant step back toward the changing room door. "I guess that's a good thing, considering we're about to spend our night at a sex club."

A sex club. With Charlie—the one person on this fucking earth his dick shouldn't get within ten feet of.

Fate had a wicked sense of humor.

CHAPTER THIRTEEN

In between their shopping trip and now, Charlie had spent most of her time trying to dig through the files she'd found on Arturo's computer. When that had yielded a jack ton of nothing, she'd changed her strategy to the first two military-linked abductions and their finances and, hours later and from the cab of their rental, she was finally making headway.

"Anything?" Vince kept half his attention on the back of the club.

They were splitting their time, staking out Sinful Delights *and* trying to find more leads. "Hold on a sec."

Charlie pulled up the bank accounts and credit card statements for each of the girls and set them side by side, until her entire computer screen was one big sheet of deposits and withdrawals.

A loud crunch broke the looming silence. Charlie ignored it, until it happened again, this time hellishly closer to her ear. "Must you do that?"

"What? Eat?" He pulled another potato chip from the bag in his lap and deliberately chomped—loudly. "Yes, I must. I'm fucking starving. You had the chance to pick the poison and didn't. Now you have to deal with it, sweetheart."

"SEALs are supposed to treat their bodies like temples, not garbage disposals, *love*."

"My body's doing just fine." He purposefully flexed his arms.

Even in the cab's dark interior there was enough light for her to catch the fluid movement of his muscles before focusing back on her laptop. *Sweet mercy, the man made her hormones go ape-crazy even while he binged sour-cream-and-yak-flavored chips.*

"Why the hell are you so goddamned twitchy tonight anyway?" Vince asked.

"Other than the fact that I don't like puzzles I can't figure out? I can tell I'm close, and it's driving me bloody crazy."

Vince tossed the chips into the back seat. Maybe she shouldn't have poked him about the chips, because now he was focused on her instead of clogging his arteries. "Although I'm sure that's the case most of the time, there's more to it than that. You've been a little off since we talked to Sarah this morning."

Did she dare?

Did she tell him? All of it—or just enough?

If she diarrhea'd everything out into the open, she chanced Vince pulling the plug on going to Sinful Delights tonight. Delaying it increased the probability that the traffickers would make another grab and add one more victim to the tally.

"I've been here before," Charlie finally admitted.

Vince, in mid-swallow, choked on his water. "Excuse me?"

Charlie rolled her eyes. "Not since it's been a sex club. Get your mind out of the gutter. It used to be an underground club called Illusions. I hung out there. A lot."

"Teenage English living up the nightlife, huh?" He peered over her shoulder at the computer screen. "What are you looking for now?"

"This." Charlie brought up the map of Ocean Drive's popular clubs and pointed to the screen. "As far as we knew until now, each of the three last abducted girls had been at different clubs, right? The pair of friends, from Pink. The second, from Poison Ivy. And even though Sarah said she and Tiffany Jansen started the night at Hot Lips, they ended at Sinful Delights."

"Clubs all owned by your uncle—except Delights. At least, as far as we know."

"Let's think about this realistically. Arturo practically has the monopoly on nightlife here in Miami Beach. No overprivileged, twenty-something young woman is going to come to Ocean Drive and not go to one of his clubs. Chances that the missing girls were at one is pretty damn high."

"So we find the metaphorical smoking gun that links all three."

"We may have already found it." Charlie nodded toward the screen. "Sarah said the regular cover charge for Sinful Delights was ten grand, right? Well, look at Ann Rittle and Genie Estevez." Charlie blew up the bank statements from the first two military-related girls. "From Ann's savings, ten grand gets withdrawn four days before she's reported missing by her uncle, and when you compare it to Genie's, it's the same ten grand, but it's a tally of a savings withdrawal and credit charge. I don't believe in coincidences that blaringly bright."

"If Genie charged part of the fee, wouldn't it come up on some kind of report?"

"Wow. Smart and buff," Charlie teased, bringing the next *coincidence* to her screen. "Sin Enterprises."

Vince's brow lifted. "Well, can't get much clearer than that, huh? So what the hell is Sin Enterprises, and who the hell owns it?"

"I'm pretty sure it's a shell company and, so far, I can't tell who owns it."

"And what the fuck does that mean?"

"It means if the real owner of the 'company' has a halfway decent computer geek on their payroll, it can be near impossible to find out who owns a shell company, or where the money's being directed. It makes laundering money ridiculously—and scarily—easy."

"Does your uncle have that kind of person?"

Charlie grimaced, hating what she was about to admit. "I *was* my uncle's person until I refused to do his dirty work anymore."

She waited for a judgmental comment, for the additional questions, but he surprised her by moving onward. "So maybe he found someone else."

Charlie contemplated it a moment. "Always possible, I suppose. But then I think about his sham security system at the house, and how he hasn't even changed the password to his computer. It's not likely. Anyone with a lick of computer sense would've made those adjustments the first chance they got. And then there's the added factor that Arturo doesn't trust easily."

"Will you be able to figure out the owner of the shell company?"

"Eventually. But we need to be prepared that Arturo may not be the one behind it all. I'm afraid if we go looking for bread crumbs that lead specifically to *his* doorstep, we may miss the real trail."

Vince nodded. "You're right."

Charlie did a double take. "I'm sorry, what was that?"

"What was what?" Vince cocked his head, looking genuinely confused.

"You just agreed with me."

"Because you're right. Narrowing our focus decreases our odds of finding the person responsible. Casting a wider net takes longer, but it has a higher success rate. It's basic search-and-rescue tactics." He glanced up at the nondescript warehouse structure and watched as a leather-clad couple approached the back door. "Fuck. We're really going to have to go in there, aren't we?"

Charlie followed his gaze and chuckled. "Afraid so, stud. And if we can link more abductions with the same MOs, I see return trips in our future. And since we only have two free passes, that's going to mean becoming official members. I wonder if that ten grand is for a person, or for a couple."

With a groan, Vince scrubbed his hand over his face. "Stone's going to shit a litter of kittens when he sees the bill for all this crap."

Charlie signed off on her computer and stuck it in the back compartment. "Then I guess it's a good thing we're out of state."

* * *

Vince's specialty on his SEAL team had been blowing shit up—a little putty, a timer, and you sat back and watched the show. The closer they got to Sinful Delights, the clearer it became that this time around, he *was* the show—a freak one, dressed up in matching leather pants and vest.

Wrapping his arm around Charlie's waist, he anchored

her close to his side. "You seriously think people are going to be having sex in there?"

Charlie's wicked smirk and eyebrow lift alerted him to the coming smart-ass comment. "No. I think they're playing cards."

"You're making fun of me now?"

"Making fun of you would be saying that they're playing Old Maid and the first loser takes a flog to the arse. Maybe that would be the winner. I don't know, with this being my first sex club appearance, all the particulars are still a little fuzzy."

As she pressed her lips together and fought not to laugh, his gaze shot down to her mouth. "*Now* you're making fun of me."

"Why yes. Yes, I am."

Vince reflexively slid his hand over the large cherry blossom tattoo her half-top left partially exposed. "We need to get one thing straight before we go walking into that club. You stay within arm's reach of me at all times. Glued to my fucking side, you got it? There's no way in hell we're chancing whoever's behind the abductions setting his sights on you, and in that getup, that chance is pretty fucking high."

Her brown eyes narrowed on him.

"Throw your daggers somewhere else. I know you can handle yourself. But we don't know who we're dealing with yet. It could one or two sick fucks, or an entire organization. I don't want to figure it out the hard way."

She looked reluctantly appeased by his explanation. "Fine. You'll have a Charlie-sized growth on your hip."

"Thank you. And besides," Vince added, "if any perv touches you, I'm going to be forced to touch them. Then cops will be called. Arrests will be made, and Stone will be up both our asses for having to bail me out of jail."

"Well, there goes my idea of jumping on the first man with nipple chains." Charlie feigned disappointment. A moment before her hand clamped on his arm in excitement, her brown eyes sparkled with a hint of mischief. "We should get you some for when we come back! You can take out those barbells and put in some hoops. Add a clip and a chain, and voilà! A dog leash for your nips! I can lead you around the club like you're my hairless poodle!"

"I'm not leashing my nipples together." Vince confined his laugh to snort. "And I'm no fucking poodle."

Her low chuckle sent a warm tingle to his dick. "Then you leave me with no choice but to get my bondage thrills elsewhere, Navy."

He gently pulled her to a stop, suddenly not caring if she was joking or not. "Let's get one thing clear right now. If you want to be hog-tied and blindfolded, you come the fuck to me. No way in hell am I going to stand by and let some twisted bastard do it—and that goes for inside this fucking club *and* out of it. *Got it*?"

Charlie's eyes widened in shock—and *heat*? Hell, his offer took *him* by surprise, but not as much as realizing he fucking meant it. The idea of her putting that kind of trust into someone who wasn't him conjured a flash of anger that took him a few minutes to get over. It took another to realize that it was because he'd never had enough emotional investment to want to slug some unknown, faceless man— not until Charlie had flipped things all the fuck around. Realizing just how much she'd come to affect his daily life was probably something he should've refrained from realizing until *after* they'd made their sex club drop-in.

Charlie laid her hand flat against his abdomen and, shirt or not, her touch seeped straight to his core. "Got it. But just so you know, I'm not into the whole blindfold thing, and definitely not hog-tying. This probably doesn't come as much of a shock, but I'm not a particularly trusting person. No way would I put myself in that kind of position with just anyone."

"And you shouldn't...but you trust me."

She studied him, her face blank way too long. Finally, she gifted him a faint nod. "You're right. I do."

Vince's chest expanded, finally taking the breath he'd been holding. "Let's get this over with."

He threaded his fingers through hers and led them to the nondescript metal door of the large warehouse structure. No neon lights. No blaring advertisements. From the outside, it looked like a run-down, forgotten, and abandoned building.

"Here it goes." Vince knocked.

A narrow slat slid open, the eyes behind it giving them a thorough once-over that turned into a second. Charlie slipped their black cards from beneath her top and flashed them, along with a charming smile. "We're here for a trial run—told this was the place to let loose and have some fun."

The peek-a-boo window snapped closed and, a moment later, the door opened. The barest hint of music wafted toward them as the bulky man ushered them into a cramped foyer. "Let me see the cards."

Charlie handed them over, her smile never wavering.

"Your sponsor?"

"Sarah. She said we could use the cards to see if the place fits our needs before we decide to put in our membership papers. These places have been either hit or miss with us."

Mountain Man gave them another cursory look before nodding. "Sinful Delights will be a hit. Can't say I've ever heard of any complaints, and I've been here since we opened. You're first-timers, correct?"

"Virgins." Charlie smiled, saddling up to Vince. "At least in some ways."

The man didn't even bat an eye. "So here's the deal; your free passes don't allow you a free pass from house rules. You don't follow them, you're out. Rules are: "No" means fuck the hell off. You don't pressure. You don't stalk. No video or audio recordings. If we find them, they're dust and you'll be blackballed from every fantasy club coast-to-coast. Front room's for observation and the crowd. If you go in the back, prepare to be approached." He gave Charlie an approving scan. "And you, hon, *will* get approached." He slid a look to Vince. "If you're not into sharing—"

"I'm not," Vince growled.

The bouncer nodded and produced a set of red plastic bands. "Anyone wearing green bands is up for anything, or at least is willing to be propositioned. Red means don't bother asking. If a green band approaches you looking for some fun, flash your band and they move on. If they don't, find the nearest employee, and we'll take care of it."

The bouncer snapped on their bands and pulled out a small gold key. "And lastly, for your locker."

"Locker?" Vince frowned, reluctantly taking the key. "What is this, an amusement park?"

"No cell phones beyond this point. You put them in the locker and you get them back when you're done for the night. Now last, I need to look at your driver's licenses."

"Surprised you don't have a goddamned metal detector," Vince grumbled, handing over their phones and IDs.

"We do. It's embedded in the frame of the front door. You were already cleared." Once satisfied they weren't in possession of any recording devices, the bouncer jotted something on a list and handed back their identification. When he opened the inner door, he finally smiled. "Have fun...and welcome to Sinful Delights."

Six deployments, not counting special assignments, and

Vince thought he'd seen it all. Boy, was he fucking wrong. He enjoyed a bit of kink as much as the next red-blooded male, but these people took the kink and slipped it into a damn knot a few dozen times over.

The deeper into the club they went, the more imaginative people became. Thick, heavy curtains cordoned off the more "active" part of the club, a setup that made him give thanks.

Half-naked, horny people surrounded them, yet there wasn't a single twitch in his pants. But one glance at the woman at his side and little Vince practically saluted the flag. He touched her arm and guided her to their right, where a large group of people huddled around a small, circular stage.

On it, a man, wearing nothing but black leather pants, circled around a naked woman. In this place, that alone wasn't cause for an eyebrow-raise, but the long, silky rope he weaved around her body in an intricate latticework of webbing, was.

"Wow," Charlie whispered. "That's...I don't know if I have the right word for that."

"*Shibari*," he answered reflexively.

Charlie's eyes widened before her mouth slid into a suggestive grin. "And you know this how?"

He shrugged. "I read—and no, not porn. It's a form of ancient Japanese art. It can look incredible when done right, or painful if done by someone who hasn't studied it their whole life."

Charlie's head swiveled back to the show, and he knew how she felt. The guy on stage, whoever he was, had definitely learned from someone skilled.

Vince scanned the room, looking for something—anything—out of the norm when his gaze stopped and rested on a lithe brunette. Her hair was twisted into an intricate braid, keeping it off her face, but there was no denying who it was.

Brushing his hand down Charlie's arm, Vince gently guided her attention toward the other side of the room. "Two-o'clock. Brunette in black leather. You'll know her when you see her."

She surveyed the room and came to an abrupt stop. "What the bloody hell is *Tina* doing here?"

"Looks like your cousin isn't as uptight as you'd like to believe, sweetheart." Judging by the waving arms and pissed-off body language, Tina Franconi's conversation with the tall man in front of her wasn't a happy one. "I feel a little sorry for the poor fuck she's castrating right now. I'm starting to see a family resemblance."

Charlie nearly neutered him with her glare. "I'm nothing like Tina. You couldn't have insulted me more if you said I smell like I bathe in garbage."

Across the room, Tina stormed away, leaving the poor fuck to watch her make a dramatic exit toward the hallway in the far back corner of the club.

"Well, isn't that interesting." This time, Charlie aimed Vince's attention at the man Tina had left behind.

Brock-fucking-Torres.

The DHS agent studied Tina's departure a beat longer before turning and stalking away in the opposite direction. Charlie's gaze bobbed back and forth.

"I know what you're thinking, and *no*. No way in hell, English. Like glue, remember?" Vince growled, reading her mind.

"It's going to have to be stretchy glue, because we need to follow them and we can't do it attached at the hip. There's no way the two of them being here is a coincidence, and even if it was, they can't stand each other."

"Well, they didn't exactly look friendly. Maybe they didn't know the other was a member." At Charlie's continued glare, Vince cursed, knowing she was right. "Goddamn it, fine. I'll take Torres, but if someone even threatens to get in your way, you lay them out. You hear me? You don't question. You don't warn."

"You worry too much, Mum."

"Damn straight I do." Vince caught her hand before she stepped away. "We're only here to watch tonight. If we draw too much attention to ourselves, we're never going to find out what's going on here."

"I'm always the picture of low-key."

Gripping the back of her neck, Vince pulled her into an automatic kiss, and despite being given no warning, Charlie not only accepted it, but returned it with a vengeance. Her tongue touched his, instantly disintegrating any will to stop.

It was a husky, "Can I get in on the action?" spoken from a leering man two feet away, that brought Vince back.

"Fuck off." Vince flashed his red band, and like the bouncer said, the guy nodded and walked away.

"That wasn't very nice," Charlie scolded him playfully. "We're here to make friends."

"You don't need any other *friends* except me." Something in his tone must've alerted Charlie to his seriousness because she gave him a probing look. "Now's not the time to hash it out, English. You follow Tina and be careful. We'll meet up at the bar."

CHAPTER FOURTEEN

With her cousin in her sights—and Vince out of it—Charlie tried dragging her mind off Vince's lips and onto the job. Hell, onto reality. Before this assignment, his broad chest and their verbal sparring matches had been an entertaining hobby.

Ogle. Verbal assault. Retreat. Repeat.

It had become their thing. At no point in time had she felt like she was putting her goal of becoming an Alpha field operative at risk. But working together side by side, seeing more of the man behind the gun?

When she least expected, snippets of what life could be like being with a man like Vince snuck their way into her subconscious. She didn't know what to do with those kinds of thoughts. It unnerved her, more than leaving Miami twelve years ago with nothing but a few changes of clothes and her laptop.

That meant she needed to drift into survival mode: *focus harder on the assignment.*

Less time sucking face with her partner and dwelling on the fine art of relationship statuses meant bringing home the abducted women.

"Head on straight, Sparks," Charlie murmured to herself as she followed Tina through the club.

Her cousin stopped to chat every few feet, a regular social butterfly among a crowd of salivating horny wolves. After ten minutes, the crowd thickened, and following at a distance became near impossible.

"Want to find an empty space, sweetheart?" A pair of wandering hands slid over Charlie's ass. When she didn't answer, the deep voice came again. "Or we could go have some fun in the back. I have a friend or two who would fucking kill for a taste of you."

Charlie barely spared him a glance and held up her red band. "Sorry. I'm not the to-be-shared type."

"I don't see him here. It's not like he'd know."

Charlie turned toward the stranger, one arse-grope away from being impolite. His heavily oiled dark hair and overabundant use of self-tanner prevented him from being labeled gorgeous. Tall and well built, a gym membership no doubt held a special place in his wallet.

And there wasn't a speck of sexual interest coming from her girl bits.

Forcing a disarming smile, she kept track of Tina in her periphery, watching as she paused to speak to one of the security staff and disappeared down a long corridor. "Like I said, I'm a taken girl, and my man isn't one to share."

He trailed his hand over her bare arm. "Maybe he's afraid you'll find something better."

"Sorry, love, but there *is* no better." She let out an internal sigh when she realized it was the truth.

No big scenes, she reminded herself, which meant breaking the guy's fingers was a no-no.

His gaze flickered from her cleavage to over her shoulder, and as suddenly as he'd appeared, he stepped back. "I'm sorry to have bothered you. You and your man have a good time."

"Was it something I said?" Amused, Charlie watched the guy disappear like someone had set his pants on fire. "Huh. Maybe I do smell like garbage."

"No, you smell fucking edible." Vince's chest warmed her back, his arms sliding around her waist. "I leave you alone for a few minutes, and you're already trying to replace me."

"As if anyone could take your place." Charlie turned into his hold. To everyone around them, it looked as if they were hugging affectionately. "You need to teach me how to perfect your Fuck-Off face. I want to scare people off as easily as you do."

"Sweetheart, you scare people just the same," Vince joked dryly. "Brock gave me the slip. I searched the club, and he's nowhere to be found."

"And now so is Tina." She nodded toward the corridor and the guard dog standing in front of the entryway.

"Wonder what Daddy Arturo would think about his little girl spending a night out at a place like this."

"I think she spends more than a night here. It was like she knew everyone, from the clients to the staff, and stopped to talk to all of them. I've seen her do it a million times at Arturo's parties—playing hostess."

"Hostess at a sex club. Wouldn't that be an interesting talking point on a resume."

Charlie snorted. "Like she needs a resume. Arturo will get her anything—including any job—that she wants. I hate to say it, but we're not going to get anything else tonight. And I *really* hate to say *this*, but we need to contact Sarah again and find out how we put our application in for membership. And then I need to start looking into the other missing girls, see if any of them may have a link to this place."

"You've got something else on your mind," Vince guessed accurately. His fingers started playing with the bare patch of skin at the small of her back.

She nodded, grim, as she thought about her next words. "That Tina and Brock being here is way too...coincidental."

"Yeah, coincidences give me a rash." Vince grimaced, shifting his balls in the leather pants. "Or maybe it's these fucking pants. Either way, you're right. We should draw straws to see who has to prep Stone about the bill."

"Aw, Navy." Charlie gave his chest an affectionate rub. "We don't have to do that. That honor is all yours. I'll even let you do it when we get back to the room because, after seeing all these...Sinful Delights, I feel like I need a shower."

* * *

Hot water. Cold. Tepid. All the varying degrees in between. Since squirreling herself away in the hotel shower, Charlie had tried each and every one and ended up with the same result: prune-y skin, and not a damn clue as what to do next.

The second she and Vince had hit their room, she'd dialed up Logan. In a combined effort searching all reported disappearances in the Miami area, she quickly realized that unless someone broke the speak-to-no-one mantra, the chance of linking Sinful Delights definitively to more than Tif Jansen's disappearance was slim to nil.

Charlie tipped her head back against the shower tile and closed her eyes. In a rare moment of klutziness, her foot slipped, and her balance evaporated. Knocked off its perch, the corner tray stand dropped onto her foot.

"Bloody freaking hell," Charlie shouted through the pain. Standing one-footed like a flamingo, she bent over to inspect her throbbing toe and, on the way down, her arse smacked against the glass door.

The damn thing sounded like an incoming train as it rattled itself open, but it was nothing compared to the bursting bathroom door. It flung open, smacking against the sink and showcasing a very tall, very armed, and very foreboding Vince.

Butt naked and shocked to be staring Vince dead in the eye, Charlie stood frozen. Neither of them moved. Or blinked. Or hell, even breathed. After what felt like an eternity, Vince's attention dropped to her breasts, snapping Charlie from her statue-like position.

"What the hell are you doing in here?" She slammed the sliding shower door closed, making it shake again.

"I heard the crash..." Vince sounded stunned. "And I thought—"

"You thought what? That someone broke into the suite without you noticing and then strutted straight into the bathroom?" She scrubbed enough steam from the door and glared through the clear spot. He'd yet to drop his gun from his at-the-ready position.

"I don't know what the hell I thought," Vince muttered. He scrubbed his palm over his face.

Five excruciatingly long seconds passed and he still didn't leave. "Why aren't you going, Navy?"

"Fuck if I know," he murmured.

Vince slowly slid the door open, giving her time to stop him if that's what she wanted. She didn't. Nothing stood between them, certainly not her clothes. It was the two of them and an insane number of bad ideas flying through her mind.

Maybe their wall interlude hadn't been enough to burn this heat out. Maybe they needed more, just *one time* to put them both out of their misery. Then they'd go on with their lives as if nothing ever happened—except she'd never heard of that working. Ask Penny. Or Elle.

Charlie took a deep breath, warding off the worst of her sudden nerves. Heat radiated from every inch of Vince's body, but his eyes? His lustful gaze lit her body up like the stroke of a match and she knew fighting it wouldn't do either of them any good.

Charlie stepped deeper into the shower, making room. "What are you waiting for? An engraved invitation?"

Vince's chest expanded as he took a deep breath. Once. Twice. He grabbed the back of his shirt and tugged it over his head in a way that only men made look easy. *Lord have mercy.* She'd seen him shirtless countless times...in the gym, on an operation. Sometimes she wondered if the guys on the team even owned clothes, they walked around headquarters half-naked so often, but only Vince made her throat dry.

The elaborate ink of his tattoos seamlessly moved with his muscular arms as if they'd always been there, one image blended into another. And then there were those small rod piercings through each nipple.

Vince reached for the buttons on his pants, but he didn't rush. He took his time undoing them one at a time, and when the last one popped through the hole, he dropped his pants and underwear to the ground. Strike that—he wasn't wearing underwear.

"Bloody hell." Charlie braced her back against the wall.

"Like what you see?" Unlike his decorated top half, Vince remained untouched and natural from the waist, down. And huge. And hard.

He crowded into the shower, and then he didn't move. He didn't lean closer, or touch her. His gaze traced up the length of her body, and by the time he reached her breasts, she felt like she'd already been devoured six times over.

Near panting, Charlie watched him slowly reach for her breasts. Their weight rested in his palms before he dropped his mouth to one tight bud, giving it a hard suck and then pulling back enough to roll the tip between his lips.

Charlie clasped the back of his shaven head. "Sweet Lord."

Vince slowly slid his mouth up her neck, her jaw. An inch away from her lips, he paused, meeting her gaze. "Are you sure about this? Because I'm telling you right now, I don't do half-ass when it comes to women in my bed. And I'm not so sure I can do soft and gentle either."

"Good. Because I didn't ask for either of those things." Charlie ran her tongue over the seam of his lips. "Less talk, more action."

Vince's gaze remained lasered to her as he flicked her nipple with the tip of his tongue. Yeah, she'd asked for this, but it was almost too much. Too much attention. Too much pleasure. Vince leaned his body against hers, anchoring her to the wall as he continued to torment her in the best way possible.

Charlie's eyes drifted closed and she focused on breathing. In and out. Slow and deep.

"Eyes on me, English," Vince demanded softly.

He stared at the cherry blossom below her left breast and took his time trailing his mouth along the path down her torso. Once on his knees, he gripped her hips and secured her into place.

"I love this fucking tattoo." He feasted on her flesh, licking and nibbling, working his way from one pink flower to another and, finally, to the one just above her mound. "One day damn soon, I'm going to taste every petal from the base of your neck to this pretty little pussy."

"I have a lot of blossoms," Charlie teased breathlessly. "That may take a while."

"I don't care if it takes all damn day. But first, I'm going to taste you straight from the source...and I want your eyes on me the entire time." Vince's gaze stayed locked on her as he brought his mouth between her legs. His tongue flicked out, skimming through her folds, and paused over her clit for a gentle rub.

Charlie's legs shook as she dropped a hand to the top of his shaved head and groaned. "Don't you dare move from that spot."

His chuckle rumbled against her sex. "You couldn't move me with a fucking bulldozer, sweetheart."

CHAPTER FIFTEEN

Charlie's soft moan snapped something in Vince—maybe his control, maybe his well-laid-out plan to stay the fuck away from her for as long as possible. Maybe it was both, along with his dick, because he'd grown so goddamn hard it fucking hurt.

No way would one time be enough. Or two. Fuck, chances were high that a weeklong marathon wouldn't get her out of his system—especially after he sampled her sweetness.

Heaven—that's what she tasted like, and he let himself feast. Her hands held onto his head like he'd for even one second think about pulling away. No way in hell. He slid his tongue through her folds, rubbed her clit with the tip, and did it all over again. With each pass, her body's trembles increased until she ground her mound onto his tongue.

Control abandoned him and empowered him at the same time because he *had* to touch her. He needed her pleasure resting in *his* hands, with *his* mouth. A few strokes of the tongue later, and he had it. Her sweetness spilled onto his tongue and he continued to savor, to tease, even when her legs buckled with the effort to stay on her feet.

Once her trembles eased up and her legs firmed, he trailed his mouth back up her body and took her in a carnal kiss.

"You taste fucking delicious," he murmured against her lips.

"Why, thank you." Grinning, she slipped her hand between their bodies and wrapped it firmly around his rock-hard cock. "Your turn."

He groaned. "No way am I lasting that way."

"Who said you were meant to last?" she teased, voice husky with desire.

"I did…because if we're going to light our own rules on fire, I want to make sure I get more than a quick fuck. I want to play."

The hand on his cock paused. "*Play*? I thought you were more of a get-straight-to-the-point kind of guy."

He grinned, knowing she was trying to goad him into action, and the action would come eventually. "When I play, it's going to be for your pleasure, babe."

He slid his hand across her back and over her ass to the backs of her thighs. "Up," he commanded firmly.

She obeyed instantly, lifting her legs around his waist by the time he opened the shower door. Fuck drying. If he did his job right, they'd be damp again in no time…this time with sweat.

"Stay here and don't move." He gently deposited her on the edge of the bed and, when her mouth opened in preparation for an argument, he pointed his finger at her and chuckled. "I know it's killing you, but shock us both and listen for once."

Surprisingly enough, her mouth snapped shut. Vince slipped back into the bathroom and grabbed what he needed from his shaving kit and from the robe hanging on the back of the door. When he returned to the room, Charlie's gaze bypassed the condom and went straight to the silky sash.

She started shaking her head. "I don't know what you have planned for that, but the answer is no. Not just no, but hell no."

He chuckled. "If you don't know what I have planned for it, then why are you saying no?"

"Because you're planning on tying me up like a bronco."

He laughed, a full-out, chest-shaking laugh, not something he'd ever pictured happening while Charlie stood naked in front of him. Everything about it felt foreign, the rumble, the shake, the slight way it made it easier to breathe. Judging by her half-shocked look, it sounded odd to her ears too.

She cleared her throat, looking uncomfortable for the first time since he'd known her. "You should do that more often."

"What? Dole out orgasms? Because if you're in the market to receive, I'm more than happy to dish out."

"Laugh."

He gently spread her thighs apart and stepped between her outspread legs. "I used to laugh."

"What happened to change that?"

"Life." He leaned over her until her back hit the mattress, caging her in with his arms. In this position, his cock brushed against the apex of her mound, and the sensation made it jerk in anticipation. "Do you trust me, English?"

Vince held his breath. He didn't realize how much her answer meant to him until there was a risk of hearing she didn't. If she'd been anyone else, he wasn't sure he would've even asked. Release, forget, and move on. That had been the theme of every sexual encounter he'd ever had—until now.

Not only did he want to remember every fucking moment, but he wanted it etched in Charlie's memory too—for all the best fucking reasons.

"I know it sounds ass-backward, but trusting you to watch my back and trusting you with *that*"—she eyed the sash in his hand—"are two different things."

"Not to me." He ran the fabric over her breasts. "It's just silk. Cool. Soft. Even with your hands tied, you're still going to be the one in control."

She cocked up an eyebrow. "Right."

He reached for her hands. "Let me show you."

Vince dampened the small thrill that shot through him when she tentatively offered him her wrists. He wasn't a kinky bastard. He didn't do whippings or pain. But a nonbinding scrap of lace or a well-positioned blindfold definitely had its perks. The mental image of Charlie wrapped up in silk was a hell of a lot more than a perk—it was one of his wet dreams come to life.

Carefully looping the sash around her wrists, he kept his large fingers beneath the band to ensure she had room to move. He gently tugged on the fabric, showing her the extra space. "If at any point in time you don't like how this feels, you can get out."

She tested the restraints before looking him in the eye. "Why have them if they're only for decoration?"

"For appearances. Sometimes your brain doesn't connect with the images you see. Logically, you know you're not tied, but seeing your wrists bound will heighten everything else around you."

Her throat convulsed. She glanced from her hands back to him.

"You okay with this?" He needed to make sure she was with him 100 percent.

Finally, she nodded. "I'm okay."

Vince forced his breathing to slow as he gently guided her arms above her head. Her back arched gracefully, pushing her bare breasts against his chest.

He slid his mouth down her neck, pausing where her red marks had already disappeared.

"Nuh-huh." Charlie gave him a knowing look. "Wherever your head is about to go, put on the brakes and reverse it. I'm naked. And under you. And I let you truss me up like poultry. Keep it moving, Navy."

Vince couldn't help but chuckle, again. He cupped one perfect breast in his palm and wrapped his mouth around its twin. "I'm going to make this feel so fucking good for you."

Charlie kept her arms above her head, even when he skated his mouth down her torso and played with the blue jewel winking in her belly button.

"Please." Charlie stared at him through heavy-lidded eyes. "I don't want slow. Not now."

"You want it fast and hard?"

Her emphatic nod nearly made him plunge into her in one swift thrust. Before he lost his shit, he sheathed his cock in the condom and grimaced at the deep throb rising up from his balls. Primed—so fucking primed and ready to be inside her.

Vince slipped his cock against her damp folds, teasing them, testing her readiness. Charlie writhed in an attempt to get closer. He couldn't hold back anymore. Sucking in a groan, he slid the tip of his cock just inside her entrance, held still, withdrew and slid in again, this time a fraction deeper. Inch by inch, he buried himself in her body.

"Too slow," Charlie complained with a squirm, trying to get him to bury himself to the hilt.

"I don't want to hurt you, babe. I'm not exactly small."

"No, you're massive." She lifted her hips. "But I can take it. Fuck me, Vince."

Fuck. Hearing her speak his name in that sexy-as-hell accent sent his hips in a thrust that seated him halfway in one shot. Her body wrapped tight around him, her breath hitching.

"More," Charlie demanded. Shifting her body, she rested her legs on the top of Vince's forearms. The change in position gave her ample leverage to glide her pelvis into a slow, deep rotation.

Soon, Vince needed more too. He anchored her hips into position and hardened his strokes, each one a little faster than the one before. Charlie's breasts bounced in front of him, nipples tightened and begging to be touched—which was exactly what he did. And the entire damn time she kept her arms high and anchored to the mattress above her head.

"Fucking-A. I love those noises you make," Vince growled.

"Then don't stop," Charlie panted. "More. Goddamn it, Vince. Harder."

Vince shifted to his knees and put his entire weight behind each thrust. He might physically have the upper position, but Charlie was the one with all the control. The mattress squeaked, the bed frame smacking against the wall.

Charlie's body bowed upward. Her half-ass-tied arms came off the bed, looped around the back of his neck, and brought him to her mouth for a savage kiss. Vince didn't stop. He let one leg slide from his shoulder, but kept her other spread wide, and thrust like they kissed: wild and barely controlled.

He couldn't hold on much longer, and he didn't have to. Her body fisted him like a vise as she erupted around him, stronger than anything he'd ever felt, and he followed right behind her.

This time, they *both* shook.

Vince nearly collapsed on top of her in a state of pure fucking bliss.

Charlie panted breathlessly, her skin sweat-glistening and damp. "I think you've turned me on to silk."

He pushed up high enough to look her in the eye. Her hair looked sex-rumpled and her lips, ravaged. "And I think you look good-and-fucked."

Charlie's mouth twisted into exhausted amusement.

"And see," Vince added. "You were in complete control the whole time."

Both her smile and her glow faded. "Somehow I doubt that."

She squirmed beneath him until he rolled away. Her walls were tossed back into place before her feet even hit the floor. His nightmares made sure he'd never been a snuggler, but damn—this was one of the fastest dodges he'd ever seen, his included.

He couldn't blame her. He'd recited the reasons why the two of them weren't a good idea so many times he'd committed them to memory, but that didn't mean he didn't want to take her again.

And again.

Charlie picked up the nearest article of clothing. One of his shirts, it hung off her smaller body, hitting her about mid-thigh. "Thank you, Navy. Not only did you prove me wrong about silk, but you gave us both what we needed to get whatever this is out of our systems. But so help me God, one mention of this to any of the guys and you'll be skulking around headquarters with extra room in your gym shorts."

He let her tug on her panties before he got out of bed. "You care to run that by me again?"

She didn't look at him until he was practically touching her. Her lips, pink and lush, were still swollen from their kissing. "Which part?"

"I'd like to address both of them"—Vince barely withheld a snarl—"but I'll start with the one that *really* pissed me off. No way in hell will the guys ever be getting a play-by-play. What happens between us is no one's business but our own."

"And the other thing you have a problem with?"

"That you're so delusional you think once and done is going to fucking work."

Her shoulders tightened up, as if she were prepping to run for the hills. "We agreed."

"Yeah, when I made you come on my hand. Newsflash, sweetheart, it didn't do jack shit because we still ended up in that shower together, *and* out here on the bed. I agreed to keeping our business *our* business and to letting it run its course for however long it takes. I also agreed it couldn't get in the way of our job, but I did not fucking agree to one and done."

"You're so sure there isn't a woman around who can resist your charming personality, aren't you?"

"No, I think *you* can't resist. And now that I know how hot you run under those camos and gym clothes, I *know* I'm not going to be able to keep my hands off you." He skimmed his mouth against the shell of her ear. On contact, her muscles went lax, and she shivered. "I promised I was going to lick every inch of that tattoo, and I'm a man of my word. It may not happen now, or in an hour, but it is going to happen, English. Consider yourself warned."

"You really are a conceited jackass," she said, but her words lacked her typical heat.

"Maybe. But I'm a truthful jackass. It's my night for the bed, but you're more than welcome to join me if you want."

Vince swatted her ass, laughing when she yelped. He ducked into the bathroom a split second before a hairbrush came flying toward his head. Being with Charlie was wild, unrestrained, and yet for the most part, safe. It got him thinking that maybe he'd been going about this control thing all wrong.

CHAPTER SIXTEEN

No less than four times since Vince had escaped the shower, both smelling and looking oh-so-lickable, Charlie had contemplated taking him up on his offer to join him in bed. But she knew her limits. She'd already crossed them with their earlier sex-fest, so far she couldn't even see the lines anymore.

Let it run its course, he'd said. In theory, it worked. But what happened if it took weeks, or *months*? The longer it took to fizzle, the greater the chances that she'd have to kiss her dream of becoming an Alpha operative good-bye.

After close to an hour of deciphering hordes of missing-person reports, Charlie's eyes got heavy. Her computer teetered on her lap, snapping them back open. And then it happened again five minutes later.

Sleep. That's what she needed. She'd plumped the couch pillow and lifted her legs up when she heard the first thump.

Faint and muffled, deep rumbles came from the bedroom. And then another loud noise.

Did she dare?

Her throat was still sore from the first time she'd interrupted one of Vince's nightmares. But no way in hell could she sit back and let him be tormented by whatever past sought him out. She tiptoed to the slightly ajar door, slipping into the room easily.

Sprawled in the middle of the king-sized bed, Vince tossed restlessly. His head turned back and forth. His lips, softly mumbling something beneath his breath, were pinched tight.

This was not an ice-cream cone and puppy dream.

After last time's debacle, Charlie had done some research on nightmares and realized her mistake had been in trying to wake him up. True to Vince's words, she should've left him alone.

"I shouldn't have done it," Vince mumbled. "I'm sorry. I'm so goddamned sorry. My fault...all my fault."

Charlie hesitated, ready to let him be, when his next words froze her still.

"It should've been me..."

Those words sat on her chest, weighting her feet to the floor. Even though she didn't know exactly what *should've* happened, she could only imagine—and the pictures weren't pleasant.

"Screw it." Going against Vince's orders and her own better judgment, she walked to the bed and, instead of waking him, gently rested her hand on his shoulder.

"It's okay, Navy." Charlie caressed his face with her knuckles and continued to soothe him. "You're right where you're supposed to be."

"He's gone," Vince mumbled. "It should be me. *My* fault."

"Nothing's your fault, Vince."

"All mine. *My* fault."

Careful not to jostle him, Charlie slid on top of the sweat-dampened covers and nestled her head against his shoulder. "It's not your fault. You're right where you're supposed to be."

And she repeated those same two sentences, over and over, eventually noticing he no longer fidgeted or talked in his sleep. His deep, regular breaths lulled her eyes closed, just as one of his arms banded around her waist and pulled her even closer.

* * *

Sweltering Miami heat, a warm ocean breeze, and the muffled crunch of firm sand beneath the soles of his sneakers... Vince hadn't felt this refreshed in God only knew how long. But it didn't have a damn thing to do with his run, or even waking up on the right side of the bed.

He'd slept through the night—no nightmares. No images from the fucking desert. No best friend lying dead in his arms. No waking up in a cold sweat. There'd only been him and the warm, pliant woman plastered to his side.

First night with Charlie wrapped in his arms and his first restful night's sleep in years. Coincidence? Vince didn't know. What he did know without a doubt was that someone had started watching him ten minutes ago.

His gut never lied.

With the sun barely peaking over the ocean and no visitors clogging his line of vision, the black town car parked in the lot above the boardwalk was easy to spot. He slowed his pace to a trot and watched as Anthony stepped out of the car and beckoned.

"Guess they aren't even hiding it," Vince mumbled, taking his time hiking up to the dune.

By the time he got there, Arturo had climbed his way from the back seat, looking weaker than he had two days ago.

"Come. Sit." Arturo motioned to the park bench and waited expectantly for him to obey.

"Here for a run on the beach?" Vince joked dryly.

Arturo chuckled. "I didn't run when I was a fit and healthy young man, much less now. Maybe if I would have, I wouldn't be sitting here with one foot in the grave. How's my niece this morning?"

Vince didn't bother giving an answer, and the look on Arturo's face said he didn't expect one.

"I know the girls are having a day at the spa today," Arturo continued, "and I wanted the chance to talk to you—man-to-man."

"Is this where you threaten what you're going to do to me if I don't take care of Charlie?"

"I don't threaten, son." Arturo's crooked smirk held a whole lot of lethal promise. "If I feel the need to threaten someone, then the deed's already been carried out."

"Comforting."

Arturo shifted backward in his seat. "I like you, Vincent. You're the exact type of man I wanted for Charlotte. She's never liked doing anything the easy way, and normal social standards never really applied. She needs someone who challenges her and who isn't afraid to tell her when she's a step from going too far. I'm not so far gone I believe she's come home to make amends...or for a vacation. I know what she thought of me when she left."

"What are you getting at here, Arturo?" Vince propped his elbows on his knees and locked gazes with the older man. Eight feet away, Anthony stood by the car, staring down the beach.

"You need to convince Charlotte to leave Miami," Arturo clarified.

Vince lifted a brow. That wasn't what he'd expected him to say. "And why would I do that?"

"Because contrary to what my niece may believe, I *am* attempting to shut down my businesses—all of them. For the most part, I haven't received much resistance. But there are some colleagues out there who aren't very thrilled about the sudden loss of income flowing into their bank accounts."

"And what does that have to do with Charlie?"

"She may not want to acknowledge it, but her aunt was the love of my life, my reason for living. My daughter and Charlotte are the only two pieces I have left of my dear Leslie, and it wouldn't take much digging for my enemies to use that against me."

Arturo stood, his gait slightly unsteady. "If you care about my niece at all, you'll convince her to head back to your quaint little bar in Pennsylvania."

"And if she won't go?" Because no way in hell was he going to be able to convince her to give up on those missing girls.

Arturo looked almost resigned. "I sure as hell hope I'm right about your character, Vincent Franklin."

"What kind of character is that?" Vince couldn't help but ask.

"The kind that would lay his life down for the woman he loves."

Vince watched as Anthony assisted Arturo back into the car, the older man's words rattling in his head.

The woman he loved?

Vince would put his life on the line for any innocent, and that included Charlie. But love? One night of nightmare-free sleep and great sex didn't change the fact that he wasn't built for lasting relationships. He'd take what they'd agreed upon and enjoy it while it lasted, because it *would* end. There was no other choice. He had to live with the nightmare that he'd caused eight years ago.

Charlie didn't.

Convince her to leave? That wasn't happening. Protect her with everything in his arsenal? *That* he could handle.

* * *

Charlie didn't know which was worse, waking up alone or waking up realizing Vince had not only tucked the blanket around her, but left a note telling her he'd gone for a run.

She hadn't meant to fall asleep next to him, but she'd been exhausted and, despite being hard as granite, his chest was really bloody comfortable. Add in the steady thump of his heart and his comforting, musky man smell, and she'd never stood a chance of staying awake.

At least with him gone, she could do what she'd tried doing last night.

Charlie booted up the computer and went right to the finances of all the last three abductees. The latest, Tiffany Jansen, as they already knew, had put a charge on her credit card for ten grand. The two friends, Ann and Genie, had also shelled out approximately ten grand each, although in varying fashions.

Coincidental? Maybe. But she wasn't putting down a check mark until she knew for certain.

First stop, Ann's banking activity—which required hacking into the bank's system. "What Stone doesn't know won't kill him," Charlie reasoned with herself, "or make him scream at me."

She cracked her fingers and got to work chipping at the bank's firewall. The ease with which she located the original scanned check was enough to make a girl want to stuff her money under the mattress.

Sin Enterprises.

Printed in Ann's handwriting, it was the link they needed to tie Tiffany's abduction to the JAG lawyer's daughter. Next up, Gina Estevez. Since she'd already linked the young coed's credit card to the same shell company, it was time to hack another bank firewall.

And there it is again.

With a budding headache brewing behind her eyes, Charlie kept digging. Sin Enterprises eventually linked up with another shell company. More digging and more muscle tension, and she found a third.

Charlie's headache had drifted into DEFCON-1 territory by the time Vince returned from his run. Workout shorts hanging low on his hips, he crossed the room and stopped a good three feet away. But she couldn't even enjoy the sweaty wonderland of his hard body.

"What's wrong?" he asked, forgoing any pleasantries.

"Good news is we can now confirm the three latest girls, the ones with military connections, are all involved with the same shell company, Sin Enterprises. I think we found our smoking gun."

Vince grabbed a towel from the bathroom, momentarily distracting her as he started mopping up his sweaty chest. "Why don't you look happy about it?"

His question snapped her away from her abs adoration. "Because beneath Sin Enterprises is another shell company, and another."

"Explain it to me again?"

"Think of it like those wooden nesting dolls—one

shadow company is cocooned by another. And then that
one is cocooned by yet another. The more times it's cocooned, the harder it is to find the true owner behind the
money associated with it. I could, quite possibly, spend years
searching and keep getting nowhere. These girls don't have
years, Navy. They don't have months, or weeks. *Days*. Every
bloody *hour* counts."

"Take a deep breath." Vince stepped up behind the couch
and dropped his hands to her shoulders.

All her tension melted away at the first squeeze of his
fingers. Her chin dropped to her chest, and a little moan escaped her throat. "Those are some really amazing hands."

"I know." He kept massaging. "Stop being so hard on
yourself. You're doing the best you can. The fact that you
found out there's something happening here is more than
DHS had. All they had were suspicions."

"Yeah, but knowing that something's happening isn't
enough. We need to *stop* it."

On cue, Charlie's computer beeped.

"Got something?" Vince asked, peering over her shoulder.

"My search got a hit." She pulled up the cross-reference
she'd started when she'd woken up, and swore. "Bloody
freaking hell in a goddamned hornet's nest! *Tropical Heat
Foundation*."

Vince sat next to her on the couch, dropped his arm behind her, and huddled close so he could see the screen.
"What's Tropical Heat?"

"Another shell company, but this one got a hit with something I already have on my computer—from Arturo's hard
drive. Tropical Heat Foundation is owned by *him*."

Vince's brows rose. "Meaning he owns Sinful Delights?"

"Or is the purse behind it, at the very least. It's making

me wonder if Tina was there last night as a participant or—"

"A manager?" Vince guessed.

Charlie swiveled her gaze to Vince. "But why would Arturo do something that would purposefully turn law enforcement his way? For his entire life, the man's been one step ahead of authorities. I just don't see him using his own stomping grounds as a stage for kidnapping. It would put him on their radar."

"But you said yourself, the trace goes back to one hell of a line of shell companies. Maybe he didn't expect anyone to find the connection."

Charlie shook her head. It didn't make sense. "DHS didn't know about the sex club, right? As far as they're concerned, those girls disappeared in Arturo's mainstream clubs. Either way, it paints him in a bad light."

"Maybe it's not Arturo. Maybe someone's using his stomping grounds to bring trouble to his doorstep. I can't imagine he's made a lot of friends in his line of business." Vince seemed to ponder something. "As a matter of fact, he told me as much about an hour ago."

Charlie took a deep breath and tried talking her head out of bursting on the spot. "And when were you going to tell me this?"

"I'm telling you now," Vince stated matter-of-factly. "He was playing the part of the concerned uncle, worrying about his enemies getting to you—either that, or he's putting doubt in place in case you happen to stumble onto his new little business venture."

A video chat request chirped to life on the laptop. Vince removed his hands and played the part of good partner as Logan's face came onto the computer screen. The Texan's gaze eased from Vince to Charlie and back. Charlie summoned an innocent expression, but Logan's smirk said it all.

He didn't believe it.

"Good morning, kids." Logan's eyes practically twinkled. As a former Marine sniper, he was trained to notice things others didn't. "How's married life treating you?"

"Engaged," Charlie corrected. "There were no crazy women fighting over a tossed bunch of wilting flowers."

"Are you sure, darlin'? Because something radiant's happening beneath that beautiful tan skin of yours."

"Bruising is going to start happening under your beautiful porcelain skin if you don't knock it the hell off, Callahan," Vince warned.

"Threatening me for complimenting your intended, Franklin?"

Vince shook his head. "Nope. Just stating the fact that the longer you speak, the more likely my fiancée's going to kick your ass. What's up? Do you have any updates?"

There was a brief, shared look. Charlie saw it, and after nearly thirty seconds of silence, realized they weren't going to disclose its meaning to her.

Logan spoke first. "Actually, I do. I've been combing over the first nine reported abductions and I emailed you a few you should take a look at. Something about them didn't seem like the others. Figured it wouldn't hurt to dig a little deeper."

"Did any of the not-quite-right feelings involve either the charging or the withdrawal of large sums of money…say, ten grand?"

Logan's brow lifted. "Uh, yeah. Fuck, how'd you know that?"

"Because Charlie found the same link between the last three girls. And she traced them to a shell company called Sin Enterprises."

Logan glanced down to a notepad in front of him and

scribbled down the name. "Let me guess, it's linked to another?"

"About ten times over, but the one I got a hit on a minute ago is owned by Arturo," Charlie explained.

Stone appeared over Logan's shoulder. "What steered you in this direction?"

"Talking to the last abductee's friend. She admitted that even though they'd been to the Ocean Drive clubs, it wasn't where they were when Tif Jansen was taken. They'd been to a club called Sinful Delights—which happens to have a ten-grand monthly membership fee."

Logan whistled. "*Day-um.* That must be one hell of a delight. What the hell kind of club is this? A freakin' sex club or something?"

"Actually...yeah."

A slow grin broke over Logan's face. He leaned closer to the screen, dropping his whiskered chin in the palm of his hand. "Go on. You have my undivided attention."

"Take a cold shower, Callahan," Vince quipped.

Stone, stern-faced and contemplative, added, "So nothing's changed. Whether the abductions are happening at the mainstream clubs or Sinful Delights, they're owned by him."

"That's how it looks from the outside"—Vince's gestured toward Charlie—"but we're not entirely convinced he's the smoking gun here. English made a good point a minute ago."

Charlie tried to appear unaffected at Vince's support, but stared at him a beat too long, noticing Logan's smug smirk. Clearing her throat, she explained. "Arturo has stayed out of the authority's crosshairs for years. Running a human-trafficking business out of one of his clubs isn't exactly going to keep him under the radar. He's a criminal, but he's not stupid."

Stone nodded, revealing nothing in the way of his thoughts. "You're right. DHS said he's sick. Someone could be using his illness as a way to start up their own organization. Or hell, it could be revenge-motivated."

Vince returned his arm to the back of the couch, just behind Charlie's shoulders. "My gut tells me we haven't even touched the surface of the shit-storm brewing down here."

"I'll try to fend off DHS, get you more time to do your thing. But if this turns into too much of a shit-storm, you bunker the hell down and call for reinforcements. Got it?"

"We got it," Charlie agreed.

"So"—Logan's widened grin hinted toward a coming smart-ass comment—"the charge I saw on the business card at someplace called Lace and Leather? Was this sex club the reason for the shopping spree? And can you model the outfit for me, darlin'?"

Vince nearly growled. "No, she can-fucking-not, Callahan, and if you don't stop picturing it in your head, I'm going to fucking neuter you."

Charlie sent Stone a look of apology. "And speaking of Lace and Leather, we're going to have to make a return trip both to the store and to the club—and the club requires a membership."

"Is this your way of preparing me for some astronomical fee?" Stone asked.

"The ten grand." Charlie grimaced. "Not sure if it's per person or couple."

Stone swallowed a curse. "Good thing we're doing this on DHS's dime, but it's worth it if you find out who's responsible and we get those girls back. Watch each other's sixes and tread lightly."

"You can call Navy Twinkle Toes, he stalks around so quietly." Charlie reached sideways, ignoring Vince's glare, and patted his cheek with a little extra oomph.

Logan burst out laughing. "Goddamn, I wish I was there.

It's got to be more entertaining than dealing with wedding bells and baby talk. Don't get me wrong, I love Penny and Elle, but with almost everyone else out on assignments, I feel like I'm starting to grow a uterus."

Vince snorted. "You do, and I'll sell you to science. Maybe we'll all manage to get some peace and quiet around the compound for once."

"Do me a favor, though? Next time the two of you go all leather-clad and shit, take pictures."

Vince flipped Logan off and leaned forward, ending the vid-chat.

"You could've at least let me say good-bye," Charlie teased.

"Over here." Moving fast, Vince hauled her into his lap.

"What are you—"

His mouth cut off her comment and when his tongue brushed against hers, he pulled back just enough to elicit a frustrated Charlie-groan. She clutched the front of his shirt. "What was that for?"

"Five hours and forty minutes."

"What the bloody hell are you talking about?"

"That's how long it's been since I've had my mouth on you, and to be this close to you and not touch? I wasn't lasting another damn second."

Charlie knew exactly what he meant. Antsy. Tense. Out of sorts. She'd felt all those things and more in the time they'd been apart. Slipping her palms over his broad shoulders, she let out a resounding sigh.

"We're going to let this ride itself out, huh?" she asked, using his earlier words.

"Damn straight. And you better prepare yourself for the possibility of it taking longer than we're going to be down here."

That was exactly what she was afraid would happen.

CHAPTER SEVENTEEN

When most people pictured hell, they envisioned raging infernos and a leather-skinned devil with horns, maybe a few floating souls screaming in agony. To Charlie, it was the pungent odor of perfumed incense and the cold massage table that had seen umpteen naked people that day alone... and having a stranger touch her.

Ten minutes ago, she'd told the masochist masseur he'd better take his wandering hands and hide, and that's exactly what he did. And the only regret Charlie had was not having threatened him sooner.

"I still can't believe you nearly made Sven cry," Tina complained—again, as they waited outside the spa for the valet to bring around the truck.

"He got too hands-y." Charlie purposefully didn't apologize.

"He's trained in the art of relaxation. It's his *job* to get hands-y," Tina said snottily.

"I don't know *what* that was, but it wasn't relaxation."

"For the love of God, you could've tried not acting like a torture victim for at least *one* of our treatments! Don't they have spas in that backwoods town of yours?"

"Sure. The bathroom in my one-bedroom apartment."

"*Your* apartment?" Tina flicked her long hair over her shoulder. "Things aren't going well with Mr. Tall, Tatted, and Terrifying? I mean, you're marrying the guy and you're still holding on to your own dumpy little place? Doesn't exactly sound like happily ever after."

"We like our own spaces. Nothing wrong with that," Charlie grumbled.

"Yes, there *is* something wrong, little cousin. Marriage means making sacrifices to be with the other person, sometimes even if you have to do things that may be uncomfortable—like sharing a living space."

"And you know this how, exactly?" Charlie snapped. After a whole day of being poked, prodded, and buffed to within an inch of her sanity, she still hadn't gotten a chance to grill Tina about Sinful Delights. Her cousin's interrogation talents, however, were starting to outshine Stone's. "If you have something to say, Tina, get it all out in the open. You never wasted pleasantries on me before, so why start now?"

Tina whirled around way too fast for a woman in six-inch heels. "Why did you really come back? Because this whole I'm-getting-married-and-I-wanted-to-show-my-fiancé-my-hometown act sounds like freaking hooey."

"What person above the age of eight says 'hooey'?"

What person who can be found in a bloody sex club?

"*I* do! When I see of a load of it staring me right in the face!"

"It's not hooey staring you in the face, Ti, it's the truth,"

Charlie lied easily. "And may I remind you, I wasn't the one who sought out a little reunion? I kept my distance when Vince and I got to town for a reason. I sure as hell didn't invite myself to brunch, or come up with this wonderful bonding excursion."

"But you came," Tina huffed.

"Like Arturo would've accepted anything else."

Even though Tina saw Arturo with Daddy Vision, her cousin wasn't stupid. No one went up against Arturo Franconi and came out unscathed.

When the valet showed up with the rental, Tina gave the pickup a disgusted eye-roll and dramatically climbed into the passenger seat.

Charlie had barely managed a right-hand turn out of the spa parking lot when Tina opened her mouth again. "I may not have run with the smart kids in school like you, but I didn't need a genius GPA to know you hated Miami. You hated living with us. You hated everything about our life here."

"I hated that I wasn't able to live with my mother," Charlie said bluntly.

Tina went quiet. Charlie didn't mention her mother often. Or ever. And she hadn't meant to do so now, either, but the constant nagging was starting to get to her, and she'd slipped.

There'd been no father growing up—just her and her mom—putting their mark on the world. Yeah, she'd hated Miami. It took away the only person who'd ever given a damn—or more accurately, who didn't have an ulterior motive for giving a damn.

Tina sure hadn't liked her home being invaded by the brainy British kid, and when Charlie's talents with a computer became obvious, Arturo's lavish attention only gave her cousin more reason to dislike her. It hadn't mattered that it had been focused on what Charlie could do for him.

And then there was Brock. Until Charlie had been given this assignment, she'd thought befriending the estranged son of her uncle's right-hand man at a local Internet café had been a happy coincidence.

Wrong—once again, used.

"I didn't fit in here, Ti." Charlie admitted, trying to ignore the slight tightening in her chest. "Arturo—"

"Is no angel. I get it." At Charlie's surprised glance, Tina rolled her eyes. "Seriously, just because I keep up to date on all the latest fashion doesn't mean I don't have a brain. I know Daddy's not the typical soccer-coach father. He looks for opportunities in everything he does—and everyone he meets. Just remember, when he first took you into our home, you were eight years old."

"I know how old I was. What's your point?"

"My point is, smart or not, the only thing an eight-year-old is good for is increasing your grocery bill."

Charlie hadn't thought about it *quite* like that. Arturo hadn't been required to take her into his home. She wasn't any blood relation to him, after all. But just because he hadn't packed her bags and sent her into the foster care system didn't mean he'd sprouted angel wings.

Charlie tried steering the topic away from herself just as she directed the truck onto the main road leading off the spa grounds. "You said at brunch that you're running your own business. How's that going?"

Tina shot her a glare. "Look. We spent the day together like Daddy wanted, but don't insult my intelligence by pretending you actually care."

The car in front of them slammed on its brakes, and Charlie swerved, narrowly missing attaching the truck to their bumper. Miami traffic sucked around the clock. There was no way to avoid it. But traffic during a burgeoning rush hour? With cars, construction, and basic bad driving, the ride home went from inhumanely long to nearly fatally long, because by the sixth heavy-breathed sigh from the passenger seat, Charlie had just about snapped.

"Feel free to hop out and hoof it back to the house if you think you can get there any faster," Charlie gritted through her teeth.

"At this rate, I could. If you don't move it along, I'm going to miss Whitney's engagement party."

"Whitney. As in Whitney Holiday?" Charlie snuck her cousin a glance. "Isn't she already married?"

"This is her fourth engagement, if you must know, but it doesn't make the celebration any less special."

"Yeah, it kind of does. '*Congratulations on finding that one special someone...for the fourth time.*' See? It doesn't have that same ring to it."

Tina scowled. "And where did you have your engagement party...in your place of employment?"

Charlie grinned, saying the first thing that came to mind that she knew would get under Tina's skin. "You can't go wrong with beer and trail mix."

Her cousin's nose wrinkled, her look of disgust making Charlie chuckle. "Ugh. I honestly don't know what happened with you. I mean, Daddy tried so damn hard to bring you up right, and you threw your life away for drunkards grabbing your ass and cleaning crushed peanuts off a dirty floor."

Maybe so, if by "right" she meant his trying to convince her to break the law and make him even richer than he already was. Oh yeah, and keep him out of jail.

Charlie forced a tight smile. "And yet I much prefer that

to subjecting myself to what we did for the last six hours."

"You could've stayed with your ruffian fiancé. Heck, I wouldn't currently be stuck in this horrific traffic if you had. I'm never going to get ready and make it to the party in enough time to be fashionably late."

"Unless you're Moses, you would've been stuck in the very same traffic. You're the one who said the only spa worth going to was the one in Shady Oaks."

"And if you'd ever been to the one near the house, you'd realize there *was* no other option. But considering you probably treat your hair with Kool-Aid and buff your nails with a chainsaw, I wouldn't expect you to know the difference."

"Then don't complain about the traffic!"

Tina muttered under her breath, folding her arms across her chest like an insolent child. Drumming her newly manicured nails on the steering wheel, Charlie caught sight of a flipped tractor trailer a dozen car-lengths ahead. After that, the road cleared—somewhat. Thirty minutes later, they passed the accident, but rush hour descended with a vengeance.

Charlie ignored Tina's irritated huffs and snorts, and switched lanes to avoid a slowing minivan. Mid lane-change, her gaze snagged on a bright blue sedan doing the same, three cars back. When she drifted to the far right to avoid a disabled car, the blue sedan did the same. Again.

Instincts blaring, Charlie took the first right with no warning.

"What the hell?" Tina dropped her hand onto the dash. "Where did you get your license? A Cracker Jack box?"

Charlie ignored Tina's tantrum as she watched the blue car make the same sharp right turn. Keeping the truck steady, her eyes flickered to the rearview mirror. Dark tinted windows made it nearly impossible to identify either of the two men inside the car, and, not much of a surprise to Charlie, it didn't have a license plate.

"Hang on a sec," Charlie warned Tina just before she made an unexpected left. She held her breath and counted— five seconds. Ten. At nearly thirty, Charlie let out a shaky sigh and mentally scolded herself for her paranoia. After three intersections, her heart rate almost returned. After the fourth, a squeal of tires pulled her attention to their rear.

Blue Bird was back.

"Bloody hell." Charlie reached for her phone, but her fingers had barely touched it when Tina snatched it.

"No! No freaking way are you going to text and drive. You can't stay on the road as it is!" Tina held it out of reach.

"Give me the phone, Tina."

Tina dangled it from her fingers and dropped it on the floor. "Whoops."

Charlie let out a growl. "Give me my phone and then snap into your seat belt."

Looking smug, Tina brought her leg down with a loud crunch. "Try and use it now. And why do you care if I'm wearing my seat belt? With the way you're driving, I could be strapped into a harness like a freaking astronaut and still get injured. You are not my keeper, Charlotte Ann *Sparks*," Tina snapped, getting back on her high horse. "I don't know what you think you can accomplish by coming back home, but it's not to get me to—"

The blue sedan nearly latched itself onto the truck's bumper. Charlie stepped on the gas, and Tina's head whipped back onto her headrest.

"Are you freaking insane?" Tina screeched.

"Shut up and get your bloody seat belt on...*now*!"

Tina finally listened. Behind them, the car rumbled as it attempted to pull alongside them. Rafe had forced her to watch enough training videos to recognize the move: it gave the car's passenger free rein to empty a round of bullets into the truck—and the truck's driver.

Charlie frog-hopped between cars, keeping the blue vehicle in her line of sight at all times—and behind them. Its passenger window dropped, and an arm emerged, holding something silver in its hand.

"Charlie!" Tina squeaked—but she wasn't staring at the gun taking aim. Up ahead, a parked delivery truck sat in their lane, ramp down in mid-delivery.

"Hold on." Charlie yanked the truck to the right, through two lanes of traffic, earning her a middle finger from a pissed-off cabbie.

"Oh my God. Oh my God." Tina clutched the oh-shit handle above the seat.

Traffic lights went from green to yellow, and the car behind them blew each one, hurtling through the intersections. She turned, they turned. She stepped heavily on the gas, and they sped up too.

"You're going too fast." Tina now sounded concerned. "Jesus, Charlie, that's a red light! Stop!"

"Can't." She floored it, almost closing her eyes as she burst through. Horns honked, and people shouted, but she didn't care... especially when the car behind them did the same.

Charlie summoned every evasive-driving lesson the guys had ever given her and put it into effect, except her goal wasn't to put their pursuers out of commission. What Charlie wanted was to get away without killing anyone, but the blue sedan didn't seem to have the same philosophy. They nearly collided with a homeless man, making his cart of belongings fly into the air and scatter.

Tina turned in her seat, looking behind them. "Is that car chasing us?"

It was Charlie's turn to roll her eyes. "Gee. What do you know. I hadn't noticed."

"Well, pull over and find out what they want before they run us off the road and kill us!"

Charlie shot her cousin an annoyed glare. "They're fucking chasing us in the middle of the city and nearly ran over a homeless man to keep up. Do you really think they're the type of guys I want to pull over for?"

"Well, they must be *your* friends, so why the hell not?" Tina yelled.

A metallic *ping* bounced off the truck and the passenger-side mirror shattered.

"What was that?" Tina asked.

"I'm pretty sure it was a bullet." Charlie's heart leapt to her throat.

Tina's head whipped in her direction. "Your friends shoot at you?"

Charlie's restraint, or what was left of it, snapped. "Your father's a bloody mob boss and you think those guys back there are because of *me*? What delusional world have you been living in, Tina?"

"I've never been shot at until you came back to town! I knew you should've stayed gone."

"For the last time, these are not my bloody friends!" Her eyes shifted left and right, looking for their next-best option.

Ping, another shot, this one somewhere near the truck bed. Either their tail wasn't aiming directly into the cab of the SUV, or they were lousy shots. Screaming, Tina clutched her expensive purse to her chest like it was an armored vest.

"Do you have a cell phone in your purse?" Charlie asked.

"You want to make a phone call while driving for our lives?"

"Phone, Tina."

Tina shuffled through her bag before pulling out the jewel-encrusted case. "Got it."

"Dial the number I tell you,"

Another *ping* smacked the truck, this one snapping off Charlie's side mirror and making an all-too-close *zing* near her left ear. Tina screamed and ducked, dropping the damn phone, and braced her hands on the dash.

Bloody. Fucking. Hell.

"All right boys"—Charlie gritted her teeth—"enough is enough. Hold on."

The truck's tires squealed as she turned in a sharp right. Charlie sped up, eyes narrowed in concentration at the two Dumpsters lining each side of the alley-like road. "Please fit. Please fit. Please bloody fit."

Metal screeched against metal as they squeezed through. The left Dumpster caught on the back bumper, tugging it off-kilter enough that their friends were forced into a shrieking stop.

Tina nervously glanced over her shoulder. "They're gone?"

"For now." Charlie used her only remaining mirror to make sure their admirers stayed behind as she directed the truck toward the freeway. Tina, atypically silent—and pale—still clutched her purse like it was her lifeline.

"Well, that was fun." Charlie sighed, releasing the tension she'd been holding since leaving the spa.

Tina turned in her seat, mouth agape. "You're crazy. You're even crazier now than you were before you left."

Charlie kept her mouth closed as she tried to decipher how to continue. This hadn't exactly been part of the plan of keeping a low profile with the family. The sun set as they approached her uncle's neighborhood, and by the time Charlie pulled up in front of the house, Tina was already sliding out.

"Tina." Charlie bent over the seat to catch her cousin's eye. "Can I trust you to—"

"Keep my mouth shut?" Tina rolled her eyes. "Please, like I *want* people to know what happened. I won't tell Daddy either, but you need to stay the hell away. Forget whatever it is that brought you back into our lives and slip out of them as easily as you did before. It shouldn't be difficult for you. After all, you seem pretty good at it."

CHAPTER EIGHTEEN

Vince paced the hotel room for the fourth time in as many minutes. After Charlie had left this morning, he'd gotten two irritated texts filled with British curses he still didn't understand, and then nothing. No call. No text. It was like she'd fallen off the fucking planet.

"You're making me motion sick, man," Logan complained from the laptop screen.

Vince shoved his face in view of the camera. "I don't give a flying monkey fuck if you're getting sick. Get a ping on her phone or the truck."

"Dude, I told you the phone's not on, and the GPS tracker isn't picking anything up. Someone either removed it or—"

"Finish that sentence, and they won't find your body, Callahan," Vince growled threateningly.

It wasn't Logan's fault Charlie had gone MIA, but fuck. He needed someone to lash out at or he'd start accosting hotel furniture.

Logan seemed to weigh his words carefully. "I was going to say that she physically disabled it. Jesus. Bloodthirsty much?"

When it came to Charlie? *Yes*. Vince never should've let her go off on her own, not after Franconi's warning earlier in the day. Images of her lying facedown on the outskirts of a bush-lined highway kept flashing through his head, each one worse than the one before.

"Hell fucking yeah!" Logan roared, fist-bumping the air in front of him. "I got a hit on the truck. Hell, man. It looks like it's at the hotel."

"Does it look like she's in the room right now?" Vince asked.

The words no sooner left his mouth than their door clicked open.

"She's here. Call you all back later," he said gruffly.

Charlie stepped into the room as he cut off the video feed.

Relief at seeing her stuck in Vince's throat. Wide eyes glanced around their suite, and her skin, usually with a healthy glow, looked pale beneath the lights. Hell, the only color on her face came from the small red knot blossoming to life on the left side of her forehead.

Vince closed the distance and touched the bump, cursing when she winced.

"What the hell happened?" Vince reluctantly pulled his hand away, letting her inspect her head with her own fingers.

"I didn't even know that was there. I guess I hit my head after all."

Vince clenched his teeth until they ached. "*How* did you hit your head?"

Charlie shimmied past him, kicking off her shoes before plopping heavily down on the couch. For once, he didn't think she'd ignored his question to be a pain in the ass. He'd seen it in the field. Acute shock. Whatever had brought it on was going to have to work its way to the surface, so he didn't push.

She dug into her purse and tossed him the truck keys. "Pretty sure Alpha purchased a very expensive piece of scrap metal from the rental company. If Stone was going to birth kittens before, he's going to have a litter of jungle cats now."

He dropped to his haunches in front of her. "You were in an accident? Why the hell didn't you call me to come to get you? Did you get your head checked out?"

"First, it definitely wasn't an accident. And I couldn't call because my phone is in about twenty different pieces from a run-in with my cousin's high heel. And there's nothing wrong with my head except for a having one hell of a headache."

He trapped her chin between his fingers and gently kept her attention focused on him. Pupils reactive. Equal. Once he was satisfied she wasn't in any immediately health jeopardy, he asked, "Are you purposefully trying to be difficult?"

"I was tailed out of the spa." Charlie melted into the couch cushions, looking drained. "When they realized they'd been spotted, it turned into a bit of a car chase. And my crazy-assed cousin was so worried about me texting while driving that she dropped—and then stepped on—my phone, so I couldn't call."

"Explain to me again why you have a goose egg?" Barely hanging on to the last string of his control, Vince retrieved ice from the small fridge, and after wrapping it in a washcloth, sat next to her and held it against her head. "Goose egg, English. How did you hit your head?"

"It must've hit the window when I made one of the sharp turns. Bloody bastards wouldn't give the hell up."

Charlie looked more shaken than he'd ever seen. Everything inside him wanted to haul her closer, but coddling her now risked her pulling away. "Tell me about the car."

"It's minus its mirrors and the paint's—"

"Not the truck—the car tailing you."

"It was a dark blue sedan, late nineties. No license plate. And because of the serious tint job, I could barely register the fact that there were two of them inside, much less see anything more identifiable. When they rolled down the window to take a shot, they made sure I still didn't have a view, so they weren't completely bloody stupid."

"They took fucking shots at you?" Vince roared, making her jump. He paced a few times, counting to ten before tacking on another five seconds. "With bullets?"

She gave him a cockeyed glare. "No, with spitballs," she said sarcastically, her voice tired. "Yes, bullets. And like I said, the truck took the worst of it. Two of their hits made it earless, and then there was an unfortunate incident of squeezing between two Dumpsters."

"Ears?"

She gestured to the sides of her head with her hands like he should know what the hell she was talking about.

"Yeah, ears. Side mirrors," she clarified. "I hope you know a good body shop."

"Cars can be fixed or replaced, Charlie. You can't."

She went quiet, maybe because of his use of her name, or the car chase starting to play on repeat in her head. Maybe both. But it gave Vince a chance to curse himself out for not being there to back her up.

He sat next to her, his thigh brushing hers because he *needed* to be touching her, somehow. "I'm sorry. I should've been there."

She gave him another one of those looks. "You wanted to go to the spa?"

Vince released a tired sigh. "You know what I mean."

She patted his knee and, before she took her hand away, Vince clasped it in his, entwining their fingers. They both studied their interlocked hands, and if Charlie's face was anything to go by, the same emotions rolling through him at mock speed were also flying through her.

Relief. Confusion. And hell, need. She didn't pull her hand away, instead leaning heavily into his side. Things were about to get a fuck-ton more complicated.

"You know," she spoke first, softly, and with a slight tremble she tried hiding behind her usual snarky tone, "we can't be attached at the hip. And being a full field operative means being able to handle things myself... which I did. So stop beating yourself up."

Vince ran his thumb over the curve of her hand. "Just because you can handle yourself doesn't mean you should have to do it all the damn time."

Tension filled the room. A gentle shudder slid through Charlie's body, and for a moment, he thought maybe he'd pushed too hard. And he didn't care. He did what he'd wanted to do since she'd walked through the door, and pulled her onto his lap.

She didn't bite or kick him. No smart-assed comment came hurtling his way. She turned in his arms, burrowing her nose in the curve of his neck, and wrapped her arms around his shoulders.

Vince held on tight and hoped he wasn't hurting her. For hours he'd been ready to tear Miami to the ground and, now that she was here, he wasn't eager to let her go. And the hell if he knew what that meant, but he wasn't about to waste his time trying to figure it out.

Stroking her back, Vince attempted to smooth the tension coiled in her muscles. Charlie Sparks wouldn't cry. Showing weakness around others wasn't something she did, and he understood the need to be strong—to *look* strong. That was why he waited until her breathing returned to normal before he carried her toward the bedroom.

"Am I being sent to my room for being out past curfew?" her voice, muffled against his shirt, teased.

"Exactly," he answered dryly. "But first you're going to take a shower."

"You realize I was just slathered in expensive oils and shite for the better part of the entire day, right?"

He gently settled her back on her feet. "And you need a hot shower to help break you out of your shock."

"I'm not—"

"Babe, I've seen the hardest of assholes go into shock for less than being in a fucking car chase. Your adrenaline's pumping right now, and you need to channel it before your body goes haywire." He nodded to her skimpy little sundress, a far cry away from her Sinful Delights leather. "Do you think you can do it alone or do you want help?"

Helping her without touching her would be the painful equivalent of having his fingernails ripped out of their nail beds, but if that was what she needed, he'd do it.

"I got it covered. Thanks for the offer."

He nodded, his voice gruff. "Fifteen minutes, and then I'm banging down the door."

Her small smile didn't reach her eyes. "We both know how it turned out the last time you did that. I imagine that's good for shock too."

"Wouldn't know. I never offered the service to any of the guys...but I could maybe be convinced to try it with you," he teased. He started the shower and tested the water. "I'll check on you in a bit."

It took more effort than he'd thought to leave her alone in

the bathroom. To distract himself, he dialed up headquarters. Stone answered on the second ring.

"What the hell's happening?" Stone's bellow made Vince pull the phone away from his ear. "You're supposed to be watching Charlie's ass, and then I find out from Logan that she's missing!"

"She fine, though someone's not going to be when I get hold of them," Vince grumbled. "When she's not so shaken up, I'll try to get more of the particulars, but some bastards tried driving *through* her and, when that didn't work, they decided to take a few potshots."

"She okay?" his boss asked.

"Like I said, a little shaken up, not that she'd admit it. But she's good. When she puts her head back on straight, I'll probably have to talk her out of going after these guys. Her cousin was in the car too, so that didn't help the whole *fitting in* goal."

Vince heard Logan's voice in the background before the other operative got on the line. "You guys going to be around later on? You know, no sex club delights or anything?"

"Callahan," Vince growled a warning.

"Dude, I'm being serious here. I don't have anything concrete on that thing you asked me to look into, but I'm close."

Fuck. Charlie's Miami exit. He'd almost forgotten that he'd conned Logan into digging into it, and with things as they were now, Vince was torn. Did he scrap the entire damn thing and focus on the here and now? Or did he go with his gut—and embrace what Charlie called his Caveman Tendencies—and tell Logan to keep at it?

He thought about tonight and not only how close he'd come to losing her, but how helpless he'd felt fucking waiting... *and not knowing*.

"Let me know what you get," Vince heard himself say.

"Will do, brother. Take care of our girl."

"And Franklin," Stone added, "I know Charlie doesn't make it easy to look out for her, but—"

"I got it, boss. I'm going to be so far up her ass she'll think she sprouted a hemorrhoid."

Vince hung up and, a few minutes later, the shower shut off. Charlie opened the door and stood in front of him, wrapped in a large, fluffy white towel. The hot water had put a little more color in her cheeks, but her eyes still resembled two big brown pools of exhaustion.

"Did you call headquarters?" she asked.

"I called. And you're not to worry about it. Up you go, English." Vince didn't bother asking for permission as he scooped her up and deposited her on the mattress's edge.

He didn't know what she wanted—or needed—in that moment, but he knew he wanted to be the one to give it to her.

They stared at one another. Seconds stretched to an eternity. Charlie reached for the towel, slowly unbinding it from around her body, and let it fall away. Every inch of her silky skin was on display for his viewing pleasure.

She slid to the center of the bed, and with a whole lot of something welling in her eyes.

"I want to give you what you need, English, but I'm not so sure this is it." Vince's voice sounded raspy even to his own ears.

"I just need you naked and against me right now. No sex. Just"—her throat convulsed as she tried to speak—"just you. Just until I fall asleep."

Fuck. Hold her? And *sleep*?

Vince warred with himself for five seconds before he stripped his clothes and climbed onto the bed. The second his back hit the mattress, Charlie curled into his side, her cheek against his chest. "You'll stay? For a little bit?"

Vince rested one hand low on her hip, and held her close.
"You couldn't move me with a forklift, baby. I'm yours—for
however long you want me."

Fucking-A. Even he couldn't ignore how fucking truthful
those words rang.

* * *

The mattress bounced, stirring Charlie awake. Goose bumps
erupted over her skin, sending a chill through her as she registered her naked body and the mound of blankets lumped
together at the foot of the bed.

Another thrash turned her gaze to the right.

Vince lay on his back, fists clenched at his sides, his head
twisting from one direction to the other. Sweat dotted his
brow and pooled at the base of his throat. Low, almost indecipherable murmurs slid from his lips and as he chanted a
name: *Rico*.

This time, Charlie didn't struggle with what to do. He'd
slept before when she'd crawled next to him, and if there
was a slight chance she could help him, she'd do it. Starting
with a soft touch, she rested her hand on top of his. He
jolted, but stayed asleep.

"You're okay, Navy," she cooed, running her palm slowly
up his arm and over his shoulder. "You're here with me,
Vince. Charlie. Nothing's happening. You're safe."

And she repeated it, over and over—the words, the
stroking. Eventually, his twitches lessened. Charlie, taking it
as a good sign, placed soft kisses along his jaw. His breathing, though still labored, eased as he turned and tucked his
head against her chest.

Charlie froze, unsure of what to do until his arm draped
her waist, holding her tight. A small smile danced on her lips

as she put her arms around his broad shoulders. Her heart beat a little faster as she continued rubbing his back in small, soothing circles.

Big man. Big nightmares. And big "aw" factor when his guard dropped—like now.

Vince Franklin was a man built on contradictions, and Charlie had to admit, they were a lot alike. Maybe too much so for anything to happen between the two of them beyond the sexual, but there was a ball of something sitting in the center of her chest, and every time she thought about their agreement to let things fizzle out, it tightened into a knot.

For someone who prided herself on independence, her first instinct after dropping Tina off at Arturo's had been to get to Vince as fast as the damn bullet-riddled truck would go. That wasn't something she should feel if they were working out a bout of sexual lust.

Sometime later, Charlie startled awake. The bedside clock read five in the morning, and both she and Vince still lay naked, their legs entwined like human pretzels. But now she was using *him* as a pillow.

Running her fingers through the dark dusting of hair between Vince's pecs, Charlie brushed her thumb against his right nipple piercing.

"This is getting to become a habit." Vince's sleepy voice rumbled his chest. His hand, draped around her torso, traced over the largest of her cherry blossom tattoos.

"You complaining about it?"

"Nope." He took a deep breath, the movement raising her cheek from his chest. "I could get used to it."

Her, too—something for which she hadn't prepared herself.

"What's the meaning behind your tattoo?" Vince asked

as he continued stroking her skin. "Out of all the things you could've gotten... why a cherry blossom tree?"

"Maybe I like flowers. Or spring. Or pink."

"Nah. You're not one of those sorority clones who want a dolphin because they're cute. For you to have gotten it etched on your skin, it needs to have meaning." His finger dipped to where one tree branch swooped below her left breast.

She wasn't sure she liked him reading her so well, and he must've read it in her silence. "You don't want to tell me," Vince guessed accurately.

After everything they'd experienced together, it was ridiculous keeping the reasoning to herself, but to admit it aloud was one more nail in the coffin of intimacy she already felt when she was in his arms.

Blowing a pink-blonde strand of hair from her face, she tucked her chin into his chest and looked him in the eye. "I got it as a reminder; a comparison."

"Of what?"

"Of the Charlie I was before Stone found me—one with all bark and bare limbs. To the Charlie I wanted to be— one who keeps coming back, time after time. Strong and resilient."

Vince's mouth spread into a slow smile. Charlie's heart stumbled, then went still as his fingers gently brushed a lock of hair off her face. "See. Told you it wasn't some drunk, bored college whim."

"You don't think it's silly?"

"Nothing about you is silly, English. That tattoo suits you perfectly—although I do want to know what about your life here made you feel like bare bark."

"Do all of your tattoos have a meaning?" She tried shifting the attention to him.

"Way to dodge."

"Vince," she warned.

"Okay. Too soon. But eventually," he warned back. "And yes, all but one." When she lifted a questioning eyebrow, he chuckled. "A drunken, bored weekend of R&R in a foreign city isn't a sailor's best friend."

Charlie ran her fingers over his arm, taking her time to admire his ink work. Everything was so beautifully blended, one image melting into another. She paused where the buxom brunette from the Archie comics perched seductively above his elbow.

"Let me guess, this one was your bored, drunken R&R weekend."

Vince chuckled. "Actually, no. Veronica's ballsy. She reminds me to never let anything or anyone get in the way of me and what I want. No matter how slick or squirmy or attitudinal she becomes."

His arms tightened around her, bringing her attention back up to his eyes. The heat radiating from them nearly melted her on the spot. *Hello, subliminal messages.*

"When did what you want become *she*?" Charlie asked, her thoughts racing.

"Thought inserting your name right off the bat would send you screaming in the other direction."

He was right. Being wanted wasn't something she was accustomed to, and it scared the hell out of her how much she liked it.

Charlie kept up her tattoo search until she fingered the Navy SEAL trident on the inside of his bicep. Half-hidden within the curves of the staff were a finely etched date and set of initials.

"What's the story about this one?" she asked.

It was Vince's turn to be uncomfortable, and for a moment he didn't answer. He looked at the tattoo, staring as if playing a movie reel in his head. "The trident came when I got my first SEAL team assignment."

"So you survived through Hell Week, huh?"

"Yeah. But it's nothing compared to what happens on the outside." Vince took his eyes off his tattoo. "The initials and date were added later."

Charlie didn't need to ask what they meant.

"I'm sorry." Her heart ached with the truth. "I can't imagine."

He nodded, his jaw flexing. But Charlie saw his emotional battle in the darkening of his eyes. Now a deep green, they held the untold sorrows that stretched straight to his core. "Thank God not everyone has to. But a SEAL knows what we're signing up for ahead of time. Still doesn't make the loss any easier...especially when it could've been prevented."

Charlie knew his basic service history from his Alpha background check, but it had been dates and locations, no stories. Although she suspected there were a lot of them. Not long after that date etched on his skin, he'd put in his papers for retirement and became bail enforcement—which was what had led to his meeting Penny, and inadvertently, signing on with Alpha.

Since day one with the team, he'd been a man of rules. He trained hard. He worked harder. And he kept to himself the hardest of all. He'd been a man of secrets, and even though it was hypocritical of her, Charlie needed to know what they were.

"That thing you said could've been prevented...that's what your nightmare is about, isn't it?" she said carefully.

Vince stiffened against her. "It's in the past. Isn't that what you once told me?"

"Except that's not really the case when you relive it every night."

"I'm not doing this right now, English," Vince warned, his voice gruff.

"If not now, then when?"

Vince pulled away, sitting up and sliding to the other edge of the bed. His massive shoulders slumped as he dropped his head to his hands, making sure to keep his back turned her way. "It only affects me when I'm sleeping."

"Maybe the flashbacks only come back when you're sleeping, but do you mean to tell me it doesn't affect your everyday life?" Charlie debated whether or not to push. And what the hell...playing it safe had never been her thing. "You're a rule follower—sometimes to the point where you begin questioning your gut. You don't do relationships—"

"Neither do you," Vince pointed out. "That's not a crime. It's called an agenda."

"For some. For others it's called avoidance." Charlie crawled next to him—and waited. When he didn't move away or tell her to get lost, she laid her hand on his knee and continued. "I don't know what happened on that mission, Vincent, but what I do know is while we've been here in Miami, I've seen what kind of an impression it's left on you. And do you know what else I've seen? Your mind quiets when I slide in bed next to you."

"I told you to leave me alone when it's happening." Instead of a growl, Vince almost sounded...tired. Beaten.

"And you know I don't always do what I'm told." Charlie gripped his chin and drew his attention toward her. The flood of emotions swimming in his eyes almost undid her right there. "Your mind quieted when you let someone in, Vince. You can do it. You can let *me* in."

CHAPTER NINETEEN

Fucking-A. He couldn't deny it. He tried avoiding it by not bringing up the fact that both times he hadn't woken up drenched in sweat, she'd been wrapped around him like a cocoon. But the jig was up. The secret was out—or at least some of it. Now it was a matter of whether or not he wanted to give her the picture in full color.

"What did I say in my sleep?" he asked, in an emotion-choked voice.

"Murmurs mostly. Something about '*your fault*.' And a name—'Rico.'"

Hearing his buddy's name said aloud fucked with his head. He closed his eyes and took a deep breath. When he opened them again, Charlie hadn't moved.

Vince warned her, "If I tell you, I don't want you worrying I'll fuck up now like I did then. Because that shit is over and done with."

"I promise, I won't think you'd fuck up any more than I do now," Charlie teased.

Vince gripped the back of her head, his heart pounding with the idea of sharing his past. "I mean it."

"Relax." Her hand reached up, stroking his arm until his fingers eased, and when he released his hold, she took his hand in hers and held on tight. "I'll deny it if you ever mention it to any of the others—because of fragile male egos—but there isn't anyone at Alpha I'd trust more to watch my arse than you."

"That may change when I tell you about Afghanistan."

Charlie squeezed his hand. "That won't change. *Ever.*"

She didn't push, goad, or try to trick him into talking. She waited in silence, something very un-Charlie-like, while Vince took his time gathering his thoughts.

"We'd just come off a mission, providing support to a village being terrorized by a local insurgency. We'd been out in the field three weeks. Maybe three and a half. We'd finally made it within sniffing distance of our base when we smelled smoke." Vince took a deep breath, almost tasting the rancid scent in the back of his throat. "They'd bombed the hell out of the place—the insurgents we'd just gotten done fighting off. I guess they wanted a little payback for ruining their plans, so they took it out on our friends while they were sleeping."

Vince heard Charlie's quick intake of breath and continued. "Our orders were to return to base...but the guys... *Rico*...they all wanted to go after the ones who did it. Hell, I did too. We didn't need to be standing next to base to know there'd be carnage down there, but we weren't medics. We couldn't have done anything except stand around with our thumbs up our asses. Going after the assholes was in our field of practice."

"So you went after them?"

At the soft declaration, Vince met her gaze. There was no disappointment, no judgment. He nodded, his throat drying to the point that his tongue stuck to the roof of his mouth.

"It was *my* call to make," Vince admitted. "I let my need for payback get in the way of orders. We tracked all the hostiles through the ravine, but when they split up, we had to do the same or risk losing them. Rico was adamant he could handle the single escapee on his own, and so I let him, and we found him an hour later, his throat slashed. Dead. Alone."

"I'm so sorry, Navy," Charlie murmured softly. She rubbed across the back of his shoulders, gaining his attention. "I know this doesn't help, but it wasn't your fault. I mean, you gave the formal order, but you said your team wanted to go after them."

"But it wasn't up to them. If I had continued on to base camp, none of it would've happened. He'd be alive, a husband to his wife and a father to his little girl."

Something clicked in Charlie's eyes. "The woman from the dock. The pretty one with dark hair."

"Dawn." Vince nodded, clutching Charlie's hand as if it was a parachute. "I haven't seen her since Rico's funeral, when I put an American flag in her hands. I knew she'd had a girl. I've been..." Vince sighed, unable to believe he was about to admit it. "I've been putting money into a special account for her since the day of Rico's funeral. It doesn't make up for getting her father killed, but I hope it'll make her life a little easier."

"I can't imagine Dawn blames you for what happened."

"She doesn't have to. Rico would still be alive today if I hadn't let my emotions get in the way."

"She gave you something before you walked away."

Vince arched a brow. Leave it to Charlie to have seen

that from dozens of yards away. "Her number. She's in town for another week or so. She wanted me to call her when I could."

"Then you should. You should meet up...and talk."

"And say what?" Vince sneered, unable to meet Charlie's eyes. "Sorry I fucked up your life?"

"Truthfully, I don't know what you should say. But I think you need some kind of closure. I think both of you do. She wouldn't have given you her number if she didn't want you to use it."

Charlie was right—on all fronts. *Way too fucking right.* He pulled away and grabbed a shirt, needing some kind of distance from the raw ache in his chest, but it followed him. Hell, it latched on with fucking claws.

"I'll tell you what, English."—he prepped to act like a world-class asshole as he yanked a T-shirt over her his head— "I'll make peace with myself the moment you do."

Eyes wide, Charlie froze in place as if she'd been slapped. But instead of getting sparking mad, she drilled him with a hard, wounded stare. "We weren't talking about me."

"You're right. We weren't. You're fine with talking about what others should and shouldn't be doing, about doling out advice and being open and honest, but you're not even being honest with yourself," Vince lashed out. "Maybe when you're finally willing to come out in the open and share some of *your* nightmares, I'll do what I have to do to get rid of mine. In the meantime, we have a sex club to visit, young women to find, and a sick bastard to sniff out."

Vince stalked toward the bedroom door, Charlie's gaze heavy on his back; and despite the severity of it, it was nothing compared to the weight pushing on his chest. He no longer knew which way was up or down, left or right. All he was certain about was that at some point during this assignment, Charlie had started seeing him more clearly than he fucking saw himself.

* * *

After being subjected to an hour-long talk with Sinful Delight's manager and then led on a tour of the club, Charlie came to two conclusions. The first: She should've done a more thorough scrubbing after their first visit. An hour-long soak in a bleach bath might have done the trick. And the second: She wasn't as good an actress as she'd thought.

Evidently, she'd done a piss-poor job of masking her irritation with Vince because the manager, homing in on the awkward silence, made sure to state that whatever happened outside the club *stayed* outside of the club. And vice versa. Meaning she needed to pull her shit together.

Had she liked Vince calling her out? No. Was he right? Yes. But just because their conversation made him uncomfortable, it didn't give him the right act like a bloody arse.

Sinful Delight's manager brought them to a stop at the main bar. "And that concludes our little tour. I hope you can see we take our clients' safety very seriously. It's our primary goal, followed immediately after everyone's enjoyment, of course."

"You guys seem to run a tight ship." Vince ran his hand down Charlie's back. It took everything in her not to turn around and bite it. "I don't foresee us running into any problems. What about you, English?"

Charlie forced a smile. "None. It seems a perfect spot to sate our needs."

"I'm so glad to hear that." The manager offered a slick smile. "Maybe on another night, our owner will be here to speak with you. She loves welcoming new members. But unfortunately, she was called away on business."

"Like I said before, it's not a problem." Vince shook the man's hand.

"Of course." The manager, a young man no older than his mid-twenties, nodded. "So you have our handbook. In it are the policies and guidelines we hold ourselves to as a club, and expect from our members. Background checks are done on all SD clients, so you never have to worry about whether you'll have a fun, safe evening. And in the odd case that a problem does arise, our security officers are efficient in handling it."

"Good to know."

"Enjoy the club…and may all your delights be sinful." He flashed them a wink and gave a slight bow before disappearing into the crowd.

Charlie counted to five before she murmured, "My delight right now would be a decontamination chamber and an eyewash station. I'm never looking at my GYN's stirrups the same way again."

Beside her, Vince snorted. "And here I thought it was pretty inventive."

"There's no real substitute for good taste—although I shouldn't project that belief onto you, should I?" Charlie said dryly. She tossed him a glare. "I wouldn't want to skew your decision, one way or another. You know, with my horrid opinions and all."

Vince's arm banded tighter around her waist as he leaned close. "Is this how it's going to be all night? You freezing me out?" he murmured against her ear.

"I'm not freezing you out. This is just me, being my secretive, dishonest self."

"You're purposefully twisting my words around," Vince growled.

"Better your words than your neck—which would be my second choice."

Even though no one could hear their low conversation amid the loud music, Charlie noted a few curious glances being shot their way. She amped up the wattage on her fake smile and curled into Vince's side. "Which of the amenities would you like to partake in first, love?" She drew a finger over his chest. "Or we could take a stroll and see what tickles your fancy."

Vince's eyes darkened, and his hand gripped her hip a little harder. "*You* tickle my fancy, sweetheart, and everything else. But I like the sound of that stroll."

Charlie told herself the innuendo and the touchiness was all for show, but the truth was, she didn't know. Lord knew each time *she* touched *him*, it felt less like a job and more like a constant need to be around him. And touch him.

And she shouldn't still want that after his jerky tantrum. *Shouldn't.*

But she still did.

They started their walk by skirting the dance floor. No less modest than they'd been the last time she and Vince had been there, people didn't bother hiding the fact that their hands, mouths, and other various body parts were busy exploring—basically every*thing* and every*one*. But the back room?

Vince and Charlie stepped through the heavy velvet curtains and, suddenly, Charlie was glad for Vince's presence.

Far from a prude, she knew her way around a good sexual romp as well as the next girl, but she didn't know her way around...*this*. Not only was the back room where inhibitions and reservations were shed, but apparently clothes, too. Even a pasty or uncomfortable G-string was a hard commodity to spot.

People strutted around, naked and free, and way more open than Charlie could have ever thought possible. Off in the far left corner, the same dark-haired man from the *shibari* demonstration their first night was in the midst of another one.

With her arms bound and straightened high above her head on a beam, a woman stood naked and exposed, her body facing the watching crowd, while the man on stage stalked around her, a leather flogger in his right hand and a feather contraption in his left.

At her side, Vince's body straightened. "Eleven o'clock."

Charlie glanced left. *Tina.*

She put Catwoman to shame, wearing a skintight black bodysuit that made Charlie wish she'd been blessed with her cousin's height. Tina strutted around the club, not looking the least bit self-conscious as she stopped and spoke to the occasional couple.

Apparently, Little Miss Hostess was back—and so was Brock. He stepped up behind her cousin, his massive arms wrapping around her waist.

"What the ever loving hell?" Charlie's mouth dropped open.

"Well, look at that. There's definitely no fighting happening now." Vince's face broke into an amused smirk. "They look awfully damn cozy, don't they? I thought they couldn't stand to be in the same room together?"

Charlie blinked a few times, hoping the scenery would change, and that her cousin and Brock weren't about to suck face. "They can't—or couldn't. Not to mention Arturo would never let someone on his payroll mess around with his daughter."

But they couldn't deny what was right there in front of them—especially when the young manager stepped up to

Tina. The two spoke in hushed tones before her cousin said something to Brock and stalked away with the younger man.

"I say we follow Loverboy this time," Vince suggested.

"You follow Brock. I'll go for Tina."

Vince all but snarled. "The last time I did, someone fucking shot at you."

Charlie turned on him, way too emotionally tired for this shite. "No affecting the job," she reminded him. "You promised me before we started this...whatever."

"That's not what I'm—"

"Yes, it bloody well is. Ask yourself, 'Would I be objecting to this if she had a penis?'" She only paused a beat before answering, "No, you wouldn't. Glad we cleared this up. Now go and stalk Brock while I find out once and for all what kind of tie my cousin has to this place."

Charlie didn't give him time to object. She followed Tina through the back of the club, making sure to keep her distance even when Tina and the manager took a right down a long corridor. Charlie waited an extra beat before following at a fast clip. Doors lined the long hall, some with titled plaques: VOYEUR. PLAYTIME. PEEPING TOM.

Charlie bypassed them all, taking the very last right into a much smaller hall. One single door stood open, with Tina's barking voice coming through it.

"I thought this was taken care of," Tina snapped, her voice rising in pitch.

"It was. They came out and assured me it was fixed. Again," the manager's voice stated.

"Did they give any reason as to why it keeps going under?"

"Not a damn one. Maybe these guys aren't as top-notch as you think. I have a friend who dabbles in alarms; I could have him take a—"

"No," Tina cut him off. "We owe our clients more than someone who *dabbles*. Call the firm again and make them send someone out. And make sure they know that I'm not handing over any kind of service fee for what should've been fixed eons ago."

"We don't have security inside the club. Do we really care what happens outside of it?"

"We don't allow video recording inside Sinful Delights to ensure our guests' privacy. But we still need to protect them—which is why we need working cameras at the exits and along the perimeter."

We. Our. It almost sounded like—

"I understand, boss," the manager agreed. "I'll call the security guys myself and get our team in their down-time positions."

Tina wasn't a guest. Or a hostess. She *owned* Sinful Delights. Charlie was still reeling from the shock when she realized someone had stepped up behind her.

"Guests aren't allowed back here." A firm hand dropped onto her bare shoulder. Her first instinct was to shrug it off and return the favor tenfold, but she kept her face devoid of emotion and turned, prepped for a performance.

"I'm sorry, love. I was looking for the loo and got turned around." Charlie amplified her accent. "My mum always told me I could get lost in a paper bag. Point me in the right direction, and I'll be on my way."

"Who is that, Rollins?" Tina's voice asked.

"A guest who's lost her way," the guard answered. "Don't worry, ma'am. I'll take her back."

"Bring her here."

Bloody hell.

"Really, I just need the ladies' room," Charlie tried bartering. But the tall security guard ushered her toward the open door. The second she stepped into the office, she chuckled at Tina's shocked expression.

To the manager and the guard, Tina ordered, "Leave us."

"Ma'am?" the manager asked.

"I said leave us alone and close the door...and for the love of God, get everyone into their positions."

Both men listened, closing the door behind them.

Charlie slid Tina a naughty smirk. "Fancy meeting you in a place like this. Guess we don't know each other as well as we thought, huh?"

"What the hell are you doing here?" Tina demanded.

"I could ask the same of you. This is a far cry away from the country club scene. Either that, or the golf club has gone through a hell of a change since I've been gone. As for what I'm doing here..." She glanced down her leather-clad body. "I should think it pretty obvious. Vince and I are soaking in the local sights."

Tina shuffled through a stack of papers on her desk and opened a manila envelope before scanning the contents, then looked up. "You're new members? You don't even live in the area. Why would you spend this amount of money for a once-in-ten-years appearance? More importantly, how can you afford the fees? You work in a freaking bar."

"Which my fiancé happens to own...and which, despite its country location, keeps quite busy, I assure you."

"I could revoke your membership right now. I *should* revoke it."

Charlie cocked an eyebrow. "And be out the money? I may have been gone a long time, but you haven't changed so much you'd walk away from something that would make your wallet fatter. Besides, it sounded like you should be focusing more on your security issues and less on my membership."

Tina tossed the file back onto the desk. "You know nothing about my security issues."

"No," she admitted, "but it sounds like you don't either. I hate to point out that if you have a weakness in one place, there are more than likely a lot more."

Tina grumbled, obviously knowing Charlie was right. She shuffled a few things around her desk before finally admitting, "It's the security detail Anthony hired to wire the club. He claims they're the best of the best, yet we've had more problems within the last six months than we've ever had before."

Charlie stepped further into the office and, God help her, sat. "What kind of problems?"

"With our cameras. We don't have them inside the club to protect our clients' privacy, but we have them pointed at every exit and around the perimeter. I mean, we're not exactly located in the ritzy part of town, and we did it for a reason. Our clients want to come here without the threat of being followed and exploited."

"How smart is it not to have cameras inside the building?"

Tina stiffened in defense, reading Charlie's neutral expression as doubt. "Our guests come to us for discretion. I can't have them constantly worried someone is going to 'leak' their videos to the press."

"So the people here are run-of-the-mill sex addicts?"

Tina drilled her with a glare. "They're not sex addicts. But they don't relish the idea of having their particular sexual proclivities announced—and photographed—for the world to see. So we have no cameras or video recording within the club. It's also why we make sure people check their cell phones before entering the building. But we *do* have cameras on our emergency entrances and exits, and outside the perimeter of the club."

"And your system's been shutting down?"

"Repeatedly, and it's becoming a nuisance. Every time I call the security firm, they send out some pimply-faced kid who ends up making the problem worse. And it keeps happening so he's obviously not fixing it at all."

Charlie glanced around the office. "Where's your security hub?"

Tina nodded toward a small side table, where three fuzzy computer monitors and a single keyboard sat, neglected.

"Everything can be accessed through here. Only a select few people have access to my office, and I'd rather not worry if someone's doing something they're not supposed to be doing." After a few silent moments, Tina let out a knowing sigh. "You want to hack into our security system, don't you? Don't I have enough problems without you going in there and doing your techie mumbo jumbo?"

"If I don't do my *techie mumbo jumbo*, you're never going to find out who's been messing with your system." Charlie leaned back in the chair, casually crossing her legs. "It's up to you."

Tina eyed her suspiciously. "What's in it for you?"

"Maybe I want to feel good about helping out family."

"Right." Tina snorted, gesturing to the laptop. "Fine. Have at it. Although I don't see how a bartender's going to be able to fix something MIT graduates haven't been able to solve."

Charlie loved proving people wrong and, less than five minutes later, she was doing just that. She shook her head, disgusted at how easily Sinful Delight's security was breached. "You should tell Anthony a kindergartner can build a better firewall than his people. They suck."

Tina's eyes widened as she came around the desk and

hovered over her shoulder. "I paid thousands of dollars for that security system."

"They took you for a ride around the globe, because it's shite. I'm surprised it ever worked to begin with." Once Charlie was through the wall, she could've done anything she wanted; embedded a virus, hacked into their live camera feeds—and altered them. *Anything.* Curious, she asked, "Do you have information on all your guests in here?"

Tina's face couldn't have gone paler. "Oh my God. Do you think all of our information was hacked?"

"I'll take that as a yes." Another click, and Charlie saw the virus embedded into the code. The alteration was slight, something even a good programmer could've missed easily if they weren't looking for the specific affected area. "Not only has someone shut off your security feed remotely, but they've left behind a back door. They could potentially get all the personal information on your guests—at least, everything they've shared. If they've linked a bank account to their membership for automatic payment they could drain their accounts dry in a single keystroke."

Tina hovered closer, crowding. "Please tell me you can fix it. I can't have everyone's business out there for any greedy lowlife. I'll lose everything."

Of course Charlie could fix it, and as she started mending the system as best as she could, she followed the bad, bad feeling in the pit of her stomach. "How often has your security footage been tapping out?"

"Often enough."

"A number, Tina." Charlie fought to keep the snap out of her voice as she continued to work.

"Three in the last two weeks. Before that, it was at least twice a month since we opened in January."

Two a month, plus the three latest . . . if each security failure meant another missing woman, they didn't have three, but twelve abductions on their hands. And that was if the assholes kept to one girl each time.

Charlie's stomach flipped on its side. Twelve girls. Twelve lives destroyed. Her fingers clacked furiously over the computer. An eternity passed until the security feed popped back up on the monitors.

Black and white images, no better than distorted white fuzz, flickered to life. Six cameras in total and, as Tina said, two were angled at a fire exit, with the remaining four located around the street surrounding the club. Charlie did a quick scan, pausing at the last monitor.

Two oversized men ambled toward the exit, their backs toward the camera—except she counted six legs.

Charlie jumped up from her seat. "Where's that camera located?"

CHAPTER TWENTY

Vince weaved his way through the dance floor, keeping back far enough not to be seen. Both women and men approached Brock as he walked deeper into the club, but with a slight shake of his head, he kept walking until he stopped on the outskirts of the dancing action.

The undercover DHS agent pulled something from his pocket.

Well, well. Looks like someone doesn't abide by the club's no-cell-phone policy.

Brock read something off his screen, typed a reply, and then the man without a mission hustled as if flames licked at his heels.

"Fuckin-A." Vince pushed people aside to keep up before he lost the slick bastard again.

Now less than three feet away, Brock nearly collided with Charlie at the mouth of a corridor. Vince temporarily banked his confusion and joined in on the party.

"What the fuck are you doing here, Sunshine?" Brock masked his own shock at their appearance with a demand: "You need to get out of here. Now."

"That's just what I'll do." Charlie grabbed Vince's hand and tugged him closer to the hall. "We'll be going. Good seeing you."

Brock stepped in their way, nodding toward where a long line of guests stood to check in their unauthorized cells—on the other side of the building. "The exit's that way."

"And there's another one down here. I'm allergic to long lines and I'd rather not stand in it."

Vince watched as they butted heads. He didn't know what the fuck was happening, but he knew Charlie wanted down that corridor for a reason, and he'd make it happen. Taking a menacing step forward, Vince distracted Brock. "You heard my lady. She wants to go out a different way. If you want to stop that from happening, you're going to have to go through me."

Charlie took the hint. Releasing her grip, she skirted past them and sprinted at a dead run. Brock turned to follow. Vince grabbed his arm and spun him around, planting him face-first into the nearby wall, but Torres flung his head back, his skull connecting with Vince's face in a loud crunch.

Vince shrugged off his star-vision.

"You have no idea what you just fucking did, asshole," Brock growled, twisting out of Vince's hold. "Get out of my fucking way. I need to get down that hall."

"Like fucking hell," Vince growled back, plow-driving his fist right into Torres's left flank. The fuckhead cursed and swung back, catching Vince in the midsection.

Evenly matched, they traded blow for blow, pounding on each other in a flail of fists and grunts—until they both heard a shout—*Charlie's* shout. And judging by the string of British curses, she was not a happy camper. Both he and Torres stopped swinging long enough to decipher the sound of fists hitting flesh—this time, not theirs.

Vince abandoned the bastard in front of him and took off down the hall, not caring that Torres was right behind him. All he wanted was to get to Charlie and get there yesterday. He turned a corner as she went flying through the emergency exit and into the alley behind the club.

Vince burst through the doors right behind her and immediately dodged an incoming fist. He tossed his assailant aside like a rag doll. A van hovered nearby, its engine rumbling and the side door hanging open. An unconscious woman lay slumped on the gravel. They needed to get her the hell out of there. He took his first step to do just that when Charlie's curse drew his attention to his right.

Locked in a fight with another goon, she circled her masked assailant, her eyes narrowed in concentration as they tracked the knife in his hand. Vince turned to intercede, but stopped at her bare shake of the head. "I got this. Get the girl back inside the club."

Fuck it all. This had been what she'd meant. *The job.* She'd taken down all of the men at Alpha at one time or another. She could handle a lone punk, and she would. He slashed out with his knife and Charlie spun, narrowly dodging the point as she strategically placed herself at her attacker's back. It was a slick move, clearly giving her an advantage against the bigger—and slower—man.

Vince ignored his visceral reaction to intervene, skirting past Brock and the thug who'd sucker-punched him moments before. The two appeared evenly matched.

Charlie shouted. "Vince! Hurry!"

Vince's gaze whipped toward the young woman now being dragged into the idling van by a third thug. He stepped once, then froze at the sound of a cocked gun.

"Move a fucking muscle and get another hole blown in your head," the owner of the gun threatened. "Seriously, man. Move and make my fucking day."

"Who the fuck are you, Dirty Harry?" Vince quipped, remaining still. Brock's thug somehow managed to free himself up.

"I'm the one with the fucking gun. You hear that, sweetheart?" he called out, flicking a glance to Charlie.

Breathing heavily, she delivered one last punch to her attacker before pulling back.

"Smart girl." The armed thug nodded. He stepped around Vince, keeping his gun directed at his face as he and his friend backed up into the van's side door—*with* the girl. The van's engine revved, and they took off in a squeal of tires.

No plate. No identification.

Charlie sucked in a hiss. Wetness coated the right side of her torso, and when she took her hand away, Vince saw red—literally. Blood coated her palm and dripped down her side.

He was on her in three long strides. "Let me see the damage."

"It's fine. Just a scratch. I dodged when I should've weaved." But no way in fucking hell was he backing down now. She must've read it in his eyes, because she sighed and removed her hand for his inspection. "I told you. It's a scratch."

He lifted the edge of her shirt. It *was* a scratch, albeit a long one. "It doesn't look too deep, but we still need to get that cleaned. Pronto."

"What we *need* to do is find these bastards before they take any more girls!" Her chest heaving, Charlie kicked a half-broken bottle, and it smashed against the brick wall in a spray of glass. "We were right there!"

"Relax before you start bleeding again." Vince stepped close, refusing to let her pull away this time as he tugged her chin up and murmured, "We have a hell of a lot more to go on now than we did before. Keep your head on straight, okay?"

Easier said than done. It hadn't gone without his notice that the man Brock had been one-upping had somehow ended up not only free, but with a gun practically pressed against Vince's head.

Tina, leather-clad and spewing flames, burst through the back door with two security guards on her flank. Her glance darted both ways before pausing on Brock and eventually sliding to Charlie.

"You're bleeding." Tina almost sounded a bit worried before she backtracked. "You better not get any of that inside my club. It's enough of a pain to keep clean, but blood's almost impossible to get out of the leather once it soaks in."

Charlie rolled her eyes. "Thanks for the concern. It's heart-melting."

"What happened? Where's the girl?"

"Gone," Brock finally spoke up.

Everyone looked his direction. He didn't appear concerned or pissed. He seemed...blank.

"You didn't want me following Charlie." Vince turned toward Torres, his anger rising notch after notch as he thought about what could've happened if he hadn't stumbled into Charlie heading to that alley. "Why?"

"This area's closed for guests. You didn't belong."

"We're not the only ones," Vince sneered.

Brock took a step forward, practically putting them nose to nose. "I'm not sure I like what you're insinuating."

"Funny how I don't give a fuck what you like or don't like."

Charlie inserted herself between them and pushed them apart. "Why are you here, Brock?"

Brock slid his gaze her way. "Are we going to do this again? You ask me a question, I throw it back, neither of us getting the answers we want?"

"Then why don't you break the bloody cycle and give me an answer."

"This is a sex club. Why would any red-blooded male be here?" Brock questioned. "What I'm interested in knowing is what you've *really* been doing for the last twelve years, Sunshine. Because when you left Miami, you couldn't have wrestled off a penguin, much less fend off a man with a knife."

"I work in a bar. Self-defense is key." Charlie didn't bat an eye.

"Test that excuse on someone who didn't teach you how to lie convincingly." Brock's lips pressed into a fine line, his body posture rigid.

"You're right. And I trusted you because you were my friend. But that mistake was all mine, wasn't it? Thinking you cared for anyone but yourself."

Tina scoffed. "You're calling someone else conceited? That's rich coming from someone who slunk away like a thief in the night, not bothering to even leave a note."

"You have no idea what you're talking about, Tina." Charlie spun toward her cousin. "None at all."

"Yeah?" Tina stepped forward, locking her cousin in her sight. "I know, to Daddy, you could do no wrong. I was his flesh and blood, but *you're* the one he always saw as indispensable. And you repaid him by sauntering out of town without so much as a good-bye."

Charlie's glare could've frozen lava. "You have no idea why or how I left—which, by the way, was *not* at a saunter. Ask Arturo. And if he tells you anything other than that I had to blackmail my freedom out of him, he's lying." She cocked her head toward Brock. "You could also ask your boyfriend, since he was there for all of it. *Or*, better yet, spend your time worrying about something important, like a young woman getting kidnapped from your club. It's the second abduction I can link to Sinful Delights right now, but I bet if I dig deeper, I'm going to find a hell of a lot more. *How* many times did you say your video system has fritzed out?"

Tina's face paled as she seemed to consider her dilemma. "Disappearances? What are you talking about?"

"Missing girls, Tina. Kidnappings. Abductions. Someone is very possibly using your club to go human-shopping."

Tina went from pale to green. Clutching her stomach, she breathed deep. "Oh, my God. I...I didn't...I didn't know. If I seriously do have some kind of weakness in-house, I can't keep Sinful Delights up and running. And before you get all holier-than-thou, it's not my reputation I'm worried about. Their safety is the last thing my clients should have to worry about when they walk through our doors. What do I do?"

Surprising to everyone, it was Charlie to whom she'd directed the question.

"I'll be back tomorrow morning," Charlie volunteered. "I'm not promising any miracles, and the damage may already be done, but I'll try to patch things up as best I can. As for the security firm Anthony hired for you? Fire them. They're not worth two pennies to rub together."

"But the owner is one of Anthony's friends." Tina worried her bottom lip.

Vince couldn't take the whining anymore. "Do you want

to have more abductions on your doorstep? Or want your guests to be blackmailed for all they're worth? Who do you think they're going to come after if that happens?"

"Fine," Tina gritted through her teeth. "You're right. Thank you, Charlie. For helping."

"Don't thank me yet." Charlie turned back toward the club, hissing through her teeth as she clutched her left side. "Bloody hell, this still hurts."

Vince rested his palm on her back. "We're getting you to a doctor."

"I don't need a doctor," she protested. At his glare, she gave an inch. "I'll let you play doctor. That's about as close as I'm going to get to a medical clinic. Deal?"

"Stubborn-ass woman," Vince muttered.

He led her around the side of the club, grabbing their cells from the front desk before leading the way to the truck. About halfway there, she elbowed him in the side, creating a distance between them he didn't like one damn bit.

"I have a little scratch, Navy. Give a girl some breathing room," she complained.

"The last time I gave you breathing room, you ran straight into an abduction and nearly got yourself gutted."

But it was exactly what he would've done if placed in the same situation Rafe, or Logan, or any of the guys on the team. Charlie waited, almost as if expecting him to whip out his club, so when he kept it tucked away, she gave him a small, approving nod.

"Baby steps," he murmured.

"It's better than standing still—or worse, going backward."

Maybe for her. Vince was pretty sure he was going to have to up his meditation regimen if they were going to be partnered on this assignment much longer.

CHAPTER TWENTY-ONE

Charlie ignored the glowering man following her into the hotel suite and headed straight to her laptop. It had no sooner booted to life than they got a video summons from Stone back at headquarters. Charlie clicked it open and immediately noticed their boss wasn't alone. Agent Dennison, Alpha's DHS contact, sat next to him.

"What the fuck are the two of you doing?" Dennison roared, red-faced and livid. "It's been less than a week, and two more fucking girls have been taken. Where's the intel we need to put Franconi away?"

"We don't have it," Charlie said simply, "and our first job was to find information on the missing girls. We're getting closer."

"Not goddamn close enough."

Suddenly, Vince popped up at Charlie's shoulder. "Did you get a positive I.D. on the girl taken tonight?"

Stone intervened, glancing down at a file. "Logan started

looking the second you called me from the car. Marie Perry had no military background except for the fact that she grew up within five miles of Fort Hood. She used to tend bar at one of the local watering holes before she packed up and moved to Florida about a year ago. Since then, Miami's become her favorite weekend getaway spot."

"There's got to be something else," Charlie ground out, getting more frustrated by the second.

"Yeah, fucking Franconi," Dennison growled.

"Arturo doesn't even own Sinful Delights. It's run entirely by his daughter."

"Then we'll bring *her* the fuck in. Truthfully, I don't fucking care who gets fitted for the handcuffs as long as Franconi is the surname."

"And what? To hell with the missing girls?" Charlie looked like she wanted the power to pull a Freddy Krueger through the damn computer screen. "I didn't risk everything I've built in my life so you could stamp '*case closed*' on a bloody file! I came here to stop these bastards from taking girls and finding the ones who've already been abducted!"

"Let's get one thing clear, Miss Sparks." Dennison leaned closer to the screen. "We contacted you to make something happen. Focus on that, and let the big boys do what we're supposed to do."

Beside her, Vince muttered a curse. He opened his mouth to come to her defense, but stopped at Charlie's subtle headshake. "Stone?"

"Yeah?" Their boss stood still, arms crossed as if he knew what was about to come out of her mouth.

"Is my job in jeopardy if I tell Dennison to go screw a light fixture?" Charlie asked.

Stone covered a laugh behind a not-very-convincing

cough. "Not a fucking chance. Do what you need to do, Charlie—for the girls. And watch your backs."

Dennison turned on Stone, red-faced and fuming. "Now wait one damn min—"

Charlie cut off the secure feed and took a deep breath. "I really can't stand that man."

Vince planted his palms on either side of her face and hauled her in for a hot, hard kiss. And he didn't let either one of them up for air until his chest ached like a bitch.

When he finally released her, Charlie panted, raising her brow in question. "You're getting a little free with your lips there."

"Damn straight I fucking am." He didn't let go of her cheeks. "Screw a light fixture?"

A smirk danced on her lips, and she shrugged. "I would've told him to screw a meat grinder but I thought that was going a hair too far."

Vince swallowed a chuckle and gestured to her abdomen. "We need to get that cut cleaned."

"Just give me one second."

Charlie was already pulling away, bringing up the cross-referencing software she'd been developing over the last year. It wasn't up to full snuff yet. It had a few kinks that needed to be smoothed with an industrial-sized iron, but at this point in the case, she'd risk being led in the wrong direction if it bumped up their chances—even a little bit—of being steered in the right one.

"English..." Vince waited impatiently, squeezing the bridge of his nose as if searching for control.

"Hold on. I need to do one more thing."

"You can't do jack shit if you bleed out."

"The bleeding stopped before we even got to the truck, Mr. Melodrama. You're going to give yourself a raging ulcer by the time you're forty if you keep this up." She started plugging keywords and names into the program, making sure not to leave one thing out. That meant all their known abductees, Sinful Delights, Arturo, even Tina and Brock—anyone and anything that had anything to do with Miami went into that damn search engine.

"English," Vince warned.

"One more minute."

"I gave you ten. Time's up." Cupping her elbow, he firmly steered her away from her computer and toward the couch. "Sit down."

"But the program—"

"Runs without you watching it, right? It'll tell us if it gets any hits." One deep breath from either of them would push their bodies together. He stared, no hint of humor or understanding or patience written anywhere on his face. "Are you planting your sweet ass, or am I going to have to sit on you?"

She glanced over to the couch in question, seeing he'd already cleaned off the coffee table, making room for the assortment of first-aid supplies spread across the surface. "Jesus. Do you think you're performing surgery or something?"

He crossed his arms over his chest and stared her down, his silence speaking a thousand words. He wasn't going to back off.

"Fine," she grumbled. "But your bedside manner sucks. Elle needs to give you lessons on how a nurse treats her patients."

"Good thing I'm not a nurse."

Charlie reluctantly settled on the couch as Vince perched himself on the edge of the coffee table. His hands, steady and sure, gently prodded the reddened area surrounding the three-inch cut.

"Half the gash is underneath your corset. The leather probably made the difference between a few butterfly bandages and being gutted like a fish."

"Hear, hear for leather bustiers," Charlie joked.

"You're going to have to take off your top so I can clean it and see exactly what we're dealing with."

"I think we've proven you don't have to talk me into taking my clothes off around you. It seems to happen naturally."

Vince didn't smile.

"Man . . . tough room."

As Charlie unhooked her top, Vince worked way too hard at prepping cotton ball swabs with Betadine—and not looking in her direction until her top was off and he'd handed her one of his shirts. She murmured a "Thanks" and tugged it on before rolling it up to expose her midriff. "The girls are restrained now, so it's safe to look."

Her comment should've gotten at least a single-lip twitch. But he was all business inspecting the wound. "We'll clean this and butterfly it. I think we can get away without stitches, but we should have Shay call in a script for antibiotics."

For once, Charlie agreed. God only knew where that thug's knife had previously been. "I'll call her when you're done."

Vince gently dragged the first cotton ball over her torso. For a man with hands as large as dinner plates, he was surprisingly gentle. She didn't realize she'd been holding her breath until her head went a little foggy. After a slow inhale, Vince's glaze slid up to hers.

"You okay?" he asked, voice hefty with concern.

"Never better."

A blatant lie, but she wasn't about to admit her head was swirling with a bit more than confusion. About everything. The missing girls. About her uncle. Tina. The club. Brock.

Vince—and their heart-to-heart talk about his SEAL team that had somehow led to an argument. Having his hands on her wasn't helping to clarify any of it.

Vince took his time, like he did with everything else, and Charlie couldn't help but watch as he finished up by taping a gauzy bandage into place.

"Done." His gaze flickered up to hers. Green. His hazel eyes turned more emerald as they studied her face.

"Thanks for the patch-up." As mesmerizing as those eyes were, Charlie looked away and stood, turning back to the computer.

But so did Vince.

One corded arm banded around her back and held her captive against him. "Are we going to talk about what happened back at the club?"

From this close, she couldn't help but look at his mouth, extremely near and well within kissing distance.

"Or what happened here before?" Vince added.

"I already updated you in the car," she said, referring to her explanation that someone had purposefully screwed with Sinful Delights' security system. "Tina may be a lot of things, but a good liar isn't one of them. She was genuinely shocked and more than a little fearful at the idea of her club being used as a hunting ground for traffickers. If she's involved with the abductions, other than being the unfortunate scapegoat, I'll hand my resignation in to Stone now."

"No, you're right. And you're also right in that Arturo doesn't seem like a likely candidate. We need to think about who would have the most to gain by making your uncle seem guilty...and who had the technical know-how."

Charlie sensed he was trying to tell her something without saying it aloud. "Which is what I'm hoping to figure out with the program you pulled me away from."

Using her superior avoidance tactics, Charlie slipped by Vince, ignoring his penetrating stare as she dropped in front of the computer. She hadn't expected any hits yet...but a girl could hope.

"What do you want me to do?" Vince finally asked from across the room.

She shrugged. "Nothing. The program's running, including the BOLO out on the van, but without a plate number, it's going to be practically impossible to track. Everyone from plumbers to flower shops to soccer moms has a commercial van."

Surprisingly, Vince didn't argue. He changed in the bedroom and came out wearing a dangerously loose pair of gym shorts and no shirt. He glanced around at the furniture pushing the coffee table out of the way and opening up the space in the middle of the room.

Charlie eyed him curiously. His muscles shifted and tightened as he stretched his body into different poses. Each would have looked like a fighting stance if he'd blend them together and sped it up a million times faster. Performed in slow, melting glides, it looked like a seductive dance.

Personally, other than the beauty of watching it, she didn't see how tai chi did a damn thing to decrease stress. Punching. Kicking. Knife-throwing. Those were the things that built up a good sweat—and yet it took only a few minutes for Vince's chest to build up a dewy glow.

Had it only been twenty-four hours since she'd had all that muscle above her? And under her? *Inside* her?

Charlie turned her attention to the computer. *Vans, thugs, missing girls*, she chanted to herself. She'd have time to picture Vince naked later and, before she realized it, time had passed and she couldn't turn her head more than twenty degrees without cringing from the sharp pain shooting through her neck.

"Come here," Vince called from his spot in the middle of the room.

"I can't throw my computer across the room if I come over there," Charlie grumbled. An hour of continuous searching, and she had as much info as when she'd started. *Stupid-bloody-program.*

"That's exactly why I told you to get your British ass over here." Vince beckoned her with a crooked finger. "You're not going to do anyone any favors by stressing yourself out."

"How is going over there going to do anything either?" she quipped.

"You can work off a little steam."

"A punching bag would help me work off a little steam, not that slow-dancing business. I can't find the van. I can't find the men. And I can't even find the girl . . . which should be the easiest task of all, considering I can't get her face out of my bloody head."

This time, Vince gave her the full brunt of his attention. His chest, dripping moisture, looked positively lickable. "Being hard on yourself isn't going to make it happen any faster. You need a break. Get over here."

She shook her head. "It's not going to work."

"Humor me, sweetheart."

She glared at him. He glowered back, hands on his trim hips. His stance almost looked comical, and she was ready to fire off a snappy remark when he took a step toward her.

"Okay, fine!" She stood, lifting her hands in surrender. "But I don't know how to do this."

"Mimic me, and you'll pick it up in no time." She stood at his shoulder and waited. "And it would help if you would erase the scowl off your face."

"I just don't get it." Charlie widened her stance to match Vince's.

He pushed his arm out, elbow barely bent, and released a deep breath. She mimicked him.

"Don't get what?"

"You're a former SEAL. A team leader. You're a demo expert, which means you like to blow things up. None of those things requires elegance and poise."

"Tai chi isn't ballet, although it does help with your balance and agility. It's also a great way to regain control and pinpoint your concentration. And babe, yours is all over the place."

"That happens when I can't do my bloody job," she muttered under her breath. A little more loudly, she said, "And playing Karate Kid isn't going to help me do it."

"Ten minutes. If you're not feeling the slightest bit calmer in ten minutes, then I'll let you go back to killing yourself hunched over the bloody computer."

She glared at him for using her own curse word. "Fine. Deal."

At first, she watched the clock, begging it to tick quicker so she could get back to work. But after five minutes, her breathing had eased, as had the weight on her shoulders. Unfortunately, the movements didn't come any more naturally to her. She tried mimicking Vince, but the harder she tried, the worse she got.

"I can't do this," she growled, letting her hands drop.

"Yes, you can." Vince eased her in front of him. His chest pushed against her back, and the heat radiating off his massive body soaked into her skin, making her shiver.

His large hands settled on her hips, and his mouth hovered an inch above her ear. "You're thinking too much instead of letting your body go with the movement."

His palms slid up her arms. The touch shouldn't have been sensual. Wearing his oversized T-shirt, the thing so baggy it slid off her left shoulder, she wasn't dressed to seduce—or be seduced. Yet it was happening. Vince slowly lifted her arms, trailing his fingertips as he guided her into movement.

This defeated the purpose of relaxation techniques because she'd never been more hyperaware of someone's close proximity—or her reaction to it—than at that moment.

"Breathe," he murmured against her ear. He slid their arms to the side. "Inhale through your nose. Exhale through your mouth. When you move your arms out, use your muscles to push them away from your body. You want each movement to glide into the next. In one. Seamless. Motion."

Closing her eyes, Charlie inhaled and tried focusing. It started working until the stress of the night began seeping back into her thoughts. Images from the alley played in her head. The fight. The gun. The innocent girl. The months—hell, years—of vigorous training had taught her how to bring down some of the hardest men that had come out of the military, yet she'd gotten bested by a pair of street thugs.

Vince's hands tracked down the length of her torso. "Empty your mind, English. I can practically hear you thinking aloud. Turn it all off except for the movement of your body."

Words of failure didn't often grace Charlie's vocabulary, but this was one of the few times it did. She dropped her hands to her side, flustered. "I can't help it. I can't. That girl's now going to be subjected to God only knows what, and doing this isn't going to bloody help her."

"We're going to get her back," Vince said, sounding sure. "We're going to get them all back and we're going to nail the bastards responsible."

"But not quickly enough."

Behind her, Vince sighed, but didn't move. "Change of tactic it is."

Before she could ask him what he meant, one wide palm slid beneath her shirt, flattening against her stomach, while his mouth slowly slid up the curve of her exposed neck.

"What are you doing?" Her voice caught on the question, turning into a soft moan.

"If you refuse to turn off your mind, I'm going to give you something else to focus on."

CHAPTER TWENTY-TWO

Outside Sinful Delights, litter danced down the street, blown around by the breeze coming off the ocean. The dockside neighborhood surrounding the club looked different during the day, although no less unsavory. Charlie kept her eyes open, her attention alert as she scanned the block.

Maybe she should've parked a little closer.

Charlie shrugged the thought off. Get to the club, do her thing, and get back to the hotel. It didn't matter that she'd sent her cross-reference program to Logan and the former Marine had promised keep tabs on it. The second any possible link blinked to life, Charlie wanted to be able to act right then and there.

Surprisingly even to herself, her tension started to dissipate. Part of that had to do with Vince's new tactic to redirect her brain waves onto something that didn't involve Miami and abductions. He'd taken matters into his own hands.

And his mouth.

And every inch of his body.

He'd been extremely thorough, making good on his promise to erase everything from her mind except the two of them. A week ago, she wouldn't have thought it possible. A week ago, there'd been no way in hell she'd get involved with any co-worker, much less Vince. And here she was, the morning after an all-night round of mind-numbing sex, and her mind kept drifting, wondering when it was going to happen again.

And when it would end.

She'd been the one who'd originally wanted to give it a hard stop date, but Vince slowly brought her around to his way of thinking—letting it fizzle its way out. With an occasional reminder about keeping their head on the job, it would be fine.

What worried her was that she wasn't so convinced it was going to fizzle out. Vince Franklin was in a league of his own. A rare breed. Possibly the only man on earth with the ability to make her question all her life's goals without forcing her to do so.

He was as alpha as the next man, a difficult, stubborn, bossy pain in the arse. But he got her. He understood her need to be strong, to attack things head-on without flinching. He got that there were things she needed to do on her own.

He understood her—at least, everything she'd been willing to show him. Maybe it was time to share more…to let him deeper into the world of Charlie Sparks.

The thought about sharing what had happened that night twelve years ago scared her to death—which is why she needed to tell him. If she explained her past, she'd finally know if he was a man who could stick around in her future in the way she needed—in a way that let her fight her own battles, without trying to fight them for her.

But for now she needed to focus on Sinful Delights.

A minute after she rapped on the front door, the guard opened up and gestured her inside. "Boss is waiting for you."

Charlie headed toward Tina's office. Her cousin's phone conversation reached her ears before she even got to the door. She looked up as Charlie entered the room and nodded for her to take a seat.

"I'm sorry you feel that way, Anthony, but like I told your friend, I've made my decision, and it's not one I've made lightly. I need to consider what's best for my club, and I believe this is it." Tina paused, listening to her father's security head. "I appreciate the concern. Really, I do, but I have everything under control."

Tina hung up the phone and, with a long sigh, tossed the receiver onto her desk.

"That went well, I take it?" Charlie sat her computer on the second desk. "Anthony didn't like being told you put his friend out of a job?"

"To put it mildly." Tina rolled her eyes. "It took about five seconds from when I notified his friend I'd no longer be needing his services to when my phone lit up. I don't get it. They're a big firm—international. The business of my small-time club isn't enough to put toothbrushes in their employees' Christmas stockings."

Tina came over to the desk while Charlie booted up the laptop. "So you're going to be able to lock everything down, right?"

"If by 'lock everything down,' you mean make it impenetrable for someone on the outside to hack their way back in? Then yes. I am. But you're going to have to do your part by not allowing half-assed security technicians to put their grubby little hands on it. *Ever.*"

"I definitely learned my lesson there," Tina grumbled, looking like she did.

"Good. But you need to realize any damage that's already been done—or information taken—is forever taken. I can't erase the months of access they've already had to your system. And I hate to be the Harbinger of Bad News, but you're going to have to tell your clients there's a possibility their information's been compromised."

Tina winced. "I've already begun talking to my PR person and company lawyer about ways to soften the blow."

"Maybe offer a free rope-tying class," Charlie suggested snarkily, earning a scowl from her cousin. "What? You're saying you wouldn't have any takers?"

"For your information, Miss Smart Aleck, Master Tekei already teaches a *shibari* class for beginners. Don't knock it until you've tried it. If you're interested, I could sign you up for the next session."

Charlie let out a string of laughing snorts. "I'll have to pass on that, but thanks."

Tina sat next to Charlie, casually studying the computer screen as if she were interested. "So after you do your techie stuff, what's preventing whoever hacked into the mainframe from doing it again?"

"First, this time *I'm* the one laying down your secure network. No one's going to get into it who I don't want there."

Tina lifted a sculpted eyebrow. "Awfully cocky, aren't you?"

Charlie shrugged. "It's the truth. And they're definitely going to try to gain access again. They just won't be able to get anywhere, because we'll be prepared." Charlie didn't dwell on the use of the plural term, and neither did Tina. "I'm going to embed a virus that's only activated if someone attempts to hack into your system. And don't worry," she added, seeing Tina's deepening frown, "it's not the kind of virus that's going to affect your computers. Once an unauthorized party tries gaining access to your system, the virus activates and, in layman's terms, becomes a leech. It'll leave me a trail to follow, and we can find out who's responsible."

"For the hacking," Tina clarified.

"And the abductions." Charlie made sure her cousin knew she was serious. "We can't overlook the fact that not only are these hackers bypassing the chance at millions of dollars, but they're attacking on every night there's a physical abduction."

And *that* little bit of information had been confirmed an hour ago when Charlie had cross-checked the list of security downtimes to their missing persons. Whoever was responsible for the hacking would lead them to the human-traffickers. And while Logan checked on Anthony's firm, Charlie was taking the more hands-on approach.

"I don't get it. What does someone get out of stealing young women from my club?" Tina, truly disturbed, bit her lower lip, as she'd done when they'd been kids.

"Other than being evil? Who knows why anyone does what they do. Their mums never hugged them. They never got a present beneath the Christmas tree. I don't really care what their bloody reason is. It's wrong, and I can't wait to bring them the hell down." Charlie's words sounded more like a growl toward the end, and Tina's surprise didn't go unnoticed.

Charlie busied herself in pulling together everything she needed to lay the groundwork for Sinful's new security system. About ten minutes in, Tina fidgeted in her seat.

"I saw the hospital band after you left." Said out of the blue, Tina's softly mumbled words shocked Charlie's fingers still.

She turned. Her heart skipped a beat and stumbled over itself to get back into rhythm—a fast one. "Excuse me?"

Tina shifted in her seat again, wringing her hands in her lap as she avoided eye contact. "The night you left Miami? After you swung by the house and picked up your things, I went back to your room. God only knows why. And I saw the patient band from Miami General in the trash—admitted from the night before."

Charlie didn't know what to say. Her throat dried, and she tried clearing it, wincing. "Where are you going with this, Tina?"

"Truthfully, I don't know. I guess I was so determined to think the worst about you, about how easily you could up and leave...but then I saw the story about the rescue in the newspaper, about the six teenage girls they'd found in freight holds, hours away from being shipped to God only knows where. They never released the names because most of them were minors, but..."

Charlie finally looked her cousin in the eye. They'd never been close. Charlie had always been envious that her cousin still had someone to call family, and Tina had never liked Charlie for invading her home territory. But there was something in her cousin's eye she couldn't remember seeing before...

Sorrow.

"I'm sure there are more reasons why you left, but I wanted to say that even though I don't know *why* you're here, I know why you are." Tina paused, scrunching her nose. "Does that make sense? I mean, I know you're not a bartender...and I think I know why you came back to Miami."

"Tina," Charlie warned.

"Oh, don't worry." Tina waved her hand. "I'm not saying anything, especially to Daddy. I figured you should hear from someone that you're doing a good thing. Those missing girls would thank you if they could."

Charlie was taken by surprise at the compliment, even having to fight through an unexpected rush of emotion. "Thanks, Ti. That means a lot, but I'm not doing this to get a thank you."

"I know. That means you should get one, all the same." Tina looked as uncomfortable as Charlie felt. Clearing her throat and nodding toward the computer, she nudged them away from a scarily family-feeling moment. "So why do you think they picked my club?"

"Piss anyone off lately?" Charlie half-teased. Her fingers, knowing exactly what to do, flew over her keyboard. She could do this kind of work with her eyes closed. "If I'm honest with you, are you going to be angry?"

"Probably, but if it's something I need to know, tell me."

"I think they hoped to link the disappearances to Arturo."

Tina did a double take. "Daddy? But Sinful Delights is all mine."

"But was it from the start-up? It used to be Illusions."

Tina seemed to contemplate her words as she fidgeted in her seat. "He sold it to me."

"Was that publicized among his business associates?"

Tina's discomfort escalated. "No. I'm not exactly proud of this, but my marketing team suggested keeping Daddy's name linked to the club for promotional purposes. It's all mine, but to anyone looking from the outside, it looks like—"

"Like he's an investor," Charlie finished. "Or at the very least, a silent partner."

Tina's pallor turned a bit green. "If you hadn't come, there's no telling how long it would've taken me to realize what's been happening, or if I ever would've realized it at all."

Charlie understood her horror. "Well, we did, and now we can do something about it."

In order to patch the network, Charlie needed to rip it down and build it back up with the new firewall in place. After an hour of silence, Tina's continued pacing started giving her a complex.

"Don't let me stop you from doing sex club things," Charlie said. "I'll find you when I'm done."

"Sex club things? What is it that you think I do during the course of a day?"

"Honestly, I *really* don't want to know."

Tina rolled her eyes. "Fine. I'll be back in a little bit."

Her cousin stood, throwing a reluctant look over her shoulder before disappearing into the club.

Finally. Peace.

Charlie cracked her neck and kept going, finally seeing the light at the end of the tunnel. Somewhere after testing the new system for the second time, Charlie's cell lit up with a voice mail. Double-tasking, she finished cleaning up her code and entered in the Alpha message password.

"All right, Franklin. I'm about to be the bearer of fucking shitty tidings," Logan's voice drawled. "First, about our girl . . . you were right to think there's a hell of a lot more to her exit from Miami than she's made known. And after digging, I can get why. She was a victim, man."

Charlie couldn't move—her fingers. Her chest. Her heart. Everything came to an abrupt stop.

"It was bad, Vince. Really. Fucking. Bad. No wonder there was no talking her out of going down to Miami." Logan blew out a heavy sigh. "And for shitty info, part two . . . I've been keeping watch on that program of Charlie's. We got a link to the latest four disappearances— which includes the one from the other night. *Brock Torres.*

I emailed you both everything I found in case you want some non-light reading. Each of the girls was somehow related to someone Torres had a run-in with during his time in the Army. We're talking a commanding officer who'd reported him for insubordination. The judge who dishonorably discharged him. The lawyer who repped him. And the other night's abduction, Marie Perry, was the niece of a former lieutenant who'd testified against him. I don't know about you, but coincidences give me the hives. Watch your ass—and Charlie's."

Charlie listened to dead air after Logan's message ended. It took a moment to digest everything she'd heard, interpret its meaning, and realize she'd somehow managed to pick up Vince's phone instead of her own.

Instead of taking her at her word, Vince had Logan look into her past.

Not look, but *dig*—and deep—and she knew it, because she'd been the one who'd buried it all. He'd made a big deal about trust among partners, but he didn't trust her to know her own head. And he'd gone one step further and broken *her* trust in *him*.

Charlie finished with the new security setup and by the time she was packing up her things, she'd developed a good steam.

Vince's cell rang in her hand. *Logan.* She answered, "Sorry, cowboy, but Navy hasn't gotten your message yet. I'll be sure to tell him it's information not to be missed."

Logan muttered a soft curse. "Charlie. Wait. Fuck. It's not what you think."

"No? Because it sounds like my teammate went behind my back with concerns he couldn't be bothered sharing with me. And not only did he reach out for accomplices, but he gave them instructions to keep quiet about it. Stop me if the truth veers off the path at any point." She waited a second. "No? Yeah, I didn't bloody think so."

She pressed End, and nearly plowed into Tina on her way down the hall.

"Is it done?" Tina asked.

Tears welled, but Charlie held them at bay. Barely. She couldn't remember the last time she'd cried, and she wasn't about to break her streak now, regardless of how much her chest bloody ached.

"It's done." Charlie pushed back a fresh wave of incoming emotions. "Your system shouldn't crash again."

Tina reached out to touch her arm, but pulled back at the last second. "Are you okay?"

"I will be," Charlie lied, stalking toward the exit. "Just remember what I said. Don't let anyone near your security system again."

This time, fresh air did squat to make breathing easier, and each step she took, the weight increased. She'd been delusional to think the guys would see her as anything but the techie behind their brawn, much less their equal. And even though it stung, she could've handled it from Logan or Rafe, or even Stone.

But *Vince*?

Being mauled by a circus animal would've hurt less than thinking he didn't have faith in her abilities. Thinking about his lack of trust, breathing became an issue, and those damn tears welled up again.

At some point in time, what Vince thought, what he believed, had begun to matter to her...and it mattered because she *cared*. About him. About *them*.

He didn't trust her to know her own mind?

Fine.

Then she was going to prove to him that she did.

CHAPTER TWENTY-THREE

Vince sat behind the wheel of a beat-up Chevy rental and continued to stare across the street at the busy coffee shop.

He'd called.

He'd dug out Dawn's number and dialed, praying to God Charlie knew what she meant when she said talking to Dawn could bring closure. And as much as he hoped that would be the case, he wasn't doing it for himself so much as for Charlie.

If he wouldn't face his nightmare head-on, how could he expect her to? He'd never thought himself a hypocrite and didn't want to start now. But there was the bigger reason—the one leading to a future he thought he'd never have... *could* never have. Straightening his shit out meant what he'd thought unattainable could be in the realm of possibility.

Like Charlie.

Like *being* with Charlie and figuring out where they stood with one another. Yeah, she pushed his buttons and kept him on his fucking toes. But she also showed him multiple times over that sometimes being a little out of control wasn't such a bad thing.

But his newfound way of thinking didn't mean jack if he didn't straighten his ass and his head out, and it wasn't going to happen by cowering in the fucking car like a toddler.

Vince jogged across the street and held the door open for an elderly couple before entering Brewed Awakenings himself. Unlike last time he'd been here, there was room to breathe. Business professionals. Gym rats. College students. The place drew a wide range of clientele.

He ordered a plain black coffee before finding an unobtrusive table tucked in the corner and moving the chair so that his back faced the wall, a habit ingrained in him since boot camp.

"Rico used to do that too." Dawn sat across from him, taking him by surprise, and graced him with a small smile. "When we first started dating, it embarrassed me, especially when he rearranged furniture in places where the chairs weren't meant to have much free range of motion. It drove me crazy."

"He drove a lot of people crazy," Vince joked, wiping his suddenly damp hands on his pants. "That was part of his charm."

Dawn's smile grew before a more somber look melted it away. "I have to admit, I didn't think you'd call."

"And I have to admit, I wasn't going to."

She offered him a knowing nod. "What changed your mind, if you don't mind my asking?"

"Something a friend said—that keeping myself chained to regrets wasn't going to get me where I want to be in life…or allow me to be *who* I want to be."

"She sounds like a smart woman. I hope you plan on holding on to her really damn tight."

Vince lifted an eyebrow. The tightening in his chest eased at her little chuckle. "How do you know that friend's a woman?"

Dawn grinned. "Because only someone you love can make you do something you don't really want to do. Well, that, and the day we ran into each other on the pier, I saw the pretty blonde you were with. She's gorgeous. And she looked like she made you happy."

Vince didn't bother setting her straight, or telling her about his and Charlie's cover. Charlie *did* make him happy. And pissed him off. And put him at ease. And drove him bat-shit crazy. He was still figuring it the hell out.

Baby steps.

Vince clutched his coffee cup a little tighter than neces-sary, not realizing it until a splash of hot liquid ran over his hand. He forced himself to lighten his grip. "Dawn, I know this isn't going to erase what happened to Rico but..."

Fuck, this was hard.

"I'm sorry." Vince pushed through the lump forming in his throat. "I promised to bring him back to you and I didn't. As a matter of fact, you were right at the funeral when you blamed me for his death. I'm the one that got him killed. You *should* hate my fucking guts."

Dawn watched him a beat longer and, when he'd prepped himself for a good grovel, she reached out and squeezed his arm. Instead of judgment in her eyes, there was concern.

"I don't hate you, Vince." Sincerity drenched her words. "And I'm sorry if I ever made you feel as though I blamed you for what happened, because I don't. I was in a bad place during Ricky's memorial service. I'd lost my best friend and husband. I was pregnant and alone, recently fired from my job for having been out for so long on bed rest. My father had just been diagnosed with colon cancer, and my mother was a wreck. It felt like entire world was against me."

"And I added to it."

She shook her head. "No. Vince, I was an emotional, hormonal mess. If anyone should be apologizing, it's me, for how I behaved."

He heard her words, but they didn't make sense. He shook his head repeatedly. "No."

"Yes." She gripped his arm tighter, regaining his attention. "Rico and I knew what his kind of life could mean for our future. I wasn't delusional. Every time he walked out the door, there was a chance he wouldn't be walking back through it. Did he ever tell you he'd wanted to put in for retirement?"

That took him by surprise, and he finally met her gaze. "He didn't say a damn thing about that."

"That's because I couldn't let him do it. I saw what making that decision did to him. If he wasn't working alongside you and the others on Team Five, he wouldn't have felt whole. I couldn't expect him to live that way. We decided— *together*—that he'd stay."

This was all news to Vince. And he wasn't sure how he felt about it.

Dawn graced him with a small, sad smile and sat back in her chair. "I don't blame you, Vincent. Of course I wish he was still here. I miss him every day, but I have a little piece of him with me forever. Richelle is so much like him that sometimes I stare into her eyes, and I swear I see him looking back at me."

She glanced at the shiny ring on her left hand, something he'd neglected to see on the pier. "I found someone who adores both Richelle and me. He's good to us. He loves Richelle as if she were his own. We're happy."

Vince worked his throat. "I told Rico I'd take care of the two of you, and I've done a piss-poor job of it, so I'm glad someone else stepped up."

She studied him carefully, so long that even Vince shifted awkwardly in his seat. Christ, the woman could have a lucrative career in interrogation and not even say a damn word.

Suddenly, her mouth went lax. "It's you, isn't it?"

"What is?"

"You're the source of the mystery account. You have no idea how long I argued with the bank when the statements first came rolling in—that it must be a mistake. That even though my dream was to find extra money lying around, it didn't happen in real life."

He couldn't deny it, but he also couldn't take credit for it. "Like I said, I needed to make sure you and the baby were taken care of."

Dawn's smile turned watery. "I'm not going to tell you that you shouldn't have done it—even though you shouldn't have. But it *did* help us, especially in the beginning while we navigated our way through Rico's benefits. But we don't need your help anymore, Vince."

She slid her hand over his fingers and squeezed. "Richelle and I are good now. What I need is for you to find your good place too . . . and something tells me you're going to find it in that pretty blonde."

Fuck. Was she right?

Vince didn't need to think about it long, because the answer flooded him like a tsunami.

Yes.

Charlie *was* his good place. She put him *in* a good place. It was why the harder he tried to stay away, the more he kept going back, whether it involved bickering, training, or hell, sex. She'd challenged him, but in a good way . . . in a way that kicked his fucking ass into gear and calmed him, both physically and mentally.

Vince blew out a slow breath, feeling like a moron for having overlooked what was right in front of him the entire time. "It's looking like that may be the case."

"Then why are you still sitting here with me?" Dawn's coy smile made him chuckle.

Vince's cell rang, and he picked it up without checking the caller I.D. "Franklin."

"Shit, man." Logan sighed heavily on the other end. "I hope you own stock in Chap Stick because you're about to be doing a lot of fucking ass-kissing."

"And who's ass am I supposed to be kissing?" Vince smirked.

"Charlie has your freaking phone, smart-ass. And you have hers."

Logan's meaning took a minute to sink in. Vince's back went ramrod straight. "What did you leave?"

"Oh, you know . . . not much. Just that her program linked Torres to the last four missing girls in some way, shape, or form—and that twelve years ago, Charlie barely escaped an abduction situation herself, which is why she's been so goddamned adamant about taking the fucking case." By the end of his rant, Logan was practically yelling.

Vince slammed his hand against the table and hissed under his breath, "Fuckin'-A, Callahan! Why would you leave that kind of information on my voice mail?"

"Do not shoot the fucking messenger, man. Look what the hell you're grabbing before you leave the room . . . or better yet, talk to your fucking partner!"

Fucking-A, he was right. "Tell Stone we may need the team here sooner rather than later. Something tells me this isn't going to end up dressed with a pretty fucking bow."

"He's already ahead of you. We're about to board the jet now...should be wheels down in Miami in a few hours. In the meantime, try and use the fire extinguisher on our girl."

Vince hung up the phone. Fuck. He'd have to find her first.

"That didn't sound good." Dawn's brow furrowed in concern.

"It's not. I'm pretty sure I fucked up my happy place."

"Then you better haul ass and fix it." She stood and she shooed him with her hands. "Go on. Get out of here. If you mess up your happy place because you're standing here with me, then I'm going to be the one who feels guilty. Besides, I'm going to want to meet the woman capable of keeping you in line."

"She may kick my ass to the curb before you get the chance."

Dawn rolled her eyes. "I have a feeling she can be persuaded to your way of thinking."

With a rushed good-bye, Vince hightailed it back to their second rental and started dialing his phone before he even turned on the ignition. When Charlie didn't pick up, he called the club. Six redials later, Tina finally picked up.

"Where's Charlie?" he asked without preamble.

"Oh, you mean Miss Personality? She finished her techie thing and booked it out of here like her panties were on fire—and not in a good way. And speaking of fire...it may have been a while since my cousin and I have spent quality time together, but I have a good enough memory to recall what it's like when she's about to go on a rampage. My guess is that you—somehow—screwed up. Am I right?"

"Did she say where she was going?" Vince ignored the banter.

"No, but I heard her mumbling something about being lied to by everyone."

"If you hear from her, tell her not to do anything stupid. And if you hear from Brock Torres, don't say *anything*, and call me. Immediately."

"Why would I—" Tina's head must've been spinning. "You can't possibly believe Brock is behind what's been happening at the club."

"He has *access* to the club. He's been *at* the club. And he has a link to the last four missing girls."

"No. You don't understand he wouldn't—"

"I mean it, Tina. Be careful." Vince hung up and dialed one more number as he navigated the busy Miami streets and headed downtown.

"Calling to apologize?" Logan's voice teased. "I'm fond of bluebonnets. They remind me of home."

"Ping my phone and tell me my gut's wrong."

Logan must've been prepped because, a few seconds later, he uttered the location Vince dreaded hearing.

"Goddamn it, English, what the fuck do you think you're doing?" he grumbled softly before addressing his teammate. "When you get here, use our phones to follow our trails. I have a feeling my hands are going to be too full to answer any calls."

"And what the fuck are you going to be doing?"

What he should've done from the very fucking beginning. "Backing up my partner. And Logan?"

"Yeah?"

"Hustle the fuck up."

Vince blew the upcoming red light and cut off a cabbie in the middle of the next. A few dozen blocks had never seemed so far away.

CHAPTER TWENTY-FOUR

Charlie parked outside of Inked Up and glanced around the block. Nothing looked out of the norm for the industrial area of town. What few cars were parked along the streets were either abandoned or belonged to city workers who'd shuttled into their work sites.

After grabbing Gregor from the glove box, Charlie checked her ammunition clip and stuffed the gun into the back of her pants. Bells jingled when she stormed into the tattoo shop, but unlike the last time she'd been there, no one blocked her route toward the back. The shop stood suspiciously empty until Eric came around the corner, eyes widening in surprise.

"Charlie! Not that I don't like seeing you, but what are you doing here?" His attention shifted toward the hall and back.

"Where's Brock?" She kept walking in the direction of his private office.

Eric hustled after her. "I think he's in the middle of something. Maybe you could try back later...or better yet, I'll tell him you stopped by." When she didn't slow, he skidded into her path. Points to him for looking a little wary, if not scared. "I'm sorry, Char, but I can't let you go back there right now."

Charlie kept her voice even. "And I'm sorry, Eric, but if you don't move aside, I'm going to have to move you myself."

Eric nibbled on his bottom lip, looking nervous. "Charlie, please."

"Sorry, love. But I'm not going to ask again."

With a hefty sigh, he stepped aside. Brock's office door hung wide open, and when she walked through, he was on the phone. He glanced up casually, almost as if he expected her visit.

"Yeah, she's here," he said to the person on the other line. "I'll call you back."

"Why?" Charlie demanded angrily. "Why the bloody hell would you do something like this? Help me understand because I'm drawing a blank."

"Why don't you explain to me what it is I've done." Brock leaned back in his seat, eerily calm as he folded his arms across his chest.

"Do not play games with me!" Charlie smacked her hands on the desk. "After everything we've been through together, are you really going to sit here and lie to me?"

He remained frustratingly quiet.

"What the hell happened to you, Brock? Huh? You went from hating everything Arturo and your father stood for to jumping on their payroll? And what about Homeland? You're seriously choosing to be one of the bastards you've sworn an oath to put in jail?"

Brock looked momentarily surprised by her knowledge,

but he reined it in quickly. "According to you, I've gone off the deep end already. Kidnapping, right? I've been luring women from my past to Sinful Delights and then nabbing them?"

Charlie's blood went cold. "Who was on the phone, Brock?"

"Does it matter? You've stormed in here, acting the part of judge and executioner." Despite the fact that Charlie had once seen the man in front of her as a brother, she prepped herself to be ready to move at a moment's notice. Brock stood, no longer laid-back and easygoing. "I'm not going to waste my time or yours in trying to convince you of my innocence. But it hurts, Sunshine...you believing I've stooped so low as to trap and sell innocent women."

"Why not? I foolishly believed you befriended me without any ulterior motive...*Agent Torres*." Charlie lifted her chin, refusing to back down. "I'd told myself I'd hallucinated you being on the dock that night because I'd wanted *so badly* to be rescued. But I didn't imagine it. You were there. You lied about who you were twelve years ago, and you're lying again. Admit it."

"You're right. I *am* lying. Because I hate my father and Arturo more than I did even back then."

"So you wanted to kill two birds with one stone? Is that it? Get back at everyone who ever did you wrong while simultaneously bringing down my uncle?" Charlie asked the question, but it lacked venom. Something in Brock's eyes didn't scream *evil human-trafficking mastermind*.

"Revenge isn't my style, Charlie. I'm a firm believer karma's going to come for people when their time's due. I don't need to do anything to help it along." Brock looked almost...weary. "And as for frequenting Sinful Delights—you're right. I do go there pretty frequently, but I'm sure as hell not scoping victims. Hell, I've been trying to end all the damn trafficking since that night I found you in that fucking crate—which by the way, I'm convinced wasn't a random occurrence."

Charlie's breath hitched. *Focus*. Head on straight—*and on the immediate problem*.

"But you guessed that already, didn't you?" Brock came around the side of his desk and leaned his ass against the edge. "Otherwise, it wouldn't have been so easy to convince you to leave Miami. Something told you that you'd pushed things too far and that if you didn't make tracks, it was a matter of time before something happened, and no one would be around to save you."

Something knotted in Charlie's stomach, bringing a wave of nausea. "I don't know what you're talking about. I wasn't the only one taken. They found five other girls."

"Runaways. Street kids. Kids who already had one foot over the border. You never fit the profile, Charlie. They were targeted because of who they *weren't*. You were targeted because of who you *were*."

"Arturo's niece."

Brock shook his head, his eyes almost returning to the warm brown of the man she used to call friend. "If they wanted to shake up Arturo, they would've nabbed Tina. They took you for a reason and, even though I can't prove it, I think it has something to do with your conspiracy theory involving your mother's death."

Charlie's blood turned to ice. "What does my mother's accident have to do with my abduction?"

"I think you got too close to finding out the truth, Sunshine," Brock stated gently. "And I think whoever was responsible for tampering with the car panicked, and tried to get rid of you to save their own ass."

* * *

Vince pointed the hunk-of-junk rental car in the direction of Inked Up, wishing like hell for the power of his truck's V-8 engine. Every second that ticked by solidified the cement brick resting in his fucking stomach.

No amount of meditation would lessen the jumble of nerves making his foot press harder on the gas pedal.

"Goddamn it," Vince growled, practically pushing the damn thing to the floorboard and getting only a faint hum for his efforts. "Hunk of fucking junk."

Vince's phone rang. He picked it up immediately. "Franklin."

"Where are you?" Logan sounded more than a little tense.

"I'm a few blocks out from Torres's tattoo shop. Why?"

"It's not Torres."

Vince held his phone so tight it creaked. "What the fuck are you talking about? You said there was a goddamned link."

"Let me rephrase that for you, it's not *Brock* Torres."

It took Vince a second to register. "Anthony. Arturo's head of security."

"Looks like he's had his eye on more than Arturo's safety for the last few years. Ever since Arturo's health began failing, the man's slowly been naming himself Franconi's successor. One guess who wasn't behind Arturo turning all his holdings on the straight and narrow?"

"How do you know this for sure?"

"Charlie had me digging into the firm currently running the club's security specs. The owner has a rap sheet a mile long that even a few name changes couldn't hide. Trey went to New Jersey and rattled the guy up a little bit. Turns out Anthony Torres paid him—and not any measly little sum—to not only tamper with the club's security system, but make it look like the goal was guest information when in reality—"

"He wanted access to the cameras. The sick fuck wanted to turn them off at will and make it easier to slip girls out of the fucking club."

Logan agreed. "Bingo. Guess he figures with Franconi's foot already half in the grave, it's a matter of time before there's a shift of power, and he wants in on it, starting with setting up his own little flesh market."

Vince could see it. Hell, it happened often enough everywhere else in the world, seconds and assistants wanting a bigger piece of the action. "But why make Brock look guilty? He's his fucking son."

"Because Brock's been digging into the very case our British Bombshell was investigating prior to her abduction twelve years ago—the *accident* that killed Mia Hughes and Leslie Franconi. If Anthony Torres wasn't involved in both of them up to his fucking eyeballs, I'll hang up my goddamned Stetson for good."

Fucking hell. Vince's grip slipped on the wheel, and the car skidded slightly into the other lane before he managed to pull it back. He took a deep breath, and then a second. *Fuck it.* It didn't goddamn work.

Charlie's adamancy about taking this assignment and seeing it through to the end, her safety be damned, suddenly made sense.

Vince gripped the steering wheel until it creaked. "Are you telling me Anthony Torres abducted Charlie when she was sixteen years old?"

"Fuck," Vince heard Logan curse. "I'm sorry, man. I forgot you never got my original message. Yeah. That's exactly what I'm saying. I don't know if Torres was behind the wave of abductions back then, but Charlie's definitely had his fingerprints all over it. She and five other girls were only hours away from being shipped across the fucking ocean when Brock Torres and his DHS unit got an anonymous tip on their whereabouts. And fuck, man. The detailed reports weren't pretty. I couldn't even...it was *bad*, Vince."

Vince's jaw was clenched so hard it ached. "Did you tell English any of this?"

"She's not picking up. Short of sending a fucking pigeon, I don't know how to get her the information. How close are you to Inked Up?"

Vince plowed his foot harder onto the gas. "Five minutes."

* * *

Charlie didn't know what to believe or whom to trust. So much of what Brock said made sense...and yet didn't. Why abduct her? If whoever was responsible for the car accident was seriously worried about being identified, why didn't they make sure to get rid of her instead of taking chances she'd be found? Brock's explanations raised more questions.

She had to ask what had been bothering her since finding out about Brock back in headquarters. "You've been with DHS since you were discharged from the Army, right?"

Brock didn't bother denying it. "Not immediately after, but close enough, yeah."

"So why didn't you get buddy-buddy with Arturo and your father right from the start? Wouldn't that have made your assignment easier?"

"Easier?" Brock's humorless laugh ended in a snort. "Fuck, yeah. Realistic? No. Anyone who knew either me or my father knew I couldn't stand him; that I hated everything he and Franconi stood for. Making a complete one-eighty would only put me into question in their eyes. I needed a realistic shift."

"But what happened after I left to shift—" It finally dawned on her. "My abduction."

Brock gave her faint nod, and points to him for looking a tad uncomfortable. "Revenge is something both my father and Arturo can understand. They knew I saw you as a little sister. So I used it. I wanted the men responsible for putting you in that cage—which was the truth. But it also gave me the motive I needed to start working with them."

"You need to listen to him, Charlie." Tina's voice turned both Brock and Charlie toward the office doorway.

"What are you doing here?" Brock stood at attention and snapped, "You need to go."

"No," Tina refused, keeping Charlie in her sights. "Vince told me what you suspect about Brock, but it isn't true. *I'm* the reason he shows up at the club."

"Tina," Brock warned.

"No! Enough is enough, okay? I'm done hiding everything." Tina, tears falling down her cheeks, didn't seem to care that she was starting to resemble a raccoon. "It's a long story, but to make it shorter, after you left, things just weren't right. There were more secrets than usual and I suspected something big had either happened or was about to happen. And I wanted to help."

Charlie fought to understand. "And what exactly does that mean?"

"It means that I contacted the feds, and I became an informant. *Brock's* informant. At least, that's how it started." Tina's chuckle held no humor as her gaze flickered between them. "I wasn't as dumb as my father would like to believe. I agreed to help Brock get on the inside as best as I could without drawing attention to either one of us. But one thing led to another and…"

Holy crap.

"You're together," Charlie heard herself say.

Tina nodded. "And we shouldn't be for an arm's length of reasons. Not only is he my handler, but I'm the daughter of one of the most notorious crime bosses east of the Mississippi. No way would his supervisors like him getting into bed with the enemy. Literally."

Charlie turned toward Brock. "Is that why you fell off the DHS radar?"

Brock's silence spoke volumes, and what remained unsaid was clarified as his gaze fell to Tina.

Love.

His dark eyes oozed his feelings, despite the fact that he kept a physical distance. "I like my job, like making the world a safer place. But no way in hell am I going to let a job get in the way of being with the person I love. I knew if they found out, they'd pull me out of the field and make me cut all ties. No way in hell was I letting that happen."

"But what about the girls?" Charlie asked, still confused. "At least four of them are linked to your past, Brock. *Four.* You have both motive and means." Charlie fought to keep her own emotions at bay. "I want to believe—"

"Then *believe* it," Tina interjected, sniffing. "You said these women were being abducted when our security system goes offline, right? During each of those times, Brock's been with me."

Brock's lies of omission had hurt. There wasn't a doubt about it. He'd pulled the wool over not only her eyes, but her uncle's…over Anthony's. Anyone who could lie so convincingly had to be looked at a little closer. Not doing so would make her negligent—and not to mention, stupid.

"But the links." Charlie shook her head, struggling between her head and her heart.

"Screw the links!" Tina shouted. "You of all people should know links can be planted for the sole purpose of throwing people off the real track. Didn't you do that for my father once or twice? You've known Brock almost your entire life. If he did something so freaking heinous as abducting those girls, do you think he'd be stupid enough to pick young women who could be traced back to him? We should be thinking about who would gain something out of setting up not only Brock, but my dad."

Charlie, ready to agree, noticed the hulking figure outside the hall a second before the shadow stepped in behind Tina.

"And who would've ever thought Tina here would be the voice of reason." Anthony, with a gun pressed against the back of Tina's head, surprised them all. His gaze snapped to where Brock's hand reached toward a desk drawer. "Move another inch and your bitch here eats a bullet, son."

Brock's nostrils flared as he glared at his father. "What the hell do you think you're doing?"

"Something I should've done a long time ago. What the hell is it with kids today not minding their own fucking business?" Anthony growled in return.

Charlie used Anthony's temporary distraction and whipped Gregor out from behind the band of her pants. Aiming the barrel of her gun at her uncle's longtime friend, she demanded, "Let her go, Anthony. You're not helping your cause by doing this now."

"Sure I am. In true Franconi fashion, I'm helping *me*."

Tina's eyes, wide as saucers, latched onto Charlie. "What are you waiting for? Shoot him!"

"She's not going to shoot," Anthony dug the barrel of the gun deeper into her temple. "She's not going to shoot, because she knows the second she does, my finger can squeeze this trigger and you'd be a goner too."

"Why are you doing this?" Tina cried. "You're Daddy's friend!"

"No, I've been his lapdog," Anthony spat. "And just when I'm about to get my payout for doing his dirty work for the last forty years, he's going to go legit? I don't fucking think so. I'm getting what I'm due, even if I have to take it for myself."

"And you don't care who you hurt in the process?" Charlie took a small side step to the right to better her aim.

"Charlie," Brock warned her.

"You have a problem with Arturo," Charlie continued. "I get it. But framing your own son for the abductions? What the hell's that about? Using innocent women? And what are you going to do now, Anthony? Get rid of all three of us?"

Anthony shrugged, not the least bit concerned. "Why not? I almost got rid of you twelve years ago when you wouldn't stop your goddamned poking in my business. If it wasn't for my traitorous son, you wouldn't be a problem now."

Charlie's breath stumbled in her chest, but Brock's head whipped toward his father. "You fucking bastard. It was you?"

"I've done a lot of shit, son, so you're going to have to be a little clearer." Anthony shook his head, laughing. "But I have to say, the one I'm proudest of the most—is taking Arturo's empire right out from under him without the bastard even knowing. I never thought in a million years that losing Leslie would make him so...careless. If I had, I would've orchestrated it a hell of a lot sooner."

"You...you caused the accident that killed my mother?" Charlie barely choked out. *He'd* been responsible for her mother's and aunt's deaths. Not Arturo. Not even one of his enemies…his best friend.

"Aw, sorry, sweetheart," Anthony apologized without a single ounce of remorse. "It wasn't personal. You know how they say all is fair in love and war? That goes for business and war, too. Word was circulating that Arturo was starting to get soft, and do you know what happens when that kind of shit starts getting out? Takeovers. Raids. People push the boundaries to see how much they can get away with. What better way to fire up Arturo's bloodlust than good old-fashioned revenge? It was a sorry happenstance that your mother was in the damn car. It was only supposed to be Leslie."

Charlie glanced over to a grief-stricken Tina. Tears poured down her cousin's face, nearly inconsolable sobs racking her body. Charlie had been so self-absorbed in her own misery that she hadn't seen her cousin's.

Charlie took another small shift to the side and fought the churn of her stomach. "You're bloody delusional if you think I'm going to let you get away with this—any of it."

Shift.

From three feet away, Brock eyed her movements. His body straightened, ready to pounce the second he had an opportunity that didn't risk Tina's life.

Anthony sent them both an evil smirk. "If either of you so much as has an eye tic, Tina won't get a chance to go to auction because her blood will be all over this fucking office."

"*Your* blood's going to be what's spilled if you don't let the girl go." Vince's voice sounded like music to Charlie's ears.

Anthony's attention flickered down the hall. The older man glanced left, then right, which meant Vince had blocked at least one of his exits. And judging by his body language, one more gun had been added to the mix.

Anthony stepped back, and Charlie took one step forward. The move caught his eye and he chuckled. "Do you even know how to use that thing, sweetheart?"

"Let Tina go, and you'll find out," Charlie cooed sweetly. "You've lost the advantage of surprise, Anthony. You can't think you're going to get away with all of this."

"I just need to get away with enough." Anthony kept his back toward the rear exit, and with every step that brought him closer to freedom, their chances of getting Tina started slipping away. "Maybe one of these days, Letty, you'll learn to keep your nose out of other people's business."

Anthony pushed through the back door, Tina's screams cut off as it slammed shut. Charlie, Vince, and Brock followed at a run, bursting outside a split second before a nondescript box truck squealed away from the curb.

"Goddamn it all to fucking hell!" Brock punched a nearby Dumpster, the metallic ring echoing in the alley.

Heart pounding, Charlie stared in the direction of Tina's disappearance, and forced her grip on Gregor to lessen.

Vince's hand landed on her shoulder, and his wall of heat moved close. "We'll get her back, English."

Charlie stood still, bombarded with two completely different needs: to fling herself into his arms, and punch him until he cried uncle. Unfortunately, neither one would get Tina back safely.

Everything that had happened in the last twenty-four hours had left her too open and raw—and now *this*. Charlie shrugged off his touch and turned to him with a hard glare.

"We'll get her back?" she questioned. "Before or after he sells her to the highest bidder? And for no other reason than having bloody sucky timing."

Pacing wildly, Brock looked the part of a man poised to do something stupid.

"Brock, I—"

He held up a hand, cutting Charlie off. "It's best not to speak, Sunshine. I love you, but I could throttle you with my bare hands right about now."

"Try it and see what happens," Vince threatened darkly.

"Fuck you and the horse you rode in on, Franklin."

The two of them stepped closer to one another, making Charlie shout, "Shut the bloody hell up already!"

Both men stopped inches shy from contact and stared at her. Chest heaving and fighting off a fresh set of freaking tears, Charlie glanced from man to man, making sure they each heard her clearly. "Blaming and finger-pointing isn't going to help us find Tina or any of the other girls. All it's going to do is take us longer."

"For all we know, it's already too late," Brock snarled. "You heard my father. He's been working on this for fucking-ever. No way in hell he's going to make tracking him easy. It's too fucking late. She's gone. They're all gone."

Charlie couldn't believe it. She *wouldn't* believe it. "Anthony spoke like we were *going* to regret messing in his business...as if he hadn't carried anything out yet. And despite being the bastard he is, I don't think he actually planned on taking Tina. If he had, he sure as hell wouldn't have done it in front of witnesses."

"You think he's holding the girls somewhere nearby?" Vince caught on quickly.

"I do. We just need to figure out where, and to do that, we need to learn a little bit more about him." Vince gave her a questioning look, and she had to push the words out, knowing they wouldn't go over well. "We're going to have to talk to Arturo."

Both Vince and Brock interjected at the same time. Charlie slipped her fingers into her mouth and let out a shrill whistle. "I didn't ask permission from either of you."

"It's a bad fucking idea." Brock shook his head.

"Don't you think that would create more trouble?" Vince didn't outright disagree, but the look on his face screamed doubt.

"Do I look stupid?" Charlie asked rhetorically. "I'm not about to tell him the closest thing he has to a friend kidnapped his daughter and is trying to stage a coup in his organization. Then we'd have to worry about dodging Arturo's men too. But if anyone knows Anthony's habits, it's him."

"I'll have Eric hack into the traffic cams and see if he can get a bead on Anthony or the truck. Maybe we'll luck out." Brock didn't sound too hopeful.

"Give him your laptop," Vince suggested to Charlie. "Maybe our facial recognition software will make it easier."

Brock glanced from Vince to Charlie, his eyes narrowed in scrutiny. "Who the fuck are you guys working for really?"

Charlie reached out and squeezed her friend's hand. "Let's split up and meet back at our hotel room in, say, two hours. Once we get things moving, we'll give you some answers."

"You mean, now that you know I'm not a dirty DHS agent?"

"Doesn't mean I suddenly like you," Vince interjected with a mutter.

"Good. Then the feeling's mutual."

Brock hustled back into Inked Up, leaving Charlie and Vince alone. Even after finding out he'd gone behind her back, once again questioning her fitness to be on this assignment, Charlie's first instinct was to turn to him for support. When she realized she couldn't, that all-consuming pain in the center of her chest came back.

Hell, maybe he'd been right to question. Not only had she accused an old friend of a heinous crime, but she'd overlooked the real culprit entirely and brought her innocent cousin along for the horror ride.

Vince's touch on her arm had her closing her eyes, hesitant to meet his gaze.

"We need to talk, English," Vince said, dropping his voice.

"Eventually." She reluctantly stared him dead in the eye, and the uncertainty she saw nearly did her in right there. "Right now, we have work to do."

He opened his mouth to say more, but Eric came flying out of the door.

"Is it true?" Eyes round like a kid on Christmas morning, he looked at Charlie eagerly. "Am I seriously going to be playing with government facial recognition programs and be allowed to hack into the city's traffic cameras?"

"I'm going to give you my laptop, Eric, and you're going to do what you need to do to help find Tina." Charlie kept her voice stern and pointed at him like a schoolteacher. "But things haven't changed so much in twelve years that I don't still view my computer as an extension of myself. If you get so much as a finger smudge on the screen, your arse is grass. You got me?"

He waved off her threat. "Yeah. Yeah. I got it. You have nothing to worry about. Where is that nice piece of fine machinery?"

Charlie nearly snorted. Vince. Anthony. The kidnapped girls. Tina.

Yeah, she had nothing to worry about.

CHAPTER TWENTY-FIVE

Vince followed Charlie's lead—metaphorically and physically—as she let herself into Arturo's house. No guards. No men with guns. They simply walked in without so much as a side-eye from the gardener pruning a row of hedges.

Vince drew his weapon, noticing that Charlie already had Gregor out, and glanced around the empty foyer. Not that he had much love for the old man, but finding her uncle's dead body might push Charlie over the edge.

"Am I the only one who thinks this looks pretty damn ominous?" Vince murmured.

"But it makes sense if Anthony's poaching staff from my uncle's arsenal," Charlie pointed out.

"Tina!" Arturo's voice, followed by the sound of rolling wheels, bellowed from inside the library.

Charlie and Vince exchanged glances as they headed in that direction. Making certain to keep their guns hidden, but nearby if needed, they stepped into the room. Arturo rested heavily on a walker, a new addition since they'd seen him last.

"Charlotte." Arturo glanced toward Vince, surprise written all over his face. "Forgive me, but I didn't expect to see either of you again."

"Because you told Vince it wasn't safe for me here?" Charlie asked brazenly.

Arturo's gaze snapped to Vince. He shrugged off the older man's displeasure. "I don't keep things from my fiancée."

Fuck him sideways and upside-fucking-down. Arturo's glare didn't hold a candle to the one Charlie shot his way. Freezing fucking lava wasn't an apt enough description and yeah, he'd earned every goddamn second of it. And probably more. Getting Logan to dig into her past was a colossal mistake, one he wasn't sure how to rectify.

"Why did you think I'd be in danger?" Charlie transferred her attention back to Arturo and stepped into the room.

Arturo directed his walker to an overstuffed chair and, after a minute, the older man slowly sat. "Things are changing, and change sometimes unsettles people. Unsettled people do crazy things. And like I told your young man, some people see my shift in business as a detriment to their overstuffed wallets. They hope to change my mind."

"Can they?" Vince asked, curious.

"No. And Anthony was supposed to make that fact unquestionably known amongst my old colleagues. I expected him here an hour ago to tell me how things went, but he's yet to show."

"You haven't seen him at all today?" Charlie asked.

Arturo shook his head. "And it's unlike him. He makes certain to give me daily updates."

"Updates?"

Arturo sighed, leaning back in his chair. "Updates. I regret not starting the conversion when I was healthier so I could oversee it through to its conclusion. I'm too incapacitated to ensure everything is done that needs to be done. Anthony has been my right hand."

"Anthony's on board with the changes?"

"Initially? No," Arturo admitted. "But he's since seen reason."

"What makes you say that?" Vince asked, beyond skeptical.

"Because this life has cost us both precious time with our family."

Anthony, concerned about losing time with his son? The one he'd pointed a gun at an hour ago and threatened to blow a hole through if he moved even a fucking inch?

Not fucking likely.

Charlie glanced his way, her eyes telling him she wasn't buying it either. "Where does Anthony like to be when he's not here with you?"

* * *

Being on the receiving end of Charlie's silent treatment put Vince in a foul mood. Follow it up with two hours of planting cameras at Anthony's well-known haunts and being subjected to Brock Torres's snarky-ass comments, and he was one dirty look away from assaulting a federal employee. And it would be a charge he'd accept with pride.

Yeah, he'd fucked up. He could own up to that. But instead of talking things out, Charlie had avoided him ever since they'd left Arturo's place. He was twenty years past that childish shit. Hell, so was she.

"That was the last one," Torres said of the camera they'd installed outside Anthony's condo. He pocketed his cell. "Eric and Charlie already have the cameras online and recording, plus they've hacked into the city's feed and got eyes on the dock. Everywhere. So far, we haven't gotten any hits."

"It's not like we expected Anthony to take a stroll down Ocean Parkway." Vince waited as a cabbie passed before crossing the street to the truck, Brock following. "Our resources will be less stretched once the rest of our team gets here. We'll mix tech power with good old-fashioned man power. In the meantime, we should head back to the hotel."

Torres cocked up an eyebrow. "You sure you want to do that, friend? If I know Charlie—and I do—a few hours isn't enough for her to work through all her mad."

Vince clenched his jaw until his teeth creaked. "You knew the Charlie from years ago. I know the one now."

"So you're saying the one back at the hotel isn't research-ing the best way to fry your balls?" Torres shook his head and laughed. "Amateur. Going behind a woman's back about anything is fucking stupid. Going behind Charlie's is a fuck-ing death wish."

"Says the man who kept shit from her too," Vince pointed out.

"Yeah, but we haven't exactly been pen pals over the course of the last few years, much less fuck buddies."

Vince snapped. Grabbing Brock's shirt, he propelled him against the truck door with a loud thud, and got right into the DHS agent's face. "Talk about her like that again and I'll rearrange your pretty-boy face. You have no fucking clue what's between us or what she means to me."

"Does she?" Brock asked bluntly. He didn't flinch or

twitch, even when Vince pushed him against the truck again before releasing his hold altogether.

Vince saw a kaleidoscope of fucking red, and through it, Torres's goddamn knowing smirk.

Torres casually fixed his shirt, still fucking grinning. "Judging by the look on your face I'd say not. Treating her like a plaything isn't exactly the way to show a woman you care."

"Fuck you." Vince stepped back before breaking the shit-head's nose started looking like a good idea.

"No, fuck *you*. At least I'm man enough to admit Tina's it for me. I'll level the entire goddamn city to make sure I get her back safely. And then no way in hell am I going to let her go—no matter what Daddy Dearest or the department may think." Brock looked him dead in the eye. "Because that's what you do when you love someone, asshole. You trust your woman to know what she can handle. You support her when she tells you what she wants to do—even if it's making a name for herself in the sex club industry. Can you say you've done the same thing?"

"Charlie's my partner, isn't she?" Vince nearly growled out the words.

"Chosen by your boss, not you. Right? If you don't want to admit it to me, at least admit it to yourself. You don't truly see her as an equal...or else you wouldn't have gone behind her back. You would've let her tell you in her own damn good time."

Vince didn't say a word. But he hadn't looked into her past wasn't because he'd believed her helpless, or an incapable operative. God—and the rest of the team—knew she'd handed him his ass a time or two...or a dozen.

He'd done it because, despite all his best efforts to avoid it, he saw her as a hell of a lot more than a teammate. She was the woman he wanted in his life—as his teammate, his lover...his *future*. And that's what you did for the woman you were falling for—you protected her at all costs. You put yourself on the line. You made tough choices, sometimes at the expense of yourself.

Except Charlie wasn't just any woman.

She was *his* woman. And his woman would sooner kick an ass than kiss it.

* * *

Charlie needed a bottle of ibuprofen and possibly a life vest, because she was sinking and sinking fast into the pile of shite that kept dropping in their laps. Even with the rest of the team having shown up an hour ago, nerves started attacking her patience. She tried telling herself it was because of what was on the line, but that went out the bloody window when Brock and Vince stepped into the suite.

One look at him, even if it was a glare, and she breathed a little easier. He headed straight for Stone and, along the way, his gaze landed on her.

She didn't even bother looking away. Yes, the silent game was childish, but she didn't know what the hell to say. He'd gone behind her back, hadn't trusted her ability, but he'd also cared. He'd have to be high to think she wouldn't eventually find out and make his life miserable, but he'd done it anyway.

"Wow." Logan shivered at her side. "Did it get cold in here, or is it just me?"

Charlie ignored the Marine's dramatics and nodded toward the second desk, where Eric was monitoring the newly placed cameras. "I'm not discussing the temperature with you, Callahan. Go help Eric."

"Then how about a future weather forecast?"

Charlie threw him a glare, enjoying when he squirmed. "You want a weather forecast? I can give you your own personal forecast—dim and gloomy, with my foot up your arse."

Logan chuckled. "Damn, darlin'. You have a way with imagery. You know that?"

It might have been a bit harsh, but at the moment, her feelings were still a bit sore that someone she called a friend would hop on the Vince-doesn't-believe-in-Charlie band-wagon. In her haste to go anywhere that didn't have a Ne-anderthal caveman presence, Charlie twisted too damn fast. The gash on her torso protested, making her hiss. And of course, Chase's medic eyes caught it.

He came over, nodding to her side. "What's wrong?"

"Nothing. I turned weird. It's fine."

"That's the cut from the knife?" *Of course he knew about it. Everyone seemed to know her business.* He cocked his hands on his hips, staring at her with those penetrating blue eyes, reminding her of a rugged-looking Bradley Cooper. Tough enough to kick any ass, but with a smile that could melt panties everywhere. "We can do this the easy way, which is you realizing I'm going to nag you to death until you let me check it out. Or we can do this the hard way."

"What's the hard way?"

Chase grinned. "Probably with my ass on the floor—but I'm still checking out that cut."

"I'm already taking the antibiotics Shay prescribed. Are you saying the good doctor doesn't know how to do her job?"

It was a low blow because Charlie knew the trauma doctor and Alpha's resident "doc" didn't always see eye-to-eye.

He seemed unfazed, not taking the bait. "I'm saying

sometimes even a broad-spectrum antibiotic isn't enough to keep away an infection. Or maybe what it needs is a stitch or two."

"You're not going to leave it alone until you check, are you?"

Stone stalked over, hearing the conversation. "No, he's not. And now it's an official order. Let Doc check it out."

Chase, obviously knowing he'd won, nodded to the kitchenette. He tugged out a chair and forced her to sit as he peeled away the old bandage and inspected the cut with a critical eye.

"I don't think it's infected." Chase gave it a poke. "But it does need a little something to keep the edges together."

"No stitches," she grumbled.

Chase sighed. "Fine. But I'm going to clean it again and, at the very least, put on some fresh butterfly bandages. You do realize this is going to scar, though."

"I'm not entering any beauty pageants anytime soon. Just do your thing so I can go do mine," Charlie ordered grumpily.

Someone else joined them in the kitchen. Charlie didn't need to look up to know it was Vince. It was like the air in the room thickened, making her work harder for each breath.

"What's wrong?" Vince's boots stopped right next to Chase, and still Charlie refused to look at him.

"Down, boy." Chase placed the last of the Steri-Strips on the gash before covering it with a fresh bit of gauze. "Just doing a little housekeeping and making sure our girl didn't do any additional damage."

Brock came over, and instead of watching the first-aid process, gave her exposed tattoo a good look-over. "Your pink's fading. When all this shit's done and over, you need to come back to the shop and I'll freshen you up. I've been dying to get a glimpse of the whole thing anyway, just gives me more of a reason."

"Like fucking hell," Vince growled.

Furniture moved. A chair overturned. Someone, who sounded like Chase, dropped a few curses. The two men were nearly nose to nose. Again. And Brock didn't shy away. He grinned—the jerk—knowing he was pushing Vince's buttons.

This time, Charlie didn't get between them. She threw up her hands, giving them each their own separate glare. "You know what? Have at it. Beat each other senseless. Pull out your juniors and have a measuring contest. I don't care! I have enough on my plate right now without having to deal with the two of you acting like oversized toddlers."

Her outburst temporarily earned her Vince's attention. "We need to talk, English. Still."

"Anthony and the girls first. And then when the real work's done, we'll talk about why you're a misogynistic arse."

Charlie fled. The bathroom wasn't far enough, but it was the only option. Closing the door behind her, she leaned against the sink and focused on her breathing. *Pull in. Push out.* Just like Vince had taught her to do during her tai chi lesson.

When did things get so complicated?

Oh, that's right.

Sex.

With Vince.

Charlie stared at her reflection, and finally admitted, "It wasn't just sex."

One breath quickly came after another, and not too much later, the tingles came—her fingers, her nose. Her entire body vibrated...

It was why she wanted to dropkick him to the ground, and then kiss him until they both passed out. It was why her chest ached at the thought of Vince not believing in her.

It had *never* been just sex.

That was what she'd told herself to put her mind at ease, and maybe, subconsciously, make her see what had been in front of her face since the first day Vince walked into Alpha, all arrogant and grumpy, and with an innate ability to drive her bloody crazy.

It was because she was falling—*hard*.

Or, more worrisome—she'd smacked into it face-first and hadn't realized it until that moment.

The bathroom door opened, and the object of her impending panic attack stepped into the small space, making it smaller as he closed the door behind him. "Hiding isn't going to make any of this go away."

Charlie, still fighting for each breath, jutted her chin toward the door. "But it delays it. Get out."

"No." Vince staunchly folded his arms and planted his feet. "I've let this slide for too long as it is."

"And I say it needs to be even longer."

She slipped past him and grabbed the door. When it was only an inch open, his hand smacked it shut. She whirled on him, ready to shout her way out, when he leaned close, effectively caging her in place.

There hadn't been time to readjust her big girl panties before he'd come storming in, oozing caveman goo all over the place.

"Let me out." Charlie's demand sounded less bossy and more...hopeful. Hopeful that he'd keep to his status quo and be his typical pain-in-her-arse self. "We're not doing this right now."

"Yes, we sure as hell are!" His outburst surprised them

both. Vince waited a few beats and looked to be trying to pull himself together. "It's killing me, English. Seeing you look at me like...like I don't know what. I feel like I'm having a fucking heart attack."

That made two of them. Charlie stayed quiet, not knowing what to say or how to respond to the emotion darkening his eyes—*a lot of bloody emotions*, and all ones that she could understand. The confusion? *She had it, too.* The anger? *Two-for-two.* The need? *Definitely there.*

The soul-ripping pain?

As if thinking about it, the harsh throb positioning dead center in her chest intensified.

No doubt about it. She felt that straight down to her soul.

Vince took her silence as an invitation to continue, and he did, locking her in his gaze and holding on. "You once accused me of being closed off, and you know what? You're fucking right. The one time I let my emotions get the best of me, one of my brothers was killed. His wife is a widow. His daughter's going to grow up without her old man breathing down her neck. All because I couldn't keep my shit together."

Seeing him still torturing himself over what had happened clawed at her throat. "It wasn't your—"

"Fault. Yeah, I get it. Logically. But that shit's going to live with me forever, and the last thing I wanted was to load it on someone else—or worse...let it happen again." Vince's Adam's apple bobbed as he tried to form more words. "It doesn't excuse going behind your back, but that's where my head was at. I *knew* something happened to you. I could see that dark shadow in your eyes because I recognized it from my own. It wasn't that I didn't trust you. It's that I wanted to protect you."

"I'm your teammate. An Alpha operative. I don't *need*

your protection," Charlie mumbled softly.

"No, but you deserve it. You're more than my teammate, Charlie."

A warmth she'd never expected blossomed in her chest at the use of her name. Vince's knuckles, slightly roughened, slipped up the length of her cheek until he palmed the side of her face. Charlie couldn't help but lean into the touch.

"Since I signed my discharge papers, I haven't had much of a problem keeping my shit together," Vince admitted. "I hauled in my scum and collected my payment. Even when everything went down with Penny and Honduras, my head stayed on straight. The only time I ever feel remotely like the man who made that bad call is when you walk into my line of sight."

Charlie furrowed her brows. "I'm not exactly sure if that's supposed to be a compliment or not."

His lips kicked up at the corners, and his fingers smoothed out her wrinkled forehead. "It means you wake me up, English. I'm more than aware you got your shit going on, babe, but the mental image of you in a dangerous situation— physically or emotionally—freaks me the fuck out."

For the first time in her life, Charlie didn't have a snappy retort. She could flip his words around and recite them herself, and they'd still be true, because it was how she felt about him. It wasn't a sexist thing.

It was a caring thing.

"I went and saw Dawn like you suggested," Vince said, surprising her yet again. "And you were right. She doesn't blame me for what happened, and looking her in the eye and seeing it for myself gives my nightmares a hell of a lot less power than they had before."

"Can you say that again?" Charlie asked, breathless.

Vince cocked up an eyebrow questioningly. "Which part?"

"The part about me being right."

Vince's lips twisted up in a small smirk, and his thumb continued to caress her lower lip. "You were right...and I'm hoping that since I haven't been kneed in the groin, I'm forgiven for being a caveman?"

Charlie pursed her lips and cocked her head to the side, as if debating. "Maybe. Partially. It's still pending."

"You realize it's going to be a work in progress, right? I'm more than likely going to fuck up again because I can't flip a switch and stop worrying about you. I want to protect you. *In* the field. *From* our pasts." Vince's throat bobbed nervously, his voice somewhat shaky. "Fuck. Are you going to say something sometime soon?"

There was a lot to say—except her words probably wouldn't come out as eloquently as his had. "You freak me the hell out, too, Navy."

And she was pretty sure she was falling in love with him.

Vince's face went blurry, and it took his thumb swiping across her cheek to realize it was due to falling tears. And then the damn man kissed the next drop away...and the next. With each brush of his lips, Charlie's emotions swelled.

"Damn it, Vince." Grabbing his face between her palms, she pulled his mouth to hers.

The kiss started sweet, turning salty from her tears. But at the first gentle swipe of Vince's tongue, it went supernova. His arms slid around her waist as he crushed her body to his.

Needing to touch him more, she skated one hand beneath his shirt, taking the time to brush against his piercing. "I need this off. Now."

A low growl rolled from Vince's throat moments before he followed through with her demand. He tossed his shirt aside. A few seconds later, hers joined his on the floor.

Vince slipped his fingers into the cup of her bra, pulling it down far enough for a nipple to escape. "You're so bloody gorgeous."

A smile quirked up her lips. "You getting British on me?"

"No other term seemed quite right." He curled his tongue around the exposed bud before giving it an erotic flick.

Charlie clutched the back of his head and panted, half-heartedly, letting reality slip into the bathroom. "This isn't a good idea...the guys...out in the main room."

"The only one out there right now's Eric, and he's wearing a headphone and geeking out over the facial programs. Everyone else hit the streets as extra pairs of eyes."

Charlie froze. "They're gone? Then maybe we should—"

Vince brought his mouth back to hers. "Do exactly what we're doing...followed by a nap. You got maybe an hour last night and not all at one shot. You can't possibly be on top of your game when you're exhausted."

"My mind's too wired to sleep right now."

He gave her a drugging kiss that fluttered her eyes closed. "Then I'm going to continue loving every inch of you until you can't keep your eyes open anymore."

"But—"

"Mind off, English." He kissed her again. "I need to have you in my arms right now, baby." Kiss. "Your pleasure in my hands." Kiss. "I need it so. Fucking. Bad." Kiss.

Charlie needed all of that too. She unclasped her bra and relished the way Vince's gaze devoured her whole. His hands slid over her torso, dropping to her hips, and guided her in a spin that propped her back against his chest.

"I've wanted to taste every single one of these flowers for over a fucking year." Vince pushed her hair off her neck, and while their eyes locked in the mirror, flicked his tongue over the largest tattooed cherry blossom.

Down the length of her back, he followed the trail of brown branches and pink flowers as it curved around her torso and over her hip. Slowly, he eased her back around. Looking up at her from his spot kneeling on the floor, Charlie nearly melted.

"Looks like I have one more flower to go," he teased gruffly.

"Looks like." She rested her hand on top of his head as he steadily worked open the front of her jeans and slid them down—panties and all—never once breaking eye contact.

Vince ran his hands over her ankle and up her calf, kissing his way up her thigh until he hooked her knee over his broad shoulder.

In this position, she was open and vulnerable...exposed as he lowered his mouth to the lone blossom flowering a few inches above her mound. The leg not draped over his shoulder trembled, threatening to give out as his lips caressed her already aching clit.

"I got you, babe." Vince anchored his hands on her thighs. "Just lean back and enjoy."

Charlie moaned, her head falling back. "No problem there."

Vince took her to some kind of pleasure dimension, first licking and then sucking, kissing her damp lower lips as he'd kiss her mouth. When her muscles tightened and prepped for release, he backed off and did it all over again. The result left her sweaty and panting, with both hands clutching his head.

"Don't stop," she pleaded on a moan. "Sweet heaven."

When he swiped his tongue through her folds, he picked up the pace. He nibbled and sucked until her hips lifted, chasing his mouth. Vince rubbed the flat of his tongue over her clit, and Charlie's pleasure went airborne. Her body clenched and released at the same time, coaxing out a keening moan that nearly made him come in his pants.

With a smug look twisting his lips, Vince got to his feet. "Heaven, huh?"

"Cocky bastard." She grabbed his nape and dragged his mouth down to hers for a hot, languorous kiss. "Don't go looking for compliments, Navy."

Chuckling, Vince palmed her ass and guided her jelly legs around his waist. "If you're still able to talk in full sentences, you're not tired enough."

CHAPTER TWENTY-SIX

Vince wanted nothing more than to sink inside Charlie and not come out, but he knew the possibility of her letting him do that was about nil. He sat her on the edge of the bed and stepped away from her wandering hands.

"Are you afraid of little ol' me?" Charlie leaned back, giving him a superb view of her breasts.

"Without a fucking doubt." He swallowed a chuckle.

A handful each, her breasts tipped upward, ripe berry-red nipples still puckered from his mouth. Vince hastily discarded his pants and kicked them away. His cock, already hard from their time in the bathroom, throbbed.

Vince wrapped an arm around her waist and gently eased them both onto the center of the bed. He wanted to take his time, but he didn't know if it was possible, especially when her nimble fingers dug into his back.

"Vince." Charlie rotated her hips. Both the brush of her

wet mound and the sound of his name made him suck in a hiss.

"Fuck, baby. I don't have any condoms in here."

She groaned, but didn't stop her gentle swivel. Each rocking motion slid his cock through her folds until it brushed against her hardened clit. "Where do you have them?"

He gritted his teeth and dropped his forehead onto the mattress, just above her shoulder. "In my bag. In the main room. With Eric."

At her sudden silence, Vince picked up his head. Charlie bit her lower lip, deep in thought.

"How are you with condoms normally?" she asked, contemplative.

Meeting her gaze, Vince damn near held his breath. "Religious—I've never gone without. And you see everyone's health screening, so you know I'm clean."

"Me too. And I'm a huge fan of the shot, so we're covered on that end."

Vince traced his thumb over her lower lip. "Fucking-A, babe. Are you saying what I think you're saying?"

Charlie rolled her hips again. This time, the tip of his cock hit just right, and he slipped inside her tight sheath, one inch at first. After another hip swivel, a second inch. Vince stayed still, afraid of shooting his load too soon.

"Make love to me, Navy." Lifting up, she ran her mouth over his, alternating between playful nips and gentle licks...and squeezed his ass.

Goddamn it, that's what he wanted to do. This wasn't about sex. It wasn't about a quick release or even savoring the moment to replay it for later. The words tightening his chest wouldn't come out, but damn it if he couldn't enact them.

He kissed her, timing the thrust of his tongue with the

slow pump of his hips. He threw into the kiss what he did with his body, going deeper until he could practically feel every inch of her wrapped around him.

Sliding his hand beneath her ass, Vince pulled back to the rim of her opening and slowly thrust again. Beneath him, Charlie squirmed and moaned, rubbing against him seductively. He rolled them over until their positions were reversed.

"Dance for me." Vince gripped her hips and encouraged her to take over the movement.

"Are you handing me the control?" she teased. A dark fire lit up in her eyes.

"You've had the control since day one, babe."

In this position, her bodyweight pushed her down on his cock until she hit the base of his balls. Vince lay on his back, enjoying the sight of her undulating body. Despite her petite size, power coiled in her slender muscles as she used her legs and hips to rock back and forth. She was a formidable woman, someone to contend with, no matter your sex or size.

She was also fucking beautiful. Inside and out. Power. Femininity. Delicateness. Strength. All wrapped into one heart-stopping package.

Charlie braced her hands on his chest as she rocked. Vince took them, entwining their fingers. It was a simple, intimate gesture that started the cascade of flutters wrapping around his cock.

"Vince." She groaned.

"Take what you need. You're in control here."

Charlie's pussy gripped him like glove. Her eyes locked on his. "With me. Together."

Once. Twice. Vince thrust into her each time she let her body fall. Wrapping his hand behind her neck, he brought her mouth to his and stopped holding back. He pulled out and thrust back to the hilt.

"Oh my God." Charlie gasped, her body erupting. Her heady moans detonated his balls, and he filled her body with his release.

Vince wasn't lying when he said she was the one in control, and he wouldn't have it any other way. She made him forget. She made him feel things he hadn't thought he could, and didn't think he had the right to feel again. She made him realize there were right times to live on the edge.

She made him feel *everything*.

* * *

Charlie stretched, extending her arms above her head and groaned when the muscles protested the move with a dull ache. That's when she realized she was alone, Vince's side of the bed still warm. Her head filled with conflicting emotions, the most prominent being guilt.

Only God and Anthony knew what was happening to Tina and the others, and she'd taken a time-out, soaking up whatever new feelings had come to the surface between her and Vince. Even after replaying their conversation, she wasn't sure where they stood, only knowing for certain it was uncharted territory.

Charlie had shimmied into a fresh pair of cargo pants and pulled a tank over her head when the door carefully opened and Vince filled the space. He propped his shoulder on the jamb and studied her carefully. "I was about to get you. You good?"

She figured he meant with them... with what'd happened and the door it had opened. Taking her time, she slunk across the room, letting his eyes drink her in until she was close enough to touch. Sliding her hands up the wall of his chest, Charlie didn't balk when Vince's arm banded possessively around her waist.

"Yeah, I'm good." She flashed him a surprisingly relaxed smile. "But I guess we're going to have to have another talk, since our last one ended with us naked."

A grin twitched his lips, but his nod was all seriousness. "If things go the way I want them to, we're going to end up naked a hell of a lot. But yeah, we're going to have to fit that talk in too."

From the main room, Eric's voice called excitedly, "Guys! Stone has something! You need to get in here!"

Eric was already putting their boss on speaker when they got there. "You're linked up to everyone, man," Eric told Stone. "Go for it."

"There's activity happening at the docks." Stone's voice filtered through the computer speakers. "I don't know if you can see from the way the surveillance cam's pointing, but we have a handful of white box trucks rumbling through, all headed toward dock seven."

"That's Arturo's dock." Charlie scanned the video feed, which showed her uncle's boat, dimly lit against the night, but not much else. "Are they headed toward the *Leslie*?"

"Stand by. Callahan's trying to get in a different position."

Charlie waited with bated breath for the former Marine to tell them what they'd found. Vince's hand landed on her shoulder, giving it a supportive squeeze as time ticked by.

"That's an affirmative," Logan's voice informed. "But I don't see any girls, or Torres."

"What the fuck do you see, because from our angle, it looks like not a damn thing." Vince leaned closer to the screen, trying to make out the dark images.

"Because the camera's not focused on the freighter ship itself. But let me tell you, the guards on this heap of metal are packing some serious fucking heat. Didn't know you need fucking AKs for guarding alcohol and shit."

Finally, the surveillance camera picked up movement. Charlie tapped the screen, directing Eric. "Right there. Zoom in on the guy standing off to the right."

Eric zoomed—and *bingo*.

"That's Anthony." Charlie identified her uncle's second-in-command, looking too much at ease for a man being hunted. "He's going to make a run for it, and using Arturo's boat. If he gets out into international waters, or worse, in Cuba's, it's over. Getting Tina and the girls back will be next to impossible."

"We're not letting that happen," Stone announced, followed by a long cadence of affirmatives. "We're rendezvousing dockside in less than thirty minutes. I don't care where everyone happens to be at the moment, or what you have to do to make it happen, but do it. This bastard's not slinking away like a fucking eel. Eric, you can be our eyes, right?"

Eric's mouth dropped before he glanced at Charlie, panicked. She offered him a supportive wink. "You got this, Eric. We just need someone to shine a light in the general vicinity. We'll do the rest."

Eric gulped. "Okay. Yeah. I can do it. No problem."

"Good," Stone added. "Let's get on the fucking ball. Everyone bring in all the artillery you have with you. We're not going into this packing light."

Everyone signed off.

Charlie turned to do what Stone said, and found her Glock being extended in her direction. Vince chuckled. "Please. I know Gregor's the first thing you reach for."

She took it and inspected the magazine clip before slipping it into a harness and buckling it into place. "What does it say that you can read me so well?"

"That we're made for each other." Vince took her mouth in a fierce kiss, only stopping at Eric's uncomfortable throat-clearing. "But I am going to ask one thing of you."

"And what's that?"

"I need you to be really fucking careful. Super alert. No hesitation. React on instinct. Watch your ass."

"Only if you watch it, too."

Vince dropped a kiss on her jaw. "There's no ass I'd rather watch more, English. Let's go fuck up some bad guys."

* * *

Vince and the team—plus Brock Torres—stood a block away from the docks and huddled over the blueprints for Arturo's ship, the *Leslie*. Like a typical freighter, it had a large underbelly and copious places for storage—and hiding human cargo. There wasn't a single person who didn't have their head in the game.

First operational goal: Remove the hostages without detection.

The second: Drag Anthony Torres off that ship by his dick and hand him over to the authorities. Vince didn't much care if his dick stayed attached to his body, so long as the bastard wasn't able to fuck with Charlie ever again.

Stone finished his conversation with the feds and, after shutting off his walkie, turned toward the group. "We got the go-ahead. DHS is waiting in the wings, and Miami PD's cleared the perimeter, making sure no one stumbles into the hot zone. It's our op—free and clear. So let's do a rundown. Teams."

Logan smacked his finger on the map, identifying his nesting perch on the dock. "I'm taking an eagle-eye position from this set of stacked cars. If any of you get into trouble, haul ass to this side of the ship, and I'll give you a helping hand—or a buzz cut."

"Next," Stone called out.

Rafe nodded toward Brock. "Torres and I are entering the vessel's port side via the dock."

"And Chase and I are frogman-ing our way onto the starboard side." Vince slid his palm over his wet suit–covered chest, and joked. "Figured we're already dressed for the job. Why the fuck not?"

"Hooyah!" Chase called out.

The former SEAL leaned in for a fist bump, and the scatter of chuckles breaking out among the team sent Charlie into an eye roll. "I swear, if I start sprouting chin hairs because of hanging around you Neanderthals, there will be hell to pay."

Logan winked. "You'd be drop-dead gorgeous even if you were part Yeti, darlin'."

The Marine's attention shifted toward Vince, and he laughed, obviously having enjoyed what he'd seen on his face.

"And you, Charlie?" Stone brought everyone's attention back to the op.

Charlie's arm brushed over Vince's as she pointed to her entry point. "Stone and I are hitting the anchor, then moving inward toward the center of the ship via this hatch."

"Exactly." Stone's stern tone demanded everyone's unwavering attention. "Remember, we're not here to rack up a body count. If it can be avoided, *avoid* it. If you stumble into Torres"—he tossed a glance at Brock—"the *other* Torres, bring the bastard in, but only if you stumble on his sorry ass.

You hear me? Our headlining goal is to find the hostages.
Once that's done, I'll consider an alternative op to hunt the
bastard down. Am I clear? Good. Let's Alpha up."

"Alpha up," everyone chimed before scattering, each of
them running through their final weapons check.

Vince caught Charlie's elbow just as she finished tucking
her throwing knives into place against her thigh, and nodded
to the side. "A minute?"

Charlie gave him a wary look as she followed him away
from prying eyes and ears. "You should probably think very
carefully about what you're about to say."

Vince snort-laughed. "I always have to think carefully
about what I'm going to say around you, but not this time.
You remember what I asked you to do back at the hotel?"

An evil glint made her brown eyes sparkle. "You told me
many things at the hotel. You may have to refresh my memory."

"Watch your ass. Stay alert. And let your instinct guide
your hand." Vince knew it was important to Charlie to keep
their private business private, but resisting the pull to draw
her into a kiss was damn fucking hard.

Charlie didn't seem to care. She grabbed his black Kevlar
and pulled him into a fierce kiss. One hand around her waist,
he kept her against him and ignored the catcalls around them
as he let her set the pace—and it was a wild one, just short of
indecent. When she finally ripped her mouth away, his chest
ached from lack of oxygen.

"Holy shit, woman." Vince panted against her mouth.

"And I need you to watch your ass too. If you get it shot,
I'll put a second bullet in the other cheek. Got me?" Char-
lie's heated brown eyes soaked him in. No smile. No joking.
Her seriousness sobered him pretty damn quick.

"Yeah, I got you." Vince nodded, watching as Charlie

strutted away toward Stone, as if she hadn't declared to God and their team what they'd been up to here in Miami. Following the sway of Charlie's hips, Vince's gaze collided with two shit-eating smirks.

"What the hell are you two looking at?" Vince barked at Logan and Chase.

Logan shook his head, looking equal parts amused and disturbed. "You guys are dropping like flies at a fucking horse show. First Rafe, then Trey...now you. *You*, man. If Stone thinks he's sending me on an operation that's not at some fucking monastery with a horde of men in robes, then I'm not taking it. Shit happens when you go off on your own."

With a laugh, Chase slapped him on the back. "You're just sad that you're our resident Romeo and haven't found a love connection."

"I have a lot of connections. That's what I do. I connect and move on."

"Your dick's connections aren't exactly what I meant, man." Laughing, Chase slapped Logan on the back as he took position on the edge of the pier, next to Vince. "Ready to swim?"

"Alpha up," Vince agreed, dropping his respirator into place.

His eye caught Charlie's a few yards away. Looking badass holding an assault rifle, and ready for anything, she flashed him a saucy wink, which he reciprocated with a faint nod—and then he dropped his big ass into the fucking ocean.

CHAPTER TWENTY-SEVEN

Charlie studied the mooring line tied to the front of the *Leslie*. Stone had lost his bloody mind—or he'd taken up comedy. But one look at the former SEAL confirmed that there still wasn't much of a funny bone in the man's well-toned body.

Scaling a mooring line almost thicker than her waist went on her list of firsts. After securing the semiautomatic on her back, she followed Stone. Gripping the heavy links with her gloved hands, she swung her legs up to lock around the line and then, hand over hand, climbed steadily up to the boat's deck.

Stone motioned for her to drop low the second her feet touched down. Keeping to the dark corners, he moved while she covered him, and then vice versa. The fact that the guards hadn't yet made their pass on this side of the boat was a bit unsettling.

Where the hell were they? They'd been on the camera

feed, heavily armed and looking obvious, and now... nothing.

As if he'd read her mind, Logan's voice chimed through their comm-links, "You got a bogie on the upper deck coming right up on your eleven, Stone Cold."

Charlie immediately spotted the armed man nearly two stories up and gestured to Stone to give him the position.

"Got him," Stone murmured. "Let's try and get by without sounding the alarm. Where are my frogs?"

"Frogs made landfall. Stowing gear and heading to first point," Vince's voice announced.

With time ticking, Charlie and Stone needed to get to the first point too. By approaching both ends of the freighter and meeting somewhere in the middle, the teams hoped to clear, locate, and extract Tina and the others without being spotted. With seven of them and a lot of ground to cover, it would be difficult but not impossible.

"The guard's heading your way, Loverboy," Stone warned Rafe as the lookout circled back around.

"Got eyes on him," Rafe confirmed.

Charlie took point this time as she and Stone reached the hatch that would lead them into the belly of the boat. Two familiar black camo'd bodies rounded the corner, guns poised and ready for action at a moment's notice.

Vince's eyes locked on her, nodding in support. Standing next to him on an op, literally and figuratively, felt...right. Normal. Like this was how they'd always been meant to interact—with some occasional good ribbing.

Jitters gone, Charlie took second in line through the door, immediately at Stone's rear. With Vince at hers and Chase at his, they stepped into the first long corridor. Rooms lined each side, almost reminding her of a waterbound dorm.

"Frog-jump it by teams," Stone murmured. "We'll clear each room as we go."

Like an adult version of the leapfrog—but without the jumping over each other's backs—they hopped from room to room, each pair providing cover for the other as they systematically cleared the main corridor. They worked in synch, barely muttering a word. After the fourth set of rooms, Vince flashed her a quick wink that shifted the world beneath her feet.

"What the fuck was that?" Brock, from the other end of the boat, cursed through the comm.

A deep rumble echoed through the hall, vibrating the floor beneath Charlie's feet. *Okay, so maybe Vince's machismo hadn't moved the earth.* "Are those—"

"Engines." Vince said what Charlie had already guessed. "They're taking us out to fucking sea."

"Fucking-A," Stone cursed. "Eric, we need a back-up extraction set up if these assholes peel away from the dock."

"On it." Eric, from the comfort of their informal command center back at the hotel, started sending out the Bat Signal. "All right, DHS and the U.S. Coast Guard are on alert. They'll stay far enough back so as not to make anyone nervous, but be close enough if we need them."

"Good. Let's keep it moving," Stone ordered, then addressed everyone. "Plans haven't changed, guys. Let's put some hustle in it."

They picked up the pace, the pressure turned up. Charlie, temporarily focused on speed, forgot to check around the corner before stepping into the corridor. Movement flashed in her periphery, and she swallowed a curse, plastering herself to the wall.

"Shit." She prayed the guard hadn't seen her. "I got a guard coming from my nine o'clock. Fifteen yards and counting."

"Let's make sure he's by himself," Vince murmured from

the comm-link. He appeared inside the entryway of the room across the corridor, giving her a hand signal—*hold*.

Charlie held her breath—even though that wasn't what he meant—and counted footsteps. One set at ten yards...at five...

Three. Two. One.

They waited until the guard was one step past them, and then they moved together, Vince wrapping a muscled arm around his neck while Charlie focused on the gun. She twisted his fingers, making him involuntarily release his hold on his weapon.

"Where'd your boss stash the girls?" Vince growled low.

The guard's face began changing to an unflattering shade of purple. "If I tell you anything, I'm a dead man," he rasped.

"That's going to be your fate if you *don't* tell us. At least if you talk, you'll have a slightly better chance at living after we throw your boss's ass in jail. Pick your odds."

Stone stood sentry, his gaze shifting back and forth to each end of the corridor. "Let's hurry it the hell up, kids."

Vince flexed his arm and practically hauled Anthony's man to his toes. "Running out of time here. What's it going to be?"

"Th-third sublevel," the guard gasped. "Next to the engine room."

"English?"

Charlie stood in front of an emergency map mounted on the wall and studied it with a critical eye. "That's three flights directly below us."

Vince tucked his mouth against the man's ear. "You better be telling us the truth, or I'm going to come back and give you more than a fucking nap."

One pressure point later and the guard slumped to the ground, unmoving and unconscious.

Charlie watched in awe. One minute standing, the next, asleep. "You really need to teach me how to do that."

Vince snorted. "Sure. If Logan volunteers to be the guinea pig."

"Like hell," Logan chuckled from the comm. "And it's not your ability I'm questioning, darlin'. It's what these assholes would do to me when I'm passed the hell out. I'd come-to without eyebrows or wearing eyeliner or some shit."

"Chicken," Vince murmured playfully.

Chase grabbed his plastic ties and bound their sleeping asshole. "I'll stand behind with our squealer and make sure he doesn't wake up prematurely and sound off the alarm."

Stone clapped him on the back as they took the stairwell and carefully maneuvered one level lower. After clearing that corridor, too, they went down another flight. At the third sublevel, the bloody boat shifted again.

"Fucking hell." Vince caught Charlie's elbow as her balance teetered. "The bastards started the propellers. They're moving us away from the dock."

In case their sleeping friend had lied, Stone directed the other pairs to continue their search. But Charlie's gut told her that wouldn't be the case. The girls would be there. She just didn't know if they'd be there alone.

* * *

As Charlie led the charge down the stairwell, Vince became painfully aware they'd still left a lot of things unsaid. Back at the hotel, he'd been about to try and put into words how he felt. But then Eric had called out, and one thing had led to another.

No way in fucking hell could he tell her now and risk distracting her. Not to mention that she'd kick his ass for doing it while they stood in the middle of a steel coffin. He'd wait, and the longer he did, the more certain he was of his feelings. Somehow, without him knowing, Charlie'd slipped into his heart and planted roots.

And that's where she was going to stay—permanently.

Breaching the third sublevel was child's play, right up until a rapid-fire string of curses bombarded them from their mics.

"We've been spotted," Rafe warned from above deck. "Fucking-A. If you guys are close to the hostages, make it closer and fucking quick. We'll try and hold them off, but I don't know how many are already heading your way to check out the merchandise."

"Got it." Stone turned toward Vince and Charlie. "Go. I'll keep the corridor clear while the two of you sweep the area. We don't have time to do it room by room. Hustle."

Vince nodded. "Tight on my six, English."

He didn't have to look over his shoulder to know she followed. He felt her at his flank, covering their asses while he focused dead ahead. Two rooms came back clear before they hit the engine room.

Nothing.

No girls. No Anthony.

"That little prick lied through his teeth," Vince growled.

"Wait." Charlie grabbed his arm and pointed to a door hatch deeper into the room, behind the main furnace. "Back there."

With Charlie covering their six, Vince tugged on the handle. Fucking stuck. "Give me a hand."

They both shouldered their weapons and tag-teamed the rusty door.

"On three," Vince started the countdown. "One. Two. Pull."

"Bloody hell," Charlie grunted, her face turning red from exertion.

"Just need a little more..." Finally, it gave way. Metal grinded on metal as the latch opened with a loud screech. Vince stepped through—and what he saw curdled his stomach.

Four cages lined the far back wall—and they were occupied. Dirty and crammed-in, three to a crate, twelve young women damn near cowered like scared pups.

Charlie came up next to him and froze in place. Her face turned almost green as she took in the sight. "Sweet Jesus. How can any human being do this to another human being?"

Vince's jaw clenched. "Easy. He's not a fucking human being."

Charlie stepped closer to the girls and they rattled, trying to scramble as far away as possible. She lifted her hands, showing them she meant no harm. "I'm not here to hurt you. See? We're here to take you home."

One of the younger girls, her fingers gripping the metal bars, trembled and sobbed. "H-he s-said we're never going h-home."

A heavy dose of sorrow softened Charlie's words as she crouched down to the young woman's eye level. "He didn't take into account that we weren't going to stop before you were."

Vince grabbed a bolt cutter hanging on the far wall and started breaking locks. Four cages. Twelve young women. And each time a new trio was released, Charlie found herself in the center of another hug.

"Gee," Vince joked, "I do the heavy lifting, and you get the credit."

Charlie chuckled, and when everyone was out, the girls

still remained huddled close, eyeing Vince warily. Reading their discomfort, Charlie started off introductions. "This is my...Navy. He's one of the many good guys flooding this ship right now. I know he's a little intimidating, but he's got a lot of heart to go along with all that brawn. We're going to get you out of here, but you all need to do everything we say—and I mean everything, okay? Friends of ours are dealing with the bad guys right now, but that doesn't mean we don't still need to be careful."

Charlie scanned the group of girls. "Tina's not here."

"You mean the other girl?" The first girl who'd spoken cradled her sobbing friend. "That old man came and took her. He said she was too mouthy."

"Well, that definitely sounds like my cousin," Charlie said dryly.

"How long ago was this?" Vince asked.

"Not long. I thought you guys were him coming back for the rest of us."

Fear plastered itself all over Charlie's face as she snapped her attention to him. "If Anthony knows we're here, there's no telling what he'll do to gain leverage."

Vince gripped her hand and squeezed. "One good thing about being on a boat that's out at sea? There's no place to fucking go. He's like a rat in a barrel."

"Unless he has metal teeth—or a life raft."

Charlie's eyes locked on his.

"Fuck," Vince cursed. Speaking into his mic, he alerted the team. "Anthony's in the wind with Tina. He knows we're on to him. Look alive." He turned toward the group of young women. "Everyone stays between me and Charlie, got it? No noise. No crying. You follow every direction we give you. Understood?"

"Is he always this bossy?" one of the girls murmured.

"Yeah"—Charlie nodded, smirking—"but it kind of grows on you."

Vince tossed a glare over his shoulder, and Charlie gave him a wink. "Lead the way, Navy."

They retraced their movements back through the engine room. Just as they reached the hatch to step back into the corridor, a gunshot rang out. Metal clanged as Stone shouted for them to take cover. The former SEAL released a round from his own AK before hissing out a string of profanities.

Vince poked his head into the corridor, gun raised and ready to intervene, and inspected the two unmoving bodies. With a red pool blossoming beneath him, the one lying face-down was thankfully one of Anthony's men. But Stone, slouched against the wall as if he'd been hit by a semi, wasn't faring much better.

"Stone's hit. Cover me," Vince hurled back at Charlie as he made a dodge for Stone. He took a knee in front of his boss, wincing at the wetness soaking his right shoulder—but hell, he was breathing. "How bad is it?"

"I'll live. Help me up," Stone ordered through gritted teeth.

Forearms clasped, Vince hauled him to his feet. "Anthony's in the wind."

"I heard." Stone grimaced, his good hand clutching his shoulder.

"I'd like permission to go after him while Charlie gets you and the girls off this fucking floating shit can."

Charlie was right there, girls in tow. If looks could kill, he'd have been a dead man walking. "Like bloody hell."

"Stone can't get them out of here on his own. He's damaged fucking goods."

"I wouldn't go that far," Stone grumbled.

Without taking his eyes off Charlie's murderous gaze,

Vince pushed a finger into his boss's bullet-torn shoulder, making the man howl out a few profanities. Thankfully, following the groan came a low chuckle. "Point fucking made. Asshole."

"See." Vince didn't blink. "Helpless as a kitten. How's he going to aim his fucking gun when that's his shooting shoulder? Someone needs to help him get these girls out, and honey, it's going to be you."

Charlie looked like she wanted to argue, but she glanced at Stone, then at the girls cowering behind her. "Fine," she said, her voice strained. "But I swear to God, Navy, if you—"

"I'm not letting anything happen to anybody."

"What do you have going on up there, Rafe?" Stone asked.

"We've rounded up all of Anthony's men, but we're minus the man himself. And we've got a ride inbound on the starboard side."

"Copy. Coming up with the precious cargo. Leave one as guard and fan out to look for Anthony and the last hostage. Remember, our ultimate goal is the hostage, so if you come across the Franconi girl first, the mission ends. We'll let the law enforcement worry about Anthony."

"Will do, boss."

Vince slipped his hand into Charlie's hair, pulling her close. His mouth brushed against hers, wrestling her attention away from Stone. "You need to be up there when the Coast Guard shows up, English."

Charlie swallowed, forcing down a large lump. "*Please* be careful. I need someone's ass to kick in training, and I can't do that if you get yourself killed. I mean, I could kick someone else's, but it's not as fun."

He chuckled at her attempt to lighten the mood. "There's

nothing I like more than getting my ass handed to me by the woman I love. You can kick it anytime, babe."

He reined her in for a quick, hard kiss, and released her with a firm swat on the ass. Before she could retaliate, he jogged off toward the stairs, looking back when he took the first step.

Charlie's gaze stayed on him, fierce and worried—and shocked. It wasn't until Vince hit the open air that he realized what he'd admitted aloud—and so fucking easily.

CHAPTER TWENTY-EIGHT

Charlie froze for a split second after registering Vince's mutter. No, it wasn't a mutter, or a murmur, or an indecipherable mumble or auditory hallucination. He'd said it loud and clear and, judging by Stone's face, for all the world—at least their team—to hear.

She didn't bother fighting the smile that slid to her face, because the more she tried, the larger it grew.

Stone attempted to look stern, but failed. "You know the three of us are going to have to have a sit-down, right? There's going to have to be some ground rules."

"Why? Just because he finds me irresistible doesn't mean the feeling's mutual," Charlie managed to say with a straight face, making her boss snort-laugh.

"Please. You two have been dancing around each other for a fucking year. Everyone put their money into a pool to see how long it took." He looked contemplative for a second. "And I think I won."

"Do you think Vince and I can talk about it first before we get the birds-and-the-bees talk from Dad?" Charlie half-teased.

Stone outright laughed. "Let's get the hell out of here."

Charlie kept her gun hand free and at the ready, and tucked her other shoulder beneath Stone's arm. He wavered slightly, his legs buckling. One of the rescued girls came up to his other side and wrapped an arm behind his waist.

"Jesus Christ," Stone grumbled, looking woozy, "it's just a shoulder hit."

"Which may have hit something pretty damn important, judging by the blood pouring out of you. Think blood-slowing thoughts," Charlie joked.

They made slow but steady progress. By the time they reached the deck, Chase had finished securing the mooring line from the Coast Guard boat to the *Leslie*. An officer met them at the edge, easing their twelve abductees safely into the other vessel.

"What's up with the shoulder, boss man?" Chase asked.

"Dodged when I should've weaved," Stone answered. "I'll live. You can take a look at it later."

Charlie rolled her eyes. "The level of machismo you guys ooze sometimes astonishes me."

"You'd get bored if we didn't." Chase grinned before getting to business. "Rafe shut down the engines so the Coast Guard could board, and Logan's helping them get our friends nice and comfy before their trip to jail. Once we're all loaded, they'll take us back to the mainland and deal with bringing the freighter back themselves."

Stone nodded. "Good. Did you tell them we have a runner?"

"Logan told them. One of the emergency rafts is missing. Torres may have hightailed it off this floating heap before we even showed up. They've already put out a search." Chase gave Charlie's arm a supportive squeeze. "Don't worry, Charlie. He couldn't have gone far. Those things are in serious need of upgrades. We're not giving up a damn thing until we find your cousin."

Charlie nodded, not trusting herself to speak. If someone would've told her a month ago she'd be worrying her stomach into knots over Tina, she would've laughed in their face.

Yet here she was, worrying not only about Tina, but for the man she'd fallen in love with.

* * *

Vince made one last pass around the deck, his frustration growing by the second. A missing raft. A missing Anthony. None of it sat well with him. The older Torres didn't strike him as a stupid man. No way could one of those outdated dinghies outmaneuver a fucking billion-ton ship. But Vince was running out of places to look.

As he passed a stacked row of shipping crates, something toppled over. Vince slowed his steps, but didn't stop, not wanting to draw attention to himself as he carefully withdrew his gun. The noise came again, fainter, but followed by the sound of a muffled struggle.

To the left and behind a pillar of crates.

Vince whipped around, gun pointed. "I know you're fucking there, Torres. Come out before I decide it's in my best interest to start shooting now."

He waited—and then started counting. "Three. Two."

Footsteps shuffled—and then there was Anthony Torres, looking like the smug bastard he was, a gun pressed against Tina's temple. "We both know you're not going to start spraying the place with bullets, Vince. Not at the risk of hurting Tina."

Anthony jostled Charlie's cousin, making her suck in a whimper. Clothes a little tattered and sporting a black eye, she didn't look too bad for having spent the last few hours with a psycho.

Vince kept his gun aimed at Torres. "Doesn't mean I'm just going to let you go scot-free either."

"What is it with people not minding their own damn business?" Anthony seethed, spittle collecting at the corners of his mouth. "This shit has nothing to do with any of you."

Vince stayed alert. "When assholes like you believe they can rule the fucking world, it becomes our business. Newsflash, Torres, but you can't."

"Who's going to stop me? A bunch of G.I. Joe wannabes? I don't fucking think so."

"Thinking isn't your strong suit, or else you wouldn't have even tried pulling something like this off in the first place. Come on. We both know you're not getting out of here, so you may as well drop the gun and take your punishment like a man."

There was a reason why Vince wasn't the Alpha negotiator. He'd sooner shoot the bastard in the head than try and talk things through, but he couldn't risk the man reflexively squeezing the trigger.

"I'm not dropping this gun. And I'm sure as hell not going to be punished... because I'm not going to be caught," Anthony snarled.

"Seriously? What the hell have you been smoking? We've got all your men. We've got your hostages. You're standing in front of me holding a fucking gun. How the hell do you think you're going to be getting away with any of it?"

"I want Charlie here. Now. Standing in front of me."

Vince was steadily losing his patience. "That's not going to fucking happen."

"Then *she* dies." Anthony cocked the trigger of his gun. "Call her. On your radio. When I see her—*alone*—and that fucking Coast Guard ship pulls away, I'll let Tina go."

"And I'm supposed to just take you at your word? Because you're so fucking trustworthy?"

"You can trust the fact that, unless I see Charlotte in front of me in one minute or less, this deck's going to need a good swabbing. You used to be a Navy boy, right? Hope you still have the knack for it, Franklin. Call Charlotte. Get her here. Alone. Unarmed. And send the ship away with everyone else on it. *Now*."

Vince considered every logistical avenue but kept coming to the same place—he needed to do what Anthony said and then pray he and Charlie could goad him into making a mistake.

Vince gritted his teeth and tapped his ear, mimicking turning on his earpiece. "Navy to Sparks."

"I heard. All of it." Charlie's voice, strained, answered immediately. "Recite his demands so he doesn't know we heard him."

Vince swallowed rising bile, wanting to tell her to get on the Coast Guard boat and leave. "I need you port side. Alone. Unarmed. And send the Coast Guard ship away with everyone on it."

Vince heard the chorus of curses from his fellow teammates as they debated how best to attack the situation. Any of his brothers would have his back, and risk their own ass for his, but the more people who involved themselves this time around, the greater the odds things went FUBAR. *Fucked Up Beyond All Repair.*

And that is definitely not what they needed right now.

"Enough!" Charlie's roar brought the loud debates to a faint grumble. "I'm going alone, just like Anthony wants. Do what he says and get everyone off the boat."

"And how the hell are you two going to get off the boat?" Stone asked.

"We don't have a choice. He's holding all the cards right now. If he didn't, Vince wouldn't be making the demand."

God, Vince wanted to kiss that woman. Hard. Frequently. Hell, once he kissed her, he didn't think he'd stop.

* * *

Charlie didn't think twice about facing off with Anthony, not with Vince's safety on the line, and ironically, she realized that was exactly what he'd done when he'd had Logan look into her past. Different circumstances, same motivation.

Charlie handed Stone her back-up gun and thigh-knife, but it wasn't until she handed him Gregor that she felt naked.

"Be careful," Stone ordered gruffly. "I mean it, Charlie. Watch your ass, or I'll have you doing bathroom duty for an entire fucking month—and that includes Logan's bathroom."

Her lips twitched at his unusual show of affection. "Careful, boss. You're going to have us thinking that you have a sense of humor. You guys should get going. I don't want to give Anthony a reason to do anything stupid."

"You heard the lady." Stone gestured to the rescue boat. "Everyone on board."

All the guys came up, almost like a greeting line, as they offered their support with a quick, "Alpha up," and boarded the Coast Guard ship.

Once they'd loaded, she tossed the mooring line overboard and watched a few seconds until the Coast Guard boat pulled away. And then instead of cutting through the width of the ship, she jogged the perimeter of the deck, where she could strategically plan her grand entrance. At the final corner, she cracked her neck and lifted her shoulders, even trying out Vince's tai chi breathing technique.

It worked right up until she stepped out into the open.

Anthony faced an unarmed Vince, Tina trapped between them and held immobile by the gun pressed against her head.

"I'm here like you wanted, Anthony." She lifted her hands, showing him she'd done as told and came empty-handed. "The Coast Guard and everyone else are gone. It's just the four of us."

He glanced at something in his hand. She realized he held a small video screen.

"You have this entire ship under surveillance?"

"Of course I do," Anthony spat. "Unlike your uncle, I like to move with the times, not go in reverse."

"Is that why you want to take over?" Charlie briefly caught Vince's eye.

He cocked his head, directing her to sidestep to the right. Making her movements small, she shifted a centimeter at a time. The more distance she put between her and Vince, the more difficult it was for Anthony to keep tabs on them both.

"I'm taking over because I fucking deserve it," Anthony growled. "I've worked for that man almost half my life. I've dirtied my hands so he can keep his clean. I've been a loyal friend and employee. I've put more blood and sweat into this business than he has, and he thinks he's going to get rid of it all? I don't think so."

Charlie took another half-step to the side. "Then why not take it? Why drag everything out. Why implicate Brock by targeting those last few girls?"

"Because my son's not as good an actor as he thinks he is. I never believed he'd had a sudden attack of family loyalty. I knew he was looking for proof I was behind what happened, and I wanted to see how far he'd go to get it."

Anthony's smile made Charlie's stomach roll. "Proof of what? That you're psychotic? I think we have it already."

Anthony let out a laugh that chilled Charlie to the bone. "You still haven't figured it out, have you? Brock did, or at least, he suspected, which is why he suddenly had a desire to take part in the *family* business after your abduction."

Charlie had never needed Vince's meditative skills as much as she did at that moment.

"You were never supposed to be found in that fucking crate twelve years ago," Anthony continued. "You were supposed to get shipped out with all those other whores, never to be seen again. And most importantly, never to get in my fucking hair."

Charlie's blood went cold at what he'd just admitted. "*You* did that? You were behind the abduction too? What? Killing my mother and aunt wasn't enough for you?"

"Not when you started digging into the accident...I couldn't risk the chance you'd find something and take it to Arturo. I had to do it to save my own fucking ass."

"And when they found me?"

"My mistake for thinking you'd been scared enough to fucking drop it. And here you come back, twelve years later. You should've stayed the fuck gone, Charlie. All of this"— Anthony gestured to an eerily silent Tina—"is on you."

In direct contrast to his words, Anthony released his grip on Tina, and Charlie's cousin dropped to her knees. Whimpering, she frantically scrambled toward Charlie.

Charlie helped her to her feet, never once taking her eyes

off the gun Anthony still aimed at Vince. "Go. Run to the other side of the boat and go down on one of the rafts."

"But—"

"*Now*," she demanded more harshly than she intended.

Tina surprised Charlie with a tight hug. "Please be careful."

Charlie fought back tears for the second time that day. Hell, it might have been the third. But she returned Tina's embrace, realizing a little slowly that her cousin slipped something into the back of her pants. It was too small to be a gun, but cool against her skin.

A knife.

Charlie didn't know how she'd gotten it, but she wasn't going to refuse it either. Swallowing a forming lump of emotion, she gently ordered, "Get on the raft and head toward the rescue boat."

Time dragged as Tina left the three of them standing on the deck of the freighter.

"She's in the water," Stone announced in their ear a few minutes later.

Good. Now with Tina safe, it was time to end this fiasco.

Charlie angled sideways, giving Vince a brief glance of Tina's gift before turning toward Anthony.

"You know there's nowhere to go," she announced. "It's over. Even if you manage to overpower us, you're not going to overpower an entire Coast Guard crew."

"I know." Anthony nodded. "And I'm sorry I have to take you with me, Charlie. I really am. But first we need to get rid of the extra baggage."

Anthony's trigger finger flexed, the gun still aimed toward Vince's chest.

Charlie ripped the knife from the small of her back and threw—hard. Hours of practice and maiming poor Scooter in the Alpha gym paid off, the blade finding its mark in Anthony's extended arm.

He screamed, pulling the knife from his forearm, and charged at Charlie. Vince lunged forward just as a red dot flickered on Anthony's chest. A shot rang out, and a split second later, her uncle's second-in-command dropped at her feet.

Shouts erupted in her head, and then slowly melted away... along with everything else, including her ability to breathe. Charlie fought against a wave of dizziness.

"Breathe, babe." Vince cupped her cheeks, pulling her close and up to his gaze.

"What the hell just happened?" Adrenaline still rushed through her veins, threatening to pound her heart straight out of her chest. Charlie let herself be tugged into Vince's arms because damn it if her legs didn't get a little wobbly.

"You're welcome, darlin'!" a familiar voice called out.

Hovering about fifty feet off the freighter's port side, Logan drifted on a commandeered speedboat. Having their attention, he waved and spoke into the comm-link. "Can't say I don't have good aim... even on the fucking water."

"That was a pretty sweet shot," Vince agreed with a chuckle.

"I didn't do it for you, asshole. I wanted to get back in Charlie's good graces."

The abrupt shift to teasing had Charlie shaking her head. "Consider yourself on my good side for life, Callahan. And as for you"—she turned toward Vince—"no more of this going solo shite. My heart can't take it, okay?"

Grinning, Vince wrapped his arm around her waist. "We are *really* fucking overdue for that talk."

"No time like the present." His warmth immediately

soaked into her body, and she melted, skimming her hands up his chest.

The ground shook beneath their feet, starting as a tremor and escalating to a steady rumble.

"What the bloody hell is that?" Charlie glanced right as a large blast on the stern side blew metal and debris into the sky.

"That's our cue to fucking leave." Vince gripped her hand and tugged her to the edge of the decking. Another detonation literally rocked the boat, close enough to their position that it almost knocked her off her feet. "We're going to have to jump."

"*Jump*? From up here?" There was no disguising her horror.

"The engines are off, so we don't have to worry about getting sucked under and shredded to pieces." His grin widened when she released a distressed moan. "Come on now, English. Straight down. Point your toes. Hold your breath. It's easy-fucking-peasy."

Vince kicked the deck's railing free, giving them ample space to maneuver to the edge.

"On three." Vince tugged her close. "One."

"Bloody hell."

"Two."

"I hate you, Navy."

His free hand pulled her into a quick kiss. "No you don't, babe, you love me. *Three*."

Charlie screamed, closing her mouth a second before they hit the water, and pointed her toes like a bloody ballerina. Her body shot into the ocean like a missile, submerging her at least a dozen or more feet below the dark water. Lights shimmered above her head, directing her back to the surface, and when she reached it, she gasped, sucking in oxygen by the mouthful.

"See. Easy-fucking-peasy." Vince was already treading water next to her.

They swam out of the debris zone and looked back at the massive fireball lighting up the sky. One explosion turned into another, each one creating a new series of waves that bobbed them up and down.

"We just jumped from a bloody freighter." Charlie stated the obvious.

"We sure as hell did. And it was a beautiful dive." He grinned. "An Olympian couldn't have done any better. Ten-point-oh, sweetheart."

Charlie was too mentally drained to dish out her usual snappy comeback. Instead, she focused on what she really needed to know. "Are you okay?"

Vince swam closer until their legs tangled together. He couldn't stop grinning. "I've never been better."

"You sure?"

"Definitely."

"Good." Charlie used every ounce of energy she had and dunked him back underwater.

He came up laughing. "What the hell was that for?"

"For calling me the woman you love and then walking the hell away." She smacked his shoulder for good measure. "What the hell was *that*? You better start thinking with your head instead of your testosterone pouch, because the man I'm in love with will *not* throw out declarations like that and then disappear."

Vince's fingers brushed the wet hair from her eyes. Now that she could see him a little better, she lost her breath all over again.

"Say that again." He palmed her cheek, brushing his thumb over her bottom lip.

"You better start thinking with your head." She knew it

wasn't what he meant, but she needed to hold on to her mad a little longer.

He smirked. "Wrong part."

"Disappearing after spewing out declarations?"

"Keep going."

Staying mad was too damn exhausting. She softened, still not fully believing she was about to say it aloud. "You mean the part about the man I'm in love with?"

Vince's eyes sparkled in the dim light. "*That* would be the one."

"Maybe I should pull a Navy and swim away now," she muttered.

Vince's attention flickered between her mouth and her face. "You're not swimming anywhere. Sorry to tell you this, English, but you're stuck with me."

"For now," Charlie teased.

"Nope. Forever." Vince slipped a hand around her waist, treading water for the both of them. "I love you, Charlotte Ann Sparks. I love the way you kick my ass. I love the way you keep me on my toes. And I love the way you make me feel. There isn't a single damn thing about you that I don't love to infinity and back."

Tears brimmed in Charlie's eyes, and she let them fall. "That's a lot of loving."

"Hell yeah. I'm a SEAL. Remember, we don't do any-thing half-assed and that includes loving our women." Vince waited for the spark to ignite her ire—which it did.

"*Your* women?" Charlie challenged teasingly. "Is that caveman mentality what I have to look forward to in this 'forever' you're talking about?"

"Maybe. But I'll try to tone it down some." Vince's lips twitched with his fight not to laugh. He dropped a line of kisses over her cheek, each one getting closer to her mouth than the one before. "And what about you? Are you going to love me even though I'm a brutish Neanderthal with severely lacking people skills?"

Charlie wrapped her legs around his waist, needing to be as close as possible. "As it happens, I already do."

"About goddamned time." Chase's voice, closer than comm-link distance, turned Vince and Charlie to the glaring light shining off the Coast Guard speeder less than three feet away.

"Pay up, man." Rafe extended his hand out to the former medic. "I won the pool."

Chase smacked his hand away. "Like hell you did. *I* won the pool."

"Oh hell, I don't think it was either of us. It was probably Rachel. She's been having some freaky ESP shit happening lately."

Everyone laughed. Rafe and Chase leaned over the boat, each grabbing onto one of Charlie's arms and tugging her out of the water. Vince easily hoisted himself over after her. His feet had barely hit the bottom of the boat when he tugged her into an intense kiss.

"Did I mention the other thing I love about you?" he murmured against her lips.

Charlie slid her arms around his neck, grinning wickedly. "No, but I could probably imagine what it is."

"I love that we can do *anything* as long as we do it together."

Charlie's heart did a somersault, and then kept flipping. She hadn't expected it. She hadn't gone searching for it. Hell, she'd run from it at every turn. But Vince Franklin had shown her that it wasn't so hard to trust and love—with the right person.

And he was hers.

EPILOGUE

Lebanon County, Pennsylvania
Six weeks later

Vince stayed alert, refusing to let his guard down for a second. His woman called for reinforcements, and he was going to provide backup, even if it meant developing hives from the amount of sugar and sweetness...and wedding cake toppers.

Voices drifted into the main storefront from a room on the left. He followed them, stepping carefully to avoid being spotted prematurely. Penny, Elle, Rachel, and Charlie huddled around an open book, flipping pages and talking excitedly.

"You must be the groom!" came an unfamiliar voice.

Vince snapped to attention. The older woman's white apron and Sweet Treats name tag identified her as one of the bakery's employees—and evident ninja-in-training as she'd taken him by surprise, something not easily done even by the best-trained soldiers.

"What?" He was slow to register her ear-to-ear smile and hopeful expression. "Oh. No. Not me."

"This one's all mine." Charlie settled herself into his side, her wide grin pulling out his own reluctant one. "Took you long enough to get here."

"It took me five minutes. You said it was urgent." Dipping his head, he murmured for her ears only, "Although I don't know what kind of emergency you can have at a freaking bakery, English."

"It's a matter of life and groom's cake." Charlie held a straight face.

Vince blinked, trying to tell if there was an underlying meaning—or alcohol involvement. But no one looked to be in distress, or inebriated. "A *what*?"

Charlie dragged him over the table where Penny pushed a book his way. Cake photos filled the pages, but unlike the elaborate ones he was used to seeing at weddings, these looked more…manly.

"A groom's cake." Penny tapped one of the many images. "I need to surprise Rafe with one, and I have no idea what to do. What do you think about this one with the boxing gloves? I mean, he's Alpha's trainer coordinator."

Elle shifted her weight from one foot to the other, hands massaging her lower back. Using anything to distract himself from the question being asked, Vince brought over a nearby chair. "Sit."

She flashed him a smile and slowly lowered her very pregnant self onto the chair. "Thanks."

"You brought me down here to pick out a cake?" Vince turned back to the others.

"A groom's cake," Charlie clarified. Under her breath, she muttered, "It matters to them, so just go the hell along with it, okay?"

"Can't they do a combat boot or something?"

Vince waited for the reaction—*any* reaction. Penny's

smile lit up her face as she glanced to the baker. "Can you?"

"Uh-oh," Elle's voice mumbled.

"We can do that." The Sweet Treat employee nodded excitedly. "We could even make it look worn and dirty—scuff it up like it's seen some action."

"Um, guys?" Elle cleared her throat nervously.

"That would be incredible!" Penny clapped her hands. "What does everyone else think?"

"I think it's an adorable idea," Rachel admitted.

"I think it's right up his alley," Charlie stated.

"I think it sounds edible." Vince received a wave of eye rolls.

"And *I* think that I'm going to have a baby." Elle spoke louder this time.

Five heads swiveled toward the mama-to-be. Grimacing, she clutched her swollen belly and threw a nervous glance to the puddle beneath her legs. "And I think my water broke."

Thirty minutes of intense cursing later—mostly from the pregnant one—Vince thankfully handed Elle over to the nurse at the Frederick Memorial Hospital labor unit.

"Father?" the nurse asked.

"Here!" Trey shouted from down the hall. He jogged toward them, Rafe, Chase, Stone, and Logan hot on his heels. When he reached his fiancée, he kissed her on the forehead. "How are you doing, baby?"

"About to pass a watermelon through my hoo-ha," Elle hissed through clenched teeth.

"Now there's a mental picture I never wanted in my head." Charlie cringed.

The rest of them settled into the waiting room as the nurse wheeled Trey and Elle into the back. *Hours*, she'd warned. First babies took a notoriously long time. Vince sank into one of the chairs, losing track of time as he played with a lock of Charlie's hair. Less than an hour later, the waiting room door opened again.

Trey stood in the threshold, the largest smile Vince had ever seen plastered on his face. "You guys ready to meet Alpha's newest addition?"

"Wow." Charlie glanced at her watch, chuckling. "Elle doesn't waste time, does she? She must've really missed her cookie dough ice cream."

They all laughed and joked around as they tromped to Elle's room, but at the door, they all sobered. Elle lay in bed, her hair plastered to her head with sweat, cheeks flushed—and looking so damn happy.

"Guys." Trey carefully took the bundle of blankets from Elle's tired arms and proudly presented the sleeping baby inside. "Say hello to Violet Mae Hanson. Violet…meet all your aunts and uncles."

A firm grip tightened around Vince's hand. He looked down at a teary-eyed Charlie.

"What?" Charlie demanded of him, noticing his attention. Sounding watery, her words lacked any kind of heat. "I'm allowed to be happy. I've never been an aunt before."

"From what I hear, it's a lot of babysitting and presents." Vince shrugged.

"I can do that." Charlie wiped her face dry with the back of her free hand.

"You know what else you can do?" When she looked up at him with a question lighting up her eyes, he added, "Give little Violet there a cousin to play with."

Charlie laughed until she realized Vince wasn't kidding. "Wait. What?"

"Not right this second," he clarified, in an attempt to stave off any panic. "Maybe not for a few years. But you're eventually going to have to make an honest man out of me, English."

He hadn't realized it until he'd said the words aloud, but suddenly, Vince wanted Charlie harassing one of the guys about a goddamn groom's cake for *him*. Maybe not next week, or next year. But he wanted to be able to put his grandmother's ring on her finger, for real this time.

"Well"—Charlie cleared her throat, searching for words—"we do already have a ring handy," she said as if reading his mind. "But little Violet's going to have to wait a bit on the whole cousin front, because her Aunt Charlie has a whole lot of arse-kicking still to do."

Vince laughed, bringing Charlie's hand up to his mouth. "*We* have a whole lot of arse-kicking to do."

Penny Kline didn't come to Honduras on a pleasure trip. But when she walks into the middle of a covert ops mission, she finds herself swept into the hard-muscled arms of Rafe Ortega—and on a thrilling ride of danger and desire...

Please see the next page for an excerpt from *Heated Pursuit*.

CHAPTER ONE

San Pedro Sula, Honduras

Penny's damp underwear stuck to her skin in an uncomfortable bunch, but it wasn't a man's skillful pair of callus-roughened hands or his dirty, talented mouth that had caused the problem. The blame lay entirely with the god-awful Honduran humidity.

It didn't matter. No degree of sweaty undies or unfortunate chafing would slow her down. *Nothing* could make her turn back, because her family meant the world to her—and Rachel was the only one she had left.

A tingle at the base of her neck made Penny skid to a stop. Her gaze snapped left and right, heart trilling as shadows stretched into human-sized figures and melted away with the twinkle of a far-off light. Nothing looked amiss, but two torturously slow seconds later, the sound of a boot scraping asphalt had her spinning around with fists raised.

Half-hidden in shadow, the man ducked her sweeping

arm and pivoted much too fast for someone his size. In a blink, he reappeared over her shoulder. Months of training and practice brought her heel down onto his large, booted foot and she turned . . . straight into a hulking black-camo-clad figure.

Holy ever-lovin' god of iron giants.

Behind his ski mask, the man's piercing blue eyes raked down the length of her body. He towered over her by more than a foot, and given the width of his broad shoulders and massive chest, he outweighed her by at least a hundred pounds of solid muscle.

Penny swallowed the fear rising in her throat and did the first thing that popped into her head—she aimed a swift kick between his legs. And then she ran like hell.

Each painful inhale rattled in her lungs as she pumped her legs harder. Her hair whipped across her line of sight, temporarily obstructing her view. Seconds ticked by at an agonizing crawl. Fifty yards. Twenty. The closer her rental Jeep came into view, the louder the echoing pound of foot-steps behind her became.

An inch away from the door, strong hands propelled her face-first into the grimy driver's side window.

"Let go of me." She twisted and squirmed, cursing as he yanked her arms sharply behind her back and pinned them into place with his two hundred–pound frame.

"*Ya era tiempo,*" her captor said, tossing a deep growl of Spanish to their left.

About damn time. Years of studying the language had Penny's heart sinking to her stomach . . . because she knew he wasn't talking to her.

One dark figure after another emerged from the shadows. They were dressed head to toe in matching black fatigues and masks with the metallic glint of weapons flickering off the four bodies like a commando's version of bling. The fact that not a single gun was pointed at her head became a small comfort when a dark van screeched to a halt in front of them.

"Oh hell." She took a deep breath and choked on burnt rubber fumes.

She needed to think, and the hard erection nestled against her ass reminded her there wasn't room for mistakes. If something happened to her, Rachel would be lost forever in the hands of a monster. She couldn't let that happen. She *wouldn't* let that happen.

As if sensing a forming plan, her assailant bent down, his mask brushing against her ear. "*Play nice and you won't get hurt, sweetheart. But if you don't stop struggling, I can't make that same promise.*"

Penny fought against the ice-cold tingle his rough whisper zipped down her spine. Her joints screamed in protest, but she edged closer to the only area susceptible to attack. The second fabric brushed against her palm, she curled her fingers and squeezed with everything she had.

"Fucking hell!" Blue Eyes wrenched her grip free of his balls and tossed her over his shoulder as if she were nothing more than a rag doll.

"Damn it! Let me go!" She elbowed the back of his head, and when that didn't get a reaction, she plowed a fist into his left flank—and the damn man kept walking, not once losing his stride. "Put me down! *Entiendes?*"

Behind her, someone bound her kicking legs while another did the same with her wrists. When a gag came next, she snapped her teeth, nearly catching the hand that tied it into place. A sack over the head later and her world plummeted into darkness before they shuffled her into the waiting van.

Between the musty, stale air and being bracketed between

her assailant's rock-hard thighs, it didn't matter that she couldn't see her snug confines. Walls closed in around her, making each breath feel as if it would be the last. She made one last-ditch effort to squirm from her captor's hold.

Blue Eyes's grip locked her into place, her back plastered against his chest.

"*Little viper,*" he murmured—in Spanish—into her ear. "*It's a damn good thing I wasn't thinking about having children anytime soon.*"

"*I'm just glad she didn't grab my balls.*" Another voice chuckled. "*Unlike you assholes, I'd like to expand my gene pool sometime down the line. But I am curious as to why she's down here.*"

"*Me, too. And I'm sure as hell going to find out.*" The familiar voice made Penny's heartbeat stumble.

The tone was the same in Spanish as it was in English—abrupt and menacing even from its distance across the van. But why would Trey be in Honduras? And why the hell had he let his friend turn her into a pancake against the side of a Jeep?

* * *

If someone had told former Delta and current Alpha Security operative Rafael Ortega that he'd have someone tied up in the unit's makeshift interrogation room, he'd have sworn it would've been the drug kingpin, Fuentes, or one of the cartel leader's many henchmen.

Now, three hours after he and his team pulled the hood off the American woman in the privacy of their inner-city headquarters, Rafe still hadn't entirely ruled out the redhead's involvement. Something didn't jibe, and when he couldn't figure things out, it made him goddamned twitchy.

A body search he'd been a lucky enough bastard to perform revealed a single steel blade tucked into her boot and a burner cell phone that hadn't sent or received any calls. No firearms. No identification. That was it, unless you counted breasts that would fit perfectly in the palms of his hands, and an ass that was made to be grabbed—or at the very least, ogled.

For the third time in as many hours, Rafe shifted himself in his pants and walked into the interrogation room. Instantly, he was bombarded with curses that would've had his fourth foster mother running to the nearest church.

"Ah. You missed me," he goaded.

His comment earned him another round of expletives, each one more inventive than the last. He smiled, loving both the challenge and the murderous glint in her blazing green eyes.

Rafe met her glare for glare, not turning when the door opened to emit Trey Hanson, his best friend and former Delta brother. His own black mask still firmly in place, Trey took a position against the far back wall.

"Are you feeling any more talkative?" asked Rafe.

"Go. To. Hell." The redhead tugged on her restraints with each word.

"I've been there. Too dry for my tastes." Rafe let out a mental sigh. This was turning out to be more work than he'd anticipated. "Why are you in Honduras?"

She gave him an eat-shit-and-choke-on-it glare and he covered her hands with his, halting both the damage to her chafing wrists and assessing her sudden surge in heart rate. "I'm losing my patience, sweetheart. Let's try this again. One. More. Time."

Her gaze darted left, to where Trey stood like a six-foot wall ornament, flipping his KA-BAR knife in his hand like

Rafe had seen him do countless times when bored. Something flashed in the redhead's eyes, but when her gaze slid back to him, it hardened to green steel.

The slow, upward curl of her lips alerted him to the smart-mouthed remark about to be unleashed. "Maybe instead of asking me stupid questions you should put some ice on your boo-boo. Untreated swelling could cause permanent damage."

He leaned to within an inch of her face. *Fuck-and-him.* Despite the layers of San Pedro Sula grime caked on her otherwise perfect porcelain skin, a vanilla scent clung to her body. It almost made him forget that her swift kick and good aim were the reason he actually did just get done icing his fucking balls.

"We have ways of making little girls talk," he warned. "And trust me, it's no day at the spa."

Her gaze flickered over his shoulder. "I've never been a spa kind of woman. Ask your mute friend there in the back. After all, we were practically raised as brother and sister."

* * *

Once Penny got over the fact that her surrogate big brother was lounging on the sofa across the room, it was easier to shift her focus—at least temporarily—to Mr. Tall, Dark, and Blue-Eyed.

Rafael Ortega looked like a walking sin stick, not a single ounce of softness anywhere on his body. His broad shoulders could perch a pair of economy-line sedans, and his snug shirt amplified a defined chest and quarter-bouncing set of abs. Everything about the man was rock hard and chiseled, but it was his biceps that had her close to drooling.

Nearly as big as her thighs, they bunched and flexed each

time he staunchly folded his arms across his chest, the movement giving her a sneak peek of the tribal tattoo hiding beneath the hem of his sleeve. He was *so* not her type—too large, too intense, and way too brooding. But that didn't stop the butterflies from forming in the pit of her stomach—and a bit lower.

Penny sat on the threadbare couch and forced a smile she hoped looked confident. "Nice place you have. A little compact for men of your size, but nice. Cozy."

"Forget the sarcastic small talk, Penn," Trey growled from across the room. "You owe me a few answers, so let's get to why the hell you're in Honduras."

Fake it till you sell it. The words of her mentor at the bail enforcement agency had her lifting her gaze to Trey's. "I don't owe you a damn thing."

"When you waltz your sweet ass into one of my missions, you most certainly do. You're a goddamned *social* worker. You have no business walking the streets of San Pedro Sula as if you're GI-fucking-Jane."

"I can count the number of emails and phone calls I've gotten from you over the last few years on one hand, so don't pretend to know my business. I'm not sixteen anymore. I don't need your lectures, and I sure as hell don't have to explain myself to you. The sooner that sinks into your head, the smoother this conversation will go."

Rafe blocked Trey's path in one step. In a low murmur, the two men exchanged words that pinched Trey's lips into a tightened frown.

A few seconds later, Rafe turned, locking her in his sight. "I think we've gone about this the wrong way, Red."

She matched his disarming half smile with one of her own and watched every line on his already chiseled face go still. "My name's *Penny*. And you didn't seem too concerned about stepping off on the wrong foot when you shoved a gag into my mouth, tossed a sack over my head, and hurled me into the back of a van."

"Had to do something before you ended up injuring yourself."

"Is that why you had me tied to a chair for hours, too? To protect me from bodily injury? You know what would've protected me even more? Not being manhandled at all."

Penny, one point. Blue Eyes, zippo.

His eyes narrowed, taking her bait. "Then the next time you get the urge to take a stroll, do it during the day and not in a seedy part of a foreign city. The only people who trample through the San Pedro Sula warehouse district are either looking for trouble or they *are* the trouble. For all we knew, you could've been a human trafficker looking to make a sale. You were someplace you didn't belong."

"*He* knew who I was." She tossed a blatant glare at Trey and got a stony look in return. "Isn't that right?"

Trey's continued silence turned Penny's insides into a pinball machine. She shifted her eyes to the plans littering the coffee table—schematics, maps, photographs, and itineraries. Considering their dark-wing commando look, none of it was surprising, except for one photo tucked beneath all the others.

Her hand reflexively reached for it, a knot instantly forming in her stomach. Gleaming back at her from the black-and-white picture were a familiar pair of cold, dark eyes.

Someone called her name, but she couldn't answer. Tunnel vision narrowed her focus, darkening the corners of her sight until the harsh stare of the man in the photo morphed into the concerned eyes of Rafael Ortega. Catching her chin between his fingers, Rafe gently forced her gaze upward.

"Talk to me, Red," he demanded gently.

"*He's* the reason I'm here." She met Rafe's gaze, lifting the picture up with a shaking hand. "Diego Fuentes has my niece, *my best friend*. And I'm not leaving Honduras without her."

ABOUT THE AUTHOR

April Hunt blames her incurable chocolate addiction on growing up in rural Pennsylvania, way too close to America's chocolate capital, Hershey. She now lives in Virginia with her college sweetheart husband, two young children, and a cat who thinks she's a human-dog hybrid. On those rare occasions she's not donning the cape of her children's personal chauffer, April's either planning, plotting, or writing about her next alpha hero and the woman he never knew he needed, but now can't live without.

You can learn more at:
AprilHuntBooks.com
Twitter: @AprilHuntBooks
Facebook.com

Fall in Love with Forever Romance

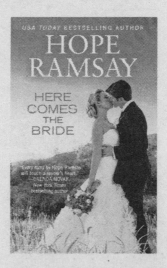

HERE COMES THE BRIDE
By Hope Ramsay

The newest novel in the Chapel of Love series from *USA Today* bestselling author Hope Ramsay will appeal to readers who love Jill Shalvis, Robyn Carr, and Brenda Novak.

Laurie Wilson is devastated when she is left at the altar. How long will it take her to realize that Best Man Andrew Lydon is actually the better man for her?

Fall in Love with Forever Romance

THE PLAYBOY BACHELOR
By Rachel Van Dyken

New from #1 *New York Times* bestselling author
Rachel Van Dyken!

Bentley Wellington's just been coerced by his grandfather to spend the next thirty days charming and romancing a reclusive red-haired beauty who hates him. The woman he abandoned when she needed him the most. Bentley knows just as much about romance as he knows about love—*nothing*—but the more time he spends with Margot, the more he realizes that "just friends" will never be enough. Now all he has to do is convince her to trust him with her heart...Fans of Jill Shalvis, Rachel Gibson, and Jennifer Probst will love this charmingly witty and heartfelt story.

Fall in Love with Forever Romance

WHEN THE SCOUNDREL SINS
By Anna Harrington

When Quinton Carlisle, eager for adventure, receives a mysterious letter from Scotland, he eagerly rides north—only to find the beautiful—and ruined—Annabelle Greene waiting for his marriage proposal. Fans of Elizabeth Hoyt, Grace Burrowes, and Madeline Hunter will love the next in the Capture the Carlisles series from Anna Harrington.

Fall in Love with Forever Romance

HARD JUSTICE
By April Hunt

Ex-SEAL commander Vince Franklin has been on some of the most
dangerous missions in the world. But pretending to be the fiancé of
fellow Alpha operative Charlotte Sparks on their latest assignment is
his toughest challenge yet. When their fake romance generates some
all-too-real heat, Vince learns that Charlie is more than just arm candy.
She's the real deal—and she's ready for some serious action. Don't
miss the next book in April Hunt's Alpha Security series, perfect for
fans of Julie Ann Walker and Rebecca Zanetti!